P a g e s

Distant Hearts | Different Worlds

Daniel Kemnitz

Pages

Distant Hearts | Different Worlds

Daniel Kemnitz

North Star Press of St. Cloud Inc.
www.northstarpress.com

ISBN: 978-1-68201-105-8

Cover Design by Elizabeth Dwyer

North Star Press of St. Cloud Inc.
www.northstarpress.com

Dedication

To God, for graciously giving me a minds eye
to see most things differently than others...
and for His patience when I'm wrong.

To Trudy, my kindergarten sweetheart and wife of 49 years,
who gave me her love and encouragement to finish
this book and help me fulfill yet another dream.

And to my thirteen grandchildren
who drive me to live large,
dream big and laugh often.

Chapter One

The fasten seatbelt sign lit up the overhead panel and the pilot began announcing the conclusion of Delta flight 1705 from Minneapolis to New York. The sudden change in pitch of the jet engines, and the soft chime of the seatbelt warning light, brought Jack Kramp back from distant thoughts to instant reality. He fumbled with his seatbelt, knowing he hadn't taken it off since the Boeing 757 jetted down the runway at Minneapolis-St. Paul International. Seated port-side, just ahead of the wing, Jack hadn't stopped gazing out the window for the past two-and-a-half hours. He wasn't thinking of the lights of New York City; tiny dots now glowing during the early fall afternoon. He didn't notice the weekend traffic snarls on the expressways below or how the trees were barren since the last of their leaves had fallen and were swept away to some distant landfill. Jack's thoughts were farther away than he was from his home and children in Minneapolis. He'd been remembering back two years. The October sky had looked the same blue-gray as this afternoon's twilight.

Jack thought about the day before that tragic Sunday. It had been a warm and sunny Saturday, even though there was already nine inches of snow on the ground. The family had a simple lunch in their small kitchen. It was an unusually warm day in Minnesota for late October and Jack had convinced his wife, Mary, that they should fire up the outside barbecue grill one last time before he stored it away for the winter. Mary looked wonderful. He remembered her standing in the doorway with a plate of brats for the grill, pausing to look over her shoulder long enough to tell one of the kids to answer the phone. She looked much younger than her 44 years--tall and blonde, toned and vibrant from hours of jogging, yoga, and aerobic classes.

Jack often warned her, "Take it a little easier, Mary, don't push yourself so hard down at the club." He would then wait for her to return his comment with twinkling blue eyes and a crooked smile.

The next day, on that cold, gray-blue Sunday, Mary died. Because of the unusually heavy snowfalls, they decided to go skiing at Buck Hill after church. On Mary's second run down the hill, her ski tip caught a rut and she tumbled fifty feet off the slope, hitting her head on a small boulder. The coroner said she had died instantly from a broken neck. It was a freak accident.

From that moment, everything changed in Jack's life. Nothing was the same. Nothing was good. He had his children, but beyond them, Jack felt he had nothing left.

Since that unforgettable, tragic Sunday, Jack was living outside of himself. He found himself watching, waiting, hoping, and expecting to wake up and find Mary poking him and laughing because he was mumbling in his sleep. Again. He was looking at his life from somewhere else, surrounded by a distant haze of complete sadness. With three teenagers and his job as a morning air personality on a popular Twin Cities radio station, Jack's life became a two-year shamble of laundry piles, missed meals, sleepless nights, forgotten PTA meetings, and empty beer bottles.

And then there were the nights. During the nights, long after Jack had checked on his sleeping children while slumber evaded him, he would quietly go down to the kitchen, pour himself a cold beer, sit at the kitchen table, and write. At first he wrote anything; grocery lists, on-air humor bits for his morning show, things to remember to do for the kids, journal entries and sometimes, he even scratched out a sad love poem. Around 2:00 a.m., Jack would switch to drinking strong, black coffee so he would be sober enough to leave for work two-and-a-half hours later. Hungover and sleepy.

Jack wasn't sure when the book began. It started with a few scribbled notes here and there, an idea, an outline, and then finally a few hundred pages bound together. Along with a half dozen bottles of cold drafts every night, the self-made novel helped Jack forget about his loss and hide his grief.

The book became Jack's twisted therapy. He went to a couple of counseling sessions with the children, but he felt they didn't help him. Skipping the sessions became a habit. It allowed his two sons and daughter to cope with their loss under the guidance of trained professionals. After all, Jack had his pens, paper, and beers. They got him through.

Jack was stumbling amid the fog of daily living. He was struggling with second year college tuition for his oldest son, the difficult teenage years of his high school daughter, and dealing with the quiet sadness of his youngest son, now thirteen. Despite all this, Jack Kramp somehow saw his rough manuscript through to fruition. He spent hours laboriously retyping it on his antiquated home computer. Alcohol was the fuel. Under the persistent urging of several close friends who read his final manuscript, Jack mailed it off to a dozen publishers for reading and review. Last spring, in late March, he received a letter of acceptance and an advance check for $5,000. He reluctantly committed to coming to New York during the first two weeks of November for final edits with his new publishing company.

The Boeing turned, banking left and started to descend, with the engines once again changing pitch. "Well," Jack thought with a deep sigh, "It's too late to turn back now. I've already spent the advance money, and we'll be landing at JFK in five minutes. I doubt the pilot will turn around and head back to Minneapolis. Not even if I said, 'Please.'"

The flight attendant calmly made her announcement over the intercom, "Ladies and gentlemen, the captain has turned on the Fasten Seatbelt sign in preparation for our final approach to JFK International. Please make sure that your seatbelts are securely fastened, seat trays up, and your carry-ons are properly stored at this time. Thank you for flying with us. We hope you enjoy the Big Apple."

"Thank God there is only 'No Smoking' on these flights," thought Jack, "If there was a 'No Drinking' policy, I would have never made it." He half grinned to himself, having ordered two scotch and waters and three beers since take off. There was an empty seat between him and the elderly lady in a purple jumpsuit sitting in the aisle seat. The only time she had spoken to him was shortly after he had ordered his second beer somewhere over Ohio.

"Do you hate flying?" She had asked sweetly, nodding to the three empty glasses from the two scotches and his first beer.

"No, I hate crashing. I drink just enough to be higher than the plane," Jack replied a bit sarcastically.

The lady returned to her knitting, but kept an eye on Jack for the remainder of the flight.

Once again, the grind of hydraulics from the wing flaps adjusting behind him brought him back to reality as the Boeing's wheels touched down with a screech. Jack became aware of that old familiar Sunday feeling that he had so often when thinking about Mary over the past twenty-five months. An indescribable, lonely hollowness that made you wish it was early morning and you still had the entire day ahead of you. But he didn't. It was 7:00 p.m. on a Sunday evening in New York City, and Jack Kramp was all alone. The blues had once again set in.

Jack finally tore his eyes away from the window when the plane came to a stop at the gate. Unlike other passengers, Jack sat patiently, his large build crammed uncomfortably in his seat. He watched the passengers scurry around like anxious raccoons as they began standing and collecting their bags. When you've watched death come unexpectedly through someone else's eyes, you tend not to be in a big hurry anymore.

Amused, Jack enjoyed the flurry of colors and changing scents: handbags, suitcases, umbrellas, purses, backpacks, coats, and duffels. The muffled grunts and impatient murmurings of people all headed in one direction; out—and out fast.

When the last passenger deplaned and the attendants were checking the seats behind him to recover forgotten articles, Jack slowly stood and retrieved his trench coat from the overhead compartment. He pulled his battered briefcase out from under his seat. It was filled with rewrite notes that he had intended to review during the flight, but somehow, he never got around to reading them.

"Good Intentions." Jack pondered quietly to himself. "What was it that my Dad had always told me about good intentions?" It was one of his little mini-sermons that he'd give when he caught Jack doing something wrong. Trying to jog his memory, Jack exited the aircraft as the senior flight attendant gave him a tired smile. "Ah yes. Good intentions. And the conversation would go something like this:"

"You're late, Jack."

"I know, Dad, I intended to be home at midnight, but then I met Ron and Doug after their dates and, well, you know how it is..."

"It's 2:00 a.m. What the hell have you been doing for two hours?"

"I really intended to be home earlier."

"Good intentions alone pave a road to hell, Jack, and you're building a damn freeway!"

"Dad's mini-sermons. They always had a way of sticking with you," muttered Jack to himself.

Jack was so deep in thought about recollecting his father's good intentions quip that he had already walked up through the jetway and out into the gate waiting area before he realized he was supposed to be looking for someone. Marsha, his publisher's agent, had told him someone would meet him at the gate, brief him, and escort him to his hotel. He'd either be paged or recognized from some of the photographs he had been asked to send for preliminary artwork and publicity planning.

Inside the terminal, a small panic seized him. Thousands of complete strangers were rushing everywhere. "And some are stranger than others," Jack muttered as a young girl in an old, long army coat and blue hair elbowed her way past him. "I feel like a country hick," Jack thought, "Everyone else in the whole damn world knows exactly where they are going, and I'm standing here with my thumb in my butt looking like I just fell off a bus from Mason City, Iowa!" He slowly walked to a large waiting area, scanning for anyone who appeared as though they might be looking for him.

"I should have told Marsha to have her greeter just look for a forty-six-year-old country bumpkin who is a little drunk, looking lost, and scared to death," Jack thought. His eyes suddenly caught a glimpse of a large, white cardboard sign. Scrawled across it in heavy black marker was written, "Jack Kramp, America's next great author!"

Momentarily, Jack stared at the sign in disbelief. His embarrassed gaze went up to the round, rather plump face of a woman in her mid-twenties. She wore thick round glasses and a blue stocking cap. Her curly black hair was pulled back and stuck out from under the fuzzy cap like the tail of an otter. Jack was fifteen feet away, but he knew as she started toward him that she already recognized him. She broke into a big smile that matched the gap between her front teeth. She extended her hand to shake his.

"Mr. Kramp?"

"Yeah, I'm Jack Kramp. Are you with Brownstone Publishing?"

"Yeah, I'm Jo. I'm one of Marsha Morrow's assistants. I'm here to brief you on your schedule for the next two weeks, take you to your hotel, and make sure I give you everything you need."

Jack raised his eyebrows just enough to cause Jo's smile to whither and her face to blush to a nice dusty red.

"I... I... I meant," she stammered.

"It's okay," Jack said as he shook her hand, "I just get a little foolish after flying and drinking." They turned and walked toward the downward arrow sign pointing to baggage claim.

"You don't like to fly, Mr. Kramp?"

"Call me Jack. And flying is okay, I just don't like not drinking. If bars had wings, I'd probably be flying off to somewhere every night."

"Oh," she said, trying not to look any more confused than he had already made her.

"What was your name again?" Jack asked as he followed her down the escalator to baggage claim.

"Jo."

Jack stopped in mid-stride to readjust his grip on his briefcase and trench coat. His sudden halt at the bottom of the escalator caused an elderly lady in an electric wheelchair to make a very sharp left turn to avoid running him over. The bun-topped grandma muttered something under her breath at Jack and brought a wrinkled right hand out from under her black shawl and confidently flipped him her middle finger.

"Welcome to New York," Jo said with an even larger school girl smile.

"What kind of name is Jo? Is it shortened for something?" Jack asked, still recovering from the shock of finding himself outside his normal habitat.

"It's short for Joanne. I'm a runner for Brownstone. You know, a gopher. I make deliveries, do a few errands, pick up people, you know?"

"I know," said Jack, his mind drifting to the fact that people often tie their name to a further explanation of their occupation, career, or position. And, anyone who had ever heard of the University of Minnesota knew that a real gopher was "Golden." Jack thought about bringing both these thoughts up to her, but as he glanced into the big eyes behind the large round glasses above the big girlish grin, Jack decided to give it up.

After picking up Jack's two large suitcases and his garment bag from baggage claim, they went outside JFK terminal and waited three minutes for a cab. As they stood near the curb, Jo chatted non-stop about the number of people she sees everyday during the course of her job. Jack stood quietly, half-listening and resisting the urge to belch. He counted his luggage again and grimaced as it was thrown into the trunk of a Yellow Cab by a short Armenian with a happy smile, a bad haircut, and poor English.

The forty minute cab ride from JFK to downtown Manhattan was not as fast and reckless as Jack thought it would be. They arrived at the West Park Plaza Hotel. It was less than ten years old and thirty-four stories tall. Central Park West was just across the street. Jo asked the cab driver to wait and ushered Jack to the front desk across the massive, elegant lobby. An impeccably dressed doorman made a quick snapping motion with his fingers and in moments a bellhop was whisking Jack's luggage away on a cart toward the elevators.

Jo signed for the room under a prearranged account. Once finished, she handed Jack a thick manila envelope with his itinerary for the next two weeks and said, "Well, Mr. Kramp, I think that about does it for me. I might see you around. You're going to be here for a couple of weeks, right?"

"Yeah, if I survive," Jack said as he looked around the hotel lobby.

"Oh, I'm sure you'll do just fine. I'm sure Ms. Lisignoli isn't always the witch everybody says she is."

"Who?" Jack came to a halt and turned to face Jo.

She bit her lower lip nervously. "Well, I... I'm sorry. I thought Marsha had told you. You've been assigned Lisa Lisignoli as your rewrite editor. She has a reputation for chewing up and spitting out aspiring new writers during their rewrites.

"She's pretty tough, huh?" Jack asked, looking for some more inside information and starting to feel a little uneasy about the entire idea.

"To her face, they call her the Tiger-Lady. Behind her back, they call her the Word-Witch."

"Thanks for the warning," Jack said, forcing a smile. He stretched out his hand, shook Jo's hand, and said good-bye. She had a firm, friendly handshake, the kind you'd expect from someone who pursued her duties with the utmost vigor.

As Jo turned and walked briskly back outside to the waiting cab, Jack headed to meet the bellhop and an open elevator. As he passed by the upscale restaurant, he noticed a bar off to his left. He tried telling his feet to turn left. He suddenly had the urge for a strong drink. One with which he could ponder over this unexpected new wrinkle; Lisa Lisignoli.

"There probably isn't enough booze in the entire hotel to prepare me for the... what do they call her? The Word-Witch? Guess I'll find out tomorrow," he thought to himself as the elevator doors closed.

Jack and the bellhop rode in silence to the top floor. He was escorted down a long, quiet and richly carpeted corridor on the 34th floor to a large suite at the very end. Suite number 3418.

"You must be a pretty good writer, sir," the bellhop said as he pulled out the room key and began unlocking the door.

"Why?" asked Jack.

"Because this is one of our best suites. Brownstone tends to use this hotel for most of their writers and the ones who usually write best sellers end up getting the royal, sweet, suite-treatment, if you know what I mean?" The bellhop grinned at his own twist on words.

"Yeah, well, that remains to be seen," Jack replied, "It's my first book and by this time tomorrow night, when the Word-Witch is done with me, I'll probably be sleeping in a cardboard box in your basement." The combination of liquor and loneliness was making Jack a little cynical.

The bellhop paused and looked at Jack, apparently not used to this kind of conversation. "Very good, sir," he said as he made a sweeping motion with his hand, indicating Jack should go in. He followed with the luggage cart.

As Jack stepped into the room, he was stunned by the plushness. He wasn't used to luxury. He thought back to the last time he had ever stayed in anything close to being this nice. It was about five years ago when he and Mary attended a radio convention in Dallas.

The carpet in suite 3418 was so thick, Jack felt like he was going to lose his shoes as he walked. Just inside the door, to the left and three steps down, was a sunken living room with two large rounded off-white sofas on either side of a matching love seat. They were arranged in a U shape and facing a massive white and gray stone fireplace. A large oak coffee table sat between the three plush seating pieces. An entertainment system, complete with a 60-inch flat screen television, was in a large white rack just to the right of the fireplace.

Across the room, near the two large French doors leading out to a walled terrace, stood a large oak desk and a new Apple monitor and keyboard. The laser printer sat next to the desk on a rather old but ornate stand. A smaller, beige desk was positioned just to the left and slightly behind the larger wooden one. The smaller desk had a stack of yellow legal pads along with pens, pencils, and highlighters neatly arranged on it.

Each desk had a standard black executive desk chair with arms. Just to the right of the French doors was a small kitchenette. To Jack's right, he noticed a double set of doors leading into the master bedroom, with an additional single entry door to the master bathroom. Also to his right, near the front door, was the entry closet.

"Well, everything is ready and in order except me," Jack muttered to himself as he looked at his fully equipped editing headquarters.

"Pardon me?" asked the bellhop.

"Nothing," replied Jack as he followed the bellhop, and his luggage, through the double set of doors into the master bedroom suite. It was spacious and elegant. "Mary would have loved it," Jack thought as he stood in the center and slowly made a 360-degree turn. There was a king-size bed, a walk-in closet, a huge chest of drawers, a dresser with a large mirror, and a vanity area. Through the other large door Jack could see the complete master bath with a glass shower and Jacuzzi tub.

Jack turned his attention back to the bellhop who had just completed arranging his luggage on the table near the foot of the bed.

"How much is this room a night?" Jack asked.

The bellhop paused for a minute, and Jack thought he saw a hint of a smile on the young man's face. "Three hundred and sixty-five dollars per night, sir."

"No shit!" Jack said aloud in surprise. "Damn!" Jack thought to himself,

"There goes my Midwest slang again." Embarrassed, he walked over to the bedroom windows. Over his shoulder, he asked, "And Brownstone Publishing is picking up the tab for all of it, huh?"

"Apparently, sir. I think they receive a special rate because they are a very good client."

The bellhop finished with the luggage, turned and walked out to stand as if at attention, just inside the front door. Jack absentmindedly followed him out, noticing for the first time a small table and two chairs in the corner near the kitchenette, just to the left of the desks.

Jack looked at the bellhop, wondering why he was waiting. Suddenly, it dawned on him. "The tip!" Jack reached into the pocket of his pants and pulled out a five dollar bill and handed it to the bellhop.

"Thank you, sir," the bellhop said in a tone of voice that Jack couldn't tell if it was genuine or mocking. The bellhop closed the door behind him, leaving Jack alone. Taking a deep breath, he walked back into the huge bedroom, sat down on the bed, and stared at the ominous pile of luggage. Reaching over and pulling the large white card Jo had with her at the airport, he read it aloud. "Jack Kramp, America's next great author... and cheap asshole," he added as he thought about the tip he had just given the bellhop.

Jack slipped off his shoes and looked at the two suitcases and garment bag he had brought with him. "I wonder how much I have packed in there that I'll never use," he thought. "Mary always said I took too much crap with me, and she was usually right."

Jack's thoughts of Mary quickly reminded him he had promised to call home as soon as he arrived in New York. He quickly pulled his cell phone from the pocket of his trench coat and dialed HOME from his Contacts.

After three rings, a voice said, "Hello?"

"Tammy?"

"Hi Daddy! Are you in New York?"

"Yes, I'm here, honey. I checked into the hotel just a little while ago. How is everything at home?"

"We're okay, Dad. We miss you. The boys got home from the Vikings game a little while ago. We ordered a pizza and had a pig-out."

"Sounds like fun. Does Michael have his homework done?"

"Yeah, I think so, and I know Jim has to study for a calculus test tomorrow."

"And, of course, YOU have all your homework done, right, Tammy?"

"Of course, Daddy!" Tammy said. Jack could almost see the smile on her face and the twinkle in her eyes, just like Mary's. Tammy always had her homework done. Her brothers would often tease her that she would have her homework half-done before the teacher even assigned it.

"I finished up my English paper this afternoon while the boys were at the game. The house is real quiet, Daddy. I miss you."

"I miss you too. All of you. What are the boys doing?"

"Jim is up in his room, and Michael's taking a shower. Should I get them?"

"No, that's okay, Tam, just tell the boys I called and that I love them. Please make sure everybody, especially Michael, gets to bed early tonight, okay?"

"Okay. Are you going to start editing your book tomorrow?"

Jack paused for a moment as images of the wicked witch from the Wizard of OZ seated on a large, black typewriter and flying around flashed through his mind.

"I guess so," Jack replied, "My editor is going to be here around 9:00 tomorrow morning. I heard she's a pretty tough cookie. I might be on a plane headed home by noon."

This time it was Tammy's turn to be silent.

"Tammy? Are you there?"

"Yeah, Daddy. I was just trying to decide if I was being too selfish by hoping you'd call from the airport here in Minneapolis tomorrow night and ask us to come pick you up. I guess I'd rather miss you for a couple of weeks so you can finish your book. I know how important it is to you."

"Tammy, I, uh..." Jack's mind was numb. He needed a drink. Right now. What could he tell her so they could quietly end this conversation? "Look, honey, please say hello to Michael and Jim for me. I'll talk to them tomorrow nigh. And you make sure you're all in bed early, okay?"

"Okay. Good-bye Dad. We love you."

"Good night, Tammy. I love you, too." Jack hung up the telephone before she could hear the cough and the gulp from the lump that had suddenly formed in his throat.

Jack sat on the bed, looking once again at his luggage. He stood to make a feeble attempt at unpacking. Suddenly, he turned toward the telephone on the nightstand and called room service. He ordered a hamburger, fries, and a six pack of beer.

While he waited for his order, Jack began to unpack, filling four of the nine drawers in the enormous dresser with his clothes. He hung three suits, six shirts, and two sweaters, along with four pairs of casual slacks, and a pair of jeans in the walk-in closet. He carried the smallest travel case into the bathroom and set it on the large vanity.

Jack stretched his lengthy six foot, four inch frame across the king size bed. He rubbed his hands across his face and noticed that it had a full days stubble.

"No reason to shave now. I'll do it early in the morning," Jack thought. He started to doze and noticed the digital clock on the nightstand read 8:39 p.m.

A knock on the door awakened Jack from his catnap. Room service had arrived. The beer was finally here. "Now I can relax," Jack mumbled to himself as he rubbed his eyes and shuffled to answer the door.

Chapter Two

Somewhere in the soft haze of early morning, between the time when the demons come out to taunt him and when Jack forces himself to conscious reality, there was an annoying ringing. It was several short, unfamiliar rings that made Jack silently wish he hadn't finished off the last two beers of last night's six pack. His memory was coming back. Slowly. There had been an old movie on television, the one about Butch Cassidy and the Sundance Kid. "Here's to you, Etta Place!" Jack recalled toasting her and Butch as they rode a bicycle across the screen in front of him around 2:00 a.m.

The incessant ringing continued. Jack opened one eye and quickly closed it. Bright sunlight streamed into the room. His memory finally returned. He was in a swank hotel in New York City. Today was Jack's first day of the edit and rewrite process with some woman that most of the literary world knew as "The Word-Witch."

Jack stared at the digital clock as he reached for the phone. 6:00 a.m. As he raised his head and felt the pain spread from his temples to the back of his head, he crackled, "Hello?"

"Good morning, Mr. Kramp, this is your wake up call. Have a wonderful day."

"But I didn't..." Jack never finished his sentence. There was a click on the other end. Jack's mouth was so dry he couldn't find the words to finish his objection. He stayed in bed for another full two minutes. Collecting more of his thoughts, he struggled to regain full consciousness. When the pebbled ceiling finally came into focus, Jack threw back the covers and stumbled out of bed to the window and closed the drapes.

Stopping in the semi-darkness to maintain his balance, Jack slowly spread the drapes apart about six inches. He was looking out over Central Park in early morning. People were walking with coats, hats, and scarves. Jack spotted a couple of joggers. He could see their breath in the crisp early morning air. "It must be cold out," Jack thought as he headed back to the bed. He looked at the clock again. 6:07 a.m. Jack rolled over, picked up the telephone, and dialed the front desk.

"Good morning, front desk, this is Rita." Her voice was warm and cheery compared to the cold scene outside. He recognized it as the same voice of the wake up call just a few minutes earlier.

"Yeah, Rita, this is Jack Kramp in 3418. I just got a wake up call."

"Yes, sir?"

"Well, I didn't order any wake up call. I was expecting to sleep in for at least another hour, and I don't appreciate being awakened."

"I'm terribly sorry, sir. I'll check on that and find out why you were on our call list for that time. I truly apologize for the inconvenience."

"Okay," said Jack, now feeling guilty for his grumpy tone. "Don't worry about it, I'll just get some early breakfast."

"Very well, Mr. Kramp. We have an excellent cafe right here in our hotel. The Garden Room is located on the main floor, just to the right as you exit the elevators."

"Thank you, Rita. I'll give it a try."

After Jack hung up, he sat on the edge of the bed, deciding what to do next. He noticed he was still wearing one sock, along with his pants. His shirt was draped over the chair by the vanity, and he was wearing his undershirt inside out. He went into the bathroom, flipped on the light, and stood in front of the mirror above the vanity and sink.

"Bright! Very Bright! Turn it off!" A little voice inside Jack's head screamed. He quickly flipped off the light, shut his eyes for a few seconds, reached for the light switch, and turned it on again. Slowly, Jack squinted and opened his eyes, first his left and then his right. "I should have known better," he thought to himself. "I've had years of practice. I've been getting up at 4:00 a.m. for the past six years, and I go through this routine every morning, five days a week. It goes with the territory when you sign-on as a morning radio personality."

Jack stared at the manufacturer's tag on his undershirt. Not only was it inside out, he also had it on backwards. Still looking at the shirt, Jack began to grin.

"It must have been one hell of a fight last night as Butch, Sundance, and I shot our way out of Bolivia!" he muttered.

Jack took off his shirt, pants, and the sock. He made a mental note to remember to look for his missing sock. As he was about to turn on the shower, the telephone rang again with several short rings in a row.

"Okay! Okay! I'm up! I'm up!" Jack mumbled to himself as he headed into the bedroom and picked up the telephone.

"Hello?" Jack answered abrasively.

"Mr. Kramp?"

"Yes, this is Jack Kramp."

"Good Morning, Mr. Kramp. This is Rita at the front desk. I'm sorry to bother you again, but I did check on that wake up call. There was one ordered for you for 6:00 a.m."

"But, I don't remember ordering any wake up call. Are you sure it was for suite 3418?"

"Yes, sir, you're right, you didn't order it. Our wake up log indicates that a Lisa Lisignoli from Brownstone Publishing called last night around 10:00 p.m. to make sure you arrived and instructed us to leave a wake up call for you at 6:00 this morning."

"I see," Jack said through clenched teeth. "Well, thank you for checking. I really appreciate that, Rita."

"You're quite welcome, Mr. Kramp. If there is anything we can do to make your stay with us more enjoyable, please let us know."

"I will. Thank you, Rita."

"Have a nice day, Mr. Kramp."

Jack sat on the bed in his boxers, thinking about the nerve of the Word-Witch. "It's starting already," he thought. "I haven't even met her yet and she is already running my life. 6:00 a.m.? On a day off? This broad must be crazy! She's not coming over until 9:00. I don't need three fricken' hours to get ready for her."

As Jack showered, he thought about how he was going to tell this Lisignoli woman in no uncertain terms that during this editing process, any time that he wasn't working on the manuscript with her, was his time. He decides when to get up, not her. And he decides when to go to bed, not her. "Who does she think she is anyway?" Jack thought feeling a great deal of irritation.

Jack was still fuming as he dressed. He put on casual slacks, a dress shirt open at the collar, and a sweater. Jack thought about wearing a necktie, but then he thought about the wake up call again and decided that this was about as dressed up for the Word-Witch as he was going to get.

Jack took the elevator down to the lobby and found a quiet corner booth in the Garden Room. He ordered two eggs over easy, bacon, three pancakes, a side of wheat toast, a large orange juice, and a black coffee.

"It would be great to have a Bloody Mary for breakfast," Jack thought. "After all, I'm not going on the air this morning. Hell, I'm not even at work." Common sense finally won out over his alcohol urge, and he decided against it. By 8:00 a.m., Jack was back up in his room. He read USA Today, fumbled around on the TV for something interesting, and finally decided to go over his rewrite notes.

"I've got an hour to kill before she gets here," Jack thought as he glanced at his cell. He put his briefcase on the small metal desk. He opened the heavy curtains on the French doors and morning sunlight streamed into the room. Looking through the windows of the doors, he noticed a growing number of people in Central Park below. Opening one of the French doors, he stepped out onto the terrace. The air was cool and crisp. Jack guessed it was in the lower forties. Not bad for early November. Jack took a deep breath. Several New York aromas permeated the air: fresh baked bread, exhaust fumes, coffee, some sort of fishy-river smell, and a few others that Jack couldn't identify. It was New York and Jack was a small town boy from the Midwest. He had a slightly sick feeling that he really didn't belong here, and he was already looking forward to the prospect of going home.

"The sooner the better," Jack mumbled as he quickly stepped back inside his suite and closed the French doors behind him. He watched the scenes of the Park through the windows and began to daydream.

The knock on the door jarred Jack's mind back to the present. He glanced at his cell again. It read 8:59 a.m. Jack was surprised at how quickly time had flown.

He crossed the room toward the door, again looking at the time on his cell phone and thinking that she was certainly punctual. Jack opened the door wide.

Only three seconds passed while they stood and looked at each other. Although to Jack, it seemed like an hour. The scene reminded him of two prize fighters, eyeing each other up before they engage in battle.

In those brief moments, Jack noticed more than he had intended. He became acutely aware of many details, more so than at any other time he had remembered when meeting a stranger.

Lisa Lisignoli looked as though she was in her late thirties, with a smooth olive complexion and high cheekbones. She looked Italian. Her long dark hair was tied neatly behind her head with a navy blue ribbon. Jack noticed her bright green eyes, with just a hint of fire behind them. Lisignoli also had full lips and just the right amount of makeup. She was about five foot, six inches tall with a slender, almost graceful figure. She wore a white lace blouse with a navy blue blazer and matching skirt just past her knees. Dark navy blue pumps set off her business ensemble. A black trench coat hung over her left arm. Jack looked back up to her face and noticed the small sparkle of diamond and blue sapphire earrings. She was one of the most beautiful women he had ever seen and Jack felt himself turning a light shade of red as he tried to refocus his eyes, locking in on hers.

"Mr. Kramp?" she asked, extending her right hand toward him. "I'm Lisa Lisignoli. I'm here to help you through the final editing process of your manuscript. Are you ready?"

"Huh, yeah, sure. Come in," Jack stuttered, feeling his anger over the wake up call go down the toilet along with his confidence.

With a professional coolness, Lisa entered the suite. She walked directly to the two desks and the Apple computer. After looking them over, she said, "Well, I suppose these will do." She tossed her coat over the love seat.

Jack was still standing near the door after closing it.

"Well, do you wish to just stand there while I edit your book for you or would you care to have some input into it?" Lisa asked as she put her briefcase on top of the old wooden desk and began sorting through it.

"No. I mean, yeah, I'm coming," Jack stumbled, trying to regain his composure as he walked over to the desks.

"I'll take the wooden one and the computer. I'll need the space. You can have the little one," Lisa said, nodding toward the smaller beige desk. She pulled the manuscript from her briefcase, gracefully sat down at the big desk, and began to thumb through it. Jack followed her lead by sitting down at his desk and pulling out his copy of the manuscript.

"*Loose Cannons*," Lisa said. "It's quite an interesting title. It fits the storyline well. We're going to keep it. It should help sell a few books. God knows, these damn western novels need all the help they can get."

Jack abruptly turned his head to look directly at Lisa. "Damn western novels?" he asked, repeating her phrase and somewhat surprised at her manner and language. Her vocabulary and directness didn't fit her impressive physical image.

Lisa swiveled around in her chair to face him. "Look, Kramp," she said firmly, "Let's get a couple of things straight from the start. First of all, editing western manuscripts is one of my least favorite things in the world. As a matter of fact, I usually place it just ahead of having my legs waxed. It was my bad luck that I was assigned this deplorable rewrite. So let's get it done quickly and maybe I can have you on a plane back home to Indianapolis by next Thursday."

"Minneapolis," Jack interrupted. "You know, the Twin Cities? Minneapolis-St. Paul? In Minnesota?" He felt he needed to start holding his ground.

"Whatever. It's out there somewhere." Lisa jerked her thumb over her shoulder, pointing west. "And I don't particularly care for people from the Midwest. They tend to be somewhat slow and slightly stupid. Now let's get this damn project completed so I can get on to more intelligent and worthwhile manuscripts."

Jack's mouth hung open as he replayed every word she had just said back in his head. "Was she trying to be funny? Did she really mean all of that?" He felt the veins in his neck begin to stick out as his anger rolled up from his stomach. "Watch yourself, Jack," he thought to himself, "Watch yourself. Don't blow up. Maybe she's had a bad experience somewhere along the line. But still," he reasoned silently, "That's no excuse for being totally rude to someone you've just met."

Lisa returned her attention to the manuscript on her desk, unaware of Jack clenching his hands into fists behind her, still fighting his anger.

"Stupid?" Jack repeated to her. But Lisa had taken out a red felt marker and was marking up his manuscript. "Stupid?" he said again, louder this time, thinking that in her concentration, she hadn't heard him the first time.

Without turning around, Lisa said, "Don't take it personally, Kramp. You can't help that you were born out in the middle of some prairie, far from schools and libraries. Midwesterners have their place, I'm sure. It's just not with me. Personal preference. Now, if you'll shut up long enough and pay attention, maybe we can get through this with the least amount of problems. If you continue to keep repeating the word 'Stupid,' I'll just assume you're trying to prove my theory as being absolutely correct. Now, do you have any further questions before we begin?"

"Yeah," Jack said as he leaned back in his chair and folded his hands across his chest. "Did you go through special training to get your abrasive attitude or does it just come naturally every time you open your mouth?"

Lisa turned in her chair. There was a fire in her eyes and Jack fully expected her to scream several four-letter expletives at him. Instead, she spoke very softly, as if she was in total control. Although, Jack noticed she spoke through slightly clenched teeth.

"Look, Kramp. Don't try to do verbal or even mental battle with me. You'll lose. It's quite simple. You wrote a book. You sold it to Brownstone. It's my job to make it better. The better it is, the more books we'll sell. The more books we sell, the more money we'll make and the more you'll earn in royalties. So, let's stop wasting each other's time and get into it, shall we?"

"Okay," Jack said, shrugging his shoulders. "But I use a yellow highlighter and a pencil to make changes."

Lisa cocked her head and gave him a sardonic look.

"Personal preference," Jack said, mimicking her. He put his head down and started to read silently from his copy of the manuscript, smiling to himself. He didn't know why, but he sensed this was going to be a challenge. Maybe he'd have a little fun in the process. At the very least, he knew he was about to learn something. And the education went beyond rewrites, edits, and revisions. He suspected he was about to see another side of human nature.

For the next three hours, they said very little to each other. Lisa would point out an awkward paragraph and Jack would rewrite it. Lisa continued to work on certain sections, pausing occasionally to bring up a page on the Apple. After making her corrections and printing them out, she carefully inserted the edited pages into a large, yellow three ring binder. Jack would occasionally get up and wander around the suite, thumbing through a dictionary, a thesaurus, or any one of several reference books that had been brought in and stacked on the floor between the two desks.

Around 11:45, Jack excused himself and went to the bathroom. Upon his return, he observed that Lisa never left her chair. "The Italian woman with the cast-iron bladder," Jack thought as he watched her work out of the corner of his eye.

Suddenly, Lisa looked up and gazed out the windows of the French doors. "What time is it?" she asked. Jack didn't answer. It crossed his mind to say something like, "Hey, I thought you knew everything. Besides, I'm just a stupid Midwesterner who hasn't learned to tell time yet." He bit his lip instead.

"It's a little after noon," Jack replied dryly.

"Give it to me in minutes, Kramp. In Minnesota, I'm sure a little can go a long way, but I have an appointment at 12:30."

"It's eleven minutes after twelve," Jack said, punching his cell on his desk.

"Thank you," Lisa said coldly as she stood and began to load her briefcase. "I'll be back at 2:00 p.m. Try to get through the paragraphs I've marked in chapters four and five."

When she reached the door, she turned, and looked directly at Jack. "Oh, and Kramp? Try to get some heat in this place. You may love to work in freezing temperatures back home in the wild woods, but I like my work environment a little warmer."

Jack stood straight up and saluted her. "Aye, aye, Captain, I'll be sure to turn up the heat a wee bit for ya afore ya return," he said in his best Scottish brogue.

Lisa was not amused. She gave him a hard look and repeated the time, "2:00 p.m., Kramp. Have your edits completed." Without hesitating, she turned, slipped into her coat, opened the door, and walked out, closing it firmly behind her.

Jack stood in the center of the sunken living room of the suite for a brief moment. Then, a full grin spread across his face. He walked over to the thermostat on the wall just to the right of the double doors leading into the bedroom. He stared at it, then twisted the dial up until it read eighty-five degrees.

"Well, some like it hot," Jack said to himself as he pulled on his sweater, grabbed his room key off the table, and trench coat from the closet. He left suite 3418 and headed for the elevators. Jack had worked up a powerful hunger.

This rewrite thing was a tedious task and the Word-Witch wasn't making the process any easier.

Jack walked outside the hotel and across the street to Central Park. He breathed in the fresh air as he watched people walking, talking, selling, and buying. He stood in uncertainty on the busy sidewalk, looking up and down the street, trying to decide where to have lunch.

"I'll eat anything as long as it's not Italian," Jack muttered as he walked south toward downtown Manhattan.

Chapter Three

After a lunch of two hot dogs and a large Pepsi from a food vendor in Central Park, Jack walked south along West Central Park Avenue in the crisp November sunshine. He bought a TIME magazine from a small newsstand and headed back to his hotel. The walk refreshed him, and he felt better. As Jack waited for an elevator in the hotel lobby, he looked at the clock behind the front desk. It was 1:35 p.m. He had just enough time to review those chapters that Lisa had left for him. As he entered his suite, his cell phone rang in his coat pocket.

"Hello?" Jack answered, slightly out of breath.

"Jack?"

"Yeah, this is Jack. Marsha?"

"Hi!" Marsha giggled on the other end. "Welcome to New York. How was your flight?"

"Wet," Jack said with a half grin. He always enjoyed these conversations with Marsha. She was one of the few people he felt at ease with since Mary's death. Jack had never met her personally, but he had spoken with her about twice a week for the past four months, ever since Brownstone had their review editors read his manuscript and recommended it for printing.

"Oh? Bad weather?"

"No, never mind. I'll explain some other time," Jack said, wishing he hadn't made the comment.

"So, how's the editing going? Isn't Lisa just the greatest?"

"At what?" Jack asked, surprised at Marsha's unexpected endorsement.

"Jack," Marsha's voice on the other end of the telephone changed. It became softer, almost a pleading tone. "Lisa can be very tough at times, but she is one of our very best. She's edited almost fifty best sellers in the past eight years."

"She hates fictional books about the old west," Jack said, wishing he hadn't mentioned Lisa's hatred for his novel.

"Lisa doesn't like anything until it's clean and ready for print. But once you're done, you'll have a manuscript you'll both be proud of. Maybe even a best seller!" Marsha added with her familiar giggle.

"She also hates Midwesterners. Maybe I should take a bath," Jack replied with a laugh.

"Oh, Jack, give her a couple of days. You'll grow on her and she'll grow on you. Just turn on that Minnesota charm." Then Marsha became serious. "She's had a rough time of it, too, Jack."

"What do you mean?" inquired Jack.

"Well, I'd rather not get into that. If she wants you to know, she'll tell you. Just cut her some slack. She's really quite good, Jack. She really is."

"Okay, okay," Jack said, "I'll give her another chance."

"Anyway, I was hoping you could join us for dinner on Friday night. You're not planning on going back to Minneapolis for the weekend, are you?"

"No, I'm not. I suspect we'll be working through the weekend. She wants my butt out of here a week from Thursday."

"I see. Well, are we on for Friday night? I'd love to finally meet you in person." Her voice was warm and sincere.

Jack thought for a minute. "Sure, Friday night is fine. Who's we?"

"Oh, possibly a couple of people from our office and me. Maybe Lisa will join us, too."

"I wouldn't hold my breath on that one," he said sarcastically.

"Jack! Minnesota charm, please?"

"All right. Friday night. What time?"

"We'll meet in your suite at, shall we say, 7:30 p.m. I'll make reservations for 8:00. I think we'll try to get into Bradburry's. It's fabulous!"

"Okay. 7:30 p.m., here. But you don't have to do anything fancy for me. Beer and burgers are fine."

"Jack, you're in New York, filled with thousands of culinary adventures for your palate. You'll love it, I promise!" her voice dripped with enthusiasm.

"See you Friday night, then," replied Jack with a deep chuckle.

"Oh, I'll likely be checking on your progress before that, at least by phone. If I'm in the neighborhood, I'll try to stop up to meet you."

"Okay," Jack hesitated for a brief moment. "And Marsha?"

"Yes?"

"Thank you very much for everything."

"You're welcome, Jack," Marsha giggled again. "Just give us a best seller."

"You didn't tell me that in order to give you a best seller, I had to let someone everyone calls the Tiger-Lady give me a constant pain in the..."

"Jack!" she cut him off with a hearty laugh, "I've read your book. It's great. Be as tough as your characters in the book. You'll survive. I've got another call holding, Jack, we'll talk soon! Good-Bye!"

"Bye," Jack said as he turned and looked out the windows of the French doors and waited for the click on the other end.

"Nice lady," Jack thought to himself as he hung up and started toward the desk to look for chapters four and five. As soon as he reached the desk, there was a knock on the door. Jack glanced at the time in the upper right corner of the Apple computer. 1:58 p.m.

"Damn!" Jack softly cursed as he turned and headed toward the door. He knew it was Lisa. The very punctual, very tough, western genre and Midwesterner-hater, all-business, yet very beautiful, Word-Witch.

"Hi!" Jack offered his best grin as he opened the door, remembering Marsha's plea to give Lisa his best efforts at being charming.

Lisa looked at him for a brief second with a confused frown of disgust that curled down the corners of her lips, then quickly walked in and went right to her desk. Jack watched her, admiring her confident stride and her trim figure.

"So, did you have a nice lunch?" Jack inquired as he slowly walked over to his desk.

"Writing a book about my dietary opinions, Kramp?" she asked cooly, without looking up. Lisa stood at her desk, head down, flipping through the pages in her briefcase.

Jack could feel the anger rising from his toes and all thoughts of turning on the charm started to leave. He was trying to be nice and create casual conversation, and Lisa refused to be anything but rude. He thought quickly. Jack's retort had to be sharp, quick, and to the point.

"No, just research for an article in the National Inquirer. They're looking for a piece on business women with cold, calculating hearts," Jack retorted.

Lisa slowly turned around to face Jack. She stuck her red marking pen behind her ear, leaned her hip on the edge of her desk, and crossed her arms.

"What is it, Kramp?" she asked slowly, her green eyes piercing Jack like hot needles. "Do you intend to deliberately anger me so you can call this entire project off and go home?"

"No," Jack replied. "I just thought that as long as we have to spend the next several days working together, we could at least be civil toward one another. What the hell did I ever do to you?" Jack was on a roll, and his voice was rising. "You've been hostile toward me since the moment you walked in here this morning. I wrote a book. Your publishing company says it's good enough to print. I didn't pick you for this assignment, your company did. If you've got a problem with that, take it up with them, but kindly leave me out of your direct line of vicious, verbal fire."

Lisa stared at him for several seconds. Her lower lip curled in and her perfect white teeth began to bite it. Her shoulders sagged ever so slightly. She turned her back to Jack and looked out the windows of the French doors. Taking a deep breath, Lisa finally spoke. "Would you like me to find another rewrite editor for you? It may take a couple of days, but I might be able to find a replacement."

Jack stood silently with his hands in his pockets. The anger drained away from him and was replaced by guilt. He said nothing because he didn't know what should be said. This was a new situation for him.

"Well?" Lisa turned and looked at him, her eyes wide, her eyebrows raised in a question.

"What do you want to do?" Jack asked softly.

"I'm not sure," she replied, shaking her head, looking a little confused. "It's your book. I presume it's your call. Marsha will need to know as soon as possible if you wish to make a change."

Jack turned and walked toward the fireplace, his hands still jammed into his pants pockets. He hadn't counted on this latest development.

"Well, maybe this is okay," he thought to himself. "Maybe I should just get someone new for the edits. After all, it's apparent that Lisa hates this assignment."

Jack heard papers rustling behind him. He turned and watched Lisa repack her briefcase, her back to him. She snapped the latches tight, turned off her computer, grabbed her coat, and walked toward the door. In that moment, something strange happened to Jack. A small bit of life drained out of him. He thought of Mary. The feeling was familiar; how he felt the days before her funeral. He'd spent a great deal of his life listening to the little voices inside him. Jack's mother often called them his guardian angels. Mary said it was a keen sixth sense. Wherever Jack's intuition was leading him, he knew it was wrong to let this person, this unusual woman, leave his suite on this cold November day in New York. Something told him not to let Lisa walk out of his life. Maybe it was because he sensed she was good at the rewrite process. Maybe it was something else. Deep down, Jack's intuition told him it wouldn't be right if that door closed and Lisa Lisignoli was on the other side of it, walking away forever.

As Lisa reached for the handle of the door, Jack was surprised at hearing the sound of his own voice. "Wait a minute. I know what I want."

Lisa stopped and turned from the door to face him, waiting, her face expressionless.

Jack walked toward her and up the three steps. He spoke as he walked. "I want to start over."

Lisa looked bewildered as Jack stopped just a couple of feet in front of her. He extended his right hand.

"Hi, I'm Jack Kramp," he said, "You must be Lisa Lisignoli, the one they assigned to help me with my rewrite."

Lisa, still looking a little uncertain, shook Jack's hand and said, "That's right, I am. Hello." A tiny smile tugged at the corners of her mouth.

"Great!" Jack said as he gently took the briefcase from Lisa's left hand and began walking toward the desks. "I've heard a lot about you, they say you're one of the best. I'm happy you'll be helping me, even though I understand western novels aren't your favorite."

With a slightly dazed look on her face, Lisa followed him to the desks. She tossed her coat across the back of the love seat again. Jack placed her briefcase back on top of her desk. Lisa sat down, still bewildered as to how it came about that she suddenly was no longer in control. She found it almost amusing and, as she watched Jack slipping off his sweater, she tightened up her lips to keep from smiling. If given the chance, she would have laughed aloud.

"This guy is really a piece of work," Lisa thought, "But he seems awkwardly genuine."

"Okay, Mr. Kramp. Shall we begin again?"

"Call me Jack. And yes, we shall."

They smiled at each other for the first time since meeting, and Jack knew this was a good decision. Lisa felt somehow refreshed. But little red warning lights began to blink in the back of her head. "Be careful," she thought. "Don't get too comfortable."

Jack looked at the time on his cell. It was 2:33 p.m. Lisa stood up abruptly and took off her blue blazer. "For heaven's sakes, Kramp! Turn down the damn heat! It must be almost 90 degrees in here." Jack remembered cranking up the thermostat at Lisa's request before he left the suite. Walking quickly, he turned it back down to 70 degrees.

"I forgot," Jack said sheepishly as he returned to his desk. "I turned it up just before I went to lunch. You were complaining about the cold, and I thought I'd make you sweat. Sorry."

"Let's open one of the French doors a little, it'll help cool things off in here," Lisa said. "Where are chapters four and five that you did over lunch?"

"Yeah, well," Jack shifted uncomfortably in his chair. "I didn't get to them. I went for a walk, had lunch and when I got back here, Marsha Morrow called and I lost track of time."

"Time is something we can't afford to lose track of around here, Jack. We've got a deadline. At exactly twelve noon, one week from this Friday, if not before, we have to turn in a completely rewritten and edited manuscript to Marsha. They want this book on the presses and a release date by February first of next year. That means everything has to continue on schedule, including our portion."

"We'll get it done," Jack said as he looked down to read the red-marked paragraphs in chapter four.

Lisa turned slightly in her chair. It was just enough to look at him. Jack didn't notice her gaze. She decided to examine this specimen from the Midwest a little closer. She knew he was tall, at least six-three or six-four. She remembered having to look up at him when she arrived this morning. Lisa took the time to study Jack Kramp from head to toe. He had a full head of slightly curly, dark brown hair with hints of gray around the temples. Jack also had a rugged, dark complexion and a strong jawline. She noticed his large steel blue eyes, an average nose, and rather sensuous full lips that looked as though they would be more natural in a permanent smile.

"He's starting to look like a writer," Lisa thought. Jack had his white shirt unbuttoned at the collar and his sleeves rolled up near the elbow. With an athletic build, he sported a slight paunch in his midsection. Jack looked relaxed as he leaned back in his chair, his feet crossed and resting on the left-hand corner of the desk. She watched and grinned as he chewed on the pencil in his mouth while feverishly lining sentences in his manuscript with the highlighter in his right hand. Lisa tried looking away, but she reviewed Jack Kramp again and again. "Not bad," she thought. "Not bad at all. In fact, he is rather handsome." Her gaze rested on his black loafers.

"What are you staring at?" Jack asked. Lisa suddenly looked into those deep blue eyes. He had caught her looking.

"Nothing," she said. "I was just thinking."

"About shoes?"

"No, of course not," she replied, feeling a slight blush in her cheeks.

"Oh, good," Jack said, breaking into a smile and letting a twinkle creep into his eyes. "Because these are size twelve and a half and I think you'd probably drown in them."

"So, Jack Kramp, where did you come up with the idea for *Loose Cannons*?" Lisa asked, changing the subject.

Jack looked at her. Lisa was completely turned around, reclining slightly in her chair and facing him. Jack noticed that she looked almost relaxed. It was a new experience for both of them.

I'm not really sure," Jack responded. "I used to read a lot as a kid. There was an elderly lady who lived next door who had boxes and boxes of books, mostly paperbacks. One entire box was westerns. I think I spent two summers reading that box of books. I carried around the idea of this story in my head for about thirty years. It's a story about a young man who is attending college out East when he gets word that his father, a U.S. Marshall in Texas, has been shot to death. Once he arrives in Texas, he meets a young, tough widow who helps him find justice, peace, and a whole lot more. *Loose Cannons* just kind of evolved from there, plus, the humor I threaded through it was therapeutic for me after Mary died. I sat down one night and started refining it. And there it is." Jack nodded to the manuscript in Lisa's hands.

"It happens like that quite often, Jack," Lisa said. "People get grandiose ideas about writing a book but very few take the time and have the dedication to actually sit down and do it. Someone once told me that eighty percent of the entire writing process is just showing up."

Jack nodded in agreement. "Yeah. Besides it gave me something to do when I couldn't sleep at night." Then Jack added quietly, "Or when I ran out of booze."

Lisa nodded up and down. Jack knew she had barely heard his last comment about the booze. She was already thinking ahead to her next question.

"Who's Mary?" her voice was soft, but direct.

"Mary was my wife. She died suddenly in a skiing accident. Two years ago last week."

"I'm sorry. I didn't know. I guess I should have read your bio more carefully."

"It's okay. My bio didn't mention that anyway." Jack was feeling uncomfortable. They were getting into areas of his life he normally never discussed with anyone.

"So," Lisa hesitated, not really knowing if she should ask her next question or even WHY she wanted to ask it. "Do you have someone special in your life now?"

Jack tilted his head back, rubbed his chin, and slowly worked through his answer. "I have three really terrific kids. Two boys and a girl. All teenagers." Realizing that he really hadn't answered her question, he went on. "I've had two dates in two years. Both of them were disasters." Jack forced a smile.

Lisa smiled back, "I think we've all been down that road a time or two, Jack. I've had some real nightmare dates myself."

"So, you're not married?" Jack asked, wishing he hadn't. He didn't want to pry.

"No. I was married at twenty-nine and divorced at thirty-one. No children. I had a two year relationship after that. It ended Christmas Day, last year. My New Year's resolution this year was to stay clear of men. So far, so good."

"I see." Jack nodded. An uncomfortable silence developed between them. Lisa wasn't sure where their conversation was going, and Jack didn't like the direction it was going in. Jack coughed and peeked at his cell again.

"Hey, it's 3:30!" Jack said as he turned his attention back to his rewrites of chapter four and five.

"Let's get back to work or we'll both be in trouble!" Lisa said as she sat up and once again positioned herself in front of her computer. Jack looked up briefly and admired her long black hair and the firm, petite figure under her white lace blouse.

"These next couple weeks could be pretty nice," he thought to himself. "At least we are being civil to each other."

Lisa stared at the computer screen in front of her, but her mind wasn't concentrating on the words she was reading. It was on the man seated behind her. "There is something intriguing about him," she thought, feeling an unexplainable sadness and an unfamiliar aura that kept drawing her softer side toward him.

"What the hell is wrong with me?" Lisa muttered as she forced herself to focus on the matter at hand. "It's a western! I must be getting old and soft," she thought. Lisa began to quickly cross out words on the manuscript with her red felt-tipped marker.

Jack and Lisa worked on edits until 6:15 p.m. They spoke very little and managed to get through chapter five. Lisa packed up her briefcase, said a hasty goodbye, and left abruptly. Jack was relieved to be alone. It had been a long day, and he needed time to think. So did Lisa.

Chapter Four

Once Lisa left, Jack stood and stretched. Feeling tired and hungry, he opened the French doors to the terrace and stepped outside. The sun had gone down, the air was cool, and street lamps glowed in Central Park. He watched two people climb into a horse drawn carriage and drape a blanket over their laps. The horse and carriage disappeared into the Park.

Jack glanced at the time on his cell. 6:45 p.m. It was 5:45 in Minneapolis. He ambled into the bedroom, slipped off his shoes, and sprawled across the bed.

"I'll just rest for a couple of minutes," Jack thought. "I'll call the kids at 6:00 their time." He drifted off, dreaming of manuscript chapters, huge yellow highlighters, and Lisa Lisignoli. "She is a pretty lady on the outside, but on the inside she has a cold personality. But what is she really like?" Jack suspected there was a lot of deep hurt and anger in her, but he was convinced somewhere within was a warm human being. As he fell asleep, he thought of how he could find the real Lisa Lisignoli and felt a bit confused as to why he even wanted to look.

Jack woke up with a start. His cell phone was ringing just a few feet away on the nightstand. After fumbling in the darkness looking for the nightstand, he finally found his phone face down on the fourth ring.

"Hello?" Jack's voice was almost a hoarse whisper.

"Dad?"

"Yeah. Jim?"

"Hey, are you okay? You sound a little groggy," Jim asked with concern.

"Yeah, I'm fine," Jack said, sorting through the cobwebs in his head. "I fell asleep. What time is it?"

"It's 9:00 p.m. here in Minnesota. So that means it's 10:00 in New York, right?"

"Yeah," Jack replied, realizing he'd slept over three hours.

"We didn't hear from you today. Michael and Tammy are getting ready for bed, so we thought we'd give you a call."

"I'm glad you did, Jim. I was planning on calling you at 6:00 p.m. your time, but I guess I fell asleep. How is everyone?"

"We're fine, Dad. I think Michael misses you a lot. He keeps talking about you and..." Jim paused, "...and Mom and how we used to go camping."

"Yeah," Jack said, fighting a small lump in his throat. "That was always a lot of fun."

"Maybe we can go again sometime, huh? Maybe next summer?"

"Sure," Jack said. "Let's plan on it. Is Michael there?"

"Yeah, just a minute, I'll put him on. Is everything going alright with the rewrite?"

"One day down, nine to go. I think I'll make it. The people here in New York are..." Jack paused, searching for a descriptive word. "...different."

"That's what I hear," Jim said, laughing. "Here's Michael. It's nice talking to you, Dad."

"Same here," sighed Jack sadly. It was hard being away from his kids.

"I love you," Jim said quietly.

"I love you, too, son," Jack replied. Then, Jim was gone.

"Hey Dad!" It was Michael, his enthusiasm in it's usual high gear. "Did you hear? The Vikings won yesterday! Jim and I went. The seats were awesome!"

"Hey, that's great, Michael! How's school going?"

"Oh, the usual freshman stuff. We burned a few books, gave a couple of seniors a swirly, helped three teachers toward nervous breakdowns, you know, same old stuff, just a different day." Michael giggled.

"Michael!" Jack tried being stern, but he couldn't help smiling broadly at his youngest son's imaginative humor, especially at the thought of a couple of freshman in high school taking a big strapping senior, tilting him upside down, and sticking his head in a toilet bowl while flushing. A "swirly." And that was pretty unlikely because the seniors were known to give them to underclassmen.

"Sorry, Dad," Michael said, but the cheerfulness never left his voice. "I was just trying to brighten up your day. Have you seen the Statue of Liberty, yet?"

"No, I haven't," Jack said with a frown, trying to remember if he had caught any glimpse of it as they landed. "But I've seen Central Park, well, at least part of it. I've been working in my hotel suite most of the day."

"Hi Dad!" Tammy's voice cut in.

"Hello, Tammy!"

"I'm on the telephone upstairs in your bedroom. How are you?"

"Hey!" Michael protested, "I'm talking to him. Get off and wait your turn. Besides, you got to talk to him last night."

"Kids, listen," Jack reasoned, "Life is too short to spend time arguing. Michael, I love you. Keep working on your home work. Remember our deal if your year-end grades are good enough."

"The camping trip to Colorado?" Michael was excited again.

"The camping trip to Colorado next summer," Jack said, then added, "As long as you get the grades and stay out of trouble."

"I will Dad. I love you. Bye."

"Good night, Michael, love you, too. Talk to you soon." Michael hung up.

"Tammy?"

"I'm here, Dad."

"How are you doing, honey?" Jack asked tenderly.

"I'm okay. The boys just don't seem to like anything I cook. I can't cook like Mom. I just can't." Jack could tell Tammy was about to cry.

"Tam, tell the boys they need to give you a hand. Go to the grocery store together and have everyone pick out things they like to eat. They should help you prepare the meals and help clean up, too."

"They helped me clear the table and load the dishwasher tonight."

"Good. There should be plenty of money for groceries. You know where it is, right?"

"Yeah. I miss you, Dad," she said softly, her voice quivering.

"I miss you too, Tammy."

"I miss Mom. I wish she were here." It was hard for her to be alone without Jack or their mother.

"I know," Jack said, fighting back tears. "Hopefully it will get easier for all of us, Tam."

"You still miss her, Dad?"

"Yeah, of course I do, Tammy," replied Jack, holding back the tears.

"Oh, well... I, we... uh, we just thought that you... well, that you were okay with it all now, because you never talk about her anymore, Dad."

Jack sat on the edge of the bed in silence. He felt himself taking a deep breath.

"Dad, I'm sorry. I really didn't mean that the way it sounded."

"It's okay, Tam," Jack spoke quietly. "There isn't a day or night that goes by that I don't think of your mother. But, you know, she would have wanted us to live on with our lives and not dwell on her death."

"I know." Tammy changed the subject. "How's the book coming along?"

"It's going pretty well. We got a little behind today, but we're really going to kick butt on it tomorrow." Jack attempted to change the mood of the conversation by sounding more confident and positive.

"How is your rewrite editor? Is she as tough as you thought she'd be?"

"Oh, yeah. And then some," he replied. Jack's thoughts turned to Lisa Lisignoli. He thought of how she looked this morning, standing in the doorway of suite 3418. "She's pretty intelligent, too."

"Is she pretty?" Tammy asked, obviously looking for more information.

"Ah," Jack paused. "She's average." He knew he was lying. "Listen, you better get to bed, okay? We'll talk again tomorrow night."

"Great, Dad. We all miss you and love you. Please come home safely to us." Jack sensed the fear in her voice. It was the same fear they had all felt after Mary died. They had all become paranoid that something tragic would happen to someone else in their family.

"I will, I promise," Jack said. "Goodbye. Love you, Tam."

"Goodnight, Dad. I love you, too."

Jack ended the call and once again fumbled in the dark for the lamp switch on the night stand. He looked at the digital clock on his way to the bathroom. It was 10:17 p.m. Jack felt his empty stomach threatening to attack his spine. He thought back to the hot dogs he'd had for lunch over nine hours ago. No wonder he felt weak.

Pulling open the drapes of his bedroom window, Jack looked out at the lights of the Big Apple. He turned, walked over to the night stand, and called down for room service. Jack decided that a large pepperoni pizza and a six pack of Budweiser would suffice. He promised himself that he would only drink three beers and put the other three in the small refrigerator in the kitchenette.

Jack flipped on the bedroom television and watched a home shopping channel as he took off his clothes. He showered and pulled on a pair of boxer shorts. Mary had always laughed at his little nuances; tight fruit-of-the-loom briefs during the day, big floppy boxers at night. Jack smiled as he caught sight of the red and green checked underwear in the mirror.

"Mary would have loved these!" Jack said aloud. He opened the door of the bedroom and noticed a draft from the main living room. One of the French doors was open about four inches. Jack closed it and pulled the heavy drapes together. After checking the thermostat, he walked down into the lower area of the suite and sat on the love seat facing the fireplace. He read the igniting instructions from the card on the coffee table and punched a red button on the hand-held remote. Instant flames ignited from the gas logs in the fireplace.

Twenty minutes later, his pizza and beer arrived. Jack sat on the love seat with his feet up on the coffee table. He devoured the pizza and washed it down with three beers while watching the fire dance around the ceramic logs.

"This is the life," Jack reflected in a soft whisper to the flickering flames. "It just doesn't feel like it's mine."

Living up to his self-made promise, Jack put the three remaining beers in the refrigerator. He brushed his teeth and went to bed. As he reached to turn out the lamp, he thought of something. Jack picked up the room telephone and called down to the front desk.

"Good evening, front desk, this is Lawrence."

"Good evening, Lawrence," Jack grinned as he tried to sound as formal as the voice on the other end of the line. "This is Mr. Kramp in suite 3418. I'd like a wake up call for 7:00 tomorrow morning."

"7:00 a.m. for suite 3418. Very good, sir. Is there anything else?"

"No, thank you," Jack said, again mimicking the proper diction of Sir Lawrence.

"Very good. Have a good evening, sir."

"Good night." Jack laid back down, turned off the lamp, and immediately fell asleep.

Chapter Five

Jack was already awake and staring at the ceiling when his wake up call came in. "It is only Tuesday," he thought. "I am starting my second day here and I already feel like I've been in this room for a week." Jack rolled over on his side and watched the digital clock tick off the minutes toward 7:05. He finally swung his legs over the edge of the bed, stood, and headed into the bathroom.

"Well, I better drag my butt into the shower. The Tiger-Lady will be here at 9:00 a.m. sharp. No doubt about it, we've got a lot of chapters to cover today." Jack was talking to himself. "Only crazy people talk to themselves, right?" he asked his image in the bathroom mirror. Jack broke into a verse from an old Jimmy Buffet song as he turned on the knobs of the shower. "If we weren't all crazy, we would go insane!"

Jack stopped for a moment of reflection before he stepped into the shower. Here he was, in New York City, on a cold Tuesday morning in early November, and he was singing.

"How long?" he wondered. "How long has it been since I caught myself singing? A long time, Jack," he answered himself in the echo chamber of the empty shower stall. "A damn long time."

Jack knew something was changing, he could feel it. Something was going to happen, and he'd never be the same again. Just like nothing had ever been the same again after Mary died.

Jack stood in the hot shower for a long time. He kept hoping the water would wash away his uncertainty of the moment, yet a part of him was feeling the excitement of the pending unknown.

"Right brain fighting left brain," Jack thought as he stood under the water. "My left brain is looking for common sense and wanting life the way it used to be: simple. My right brain wants excitement, color, and changes." Jack leaned against the tiles in the shower. "Okay, okay," he said. "Tonight, I'll drink myself into a stupor and then tomorrow morning, I'll feel like my shitty old self again."

Having solved his temporary problem with a plan, Jack stepped out of the shower, toweled himself off, and began to dress. Knowing it was going to be a long day, he selected blue jeans and a gray sweatshirt.

"Editing working garb," Jack said as he caught his reflection in the bedroom mirror. "She'll show up dressed to the nines again, but I'll be the one who's comfortable all day!" Jack grabbed his room key and headed down to the cafe on the main floor for breakfast. While waiting for the elevator, he caught himself humming again. "If we weren't all crazy, we would go insane."

Jack found a table in the corner and ordered a double waffle platter and a large orange juice. He read USA TODAY while he ate, paying little attention to the other people around him. He signed the ticket for his breakfast and wondered if he was to pay for his meals or if it was all included in the hotel bill and the charges picked up by Brownstone Publishing. "Well," Jack thought as he headed back to the elevators, "I'm sure we'll sort it all out when I checkout next week."

As Jack rode the elevator back up to his suite, he tried to recollect what Marsha Morrow had told him about the expenses. Somewhere, he had a letter from her which explained it all. He probably placed it in his briefcase. Jack got off the elevator on the 34th floor and headed down the hall to suite 3418. He glanced at his cell and saw it was already 8:25. He had thirty-five minutes before Lisa arrived for day two of the rewrite. "Today, I'll be ready for her," Jack said aloud as he closed the door of the suite behind him.

"Oh, pardon me, sir," whispered a soft voice with a slight Spanish accent. Jack jumped and quickly turned around to face the person behind him.

"Huh?"

"I'm sorry, sir. I did not mean to frighten you. I thought you were speaking to me. I did not hear what you were saying." It was one of the maids from housekeeping. She went on, "I saw you leave your room this morning, so I thought I'd come in and clean before you got back."

"Oh," Jack said, his heart returning to its normal rate. "That's fine. I just didn't expect anyone here."

"I am sorry, sir," she apologized again. "It happens sometimes." She turned her attention to the pile of dirty linens and towels on the floor.

Jack headed over to his briefcase near the small metal desk, calling back to the maid over his shoulder. "What's your name?"

"Anita. Are you going to report me for scaring you?" she asked in a near-panicked voice, her eyes wide with concern.

"Report you?" Jack turned around, looking surprised. "Oh, hell... huh, I mean, heck no... I remember seeing you in the hall yesterday. I'm going to be here for several days, and I like to call people by name whenever possible."

"Oh, well, thank you!" Anita said with a smile of relief. Jack studied her for a moment. She was short, plump, and about fifty. She looked Hispanic with big brown eyes and perfect white teeth. Jack liked her smile. He could tell she worked hard, and he wanted her to know he appreciated it. Especially since he was known for not keeping a clean room at home. More than once Mary had called him a slob. "Not a bad slob, mind you," Mary would say, "Just enough of a slob to make me want to reform you."

"You do a very nice job, Anita. I appreciate your tidiness. I'll make it a point to tell the people at the front desk, and the hotel manager, how pleased I am with your housekeeping." Jack gave her his best sincere grin.

Smiling back with her beautiful pearls, Anita said, "Oh, thank you very much. Thank YOU!" She hurried into the bedroom to put fresh sheets on the bed and hang new towels in the bathroom.

Once again, Jack turned his attention to the cluttered contents of his briefcase. "I'm sure I put that letter in here somewhere..." Jack quietly cursed to himself. Anita came out of the bedroom area and started to push her utility cart toward the front door of the suite.

Jack called to her. "Say, Anita? Did you find a dark blue sock lying around?"

"Oh, yes, sir," she replied, eager to help. "I put it on top of your dresser."

"Thank you, Anita."

"You are welcome, sir." Anita turned, opened the front door, and pulled the housekeeping cart behind her. Jack couldn't resist, he wanted to see that genuine, friendly smile one more time. "Anita?"

Once more, she stopped. This time it was in the doorway of the suite.

"Yes sir?" Anita looked at him solemnly, not knowing what to expect from this big, unusually friendly stranger.

"You can call me Jack," he replied, still grinning.

Anita smiled back. "Yes sir, Mr. Jack." She turned and pulled the cart out into the hall. As she was about to close the door, she looked in one last time. Jack was still watching her. She paused.

"Do you need anything else, Mr. Jack?"

"No, thank you, Anita. I'll see you around."

"Okay, Mr. Jack." Anita closed the door. Jack chuckled to himself. He picked up his copy of the manuscript and walked toward the French doors leading out to the terrace.

"Let's see what the weather is like in Central Park this morning," Jack mumbled as he opened the heavy drapes and unlocked one of the French doors. Jack stepped out into dim sunlight. A cold, chilly wind greeted him. He looked over the four foot brick wall that surrounded his private terrace and noticed that Central Park was looking rather deserted.

"Okay, that's long enough," Jack said as the bitter wind blew through his sweatshirt. Jack shivered and quickly stepped back into the room, closed the French door, and looked at the time on his cell phone. 8:59 a.m. He grinned.

Jack walked over to the center of the room and stood just five feet in front of the door. His grin widened as he softly started counting backwards. "10, 9, 8, 7, 6, 5, 4, 3, 2, 1." Upon his count of one, there was a knock on the door.

"Right on cue," Jack said with a self-assured smile as he swung the suite door wide open.

"Good morning, Lisa Lisignoli!" Jack sang out to her with a wide grin.

Having been completely caught off guard, Lisa stood frozen, blinking her deep green eyes at him. Jack thought he noticed a hint of a smile starting to curl at the corners of her lips, but she maintained total control.

"A little early to be intoxicated, don't you think, Kramp?" she said coolly as she stepped in. Jack closed the door behind them.

"It's Jack, remember? And I've had nothing but fresh squeezed orange juice," Jack replied. He grinned again as he discreetly looked her over from head to toe. Lisa was wearing a simple long sleeved red dress with rows of large double breasted gold buttons down the front. A beige trench coat was neatly draped over one arm. Her ensemble was accented by black high heels and gold hoop earrings. Jack wondered if she had been a model at some point in her life. "She certainly is breathtaking enough to be one now," he thought.

Lisa set her briefcase down and fumbled with her trench coat. Jack was standing with his hand out, ready to take it. She gave him an odd look and slowly handed her coat over to him.

As she picked up her briefcase and headed to the desks, she said over her shoulder, "I feel like we are really behind, Kramp. We have to make major headway today with our corrections."

"I know," Jack replied from the far corner of the room as he hung Lisa's coat in the small entry closet. "And it's Jack," he repeated again.

Lisa ignored his last comment but looked at Jack, noticing how casual he had dressed. "So you threw on a few things from your native Minnesotan wardrobe?" she asked, nodding in his direction.

"My workin' clothes," Jack said, turning around to look at her again. "I thought I might as well be comfortable. It's going to be a long day."

Lisa nodded and looked down at her dress, feeling like she needed to offer some sort of explanation.

"I have a luncheon appointment at 12:15 today," Lisa said as she started to sort through her open briefcase on the big wooden desk. "I'm certain I'll be back by 1:15. It's just down the street. Let's plan to work until at least 7:00 this evening."

"Sounds fine to me," Jack replied as he crossed over to her and the desks. Without looking at him, Lisa handed him three pages out of the printer. "Here, start on chapter six, and I'll make the finals in five."

"Sure," replied Jack as he sat down in his desk chair, pulled out his sharpened pencils and yellow highlighter, and started working. Lisa turned her attention to the computer screen and chapter five.

For the next hour and a half, Jack and Lisa concentrated on reworking their respective manuscript sections without speaking. Occasionally, Jack would look over to admire Lisa's long black hair that cascaded down her back and shoulders.

"There's gotta be some natural curl in there," Jack thought, "Because she doesn't seem like the type who would mess with a curling iron on all that hair." Jack would quickly look back down at his papers whenever Lisa made any movements with her head. He didn't want her to catch him staring at her. He felt like a young adolescent who had just discovered girls and training bras.

Lisa tried desperately to concentrate on her edits and the rewrite, but her thoughts kept turning to the tall, unpredictable stranger seated just behind her.

"What's wrong with you, girl?" Lisa asked herself. "You swore off men for a full year. Remember your New Year's resolution?" Lisa watched Jack out of the corner of her eye, tilting her head to the left, just enough to see him in his usual position; feet propped up and crossed on the corner of his desk, his body reclined in his chair, a pencil tucked behind his right ear, and a highlighter occasionally in and out of his mouth. Once, Lisa thought she caught him looking at her. She smiled, turning her head away from him, and looked out the windows of the French doors so that Jack wouldn't notice.

"It's not an attraction. It's just curiosity," Lisa told herself, not realizing that she had said her thoughts aloud until she heard Jack's voice.

"What?" Jack asked, raising his head to look at her, hoping it was the beginning of a conversation.

"Oh, nothing," Lisa said, without turning to look at him. "I was just reading out loud." She hoped he hadn't heard her exact words or, even worse, noticed that she slightly blushed. She quickly changed the subject.

"Do you have any coffee up here, Kramp?"

"Yeah, I think there is some." Jack looked up into the kitchenette. He remembered seeing a couple of small, silver bags of premium coffee and an automatic coffee maker. "I only drink the stuff during a hangover," Jack added as he stood and headed toward the coffee maker, "But I'll make some for you."

"That would be lovely," Lisa said, glancing at the time on her computer. "It's 10:45 a.m. I have to leave no later than noon, so if I get too involved here and lose track of the time, please remind me."

"Sure thing," Jack said as he poured fresh water from the coffee pot into the coffee maker. "Do you like your coffee black?"

"Black will be fine."

"That's good, because I don't see any cream or sugar here. Oh, wait a minute. Here's some." Jack had his back to her, bent over the counter in the kitchen and digging through some woven baskets. Lisa broke into a broad grin as she looked over at him.

"Mr. Midwest nice guy," Lisa thought. Then she remembered Jack's quick temper yesterday and her smile vanished. "A nice guy who isn't so nice when he is pushed," she thought. "But then, I'm the one who set him off." A glimmer of guilt crept into her mind. Lisa shook her head in an effort to erase the feeling. "Keep things in perspective," she said to herself, making sure Jack didn't hear her this time. "He's just another writer. It's just another book. It's a paperback western, for pete's sake!" Lisa shook these thoughts from her head and turned her attention back to the computer.

Jack returned to his desk, and worked for about ten more minutes, while the coffee brewed. When it finished, Jack poured a large blue mug full of hot black coffee and brought it over to Lisa.

"Thank you," she said, pausing to look up at him. Lisa stared deeply into his blue eyes. They seemed to hold a distant pain. She suddenly felt an overwhelming urge to know the cause. She felt needed, a feeling she hadn't had in a long time.

Jack caught Lisa's deep emerald green eyes with his own as he set the coffee mug down on the edge of her desk. "They look softer, today," he thought. There was a little more warmth in them. A glimmer of friendliness that he hadn't seen before. "Oh, hell," he thought, "It's just my imagination. After all, she's best known in all the literary circles as 'the Word Witch.'"

"Be careful," Jack warned. "It's hot."

"So are you," Lisa caught herself thinking as she watched Jack turn his back and walk over to the French doors. She quickly looked down in embarrassment. Jack opened one of the French doors a crack to let in some fresh air. He returned to his desk, sat down, and picked up the final three paragraphs of chapter six. Jack put his highlighter and pencil back to work. Lisa returned to her computer and opened chapter seven.

At 11:55 a.m., Jack looked up and watched Lisa bend over to retrieve three pages from the printer. He noticed her long shapely legs. "Perfect," he thought. Jack glanced at his cell phone. "It's 11:55," he said softly, not taking his eyes off the back of her red dress.

"Thank you," replied Lisa, turning to look at him. She picked up her brief-case and paused. "I think I'll just leave my briefcase here. I don't need to drag it along to my luncheon appointment."

"I'll keep a close eye on it," Jack said with a grin. Lisa turned and started walking toward the closet. Jack followed, and as she removed her coat from the hanger, Jack reached out and took it. Lisa shot him a brief quizzical look, but said nothing, as she gracefully slipped into it.

"Thank you," Lisa said softly. She walked over to the door and opened it. "I'll see you back here at 1:15, okay?"

"Sure," Jack said, shrugging his shoulders. "1:15 p.m. Is there any chapter you want me to review?"

"No, we'll finish six and seven this afternoon. Since we are working later today, be sure to eat a good lunch. Oh, but don't stray too far from the hotel." Lisa turned and walked out of suite 3418, calling a nonchalant goodbye over her shoulder to Jack as she closed the door. Jack stood and stared at the door. "Goodbye," he murmured. The room suddenly seemed big and lonely to Jack. "I need some lunch," he thought to himself.

Jack went into the bedroom's large walk-in closet and grabbed his long black trench coat from the hanger. He paused for a moment as he thought of Lisa's advice about not straying too far from the hotel. He shrugged his shoulders and turned his attention back to the coat in his hands. "A trench coat with blue jeans, sweatshirt, and white Nikes?" Jack thought a minute about his ensemble. "Oh, what the hell," he said aloud. "It's New York. No one will even notice."

Jack grabbed his room key from the small table in the kitchenette, made sure his suite door was locked, and took the elevator down to the lobby. The air was bitterly cold from a wild wind along Central Park West. Jack remembered seeing a deli a few blocks south on West 57th, just past Trump Tower and he headed for it, walking briskly with the rest of the lunch hour people on the crowded sidewalks in the chilly noon air. He found the deli on the corner just three blocks down from his hotel. He waited in line for a couple of minutes, enjoying the different accents of the people around him as they ordered their lunches.

When it was Jack's turn, he decided on a ham and Swiss on rye, a large dill pickle, a bag of potato chips, and a large hot chocolate. He walked across the street to the park, found a deserted bench, and ate his lunch. The sun was beginning to peek through the clouds and Jack felt the air getting warmer.

A bus went by and Jack noticed a large billboard on the side promoting a local country station. He suddenly realized that it was his second full day in New York City and he hadn't attempted to enjoy his hobby of listening to radio stations in other markets. He made a mental note to tune in the radio when he returned to his room. Jack was always fascinated with the humor and delivery styles of on-air personalities from other radio stations, especially in other parts of the country.

"I must have too many things on my mind," Jack said to about a dozen pigeons who had congregated around him, looking for crumbs. "I'd feed you, boys and girls, but then you'd probably thank me by crapping all over my head," Jack said as he carefully rolled up the wrappers from his sandwich and stuffed them into the large styrofoam cup from his hot chocolate. He stood and, noticing a large green trash can about eight feet away near the edge of the sidewalk, made a quick turn and a fake jump shot with his wad of garbage. "From the top of the key... Swoosh! Two Points!" Jack said, grinning as he completed his shot into the can and headed back up the street toward the West Park Plaza Hotel.

"Those were the days, Jack," he said under his breath as he stuffed his hands in the pockets of his trench coat. "The glory days. Basketball games, pep rallies, championships, cheerleaders in tight sweaters, and Mary."

As Jack's thoughts turned to Mary, he thought of the kids. He made another mental note to call them again tonight. As he neared the hotel, Jack noticed a liquor store across the street. He crossed over and bought a twelve pack of beer. "I'll put it in the refrigerator and not have to pay the high prices charged by hotel room service," Jack reasoned.

Back inside the hotel, Jack punched the elevator button for the 34th floor and tucked the twelve pack of beer in the heavy brown paper bag under his right arm. As the elevator glided up, Jack glanced at the time on his cell. In disbelief, he looked again, holding it closer to his face with hopes he had read it incorrectly. It still read 1:35 p.m.

"Oh, shit!" Jack cursed aloud in the empty elevator. "Where'd the time go?" Jack groaned as he reached his floor, and the doors opened. He leaned out of the elevator and looked down the hall toward his suite. "Thank God," he whispered to himself. "She isn't there yet." Jack hustled down to his suite, unlocked the door, and stepped inside.

"Where the hell have you been?" Lisa was standing in the middle of the suite, on the lower level between the two sofas in front of the fireplace, hands on her hips, fire shooting from her green eyes.

Remembering how Anita had startled him earlier that same morning, Jack said, "Holy Crap! Can anyone just come into this suite any time they damn please?"

"You're a half hour late, Kramp. What's the matter, did you get lost in the big city?" Lisa hadn't moved, but her eyes narrowed.

"I'm only twenty minutes late, and I wasn't lost," Jack snapped back at her as he headed toward the refrigerator with his beer.

"What's in the bag, Kramp?"

"None of your business." Jack had his back to her. Lisa stomped up the three steps to the kitchenette just in time to see Jack stuffing the twelve pack into the bottom shelf of the refrigerator next to the three bottles left over from the night before.

"Beer? Beer!" Lisa queried, raising her voice from an indignant whisper to almost a full blown shout. "You kept me waiting while you were out buying beer?" She turned and walked to the desks. "We don't have any time to waste on this project, Kramp. I believe I explained the situation to you yesterday. We're behind schedule. If you want to waste our time getting ready for your own private beer-fest, do it on your own time, okay?" Her voice was calming down, but her teeth were still slightly clenched.

"Look," Jack said as he took off his trench coat and flung it over the love seat in the lower level. "I was late because there was this fire down the street, and I had to rescue three elderly nuns." Lisa sat down at her desk and looked at him, expressionless.

"They were in wheelchairs," Jack continued, "And there was this cute little puppy with them who kept barking because he was trying to tell us about the twin orphans who had been visiting the nuns on the second floor. The orphans were trapped by this fire, and the fire escape was so old and rusted, it just fell off the building, and then there was the fireman I had to resuscitate because he had suffered smoke inhalation. And then… oh yeah, and then there were the five looters who made off with the nuns' only TV, and by the time I caught up with them three blocks away, there was a helluva fight and I..." Jack paused to catch his breath, his arms spread wide in the air extending out from his sides, palms up.

Lisa crossed her arms and tilted her head down, her hair flowed in front of her. Jack looked at her, but couldn't see her face. "Are you buying ANY of this?" he asked quietly. Jack thought he noticed her shoulders shaking and wondered if he had gone too far. Lisa looked like she was in the middle of an angry meltdown.

"Well?" he asked again.

When Lisa raised her head, there were tears in her eyes. But there was also something else. Her mouth was open wide with laughter. She was able to gurgle out a "No" from her explosive giggles as she shook her head from side to side. Lisa bent over, holding her stomach, still laughing happily in a somewhat dignified manner.

In a few seconds, Lisa regained her composure. Standing near her desk, she looked at Jack, shaking her head. "That was the longest yard of bull I've heard in years, Kramp. Where did you come up with that?" Her eyes narrowed, again. "Were you already into the beer over lunch?"

"No, I swear," Jack said, holding his left hand up and placing his right hand over his heart. "That kind of stuff just comes naturally to me. It rolls out of my mouth without me really thinking about it. It always has. Sometimes I'll ad-lib stories like that when I'm doing my radio show in the morning. It's actually quite fun."

"I'm sure it is," Lisa said, brushing her long black hair back with her hands as she continued to gain control over her sudden outburst.

Jack walked over and sat down in his desk chair. "So, still upset with me?" he asked, raising his eyebrows as he leaned forward, resting his elbows on his knees.

"No," she said slowly. "No, I'm not angry anymore. Let's get to work." Lisa turned her back to him and looked at her computer screen. Jack picked up his copy of chapter seven and hunted for his highlighter. They worked quietly for the next twenty minutes, neither one breaking the unfamiliar yet comfortable silence that enveloped them.

Suddenly, Lisa looked up and stared out the windows of the French doors.

"Jack?"

"Yeah?" Surprised at the new softness in her voice, he gave her his full attention.

Without turning to look at him, she said, "Thank you."

"You're welcome." Jack was even more surprised. He paused and then added, "For what?"

"Making me laugh. I haven't laughed like that for a long, long time."

"You should," Jack said, staring at the back of her head, wishing she would turn around so he could see those beautiful green eyes again. "Laughter becomes you. It makes you..." Jack paused and sucked in his breath, refusing to believe he was actually going to say it, "...look younger."

"Younger?" Lisa asked continuing to look out the windows, not wanting to let him see her blushing.

"Yeah. Not that you look old. I mean, you look great. It's just that I've never seen you laugh before, and well, happiness makes you even more beautiful." It was Jack's turn to feel redness seep into his cheeks.

"Well, thank you. It felt good to laugh like that again. And thank you for the compliment."

"We'll do it again sometime, okay?"

"Sure." Lisa refused to allow herself to turn and look at this big stranger who had just made her laugh. She felt relaxed. Gone was the tension of his being inconsiderately late. Gone, too, was the remorse for having been assigned to work on a western novel. "As long as this is my assignment, I might as well make the best of it," she thought.

Jack's stomach growled loudly, and Lisa looked at her watch.

"It's 7:15p.m., Kramp," Lisa said as she stretched her hands high above her head. "Let's call it a day."

"Okay, it's a day," Jack said cheerfully as he put down the final paragraph of chapter seven. "How far are you?"

"Six is done. I'll take seven's changes home with me to review if you are finished with them and enter them onto the jump drive tomorrow morning."

"Here they are," Jack handed the twenty-two pages to Lisa, and she stuffed them into her briefcase. He went to the entry closet and retrieved Lisa's trench coat. He held it for her as she crossed to him near the door.

"What time do you want to get started tomorrow morning?" Jack asked.

"Same time, Kramp. 9:00 a.m. It's always a 9:00 a.m. start time." Lisa put her hand on the door handle and then added, "I'm not exactly a morning person."

She smiled. Jack flashed a broad smile back.

"To some people, it's the best part of the day," Jack said.

"Not for me. Goodnight, Kramp," Lisa said as she opened the door. "I'll see you tomorrow."

"9:00 a.m.," Jack said, holding the door as Lisa stepped out into the large corridor. "9:00 a.m. sharp," he said again, "Unless I come across three nuns in a fire."

Lisa's eyes danced as she laughed, throwing her head back, her long black hair tumbled down her back. She closed the door behind her and headed for the elevators. Jack was left standing with a broad grin on his face, lost in his thoughts about how he had finally made her laugh today. As Lisa waited for the elevator, she found herself smiling, too.

"I'm going to sleep well tonight," she said to herself. "I'll have a nice hot shower, some pasta, and a good night's sleep for once."

Chapter Six

Jack's cell phone rang, and he glanced at the time as he picked it up. "7:30 p.m., dinner time in Minnesota," he said to himself quietly. "It's the kids."

"Hello, youngin's!"

"Hi, Dad!"

"Hey, Tammy, I was just about to call you guys. How's it going at home?" Jack was feeling light hearted and the sound of Tammy's voice made him even happier.

"Just fine, Daddy, although the way the boys are eating, I don't know if the grocery money is going to last."

"Oh? If you guys need more money, use my cash card. You know how to use it, right?"

"Sure. I think we'll be okay. It's just kind of scary without you here."

"Sorry, hon. I'll be home in about a week and a half. Maybe sooner."

"How is your book going?" Tammy asked, changing the subject.

"Slow, until this afternoon. We made better progress. At least we are through chapter seven. Only nineteen more to go."

"That's great, Dad."

Jack listened to Tammy chat on about school, homework, the boys, and the meals they had cooked together. Jack was relieved to hear the cheerfulness back in Tammy's voice. He grinned as he reclined in the love seat, his feet up on the coffee table. Later in the conversation, Michael and Jim took turns on the extension phone in the master bedroom. They were all in good spirits. Jack relaxed, knowing that all seemed to be going well on the home front.

After saying good-bye, Jack felt very tired. He closed his eyes and felt himself drifting off. Suddenly, his stomach growled loudly, waking him up from his short nap. He opened his eyes and began to sit up just as a gust of wind blew open one of the French doors, making the room temperature drop instantly.

"Brrr," Jack said as he bounded up the steps to the terrace doors. Jack shivered as he remembered that he had slightly opened the one door earlier in the afternoon to let in fresh air. Jack closed the door and locked the deadbolt. He stood for a moment and looked out over the lights of New York City.

"It's nice, but it isn't home. It's not the Twin Cities," Jack sighed to himself as he closed the thick drapes of the French doors. He strolled over to the desks and turned off the two lamps. Noticing Lisa had left the printer on, he flipped off the switch. His stomach growled again. "Okay, big fella, I'll get something down to you real soon," Jack said, patting his midsection.

Remembering the mental note Jack had made to himself during his lunch in Central Park, he went down into the sunken living area again and stood in front of the television and entertainment system.

"There must be a radio in this somewhere," Jack muttered to himself as he looked at the tuner, the DVD player, and the compact disc system. When he finally found the on/off button for the stereo radio, he tuned in on a country station and cranked up the volume.

Jack headed up to his bedroom, smiling at the announcer's introduction for the next music set. He sat down on the bed, picked up the hotel telephone, and dialed the front desk.

"Good evening, this is Jason. How may I help you?"

"Good evening, Jason, Jack Kramp here in suite 3418."

"Yes, Mr. Kramp, what can we do for you this evening?"

"Well, just between you and me, Jason," Jack said, lowering his voice to a soft whisper, "Suppose I wanted a really good pizza. I've already had one from the hotel that didn't even come close to fitting that description. Where would I call to order one?"

Jason chuckled, "Louie's, Mr. Kramp. Louie's Pizza is the best. It's just a few blocks away and they deliver. It's the pizza of choice for our entire staff. I'll be happy to give you the number."

"Good enough for me," Jack said. He took the number, repeated it back to Jason, hung up briefly, then dialed Louie's. Jack looked at the time on his cell. "No wonder I'm hungry," he thought, "It's already after 8:00 p.m." Jack ordered a medium with the works, no anchovies. It was guaranteed to be delivered to his room within thirty minutes.

"That's just enough time to jump in the shower," Jack said as he started to undress. He spotted the blue sock lying on top of the dresser where Anita had placed it earlier that morning. After a long, hot shower, Jack was about to put on his robe but changed his mind and opted for a pair of gray dress slacks, an under shirt, and a navy sweater. He thought, "Maybe I'll go out later."

The pizza arrived. Jack tipped the delivery boy and opened the pizza on the small table in the kitchenette. He pulled a beer out of the refrigerator and ate his pizza. While opening his second beer, he thought the country music coming from the radio sounded odd against the scene of the plush suite and eating pizza. It reminded him of the old Sesame Street song in the learning cartoon: "One of these things is not like the others..."

"Only which one of us is out of place?" Jack questioned himself as he leaned back in his chair, draining the last of the second beer. He stood and reached into the small refrigerator for another beer. Popping it open, he walked over to his metal desk and stared at his open briefcase. Jack remembered that he had been looking for a detailed itinerary from Marsha Morrow. After ruffling through the cluttered contents of his over-sized briefcase, Jack threw up his arms in disgust and shook his head.

"Maybe I left it on my desk at home," Jack said aloud, rubbing his right hand across the stubble on his face. While Jack was searching his memory banks for places he might have left the Brownstone itinerary, he heard sirens outside. He turned and headed back into his bedroom, thinking that there was a great deal of crime, drama, and accidents in New York. He had come to expect to hear a siren of some sort, somewhere, every few minutes.

Jack picked up the blue sock off the dresser and threw it into the dirty clothes bag. "I'll either have to wash clothes or send them out to be laundered before the end of the week," he muttered to himself as he went into the bathroom to shave.

Jack stood in the center of the huge master bath, feeling restless again. Suddenly, he slapped on some cologne, looked at himself in the mirror, and spoke to his reflection, "Thanks, I needed that, but right now, I think I need a strong scotch and water even more."

Jack stuffed his room key into his pocket, shut the door to his suite tightly behind him, and headed to the elevators that would take him down to the hotel lobby and the bar. As Jack waited for the elevator to arrive, he thought about Lisa. He had wanted to ask her how she got into his suite after lunch when he wasn't there. He'd thought of it earlier, but during her angry outburst over his tardiness and his impromptu nuns-on-fire excuse, he had forgotten.

"Maybe she has her own key?" Jack questioned during the ride down to the main floor. "Nothing would surprise me with her."

Bannigan's Bar was located just to the right, around the corner from the elevators. It was crowded for 10:00 p.m. on a Tuesday night, but Jack found a stool, second from the end on the left side of the large horseshoe-shaped bar. A tall, sandy haired young man named Eric was behind the bar, walking toward him with a white apron around his waist and a small white towel in his hand. He reached for a drink napkin and placed it in front of Jack.

"And what will you have tonight?" Eric asked, flashing a wide grin at the big stranger.

"Scotch and water."

"Right away." Eric turned and headed to the nearest setup area to make the cocktail.

While Jack waited for his drink, he surveyed the dimly lit bar. It was typical, with patrons seated on stools surrounding three sides of the dark oak bar trimmed with polished brass. There was a huge mirror on the back wall along with shelves filled with famous brand name liquors. Ornate glasses on crisp white linens lined the counter in front of the mirror. The rest of the room was surrounded by high-backed booths finished in dark oak with their benches trimmed in padded red leather. Within the twenty foot space that separated the booths from the three sided bar were about a dozen round oak wooden tables with at least four barrel chairs at each one. Each chair stained in matching dark oak on the outside back and bottom, the inside seating and back areas were upholstered in the same padded red leather as the booths.

Jack noticed that nearly every booth and table was filled. Bits and pieces of conversation, incessant chatter, and laughter erupted sporadically and blended into a familiar hum that one becomes accustomed to hearing in their favorite watering holes.

When Eric delivered Jack's scotch and water, Jack paid cash and left a two dollar tip. Jack looked up at the basketball game on the television in the far corner of the bar. He squinted, trying to focus his eyes in an attempt to determine what teams were playing.

"I should have gotten those trifocals last month when my ophthalmologist said I was borderline," Jack thought as he continued to squint at the television. He leaned forward on the bar, slightly raising himself up off his stool, yet being careful not to spill his drink.

"It's the Knicks and the Celtics," said a voice to his right. "The Knicks are up, 97 to 93, with three minutes left."

Jack sat back down on his bar stool and turned to look at the slightly bald, grey-templed older gentleman seated on his right.

"Thank you," Jack said, noticing that the man wore a blue uniform. The shoulder patch indicated that he worked for Midtown Security. The old man nodded, paused momentarily to look at Jack, then turned his attention back to his brandy and the game.

Finally, Jack's curiosity got the best of him. "So, you're a security officer?" Jack asked, in a half question, half statement.

"Yup. Ten years. I was with the NYPD for thirty-seven years. I retired. For five days. Drove myself nuts. And my wife, too. Then I started working for Midtown," replied the old man without taking his eyes off the television set.

Jack nodded, appreciating his friendly, yet matter-of-fact nature. There was a certain amount of pride and confidence in his voice as he spoke.

"Been a security guard for the hotel for eight years. Work Sunday through Thursday afternoons from two 'till ten. Off every Friday and Saturday."

Again, Jack nodded. He liked listening to the Brooklyn accent of his new bar friend. He was either Italian or Jewish, or both, Jack thought.

"Fridays and Saturdays off, huh?" Jack repeated.

"Yup." The old man took a sip of his brandy. "That way, I can spend time with my grandchildren. I have thirty-one, you know."

Jack raised his eyebrows. "Thirty-one?"

"Yup. 'Course, we had nine of our own."

"Really?" Jack, astonished, was beginning to like this guy and felt he could learn something interesting from him.

"Yup," the old man went on, "We lived next to the railroad tracks during the first fifteen years of our marriage. The train always went by at 5:00 a.m. and woke us up. And I didn't need to go to work 'till 7:00."

Jack stared at the old man, not quite sure how he should react to his last statement. He wanted to laugh, but didn't want to offend him.

The old man raised both hands, spread them apart, palms open over his drink. "Well, we had to do something to pass the time!" His wrinkled, weathered face cracked with laughter.

Jack joined in, laughing heartily and noticing the gold in his teeth.

Still grinning, the old security guard stared at his drink. He began shaking his head. Quietly, yet happily, he said, "Yup, I always get 'em with that one!"

"Great story!" Jack said, still grinning. "I'll have to remember that one."

"Name's Avery," the elderly gentleman said, extending his right hand toward Jack. "Avery Schneider."

Jack shook the wrinkled, yet surprisingly strong hand of Avery Schneider. "I'm Jack Kramp. I'm staying here at the hotel," he said.

"You're from somewhere in the midwest, right?"

"Yeah," Jack replied, pausing to take a sip of his scotch. "Minneapolis."

Avery smiled and nodded, a confusing frown spread across his forehead.

"Minnesota," Jack said, trying to clarify.

"Yup, I thought so," Avery nodded again, pleased with himself. "I can always spot where people are from."

"Really? How?" Jack was interested.

"Oh, by the way they dress, how they walk, and how they talk. Never been out of New York much, except back in '78, I had to take a prisoner to Milwaukee. Never been west of the Mississippi, though."

"It's really nice in Minnesota. Green, clean, and fresh. And the winters aren't nearly as bad as everyone makes them out to be."

"About like Buffalo, eh?" Avery said, trying to draw a similarity to someplace closer and identifiable to his home.

"Yeah, like Buffalo," Jack said, turning his attention back to his final swallow of scotch.

Avery drained the last of his brandy, looked at the television, and said, "Well, chalk up another one for the Celtics. 105 to 101. Final."

"Can I buy you another brandy?" Jack asked. He was enjoying the conversation with this unusual character and didn't want it to end.

"Nope. Thanks anyway. I stop in every night right after I get off work for one night cap. And at my age, believe me, one is enough." Avery smiled at Jack and eased off his bar stool. "I better be gettin' home to the misses. She worries after 11:00 if I'm not there. Was nice talkin' to ya." Avery extended his right hand again and Jack shook it firmly. "Good night," Avery said, putting his security officers hat squarely on his head and walking toward the door.

"Good night. It was nice meeting you, too," Jack called to Avery's back.

Jack turned his attention back to the bar. He waved to Eric and ordered another scotch and water. "Make it a double," Jack added. He glanced at his watch. "10:45 p.m. Still early," Jack mumbled under his breath.

He had just ordered his fourth double scotch and water when he saw her. She was standing in the doorway wearing a blue dress, her back to him. She had the same petite waist, graceful long legs, and soft blonde hair. Jack stared hard at her. He looked away, hoping that it was just his imagination or too much scotch. He looked back. She was still there. Mary! His Mary, was there in Bannigan's Bar. Right here, in New York City. Jack closed his eyes and then opened them again. She was gone. He slowly eased himself off his bar stool, fighting the urge to run after her.

"Jack, sometimes I think you drink a little too much." That's what Mary would say. Jack never admitted to anyone that he might be a candidate for AA with an alcohol addiction, but he knew it. And so did Mary. But after her death, he did little to fight it. He pretty much got into the beer and booze whenever he wanted, yet he was always careful to make sure the children were never around to see him. But he often wondered if they suspected.

Jack turned back and looked at his full drink waiting for him on the bar. He looked back at the empty doorway. He gazed slowly around the bar, noticing that almost everyone had left. Only a handful of semi-quiet drunks remained. His gaze came to rest on Eric, who was stacking dirty glasses in plastic racks. Eric looked up at Jack.

"That was last call, sir," Eric said, nodding toward the drink he had just served Jack, still sitting on the bar. Jack nodded, not wanting to explain that he really wasn't attempting to order another one. He reached over and picked up the scotch. He raised it to his lips and stopped. He saw her again. This time it was her reflection in the mirror behind the bar. She was staring at him, still standing in the doorway. It definitely was Mary. Jack whirled around to see her, but again, she was gone. Jack stared down at the drink in his right hand. He closed his eyes, counted slowly to five, and opened them. He looked in the mirror with hope. No one was there. Jack took a deep breath, set his still-full scotch and water back down on top of the bar, and walked out. He floated to the elevators on weak and wobbly knees and punched the UP button.

Jack tried to read the time on his cell during the ride up to the 34th floor, but he couldn't focus his eyes in the dim light of the elevator. Outside his suite, he fumbled for his keys, opened the door and, on his third attempt, found the light switch.

"Balls on a goose, Kramp," Jack mumbled to himself as he stumbled toward the bedroom. "It sure doesn't take much to get you drunk these days. It must be the altitude. After all, I am on the 34th floor!" Jack laughed at his own joke. He paused in the doorway of the bedroom and held up his cell in another attempt to see the time. "2:15 a.m. Not bad. Hell, it's still early!" Jack said again, laughing. But his laughter suddenly died when he thought of the apparitions of his deceased wife. "It's happened before," Jack said. "It's just the scotch." Jack flopped himself face down on the large bed, still in his clothes.

"Maybe I should switch to gin and tonics. I wonder who the hell I'd see then?" Jack slurred from his non-functioning lips as darkness overtook him and he fell into a deep, fitful sleep.

Chapter Seven

Out of the fogginess of a deeply troubled sleep, where the usual monsters of uncertainty and guilt often came to tread on his soul, Jack could hear the faint calling of his name.

"Mary?" he murmured. Jack's dry mouth handicapped his speech.

"Kramp? Jack! Come on, Kramp! Wake up and get with it!"

Jack's eyes fluttered open briefly, closed, and then slowly opened again, first the right, then the left. Still stretched out on his stomach, his left arm was tucked under his waist and tingling, having fallen asleep hours ago. He turned his head slightly to look at the person standing over him. It certainly wasn't Mary.

It was Lisa Lisignoli leaning over him with her left hand resting on the back of his right shoulder. Jack closed his eyes again, hoping he would wake up from this dream. His head was pounding, and he felt a slight wave of nausea crash against the linings of his empty stomach. He also had a strong sensation to empty his full bladder.

"Come on Kramp, it's not in my job description to have to play nurse to our aspiring authors. You should have left a wake up call." Lisa stood up, placing both hands on her hips.

Jack slowly rolled over on his back. Squinting, he brought Lisa into focus. "You're much better than a wake up call, Lisa." Jack couldn't believe his own ears; he said the first thing that had come into his pounding, cobwebbed head. "What time is it?" he semi-consciously changed the subject.

"9:15. And cut the bullshit, Kramp. At this rate, we won't have the edits completed on your damn book until Christmas!" Lisa's voice was rising again. She was getting angry, and Jack knew it. He witnessed it before and it wasn't pretty. "What'd you do last night?" she demanded. "Drink that entire twelve pack before going to bed?"

"No," Jack replied, trying to raise himself up on his elbows, hoping the room would stop spinning. "Although my bladder feels like I drank about ten gallons of something." Jack prided himself on being brutally honest with the entire world, especially early in the morning. He often thought it was possibly one of the reasons why his morning radio show was so popular.

"Well, you're still dressed, Kramp, either from last night's drinking or else you arose early this morning, got dressed, and then fell back asleep." Lisa nodded at Jack's feet. Jack looked down to discover he still had on his black wing tipped shoes. He managed a weak grin at Lisa.

"Would you believe me if I told you I got up early this morning, got dressed, and fell back asleep?"

"Not for a second!" Lisa backed away from the bed, her hands still resting on her slim hips. "You have five minutes to get it together. I'm going to get started." She turned and headed out the door. Jack watched her. He hadn't moved a muscle.

Lisa paused in the doorway, turned slightly to look over her shoulder at Jack, and quietly said, "I'll brew some strong coffee for you." Before Jack could reply, she was gone. He let his head fall back down on his pillow. He closed his eyes tightly.

"I'll just lay here for a minute, then I'll get up," he said softly, his throat and mouth cracking from the dryness within.

"Good morning, Mr. Jack."

Jack opened his left eye to see Anita, the maid from housekeeping, standing just inside the bedroom door.

"Morning, Anita," Jack struggled with the words.

"You want I should maybe come back a little later, Mr. Jack?"

"Yeah, that would be nice, Anita. A little later. I've got to go find the horse that crapped in my mouth last night and shoot him."

Anita nodded in understanding, placed both hands on top of her head, and giggled loudly as she darted back out into the other room. Jack slowly swung his legs off the bed and eased himself into an upright position. The clanging in his head sounded like the large bells of the sea buoys in Lake Superior. He closed his eyes and rolled his head around on his neck. "It's going to be a long day," Jack said aloud, "But the best thing about waking up with a hangover is with each hour that passes, you feel better and better."

Jack stood and stretched, rotating his left arm to get the blood circulating again. Glancing at his cell, he noticed it was 9:24. He walked over and closed the bedroom door, impulsively opening it again just a crack to see the back of Lisa, seated at the desk, already working. He closed the door and started taking off his clothes, feeling like he was moving in slow motion. Jack thought about Lisa in the next room.

"What was she wearing today?" Jack asked himself as he hung up his slacks and sweater. He had been so groggy earlier that he hadn't taken the time to notice.

After a hot shower, a shave, and a brief worship ritual of retching while bent over the ceramic god, Jack felt and looked much better. He threw on a pair of blue briefs, along with blue socks, and stood in front of his selection of clothes in the small closet. "I need to make a better impression," Jack muttered to himself. "No native Minnesota garb today, Jack." He chose a white shirt, a blue and grey tie, and a pair of blue dress slacks. He slipped into his wing tips, poked his head into the bathroom for one final review of his appearance, and headed into the other room to face Lisa.

The aroma of freshly brewed coffee met him as he entered the kitchenette. He found a large ceramic mug and poured the steaming black coffee into it. "I normally only drink coffee during emergencies," Jack said, leaning on the counter and sipping his coffee carefully to avoid burning his tongue. "And this is one of them."

"And I normally don't have to wake up my authors." Lisa replied coolly, keeping her back to him. "There is a box of fresh pastries on the table. Help yourself."

"Hey, thanks," Jack said, shuffling over to the table. "Any buttered-rum donuts?" placing his emphasis on the word rum. He watched Lisa's back. She stiffened, stopped typing on the computer keyboard, and held her head still as though she were looking straight ahead, her gaze fixed on some distant skyscraper outside the windows of the French doors.

"It's a joke," Jack said quickly, not wanting to see her temper flare up again.

"Not funny," Lisa said, returning her attention to the computer screen. "Now, if you'll drag your slowly sobering ass over here, I need your help on chapter eight. I've marked the areas that need work." Lisa nodded to a stack of papers on the edge of Jack's desk. With his head still pounding, Jack walked over to his desk, the coffee in one hand and a danish in the other. He sat down in his chair and looked at Lisa.

"Damn!" she said. Lisa's sudden outburst startled Jack. She stood up and went over to the printer. She opened up the paper tray and frowned, biting on her lower lip. "We're out of paper, Kramp. Do you know where we might have some more?"

Jack studied her. Lisa was wearing tight blue jeans, a gray Yale sweatshirt, and white running shoes. Her hair was pulled back by a gray, blue, and white clip. She looked very slender, her high, smooth cheek bones even more prominent with her long black hair swept away from her face. "No doubt about it, she's a looker," Jack thought.

"Well?" Lisa was staring at him, waiting for an answer.

"Sorry," Jack said, "I was just surprised. Something from your native New York City wardrobe?" Jack asked, nodding in Lisa's direction.

"Are you mocking me, Kramp?" Lisa asked, her right index finger pointing at him in defense.

"No, Miss Lisignoli, I don't believe I could ever do that and get away with it," Jack replied, watching her as a grin spread over his face. "As a dumb Midwesterner, I just don't think I'd have the smarts to do that and not have you catch on."

"Watch your step, Kramp. You and your alcohol-riddled manuscript wouldn't be the first to be thrown off the 34th floor terrace of this hotel," Lisa replied, a smile tugging at the corners of her lips.

"I should have remembered, "Jack said, his smile widening.

"Remembered what?"

"I forgot for a minute. You're Italian. And one should never mess with an Italian. Especially if she's a woman."

"You're really treading on thin ice, Kramp. I don't know whether to laugh, cry, or just shoot you. You're beginning to wear on me."

"An hour ago, I would have begged you to shoot me, but I'm feeling better now." Jack flashed her his most engaging grin. "I think it's in the white box on the floor, next to your desk."

"What?" asked Lisa looking confused. It was a look that Jack found to be rare on her normally confident face.

"The printer paper. I think it's in that white box on the floor, next to your desk," he repeated, pointing to it.

"Oh, thank you," Lisa replied, still a little bewildered from the latest twist in conversation with this big stranger from Minnesota. She bent down, pulled a half ream from the box, and placed it in the printer tray.

Lisa paused for a moment at the printer and studied Jack, noticing how he was dressed. She nodded in his direction. "Expecting some special guests today, Kramp?"

"It's Jack," he said again, looking down at his tie, slacks, and shoes. He looked back up at Lisa with an expression of mock surprise on his face. "How did that happen?" he exclaimed. "The last thing I remember, I was in my sweater and gray slack wing-tipped shoe pajama outfit!"

Lisa shook her head in frustration and looked at her watch as she seated herself once again at her desk. "It's almost 10:30," she said, no longer wishing to pursue the subject of their respective wardrobes. "Let's work through lunch today. Maybe we can order in a pizza."

"Sounds great. Louie's Pizza, just a few blocks away, is the best."

Lisa turned her head and shot Jack a questioningly look. "For just being in town a couple of days, Kramp, you sure seem to know your way around."

Jack shrugged his shoulders, smiled at Lisa, and picked up his highlighter. After realizing that she wasn't going to get any further response out of him, Lisa turned back to working on chapter nine.

Lisa shook her head slightly. "He's a different one, this Jack Kramp. I've worked with unusual personalities before, but this one's a little harder to figure out," she thought to herself. She sighed and tried to concentrate on the corrections before her.

The balance of the morning flew by quickly. Lisa and Jack worked independently on their respective chapters of *Loose Cannons*. They said very little to each other, but somehow, each of them sensed the other was occasionally lost in thought about the other. There was an air of comfortableness between them, in spite of each coming from very different worlds. Sensing hints of excitement, they each longed to ask more questions of the other in search for more answers. However, Lisa and Jack were also individually aware that oftentimes personal lives were better left alone and uncomplicated. Private thoughts held inside a person can only hurt those who think them.

"Geez, I'm hungry!" Jack announced loudly, breaking the silence as he stretched in his chair. Lisa flinched in surprise at his sudden outburst.

"Dammit, Kramp! Don't do that! You frightened me!"

"Sorry," Jack said apologetically. "It's 12:30 p.m. already. That danish I had for breakfast is not even a faint memory in my stomach. Can we get some lunch?"

"Sure. What would you like?" Lisa stood up, stretched her arms behind her head, and picked up her cell phone.

"Well," Jack hesitated, "Pizza is okay, but I just had it last night. What else do you suggest?"

Lisa snapped her fingers and said, "I've got it! Do you like turkey?"

"Sure."

"Okay. Good." Lisa punched a number into her cell. "Hello, Sammy? Lisa Lisignoli here. Listen, could you please have someone run a couple of your boxed lunches over to me? Yes, the West Park Plaza Hotel. Suite 3418. Turkey croissants. Yes. Everything in the box. Oh, and Sammy? Include a couple of spring waters and a diet Pepsi, too. Okay. Thank you."

She ended the call and turned to find Jack sprawled out on one of the sofas in the lower level. He was holding his head with both hands. His eyes were closed. Lisa smiled, crossed her arms in front of her, and quietly walked down to stand at the foot of the sofa. "Headache?" she asked softly.

"I have the entire United States Navy Drum and Bugle Corp marching in tight formation. They're doing figure eights in my cranium right now, Lisa."

"Would you like some ibuprofen? I think I have a bottle in my purse."

Jack opened one eye and looked at her. Lisa's head was cocked to one side. She looked concerned, almost maternal. He paused to relish the moment. "Yeah. I could use a couple. Thanks."

Lisa turned and walked up the steps, heading for her purse on the floor near her desk. Jack closed his eyes again and waited for the shooting stars to fizzle in front of him. Lisa returned with the two tablets and a large cup of water. She handed them to Jack without saying a word. Jack sat up, his back resting on the arm of the sofa.

"Are you sure these are ibuprofen?"

"Yes, of course. Why?"

"Oh, well, a few years ago, after an all night drinking binge, I was pretty groggy the next morning and I accidentally took four Mydol tablets."

Lisa snickered, covering her mouth with the palm of her hand.

"It wasn't funny. For the next six months, every twenty-eight days, I got really irritable."

"Wow, you're crude. But you certainly have a way with words, Kramp," Lisa said as she picked a small pillow off the love seat and flung it at Jack, causing him to spill the rest of his water on his shirt and tie. Jack looked down at his wet shirt and water stained tie.

"Well, that might help, too," he said slowly. They both laughed, and Jack closed his eyes again in pain.

Just ten minutes later came a knock on the door. "Lunch is here!" Lisa said and bounded up the steps to open the door. She signed for the lunches, added the tip, and brought a bag filled with two large white boxes and the beverages down into the lower level, placing them on the coffee table.

"I'm too hungry to eat," Jack groaned as he pulled himself up to a sitting position again on the sofa, rubbing his hand through his hair.

"You'll love it!" Lisa was obviously excited about this lunch.

She was right; Jack enjoyed the lunch. Thinly sliced turkey on a flakey croissant, a huge dill pickle, a bag of chips, a brownie, and an apple; all washed down with a bottle of spring water. Lisa had the diet Pepsi. "As though she really needs to drink or eat diet anything," Jack thought.

As they munched, Lisa finally said, "Okay, Kramp, so what did you really do last night to put yourself in such a serious, intensive care condition this morning?"

Jack recounted the events of the prior evening, starting with his children's phone call shortly after she left, the beer, pizza, and the trip downstairs to Bannigan's Bar. Lisa listened with interest as Jack told her about meeting Avery Schneider. He told her everything, except for the brief sightings of his wife or why he left the bar suddenly right at closing time.

"The last thing I sort of remember was trying to get the room key out of my pocket and into the lock on the door of the suite. Everything after that is pretty foggy. And then, there you were, waking me up. How long did it take?"

Lisa, still sipping her diet Pepsi, had curled her legs up under her as she sat on the large sofa opposite Jack. She smiled. "Let me put it this way. Three more minutes and I would have decided you were unconscious. I even considered calling an ambulance."

Jack looked down at his napkin. Every time he heard the word ambulance or heard sirens, Jack thought of Mary. If only he would have acted faster. If the ambulance could have gotten there just a few minutes sooner. Jack blamed Mary's death on a lot of things and a few people. But often, he blamed himself.

"Are you okay, Kramp?"

"Yeah. I was just thinking."

"For a moment there, I thought you'd gone into some sort of trance."

"No, I was just thinking," Jack repeated slowly. He changed the subject. "So how did you get in here this morning? Or yesterday after lunch for that matter," he added.

"I have a master key to this suite. Publisher's privilege." Lisa smiled coyly. "I was going to use it this morning, but then Anita came in to clean, so I entered with her."

"You know Anita?"

"We've been using this hotel for edits and rewrites for the past six years, Kramp. We get to know a lot of people."

"What about Avery, the security guard downstairs?" Jack asked.

"The way you've described him, I'm sure I've seen him around. I've just never had an occasion to speak with him."

Jack nodded. Lisa glanced at her watch, stood up, and began packing her trash back into her little white box. "It's 1:30, Kramp, we better get back to work."

Jack stood, removed his tie, and hung it over the back of the love seat to dry. His shirt was still a little damp. He watched Lisa as she walked up into the kitchenette and deposited her lunch box into the trash. Jack followed after picking up his own leftovers and white box. He took the unopened bottle of spring water and put it into the refrigerator next to the remaining beers.

He stood motionless for a brief moment, staring at the beers in the refrigerator. For the first time in a long time, he didn't have an urge to open one. It felt good; this fleeting loss of desire for a beer. "Maybe I have a fighting chance of licking this thing on my own," Jack thought. "If not, my next stop will have to be AA."

"Come on, Kramp. If you don't start putting the time in during your own rewrite, I'll insist my name go on the cover as co-author." Lisa, looking down, was standing at her desk and thumbing through more of the manuscript.

Jack headed to his desk and eased himself into his chair, propping his feet up in their usual position on the corner. Picking up his highlighter and pencil, Jack shot one last look over at Lisa. "She is truly beautiful," he thought. He felt himself turn warm as the redness seemed to seep up from his neck into his cheeks. He simultaneously felt embarrassed, guilty, and appreciative. He hadn't looked this way at another woman since Mary. It felt odd and yet, wonderfully strange.

Lisa was seated at her desk with a red felt marker in her mouth. She was typing feverishly on chapter eight. Jack held number nine in his hands. Lisa was really talented. Jack's mind started to wander. Suddenly, he expressed his thoughts out loud.

"Lisa?"

"Yes?" she answered, not taking her eyes off the screen or her fingers from the keyboard.

"Do you write?"

"Why?" Lisa stopped. Once again her back stiffened and she stared out the windows of the French doors.

"I was just wondering. You're very talented. I figured you had probably written a couple of novels yourself. But I never heard your name before. Are you using a pseudonym?" Jack was sincere in his questions and Lisa knew it.

Lisa took a deep breath, her shoulders sagged a little as she exhaled. She continued to look out the window and spoke very softly.

"I'm trying. In the last four years, I've submitted three manuscripts to over a dozen different publishers. They were all rejected for one reason or another. I'm using a different name. I am still waiting to hear from one publisher on my last submission." Lisa suddenly swiveled in her chair to face Jack. "No one at Brownstone knows about them. The one publisher I'm waiting to hear from is one of our main competitors. Please don't tell anyone, Kramp."

"I won't tell anyone," Jack said assuredly, trying to cover his surprise of Lisa spilling what appeared to be her very deep, very dark secret.

"I can't believe I told you," Lisa added, once again biting her lower lip.

"Look, Lisa," Jack leaned forward in his chair and lowered his voice as he searched her green eyes. "Whatever is said here between us, stays between us. I want you to know that you can trust me. If I can help you in any way, please don't hesitate to ask." Jack felt that there was more she was not telling him, but he didn't want to push her. He had learned enough for one afternoon.

"Thank you, Jack." Lisa sighed again, looked Jack in the eye, and added, "I feel I can trust you. I don't know why. I normally don't trust many people. I just hope your Midwestern charm isn't fooling me."

"So now I have Midwestern charm, huh?" teased Jack, deciding to bring some levity to the conversation. He wanted to cheer Lisa up and remove all traces of sadness from her face.

Lisa smiled at him. "Yes, charm. Or something oddly close to it."

"Thank you," Jack replied, settling back in his chair with his feet up.

"Let's get back to our edits," she said. "At this rate, we're going to be here until late tonight in order to stay on schedule."

"I hope it's not too late," Jack said, looking down at the papers on his lap. "I have an appointment at 8:00 tonight."

Lisa turned to look at him, her eyebrows raised in a silent question. Jack felt her icy stare, so he played it for just a few seconds longer. "A bunch of my barfly buddies and I are planning a drunken brawl again downstairs in Bannigan's." Jack threw his head back in a deep laugh.

Lisa wrinkled up her nose, shook her head at him, and turned back to her computer screen. She refused to let him see her smiling. Deep down, she was beginning to enjoy his slightly warped sense of humor. Then she sobered, wondering if she was getting warped, too.

Chapter Eight

Lisa and Jack worked long and hard for the next two and a half hours, their conversation limited to only editing details. Jack had come to appreciate Lisa's uncanny ability to clean up paragraphs and rearrange sentences so they became simple and crystal clear to the reader. Even though this was her second time reading through Jack's manuscript, Lisa continued to be impressed with Jack's writing style and ability for story telling. His ideas were good, the plot was clear, and his unexpected humorous inserts were exceptional. Although, Lisa noted that he could use a little more instruction in grammar, punctuation, and sentence structure.

"I need some air," Jack said, standing and once again stretching his lanky frame. He ambled toward the doors leading to the terrace. There was a dim, late afternoon sun over Central Park. Jack opened a door and stepped outside into the crisp air, but not quite as cold as the day before. Walking to the outer edge of the four foot stone wall that surrounded the private terrace, he leaned on it with both elbows and surveyed the park below.

"Even in winter, it's pretty, isn't it?" Lisa's voice startled Jack. He was suddenly aware of her standing next to him and looking down at the park, too.

"Yeah," Jack replied. "I was just wondering what it would be like to take a ride in one of those horse drawn carriages."

Lisa looked at him in surprise. "You've never been in a horse and carriage before? I thought that was a way of life back in Minnesota," she said teasingly, much to Jack's surprise.

"Nope," replied Jack. "I've been on horseback several times, but I've never had an opportunity to ride in a carriage, especially through Central Park. Have you?"

Lisa swung her gaze back to the park and stood in pensive silence for a brief moment before answering. "Once. A long time ago. It's a lovely ride," she said softly, keeping her eyes fixed on the park below. Jack studied her face, searching for a reason for her sudden sadness. Lisa turned to look at him and forced a smile. "Maybe you'll get a chance to take a ride sometime before you go," she said, nodding toward the park.

"Yeah, maybe," Jack said, returning his eyes to the line up of carriages.

"Let's get back to work, Kramp," Lisa called over her shoulder as she turned and headed back into the suite, "I've had enough fresh air."

Jack stood for a moment longer, watching Lisa's back. He turned to take one last look down into Central Park. "You have trouble in your life, too, don't you Lisa Lisignoli," Jack whispered to himself. He quickly walked back into the suite, closed and locked the French doors, and returned to his chair. He glanced at his cell. It was 4:10. He looked at Lisa. She was squinting at the computer, moving her lips quietly.

It was 5:50 p.m. when Lisa leaned back in her desk chair, rubbed the back of her neck with both of her hands, and said, "There. That completes eight and nine." She glanced at her watch. "I'd like to get us through at least ten and eleven before we call it a night, okay?"

"Fine with me," Jack replied, standing to stretch and walk around a bit. "Wanna order something up from room service?"

"Sure," Lisa nodded. She stood, pushed the sleeves of her sweatshirt up to her elbows, crossed her arms, and leaned with her backside against her desk. "Since I selected lunch, you can choose dinner."

"You've got it," Jack replied.

"Only one thing, Kramp," Lisa said as she headed toward the bathroom door. "I don't eat pork."

"I didn't know you were Jewish," Jack called after her.

Lisa turned in the doorway and smiled at him. "I'm not," she said, shaking her head. "I just try to avoid pork and red meat whenever possible."

"Okay, I'll try to remember that," Jack grinned back as he walked over to one of the drawers in the kitchenette and removed a green vinyl-covered room service menu. After making his selections, he dialed room service on his cell and ordered.

"Hello? This is Jack Kramp in suite 3418. I'd like to order two shrimp cocktails, a double veggie platter, a basket of clam strips, and a couple of desserts. How is your chocolate mousse? Fine. Send up two. Forty-five minutes? Okay, fine. Thank you."

Lisa exited the bathroom and walked into the kitchenette. She picked up a clean cup, filled it with cold water, and carried it back to her desk. "So what did you order for us?" Lisa asked as she sorted through uncorrected chapters of the manuscript.

Jack was leaning against the love seat, his back toward the fireplace, facing the steps. He glanced at Lisa and grinned. "Chicken of the Sea in a garden and a couple of whipped Hershey candy bars." Jack enjoyed his description of dinner more than Lisa. She wrinkled her nose, sipped her water, and sat down at her desk.

"How soon?" she asked.

"Forty-five minutes," Jack replied as he lumbered down the stairs and headed for his desk.

"Good. Maybe we can get through at least half a chapter before our food arrives." Lisa held out another set of pages to Jack. He took them, sat down in his familiar position, and started reading. Fifteen minutes passed slowly. Jack was having a difficult time concentrating. Out of the corner of his eye, he watched Lisa, red pen in hand, writing in the margins of the manuscript. Jack carefully tore a corner off of one of his pages, quietly rolled it into a small ball, placed it in the open palm of his left hand, and held it at chest level. Taking his index finger and thumb of his right hand, he skillfully flicked the paper ball toward Lisa. A direct hit. It bounced off her computer screen, ricocheted into her chest, just below her chin, and landed in her lap. Lisa flinched, turned, and shot an annoyed look at Jack, but said nothing. She returned her attention to the papers in front of her.

Undaunted, Jack tore off another small corner, rolled it up, and repeated the action. This time it bounced off the top of Lisa's computer monitor and sailed into the air, hitting the windows of the French doors in front of her.

Again, Lisa jumped. Jack reared back his head and laughed loudly. He was still laughing, his head back, eyes closed, when he suddenly felt the cold water hit him in the face. The shock stifled his laughter immediately. Gasping for breath, he sat upright reeling from the unexpected drenching. Lisa was standing three feet in front of him, empty cup in hand, nearly doubled over from her own laughter. In an instant, Jack was on his feet running toward the kitchenette. He grabbed a cup and grinned as he turned toward Lisa. "That makes twice today!" Jack yelled as he raced toward her. Lisa managed a scream through her loud giggles and jumped down into the sunken living room, rolled over a sofa, and ran around to the opposite side of the coffee table. Jack ran down the steps and started to circle the coffee table.

"Kramp, you wouldn't dare get me wet!" Lisa yelled while simultaneously laughing. Jack continued to chuckle loudly as he crouched, water cup in hand, stalking her.

Suddenly, Lisa made her move. She jumped behind the second sofa and made a dash for the steps and the bedroom door. Jack threw the full cup of water. At the top of the steps, Lisa ducked to avoid it, but the full stream caught her square in the face. She went down on her knees, laughing hysterically. Her hair and face were wet, as well as the front of her sweatshirt. Jack glanced at his own shirt. It, too, along with his face and hair, was soaking wet.

There was a knock on the door. Lisa and Jack looked at each other and grinned. Lisa rolled off her knees and sat down on the steps.

"Room service is early," Jack said, glancing at his cell phone as he passed by her to answer the door.

Jack flung the door to the suite open, expecting a service cart full of food delivered by a hotel employee. Instead, he was staring into the face of a well dressed woman. She was about fifty years old with a firm figure and perfect auburn hair. She had on a heavy green wool business suit with an ankle length skirt and a small matching hat. She studied Jack from head to toe before speaking. "Mr. Jack Kramp?" she inquired with raised eyebrows as if perhaps she had the wrong room.

"Yes, I'm Jack Kramp," he replied, wiping dripping water from his chin with the back of his hand. The woman's voice was oddly familiar to him.

"I'm Marsha Morrow from Brownstone Publishing. It's a pleasure to finally meet you in person," she said, extending her right hand.

Jack rolled his eyes up into his head and let out a slow, embarrassed groan. "Come in, come in," Jack said, wiping his right hand on his pant leg before accepting her hand shake.

Marsha entered the suite to find Lisa still sitting on the floor at the top of the steps leading into the sunken living room. Lisa had her knees propped up, head down, and her hands holding the back of her neck. Marsha Morrow stopped in her tracks when she spotted Lisa.

"Lisa! What on earth happened to you?" she asked with surprise. Lisa raised her head and looked at Marsha with embarrassment. Her damp hair hanging down around her cheeks was beginning to curl into small ringlets. Marsha turned and looked at Jack, her eyebrows raised in an unspoken question.

"Water fight," Jack said simply, shrugging his shoulders. He felt as though he was a little boy in elementary school who was about to be sent to detention.

"A water fight?" Marsha repeated, a note of disbelief in her voice.

"I'm afraid so," Lisa said, speaking for the first time from her position on the floor. "We had a water fight. I started it."

"You started a water fight with Jack?" Marsha asked, still recovering from her shock. There was a twinkle in her eyes and a smile erupted on her mouth.

"That's not exactly true," Jack protested, "I started it. I was shooting paper wads at her."

Marsha turned her attention back to Jack. "Paper wads?"

"Yeah. It's been a long day, so to break up the tension, I started shooting paper wads at Lisa," Jack explained as he leaned over and offered a hand to help Lisa up off the floor. "Lisa retaliated by throwing a cup of water on me."

Lisa accepted Jack's help and rose to face Marsha.

Marsha nodded. She giggled warmly. "From outside the door, it sounded like quite a ruckus in here. I was quite sure I had the wrong suite."

"Well, this is certainly a surprise," Lisa said, changing the subject. "We weren't expecting you."

"Oh, I'm terribly sorry. The other day I mentioned to Jack that if I had an opportunity this week, I would stop by to meet him. I was in the neighborhood, and on my way home from the office, so I decided to take a chance and drop in to see how the final edits were going."

"Not as smoothly as you would have thought, huh?" Jack said, grinning. Marsha shook her head again and smiled. "Would you like to sit down?" Jack asked, gesturing toward the sofas and love seat in the living area.

"Oh, that would be lovely, however, I can't stay very long. I would love to hear about the book."

The three of them walked down into the living area. Jack sat on one sofa, Lisa on the love seat between them, and Marsha on the sofa opposite Jack.

"So how far are you?" Marsha asked after she settled herself.

"We'll be finished with chapter eleven in a couple hours," Lisa said, flashing a quick look at Jack that seemed to say, "Be careful what you say."

"That's wonderful!" Marsha said with a great deal of enthusiasm. "If you can, Lisa, please send over all the corrections on the first twelve chapters tomorrow morning. Peter wants to see them."

"Who's Peter?" Jack asked.

"Peter Tunnell," Lisa answered, an astonished expression filling her face. "He's the president and publisher at Brownstone." She turned to Marsha, "Why does he want to read the corrected manuscript of *Loose Cannons*?"

Marsha smiled knowingly before explaining. It was obvious Marsha thought she had good news and she was about to burst if she couldn't tell them soon. "Well, one of our manuscript readers apparently had lunch with Peter last week and told him about the wonderful storyline of Jack's book. Peter wants to review it himself. I think he wants to determine if we should bring it out immediately in hardcover!" Marsha was beaming.

"Hardcover?" Lisa and Jack both said simultaneously.

"Of course, it's purely speculation on my part, but I've worked with Peter Tunnell for over fifteen years, and when he shows this much interest in a manuscript that was originally designated for paperback, I think it's a very good sign!" Marsha's confident smile became even larger.

"Wait, wait!" Jack was on the edge of the sofa, frantically waving his hands in the air. "What does all this mean?"

Lisa turned to Jack and explained, through a smile equal in size to Marsha's, "It means more promotion, a larger press run, and more money for you. Well, actually, more money for all of us."

"Jack, Peter wants to meet you. I told him about the dinner party on Friday evening. He is planning on attending." Marsha turned to Lisa. "Of course, Lisa, you'll be there, too, won't you?"

Lisa looked at Marsha, then to Jack, and back to Marsha.

"I promise, no water fights, Lisa," Jack grinned.

"All right. Fine. Yes, I'll be there. Where and what time?"

"Bradburry's, darling, at 8:00 p.m. Oh, and Lisa, would you be a dear and come by here to escort Jack to the restaurant? He is our out of town guest. I'm sure it seems rather daunting here in downtown Manhattan."

Lisa smiled at Marsha. "Oh, I don't know," she said, "Jack seems to be finding his way around the city quite well. Almost too well. But, certainly, I'll come by and pick him up. That way, we'll be sure to be at Bradburry's on time." Lisa couldn't resist a small jab at Jack.

"Wonderful!" Marsha exclaimed again, clapping her hands together. "Then it's all settled. We'll see the two of you Friday at eight."

"Unless I fall asleep," Jack said, grinning at Lisa.

"Pardon me?" Marsha leaned forward, waiting for Jack to repeat his statement.

Lisa interrupted. "Nothing, Marsha. It was just one of Jack's little inside jokes." Marsha nodded, still looking a bit confused.

There was a knock on the door. Marsha stood and said, "I had better be going."

"It must be room service with our dinner," Jack said as he and Lisa walked Marsha toward the door.

Marsha turned to them at the door and once again extended her hand to Jack. "It was so nice to finally meet you in person, Jack. You're even larger than you sound on the phone." She winked and smiled at Lisa. "Oh, and I do hope you two will try to stay dry."

Lisa and Jack exchanged brief smiles and said their final goodbyes to Marsha as she exited the suite. Immediately after, a well dressed waiter wheeled in a white linen covered cart.

Lisa and Jack spread the dinner out on the coffee table in the lower level. Lisa said she loved seafood and that the shrimp cocktail was a special treat. Jack was proud of himself. They munched on veggies, and Lisa explained in further detail about the major differences between publishing paperback and hardcover books.

"Let's hurry and finish our dessert while we get into chapter eleven," Lisa said as she headed toward the desks, her chocolate mousse in her hand. "Remember, the first twelve chapters have to be totally corrected and in Marsha's hands by tomorrow morning. I'll have Jo come pick them up and deliver them to Brownstone. It's going to be a longer night than we planned, Kramp."

"Well, let's get started," Jack said. "It's already 7:30."

"Okay," Lisa replied, sitting down at her desk chair and turning her attention to the computer screen.

Jack started toward the desks, but suddenly changed direction, went back down to the room phone in the lower level, and dialed room service again.

"Hello. This is Jack Kramp in suite 3418. Could you send up two cans of Diet Pepsi and a couple cans of... " Jack paused and looked at Lisa. She turned in her chair to look at him. She sat motionless, holding her breath while she waited for him to finish his order. At last he said, "...a couple cans of Coke or regular Pepsi, whichever you have."

"That was nice of you, Kramp," Lisa said sincerely.

"If we are going to stay awake and alert, I thought we might need some caffeine," Jack said as he walked to his desk and assumed his position.

"Here's the rest of eleven. Have at it," Lisa said, handing pages over her left shoulder to Jack. "I'll read through twelve and do the initial markings."

Jack took the eighteen pages from Lisa and began to read, blocking each paragraph with his pencil and underlining possible problem areas for corrections with his highlighter. Jack was starting his third page when he looked up at Lisa. "It's too quiet in here," he said.

"What do want to do?" Lisa asked, keeping her eyes focused on her computer screen. "Order up a six piece polka band to perform for us?"

"I was thinking more like turning on the radio."

"Fine. Nothing sleepy, no rap, no hard rock. And not too loud."

"How about country?"

Lisa turned her head, looked at Jack, and shrugged her shoulders. "I don't know. I never listen to it."

"What do you listen to?" Jack was on his feet, standing at the top of the steps, poised to head down into the sunken living area. He stared at Lisa, waiting for her answer.

"News-talk, sometimes classical. Never country." Lisa flashed a quick smile at Jack. "But, I'm willing to give it a try if you keep the volume low."

"All right," Jack said as he headed toward the entertainment system. "Let's try a little country. If you start to cry, I'll switch it over to classical." Jack grinned to himself as he flipped on the tuner. It was still on the country station he had found the night before. He set the volume on low. Garth Brooks was in the middle of one of his ballads.

"Well this is going to be interesting," Jack said under his breath as he eased himself into his desk chair.

"Pardon?" Lisa asked quietly from her desk.

"Nothing," Jack replied.

"I think Marsha likes you," Lisa spoke, still inputting their edits on the Mac.

Unsure of how to respond, Jack paused for a moment before answering. "She's a nice lady. I've gotten to know her by phone since my initial acceptance letter from Brownstone. I think we've talked at least once a week for the past few months while we made arrangements for this rewrite."

"Marsha is a very bright woman. She is one of the best editors we have at Brownstone."

"Gee, that's what she said about you." Jack wanted to change the subject.

Lisa turned and flashed a quick smile at Jack. "Marsha is always very gracious. She's well liked at Brownstone. Everyone thinks she is really sweet and wonderful."

Jack thought he detected a note of jealousy in Lisa's voice.

"She's married," Lisa added as an afterthought. "Her husband is a successful stockbroker on Wall Street."

"He's a lucky man," Jack bit his lip. He suddenly wondered if Lisa was sharing the news of Marsha's marital status for only his benefit. Or, was she jealous for other reasons?

"Yes," Lisa agreed, continuing to work. "He's a nice guy. I've met him a few times."

Jack said nothing. He grunted an acknowledgment, put his head down, and pretended to concentrate on the papers in his lap. He felt Lisa's eyes on him. He refused to allow himself to look up at her. Jack was suddenly feeling very uncomfortable. To him, Marsha was a nice lady who helped him get to New York and get his book published. A business friend, nothing more. And here, at this moment, Lisa seemed to be fishing for information on Jack's feelings toward Marsha. Jack smiled and shook his head slowly. "I'm not sure if I'll be able to figure this one out," he thought.

Lisa had turned to look at Jack. When he didn't respond, she decided to let the conversation hang. She felt both guilt and uncertainty as to why she had suddenly found herself running on at the mouth about Marsha. She admitted to herself that she was curious how Jack felt about Marsha. He seemed to be very nice to her. "Too nice," Lisa thought. She took a deep breath and told herself that Jack's kindness was simply due to the fact that he was from the Midwest. "After all, everyone from Minnesota is nice, right?"

Lisa shook all thoughts of Marsha and Jack from her head and placed her energy and concentration into the rewrite. It worked, for the next two and a half hours, at least.

"Here is twelve," Jack broke the silence as he leaned over and handed the chapter to Lisa.

Lisa took the pages, gave Jack a quick smile, nodded her approval, and said, "I've just finished inputting all the changes for eleven. While I'm entering these, could you proofread it one final time for me?"

"Sure," Jack said as he stood, taking the pages from her and glancing at his watch. "It's only 10:15. We did pretty well."

"Yes, we did," Lisa said as she hammered away at the Mac. "It must be the tempo of that country music that kept us moving."

"So what do you think of country?" Jack asked, stretching his hands over his head and raising himself up on his tiptoes.

Lisa paused for a moment, looking out at the lights of New York City through the windows of the French doors as though hoping to gain her answer from them.

"Not bad, Kramp. Better than I expected." Lisa turned to look at Jack, adding a grin. "Although, I'm not ready to go out and purchase a ten gallon hat and cowboy boots just yet."

Jack sat down on the farthest sofa, facing the desks, kicked his shoes off and propped his feet up on the coffee table. He returned Lisa's smile and said, "There is a big difference between western music and country music. What you've been listening to is pure country. Someday, I'll take you to a ranch in Colorado where you can hear real western music."

Once again, Jack bit his lower lip. "Now where the hell did that assumptive invitation come from?" Jack thought to himself. He waited for a response from Lisa.

Lisa continued to stare at him, saying nothing for several seconds. Finally, she nodded, looking a little perplexed. "That would be a new experience," she said slowly. "I've been to L.A., Las Vegas, and, oh yes, once I went to St. Louis with my father. I've never truly been out west." As Lisa said, "Out west," she held up both hands and made quotation marks in the air with her fingers.

Jack nodded. "It's really beautiful out there. My favorite is the Grand Canyon." Jack was trying to figure out a way to change the subject, or at least broaden it a bit, in an attempt to steer away from his comment about taking her to Colorado.

Lisa nodded again, glanced at the time on the computer, and resumed her typing.

Jack picked up his pages and began to read, trying to keep his thoughts away from imagining how Lisa would look in a pair of cowboy boots and standing amidst the Garden of the Gods in Colorado Springs.

It was 10:45 p.m. when Lisa finally stood, drained the last of her diet Pepsi, and switched off the computer. Jack had been very quiet during the last half hour. She turned to look at him and realized why he had become so silent. Jack had fallen asleep. Chapter eleven was sprawled across his chest as he slouched deep into the sofa, his feet crossed and draped across the coffee table.

Lisa stood at the top of the steps leading down into the lower living area and watched him sleep. "He is a big man," she thought, looking at his long legs. "He seems to have a very good build and just a slight paunch." Lisa was guessing him to be in his mid-to-late forties. She carefully surveyed his facial features; deep set eyes, a strong jaw bone with a mouth that seemed to turn up in an almost natural smile. She focused on his full lips. His sandy brown hair was curly on top and long in the back, well over his collar. There was a hint of gray around his temples.

Lisa looked away, then back again, taking a deep breath. "He certainly is a handsome specimen," she thought. "I don't remember him being this attractive when I first met him on Monday morning. Apparently, personality adds to physical beauty," she mused as she started down the steps toward Jack's sprawling, slumbering body. "Or maybe he just sort of grows on you," she added, smiling to herself at the insanity of it all.

Lisa leaned over the sofa and gently shook Jack on his right forearm. "Hey, Kramp, wake up. This is getting to be a habit, isn't it?"

Jack's eyes fluttered open. "Huh?" he mumbled. "What time is it?"

"It's 10:50. I'm finished with twelve. Did you proofread all of eleven?"

"Yeah, I think so," Jack said slowly as he struggled to sit up straight on the sofa. He rubbed his eyes, looked at Lisa disconcertedly, and muttered, "I must have dozed off."

"Let's hope your book doesn't do that to the readers," Lisa chuckled as she gathered up the pages scattered around Jack's feet.

"At least we'd have captured the insomniac market," Jack said, managing a sleepy smile.

"It's getting late, Kramp, and I have to leave." Lisa picked up the stack of pages and returned to her desk where she began packing them into her briefcase. Jack came up from the living area and leaned against his desk, never taking his eyes off her. He crossed his arms over his wrinkled shirt. He spotted her coat hanging in the open closet and quickly went to retrieve it. As Lisa turned with her briefcase and purse in hand, Jack held her coat out for her.

"Would you like to have a nightcap downstairs in Bannigan's before heading home?" Jack tried to pose the question as nonchalantly as he could.

Lisa paused and stared at him. She turned and allowed Jack to help her on with her coat before answering. "I can't," she replied, "I'm not much of a social drinker, Jack. It's pretty late." She turned to face him as they reached the door. She could see a trace of disappointment in his eyes. "Maybe another time when we aren't so exhausted. It's been a long day for us," she added.

"Okay," Jack said, grinning and stuffing his hands into the pockets of his slacks. "Another time."

"Besides, after last night, I think you had better get to bed. Tomorrow could be another rough one." Lisa gave Jack a knowing smile.

"Right," Jack said as he opened the door for her. "9:00 a.m. sharp tomorrow, then?"

"9:00 sharp, Kramp. Be up. Be ready. And don't dress so damn formal. Be comfortable. You never know when a water fight might break out." Lisa chuckled softly as she stepped out into the hallway of the hotel.

Jack nodded in her direction from the door. "Yeah, like you knew we were going to have a water fight today!" laughed Jack. They both snickered at the thought of the water fight and how they apparently looked when Marsha Morrow dropped in to visit.

"Can I escort you downstairs?" Jack said suddenly, looking more serious.

"Oh, no," Lisa said. "They know me here. The doorman will hail a cab for me. I live just twelve minutes from here. I'll be fine."

"Are you sure?" Jack was insistent.

"Really, I'll be fine. But thank you for the offer. Good night, Jack." Lisa turned and headed for the elevators. Jack said good night, closed the door, and locked it. He leaned against it momentarily. "Wow. Maybe she finally decided to stop calling me Kramp," he murmured to himself, remembering how she kept referring to him as "Jack" when Marsha was there. And again, she called him Jack just a few minutes ago when she had said good night.

Jack's thoughts of Lisa were interrupted as his cell phone rang. Jack looked at his watch as he crossed to the kitchenette to answer it. "I'll bet it's the kids," he said happily. Once again, Jack Kramp was temporarily feeling light hearted, but he didn't want to look too far down into his soul for the reasons why. He just wanted to enjoy the feeling for as long as he could have it, afraid it might go away as it had done so often in the past. And he made a small mental note of his sudden elation; he did it without alcohol.

Chapter Nine

Jack was stepping out of the shower when his 7:00 a.m. wake up call came from the front desk. He'd been awake for an hour, replaying all the events of yesterday in his mind as he sprawled across the king size bed. He smiled to himself as he thought of Lisa and their water fight. He chuckled aloud when he remembered the look on Marsha's face when she met him, and then again when she found Lisa sitting on the floor, dripping wet. Hurriedly wrapping a towel around himself, Jack raced into the bedroom and answered the telephone on it's fourth ring.

"Hello?"

"Good morning, Mr. Kramp, this is your wake up call. Have a wonderful day." It was a woman's cheerful voice on the other end of the phone. Jack recognized the voice of Rita of the hotel's front desk.

"Good morning, Rita. You have a wonderful day, too!" Jack looked out his bedroom window and noticed the sun was beginning to rise. There was a long pause on the other end of the telephone.

"Well, thank you, Mr. Kramp," replied Rita, caught off-guard. "How did you know it was me?"

"I never forget a voice," Jack replied, pleased with himself that he had recognized hers. "Especially a pleasant one," he added.

"Well you certainly surprised me," she replied, giggling. "I don't believe anyone has ever said that to me during a wake up call!"

"That's because I've never stayed in this hotel before," Jack said, still grinning at Rita's reaction.

"Well, it's our pleasure to have you with us now, Mr. Kramp. If there is anything we can do for you, please let us know."

"There is one thing, Rita," Jack said slowly, "I've eaten breakfast in the hotel for the past two mornings. Could you suggest somewhere else I might go this morning for good food?"

"Oh, heavens yes!" she exclaimed. Then in a near whisper she said, "Just around the corner on 59th street there is a little place called The Basket. It has homemade bagels, fresh omelets, steak and eggs... just about anything you want. It's very good. My husband and I eat there almost every Saturday morning."

"Great!" Jack said, "The Basket, just around the corner on 59th street. I'll find it. I appreciate the tip, Rita. Thank you."

"It's my pleasure, Mr. Kramp. Have a nice day!"

"You too, good-bye." Jack hung up the telephone, patted his stomach, and said, "You'll feast this morning, my friend."

Jack returned to the bathroom to finish dressing. He selected a clean pair of casual slacks and a sweater. He slipped into his wing-tipped shoes, grabbed his trench coat from the hall closet, double checked to make sure he had his room key, and left his suite. As Jack closed the door to his room, he caught a quick movement out of the corner of his eye. He noticed a rather short, fat man in a rumpled brown suit quickly turn and disappear down a narrow hall behind him. Jack paused for a moment, listening to his sixth sense. His suite was at the far end of the corridor. There were no more rooms beyond his. Jack walked the fifteen steps to the very end of the hall and saw another shorter hallway to the right. At the end were a set of green double swinging doors marked "Laundry" and "Freight Elevator." Just inside to the left of the double doors was a third single door marked "Stairs" with the required red "EXIT" light above it.

Jack stood at the end of the short hall for a brief moment, sensing that something wasn't quite right. Mr. brown-suit had either gone down the stairwell or through the double doors to the laundry or freight elevator. As he was turning to leave, the double doors swung open. Jack whirled around to see a housekeeping service cart being pushed through the doors by Anita.

Halfway down the small, dimly lit hallway, Anita noticed Jack and stopped. "Good morning, Mr. Jack. Can I help you find something?"

"Good morning, Anita. No, I was just looking. Actually, I was wondering where this hall went."

"Oh, just back there, to the supply room and the big elevator," Anita said, nodding her head over her shoulder. "Are you leaving your room?"

"Yeah, I'm going out for breakfast. You can go ahead and clean it if you like."

"Very good, Mr. Jack. I'll be done before you get back." Anita flashed a big smile at Jack.

Trusting the tiny hairs that were still standing straight up on the back of his neck, Jack looked at Anita one more time and finally gave into his urge to ask a question, being as nonchalant as he could so as not to arouse suspicion.

"Say, Anita, did you see a short, plump guy in a brown suit come through there just a minute ago?" Jack nodded toward the double green doors behind her.

Anita's eyes widened a bit at Jack's question. "Oh, no, Mr. Jack. I didn't see anyone come through there. I was in the supply room. There was nobody. Why do you ask?"

"No special reason. I just saw a guy come down this hall, and I was just curious where he was going. He seemed to be in a hurry."

"Nobody came through here. I woulda seen him," Anita said again, confidently shaking her head.

"Okay, thanks, Anita." Jack waved and headed down the main corridor to the elevators. He hit the DOWN button. While Jack waited for the elevator to arrive, he tried to shake off the nagging feeling that the little fat guy in the brown suit didn't belong on the 34th floor outside his suite. He made a mental note to mention it to Avery Schneider if and when he saw him again.

Jack enjoyed his breakfast at The Basket. He ordered the "Big Morning" special: a steak, two eggs, toast, hash browns, and a large orange juice. The service was fast and friendly. Jack left a large tip. Standing back outdoors on the sidewalk, Jack noticed that it was 8:10 a.m. according to the flashing time and temp clock on the bank across the street. He checked the time against his cell phone and slowly headed back toward the hotel. Although the temp was supposed to be only 48 degrees, he thought it felt warmer than that. The sun was up and very bright against a cloudless sky. Jack kept to the outer edge of the sidewalk to avoid being bumped into or run over by the people who were in a hurry to get to their offices on time.

"Don't let your life go by so fast," Jack said under his breath to the bustling throngs. "You'll miss it."

Having enjoyed his morning walk back to the hotel, Jack entered the lobby, walked up to the front desk, and noticed there weren't any guests checking in or out. He spotted Rita almost immediately. She was short, about forty years old, with cropped dark hair and big brown eyes. She smiled at him through perfect white teeth as he approached her. Rita wore a small name tag, confirming Jack's intuition.

"Good morning, may I help you?" Rita asked Jack from behind the large oak counter.

"You already did," Jack said, returning her smile. "Breakfast at The Basket was great." He looked around to see if any other employees were nearby. Leaning over the counter, he continued, "Thanks for the tip, Rita. I'm Jack Kramp, suite 3418," Jack whispered as he extended his hand out to her.

She shook his hand, broadening her smile. "Well, it certainly is a pleasure to meet you in person, Mr. Kramp. I'm so happy you enjoyed breakfast. Isn't it wonderful?" Her eyes were beaming.

"It sure was. And call me Jack."

"I'd really like to," Rita said, her smile diminishing slightly and a small frown forming on her face. "But we are not to address our guests by their first name. Hotel policy. I'm sorry."

"I understand. I just wanted to stop by and thank you for suggesting The Basket. I'll be going back there a few more times before I head home."

"Their lunches and dinners are great, too. I think they close early, about 10:00 p.m., though."

Jack nodded and looked around the lobby. "Is Avery Schneider, your security guard, around somewhere this morning?"

Rita gave Jack a quizzical look. "Avery? Let's see, today is Thursday, so he'll be in at 2:00 this afternoon. I think he is off on Fridays, though. Is there a problem?" Rita looked concerned.

"Oh, no," Jack laughed and waved his hand as he started to leave the front desk. "I just met him the other night and was going to swap another basketball story with him."

"Oh. Shall I leave word and have him call you?"

Jack pondered Rita's offer for a brief moment. "No, that's fine. I'll just catch up with him some time. It was nothing important." He flashed another grin at Rita and said good-bye. He headed for the elevators, mumbling to himself. "At least I hope it's nothing important. No need to get everyone excited. Maybe I'm just getting paranoid in my old age." Jack hit the UP button, still feeling there was more to the short fat man in the brown suit than he probably cared to know.

Jack stopped outside the door to his suite. Suddenly, he turned and headed toward the small hall to the right of the main corridor. The hallway was empty. Jack opened the door to the stairwell and surveyed the layout. To the left was a smaller set of steps leading up. There was a sign painted on the wall with an arrow that said "Roof." A small chain hung across the two handrails of the steps going up with another sign reading; "CLOSED. NO ACCESS."

The stairwell to the right was wider and better lit. Jack assumed it simply led down and outside, floor by floor. Jack pulled down on the levered handle of the stair door from inside the stairwell. It turned easily.

"They probably can't lock them because it would be a fire hazard," Jack thought. He shrugged his shoulders and headed back to his suite. Once inside, Jack hung his trench coat in the closet and walked over to the French doors. He pulled open the heavy drapes and appreciated the explosion of bright sunlight that embodied the room. After unlocking one of the double doors, Jack stepped onto the open terrace and took a deep breath of fresh New York air. Once again, several aromas from around the city permeated his nostrils.

"It's good to be alive, Jack," he said to himself as he looked out over Manhattan and the bright blue, late autumn sky. He glanced down at Central Park. "More people down there than usual this morning. It must be due to the warmer weather."

Jack turned and cocked his head as he heard a faint knocking. After determining that it was coming from the direction of the door to his suite, he turned and headed to answer it. He glanced at his cell. 9:00 a.m. "The Word-Witch. Punctual as always," Jack said, smiling as he reached the door handle and swung it open.

"Thanks, Kramp. What took you so long? I was beginning to think you were still asleep and I'd have to use my key again," Lisa grumbled as she walked in.

In one hand she held her briefcase and a large black purse. Her other arm was wrapped around a large box.

"What did you use to knock with? Your head?" Jack asked as he grinned and took the box from under her arm.

"Actually, my foot. Where were you?" She sounded out of breath as she let her purse fall to the floor near her desk and set her briefcase on her chair.

"I was out on the terrace watching the squirrels mate in Central Park." Jack was still smiling at Lisa as she took off her trench coat and flung it over the nearest sofa. She was wearing a pair of brown corduroy slacks, a beige blouse, and a matching brown corduroy vest. Her long hair hung loose, making large waves and sweeps around her cheeks and over her shoulders. "She looks a little tired," Jack thought as he gave her one more approving look, then turned his attention to the large box he was still holding.

"What's in the box?" he asked, bringing it over to her desk.

"Another ream of paper and a bunch of layout sketches with ideas for the front and back covers of your book. Geri Parsons, the head of layout and design for Brownstone, wants our thoughts on them. They were waiting for me at my office when I stopped by this morning. Go ahead, open it." Jack noticed that Lisa seemed a little cool toward him this morning.

As Jack put the box down on the floor between their desks and began to open it, Lisa placed her briefcase on her desk, flipped it open, and began to shuffle papers. She spoke to Jack without looking at him, even though he was just a few feet away.

"Is that how you get your kicks these days, Kramp?" Her voice was as cold as ice.

Jack stood up, looking bewildered. "Come again?"

"Arising early to watch squirrels fornicate?" Lisa asked with an icy sarcasm.

Jack remembered his earlier comment. "Naw, I was just kidding. I've been up since 6:00 a.m. I went out for an awesome breakfast this morning. You might know the place. Just around the corner from the hotel, on 59th, is a nice little eatery called 'The Basket.'"

Lisa shot Jack a look that left him totally confused.

"What?" Jack asked. "What's wrong?" He sensed he had struck a nerve with her, somehow, somewhere, but he wasn't sure what he had done or said to put her in a foul mood. "Maybe she just got up on the wrong side of the bed this morning," Jack reasoned with himself.

"You're just a regular little boy scout, aren't you Kramp?" Lisa snorted at him, her lips curled in disgust.

"What the hell are you talking about?" asked Jack feeling a slight rage building inside. He was obviously the target of her morning wrath, and he wanted to know why.

"You were out exploring again," she retorted, "Just like a boy scout. This is New York City, Kramp. It can be very dangerous for country bumpkins."

"It was 7:30 in the morning, for God's sake! How dangerous can that be? It was breakfast! It was three blocks away!" Jack's voice was rising. He could feel his neck veins beginning to pop.

"This city can be dangerous anytime of the day or night," Lisa said, glaring at him from her position at her desk, her arms folded in front of her. "You have to learn to be more careful."

"I can take care of myself, Tiger-Lady. Don't worry about me," Jack retorted, with frustration in his voice.

"We have to finish this rewrite, Kramp," Lisa said, a calm slowly returning to her voice. "After that, you can go anywhere you want, do anything you want, at anytime you wish to do it."

"Is that what you're worried about?" Jack was indignant. "You're worried that I'm going to get mugged or something before we are able to finish the rewrite?"

"Or killed. Dammit, Kramp. You're my responsibility while you are here in New York," Lisa lowered her voice to a whisper. "Just be more careful, okay?"

"Yeah. Sure. Whatever you say," Jack was feeling sarcastic. He was bewildered by Lisa's sudden abrasive attitude to the point of feeling hurt or betrayed. He scratched his head in disbelief and sat down in his chair.

"Let's get to work," Lisa said as she flipped on the Mac. "Jo will be here in less than an hour to pick up the first twelve chapters, and we still have to proof the last two. Here is eleven. I'll take twelve." Lisa handed Jack his set of pages over her shoulder. Jack took them without saying a word.

There was an unnatural silence between them, and time passed slowly during the final edits of chapters eleven and twelve. As Jack poured himself into the proofing process, he was pleased to find there weren't any mistakes.

Lisa concentrated on proofing her chapter and purposefully avoided any conversation with Jack. She was angry and she knew it. She woke up this morning feeling angry at Jack and at herself. Deep down, Lisa knew why, but simply being angry was much easier than facing the truth about how she felt. She wanted to deny the fact that she found herself starting to really like this big stranger seated just behind her.

At 10:05, Jo arrived to pick up the first twelve rewritten and double proofed chapters of *Loose Cannons* and take them back to Marsha Morrow at Brownstone Publishing.

"Are you enjoying New York, Mr. Kramp?" Jo asked as she waited for Lisa to pack up the chapters.

"Yes, I am," replied Jack, "Every day is a new adventure around here." He rolled his eyes toward Lisa.

Jo's grin broadened into a knowing smile as she nodded, having shared the secrets of the "Word-Witch" with Jack on Sunday night. Lisa glanced up at them momentarily, but said nothing.

"Have you been over to Central Park, yet?" Jo inquired.

"No," Jack replied, adding mock sadness to his voice. "I'm not allowed to go to the park alone."

When Jack looked back up at Jo, she was glancing nervously back and forth between him and Lisa. Jack could tell she had become apprehensive and could sense tension building in the room.

"I've been instructed to have these chapters on Marsha's desk by 11:00 a.m." Jo said, hoping Lisa would hurry with the manuscript so she could make a hasty exit.

Lisa spoke for the first time. "She'll have them. Here. I've included a copy of the jump drive as well. I'll keep the master here." Lisa handed Jo a large manila envelope. Jo nodded, gave Jack a parting smile, and headed for the door.

"Have a nice day, Jo. It was nice seeing you again," Jack said from his feet-up-and-crossed position on his desk chair.

Jo waved and hurried out the door. Lisa turned to Jack, her nostrils were flaring and she had fire in her eyes. "I'm not your mother, Kramp. Don't make me out to be."

"What do you mean?" Jack asked innocently.

"You know damn well what I mean. You can go to Central Park at midnight for all I care. Right after we finish your manuscript. Now, let's get the next three chapters completed by 6:00 p.m." Lisa glanced at her watch. Jack nodded and held out his hand for the next chapter.

"I have a lunch meeting at 12:30," Lisa said cooly, "I'll meet you back here at 1:45 p.m."

"Fine," Jack replied dryly.

"And don't lose track of the time. We can't afford to waste any more of it. We are going right up against our deadline."

"I'll be here," Jack said, trying to match Lisa's coldness.

"Oh, and we'd better plan on working Saturday morning. I have a strong feeling Peter and Marsha are going to want everything by next Thursday."

"Saturday is fine with me," Jack said, trying not to show any emotion in his voice, "But why Thursday? I thought we had two full weeks?"

"Things change, Kramp. I suspect all the deadlines will be pushed up significantly if Peter Tunnell authorizes your book to be released in hardcover. It takes several more days to push out a press run, especially for the Advance Reader Copies. This morning, Marsha mentioned that they might shoot for a preliminary debut right before Christmas." Lisa was seated at her desk, her back to him again as she spoke.

"Christmas!" Jack exclaimed as he sat upright in his chair, his feet planted firmly on the floor. "That's just a little over a month away!"

"I see you have a firm grasp of the concept for calendar time as well, Kramp." Lisa continued to separate the next three chapters, keeping her back to Jack. "Now maybe you'll understand the urgency for us to get this project done. Here is thirteen. I'll start the markups on fourteen."

Lisa handed Jack the pages, then turned once again to the computer. He stared at her back for a full minute after he had accepted the chapter. "Something happened to Lisa between the time she left last night and when she arrived this morning," Jack thought, "And I'm going to find out what the hell is going on in her life. She's an emotional puzzle, and I might be a small piece of it."

The balance of the morning passed quietly and slowly. Conversation between Lisa and Jack was limited to grunts of acknowledgments as they swapped papers, made three word sentence suggestions, and scribbled corrections in the margins of the manuscript.

At 12:15, Lisa mumbled something to Jack and excused herself to the bathroom. Jack stood up and tossed chapter thirteen's edits on Lisa's desk. He stepped outside to enjoy the bright noon sun on the terrace. Looking down, Central Park was full of activity. It almost appeared to be a scene from summer, except for the people with jackets and coats and the barren trees. Jack spotted a few people having a bench picnic and two guys tossing a Frisbee. He rested his elbows on the stone ledge and looked out over the Manhattan skyline.

"It's a beautiful, cold blue sky today," Jack said to himself. "The only thing colder today is Lisa's heart. Hell, I bet I could pull those beers out of the refrigerator and place them next to Lisa and they'd never get warm." Jack was lost in his thoughts about Lisa's strange new attitude when her voice broke the silence behind him.

"1:45 p.m. Kramp. Don't forget. If you're not here when I return, I will leave and you're on your own. Got it?"

Jack turned and looked at her. Lisa was standing in the doorway, her trench coat on, shielding her eyes with her right hand from the reflection of the bright sunlight streaming in from the terrace.

"I'll be here, Tiger-Lady," Jack said, raising both arms in the air and letting them drop to his sides.

Lisa gave him one final look then turned and disappeared into the shadows of the hall, the door slamming behind her. Moments later, Jack heard the distant chime of the elevator.

After another ten minutes of enjoying the warmth of the sun and listening to the sounds of the noon hour in downtown Manhattan, Jack stepped back inside his suite, leaving the French doors wide open. He called Louie's Pizza and ordered a medium cheese and pepperoni. Jack stood for a minute in the center of the kitchenette. Then, he opened the refrigerator door, pulled out a can of beer, and popped the tab.

Jack held the open beer up in a toast toward Lisa's desk. "Here's lookin' at you, kid," he said, mimicking Humphrey Bogart. "I thought I was getting to know you. Guess I was wrong." Jack took a long, hard swallow of beer and stepped back out on the terrace.

Jack had stuffed the last piece of pizza in his mouth, and was about to wash it down with the last of his second beer, when he heard the door to the suite open. He had pulled his desk chair out on the terrace and had propped his feet up on the ledge, watching the sky and the Manhattan skyline while he ate. Around his feet were the remnants of his lunch: a pizza box, napkins, crust, and an empty beer can. Jack adjusted his body in his chair so he could see the door to the suite. He watched Lisa let herself in, take off her coat, and throw it over the same sofa as this morning. She glanced at him, but made no acknowledgment. She went directly to her desk, sat down, and began to work.

Jack stood, downed the last of his beer, and tossed the can in the corner next to the other one. He thrust both his hands into his front pants pockets and leaned on the door frame, looking at Lisa. As he was consciously trying to come up with the right words for an ice-breaker, he heard his own unrehearsed words pour out of his mouth.

"I was just wondering..." he said slowly, never taking his eyes off the Tiger-Lady.

"What about?" Lisa snapped, the iceberg still nicely lodged in her throat.

"How big was it?"

Lisa sighed. "How big was what, Kramp?" She sounded exasperated, but still didn't look at Jack.

"How big was the dill pickle you sucked on all night to put you in this sour mood?"

Lisa paused, put her red marker down, and looked at Jack for the first time since he had started speaking. She cocked her head to one side. "Is that some sort of sexual remark, Kramp?"

Jack thought about what he had just said to her. A deep crimson rose from his neck and spread throughout his cheeks. The hotness of his embarrassment boiled his skin. "Oh, no. Hell NO!" Jack protested. "It's just something my father used to say to us kids when we had on sour pusses."

"Sour pusses?" Lisa repeated, chin lowered and eyebrows raised in deeper shock.

Jack turned an even deeper shade of magenta. "No, no, you see, I... I" Jack was stuttering, trying to figure out how the conversation had suddenly shifted in the wrong direction. One minute he was going to be cute, the next minute he was asking for a black eye or worse, a sexual harassment suit.

"You should have quit while you were ahead, Kramp," Lisa said cooly.

"Yeah. I guess," Jack mumbled and walked sheepishly back to his desk, head down. He suddenly reversed directions. "I, uh, I forgot my chair. I left it out on the terrace. I had lunch out there and didn't want to take the chance of being late, you know?" Jack continued to mumble in Lisa's direction as he passed by her on his way out through the French doors. "Hell, I even had two beers on the terrace. Wait till the Tiger-Lady finds that out!" Jack chuckled to himself at the thought.

A cool breeze blew the French door curtains inward, making the room chilly. Jack looked at his cell phone. It was just a little past 5:00 p.m. The last rays of the sun were catching the few clouds that had crept in over the East River during the late afternoon. It had been over three hours since either of them had spoken. They had passed chapters and rewrite notes back and forth to each other in complete silence. Jack stood up, stretched, and tossed several pages clipped together on top of Lisa's monitor.

"Fourteen?" Lisa asked, not looking up, but continuing to enter thirteen's changes on the screen in front of her.

"Yeah. Fourteen," Jack replied. He ambled down into the lower living area and switched on a lamp, then crossed over to the entertainment system and flipped on the radio.

"It's quite cold in here," Lisa said, "Can you close the terrace door?"

Without replying, Jack went up the three steps in a single bound, closed the door, locked it, and drew the heavy drapes together. As he passed by Lisa on his way back down to the living area, he noticed she appeared to be almost shivering. She was huddled close to her computer, arms pulled together in her lap while she stared at the screen, silently proofing her work. Jack found the remote control for the gas logs in the fireplace and hit the switch. In an instant, a warm blue flame was burning. A small fan from somewhere in the back kicked in and he soon felt waves of heat blowing toward him.

"Okay," Lisa said, standing abruptly and shutting down her computer. "That's it for today. We'll take on chapters fifteen and sixteen tomorrow morning." As she began packing up her briefcase, she noticed the box on the floor. "If you can take some time tonight, look over the cover designs. We didn't have a chance to review them today. Maybe we can tomorrow morning. Art and Production will want our suggestions and approvals by noon on Monday at the latest."

Lisa was all business. Jack just nodded at her and she barely looked at him. He glanced at her coat on the sofa, turned and started to reach for it, but she had already picked it up.

"9:00 a.m. tomorrow morning, Kramp."

"Like always," he said flatly.

At the door, Lisa turned to Jack. She took a deep breath and looked directly into his blue eyes. "Be careful tonight. Don't go out walking the city alone."

Jack walked up to her and opened the door, forcing himself to hold his tongue. As Lisa stepped out into the hall, she continued speaking, "New York can be a dangerous place if you don't know your way around, Kramp."

"I can handle myself," Jack replied quietly.

"I'm sure you can. In Minnesota. But this isn't Minneapolis, it's New York City. Although now lower than the national average, there is still violent crime here. I don't want you to be a statistic."

Jack walked down the hall toward the elevators with Lisa. He was listening carefully, not just to what she was saying. He was also trying to process the reasons why she was saying it. At first he thought she was treating him like a juvenile, but then he sensed there was some sort of logic behind her warnings. There was something that he was just not getting.

As they reached the elevators, Lisa continued her sermon. "Stay within a few blocks of the hotel. It's a safer area. And don't carry a lot of money with you. And if you get mugged, don't put up a fight, you could get seriously hurt or even killed." The elevator arrived.

"You're starting to sound like my mother, again." Jack forced a small grin.

"Look, Kramp. You are a stranger in a large, strange city. I'm just trying to help you." Lisa's voice began to rise with anger and frustration. "And if you don't like it, you can just kiss my ass!"

Lisa stepped into the elevator, totally ignoring the three people who were trying to get off, and turned to face him. Impulsively, Jack grabbed Lisa by both shoulders. He gently pulled her out of the elevator toward him. He bent down, kissed her forehead, and gently eased her back into the elevator.

"I just did," he said. The elevator doors closed quietly, covering the stunned expression that immediately overwhelmed Lisa Lisignoli's face. The three guests in the hall who had just exited the elevator snickered. Jack looked at them, raised his hands in the air, and shook his head. "Shit happens," he said.

He smiled all the way back to his room, imagining the blue smoke exploding from Lisa's ears right about now as she descended past the 21st floor.

Chapter Ten

When Jack reached the door of his suite, he instinctively reached into his pocket for his room key, then he suddenly realized that he had forgotten to take it with him before he walked Lisa to the elevators.

"Damn!" Jack swore aloud, letting his forehead bang softly against the door of suite 3418. He heard the telephone ringing inside his suite. He tried the knob with a small prayer of hope and softly swore again when it failed to open. He looked at his cell. It was 5:15 p.m. The telephone continued to ring.

"It's either the kids or Lisa calling from a house phone in the lobby," Jack thought as he turned and walked back toward the elevators.

Once downstairs in the lobby, Jack kept his eye out for Lisa as he headed to the front desk to get a duplicate key to suite 3418. She was nowhere to be found. Jack grinned broadly to himself as he thought of his kiss on her forehead at the elevator.

"I'll bet I hear about that one tomorrow morning," Jack thought. "Maybe even tonight yet if she's really upset."

After a brief explanation, and showing two forms of I.D. to a young blonde woman named Jessica behind the front desk, Jack was given a second key to his suite. As he walked briskly back toward the elevators, he spotted Avery Schneider talking to a bellhop near the front entrance of the hotel. Jack changed directions and headed toward him. Avery turned and watched Jack approach. Jack extended his right hand toward him.

"Hello, Avery. I'm Jack Kramp from suite 3418. We met the other night in Bannigan's," Jack said, nodding his head in the direction of the bar.

"I remember," Avery replied slowly, nodding his head as he looked Jack up and down. "You're that tall drink of water who couldn't see the Knicks game on the television."

Jack nodded. "Listen, can I talk to you a minute?"

"Sure," Avery said, gesturing toward two empty chairs in the corner of the lobby, far away from other groups of people.

Jack told Avery the story of the short fat man in the brown suit he had seen early that morning scurrying down the back hall on the 34th floor. Jack paused occasionally, making sure he included every detail. Avery listened intently, his eyes burrowing into Jack's, looking for any clues that Jack might need to expand upon. When Jack was finished, Avery sat back in his chair and rubbed his chin thoughtfully.

"I don't recall seeing anyone like that around. But I'll keep my eyes out for him. And you say you didn't get any kind of look at his face, huh?"

Jack shook his head. "Just a glance. I caught his side profile as he was turning and his back as he rushed down the hall. He moved pretty fast for a fat little guy."

Avery smiled and stood up. He shook Jack's hand and promised to let him know of any further developments and asked Jack to do the same. As Jack waited for the elevator, a wave of homesickness came over him.

"God, I wish I was home right now. There'd be no New York, no cold hearted Tiger-Lady, and no short fat man sneaking around outside my suite. I could be with the kids and having a beer." For the very first time since he started writing, Jack Kramp regretted Brownstone's acceptance of his *Loose Cannons* manuscript.

It was almost 6:00 p.m. when Jack finally arrived back in his suite. He had just closed and locked the door when the hotel telephone rang again. Jack caught it on the second ring.

"Hello?"

"Jack?"

"Speaking. Marsha?" There was a giggle on the other end and Jack knew that it was definitely Marsha Morrow.

"How did you know?" she asked. Jack felt the warmth of her smile through the telephone receiver.

"I never forget a voice," he said. "What's up?"

"Is Lisa there with you yet?"

"Huh, no, she left about an hour ago. I don't expect to see her until tomorrow morning around 9:00. Can I leave her a message?"

"No, that's OK, Jack. Geri Parsons and I were just wondering if she had copies of the layouts for the cover design with her."

"They are right here in a box. Lisa brought them with her this morning," Jack said, already anticipating Marsha's next question and wondering how he should answer it.

"Well? What do you think of them?"

Jack cleared his throat and decided on the truth. "Well, Marsha, the fact of the matter is, we never got a chance to look at them."

"Really?" Jack sensed both surprise and disappointment in Marsha's voice.

"We covered a lot of ground today," Jack went on, feeling defensive but not knowing for certain why, "And Lisa was in a, well, a pretty bad mood."

"No water fights today, Jack?" Marsha teased.

"She was more like a giant ice cube."

There was silence on the other end of the phone. Marsha was obviously waiting for Jack to continue. She suspected there was more he wanted to say.

"And, wow, is she ever concerned about where, when, and how I go around New York City. She is turning into a real motherly type." Jack suddenly felt like he was whining. He cleared his throat and added, "I was on the receiving end of one heck of a safety sermon from her tonight as she was leaving. Second one of the day."

Again, Marsha said nothing. Jack waited, feeling like he had said enough. Finally, Marsha spoke. There was a new softness to her voice.

"Buddy," she said quietly, almost to herself as though she had arrived at a conclusion.

"What? Who?" Jack felt there had been a sudden shift in the conversation and he'd missed a gear or two.

"Buddy Shepard," Marsha said. "He was a writer under contract with Brownstone. Murder mysteries, mainly. A little over three years ago, Lisa was helping him with edits on, gee, I think it was either his fourth or fifth book, and he died."

"What do you mean, he died?" Jack was very interested now.

"Well," Marsha took a deep breath, "He was murdered, actually. He left the hotel one night and went for a walk. They found his body buried under some trash in an alley about ten blocks north of the hotel three days later."

Jack made a short whistling noise as he sucked in his breath after Marsha's shocking story.

"Somehow, I think Lisa still blames herself for Buddy's death," Marsha said, sadly.

Jack cleared his throat. "Was Lisa, uh, was she… involved with this Buddy Shepard guy?" Jack asked, searching for more answers.

"Lisa? Romantically? Oh, heavens, no!" Marsha exclaimed through a nervous giggle. "Buddy was almost sixty years old and married. But he had a zest for adventure. He used to say the best storylines were the real ones you could pick up on the street. We think he might have been out looking for material for his next book when he was killed."

Jack was silent for a moment longer, then shot his final question at Marsha. "Was Buddy a Boy Scout?"

"Why?" Marsha paused in amazement, "Yes. He was an Eagle Scout. I think he was still very active in the scouting programs somewhere in New Hampshire. But… how on earth did you guess that?"

"Oh, just something Lisa said this afternoon. Forget it. Shall I tell Lisa you called?"

"No, Jack. I'll just leave a message on her voice mail at the office. It was nice to speak with you again. Let's keep our fingers crossed for that hardcover. I saw Peter Tunnell reading your corrected chapters this afternoon. I have a good feeling about this one, Jack!" Marsha was back to sounding like her old, happy self.

"OK, Marsha, thank you for calling. I guess we'll see you tomorrow night."

"Oh yes! It's going to be great fun!"

"I'm sure it will be. I'll be there, even if Lisa changes her mind and decides not to come."

"Oh, she'll be there, Jack." Marsha sounded very confident. Jack wondered why as he said good-bye and hung up the telephone.

Jack stuffed his hands in his pants pockets and leaned against the small counter in the kitchenette. He thought about Buddy Shepard and how he might have died. Who killed him, and why? He thought of Lisa and how she must of felt. "Well, that explains a lot of things about her sermon tonight. But it still can't be the entire reason why she turned from the Tiger-Lady into a cold mackerel from the moment she set foot inside the room this morning," Jack mused as he studied the floor.

His gaze drifted toward the small refrigerator. He reached over, opened the door, and pulled out a beer, noting that there were still nine left. Cracking the tab on his beer, he headed for the French doors. Jack drew the heavy drapes back and looked out over the lights of New York City. He lifted the beer in another toast, this time in the direction of the streets and alleys below. He spoke softly to the windows of the French doors.

"To you, Buddy Shepard, and all the other Boy Scouts down there who have a penchant for writing adventure. May you never run out of ink." Jack tilted the can to his lips and took three long swallows. As he took another look at the city lights, Jack noticed the trash from his lunch still scattered in the corner of the terrace. He set his beer can down on Lisa's desk, unlocked the French doors, and stepped out to clean it up.

Jack's cell rang as he finished stuffing the pizza box into the wastebasket in the kitchenette and reached into his pocket to answer it.

"Hello?"

"Hey, Dad. How's it going in the Big Apple?"

"Jim! It's fine. Just fine. I wish I were home with you guys, but I'm learning a lot here. How are things at home?"

The conversation between Jack and his three children lasted over a half hour. They filled him in with details of school, homework, chores around the house, and the ever increasing grocery bill. Jack complimented each of them on their maturity, and how proud he was of their responsibilities, while he was away. Jack almost told them about the possibility of his book coming out in hardcover but decided against it, just in case Tunnell didn't come through.

Jack's stomach growled and he glanced at the time. Almost 7:00 p.m. He finally said good-bye to his children and promised he would call tomorrow night before he went out for dinner with the people from Brownstone. He walked down into the living room and switched off the gas fireplace.

Heading toward the bedroom, Jack decided to take a shower while determining where he should eat tonight. Earlier, he had thought about going back over to The Basket, but after Marsha's story of Buddy Shepard, and all of Lisa's near-hysterical warnings, he wasn't too sure about leaving the hotel. He was standing in his briefs, and was about to turn on the shower, when his cell phone rang again.

"You're a popular guy, Jack," he sang to himself as he walked over to the bed, pulled it out of his pants pocket, and answered.

"Hello!" Jack said brightly.

"You are one arrogant son-of-bitch, Jack Kramp!"

Jack grimaced as he recognized the deafening voice of Lisa Lisignoli on the other end. He decided to reply with the confused approach.

"Hillary?"

"No. It's not Hillary. It's Lisa. And you are in so much damn trouble with me, buster, that I... I..." Lisa was livid. She was so angry that she had difficulty finding her words.

"So, you've been stewing about that kiss on your frontal lobe for awhile, huh?" Jack tried hard to keep his voice calm, forcing himself to smile as he imagined her stomping around her condo with her cell phone in one hand and a meat cleaver in the other.

"You're damn right about that one, Kramp. Who do you think you are, kissing me in front of everyone like that? And who do you think you are that you don't need advice about your safety? And what about your stupid little games and your stupid little comments?" Lisa was on a roll. She paused to catch her breath, then screamed at him again, "And who the hell is Hillary?"

"Just a screamer. A producer at the radio station back in Minneapolis," Jack said placidly.

"I hate you, Jack Kramp. I truly wish I had never accepted this assignment. Ignorance can be fixed, but stupid lasts forever!" Lisa paused again, as though she had just processed Jack's last response.

"Hillary? You were expecting a call from some woman you work with?" Lisa's voice lowered to a more resonating calm.

"No," Jack replied, "But for a second, you sounded just like her."

There was dead silence on the other end. Jack could hear Lisa breathing, the wheels turning rapidly in her head. When Lisa spoke, her voice was finally complacent, but Jack could still feel the heat of her rage in his ear.

"Like I said, stupid lasts forever, Jack. In your case, it's beyond eternity."

"What happened last night, Lisa?" Jack decided to try reason.

"Nothing. Why? What do you mean?"

"I mean, why did you come in this morning looking for trouble? You just became angrier with me as the day went on? I don't understand, Lisa. What'd I do? I had breakfast at The Basket, so what?"

"Forget it, Kramp. It isn't just you. I, uh I, well, there are some things going on in my life right now and..." Jack pictured Lisa biting her lower lip as she spoke.

"I understand. We all have problems. I appreciate your concern over my safety while I'm in New York, but Lisa, I'm not Buddy Shepard." Jack winced as he found himself accidentally blurting out his name.

"How the...?" Lisa became silent for a long time. Jack said nothing. He listened to her breathing. He felt her remembering. He knew she was hurting again, and he once again felt guilty for causing her pain.

"I'm sorry," Jack said quietly.

"You're an asshole, Kramp," Lisa finally whispered as tears began to trickle down her cheeks. Then Jack heard nothing but silence as Lisa ended the call.

He sat on the edge of the bed for several minutes, staring at his cell still in his hand. He finally spoke aloud to himself. "You're right, Lisa. I'm an asshole." He sighed, threw his cell on the bed, and headed for the bathroom. Jack had just stepped into the shower when he heard the faint ringing of the hotel telephone on the nightstand.

"This is getting ridiculous!" Jack said as he turned off the shower, wrapped a towel around his wet body, and headed back into the bedroom to answer it.

"Hello, asshole here, which hemorrhoid would you like to speak with now?" He expected to hear Lisa on the other end and his annoyance and overwhelming guilt had made him grouchy.

"Ah, excuse me, I believe I have the wrong room." It was a man's voice.

"That's OK, pal. Happens to me all the time. Who are you trying to reach?" Jack was searching his vocal memory bank, trying to identify the man's voice, but he kept coming up blank.

"I wanted suite 3418. I'm looking for a Mr. Jack Kramp."

A sobering thought came over Jack. He quietly groaned and sat down on the edge of the bed. "This is 3418. And, unfortunately, I'm Jack Kramp. I thought you were somebody else."

There was a hearty laugh from the other end. "Apparently so, Mr. Kramp. Think nothing of it. It was a delightful and unexpected end to an already extraordinary day."

"Good, so who are you, pal?" asked Jack, beginning to get suspicious. "This guy sounds like he is setting me up to buy life insurance," Jack thought.

"Oh, I'm terribly sorry, Mr. Kramp. I'm Peter Tunnell from Brownstone Publishing."

Jack groaned again, louder and longer. "I'm dead meat," he thought as he gradually laid down on the bed and stared at the ceiling.

"I apologize for calling you so late in the day, but I had hoped to catch you before you went out for the evening. Do you have a few minutes?"

"Yeah, sure. Of course, and call me Jack," Jack said, trying to erase the entire opening conversation from his mind while silently praying Peter Tunnell would do the same.

"I've just read the first dozen chapters of your book, *Loose Cannons*. I must say, it's both entertaining and intriguing. A perfect blend of old west charm, action, and romance wrapped in subtle humor. A bit unusual, but I think it will move well."

"Thank you," Jack said, sitting back up.

"I have only one question about *Loose Cannons*."

"Fire away," Jack said off handedly.

"Very clever, Jack," Peter chuckled. "Here is my question, how does it end?"

"You mean the book?"

"Yes, of course. You don't have to give it to me word for word, but just outline the basic conclusion for me. I need to make a few decisions by Monday afternoon, and I understand we won't have all the final edits by then. But, then, I suppose I could read the final chapters of the original manuscript, too..."

"Oh, no, that's all right," Jack interrupted. "I'll try to tell you about the ending." He was still recovering from the surprise call from Peter Tunnell.

"Splendid!" Peter said. "I have a dinner engagement tonight at 8:30 with Lisa Lisignoli. I want her input as well, but I'd really like to hear the rest of the storyline from you. Just pick it up from chapter twelve."

For the next thirty-five minutes, Jack explained the ending of *Loose Cannons* to Peter Tunnell. Occasionally, Peter would ask a question, but basically he listened intently. A few times, he laughed at the situations as Jack described them. Jack sensed that Peter was making notes as he talked him through to the ending of the book.

When Jack had finished, Peter thanked him and said he was looking forward to meeting him tomorrow night. Jack apologized once again for the way he had answered the telephone. Peter laughed it off and said there must be a good story behind his initial response and that someday, maybe Jack would share it with him. They said their mutual good-byes and Jack hung up the phone. Although he hadn't met the man face to face yet, Jack already liked him.

"So, Lisa is having dinner with the top brass tonight to discuss my book," Jack muttered to himself as he went back into the bathroom to finish his shower. "I'm dead," he said. He thought of Buddy Shepard. He quickly changed his thought pattern. "I'm finished. I'm done. Gone."

It was almost 9:00 p.m. by the time Jack finished showering, shaving, and dressing. Having decided to try the formal menu downstairs in the Madison Room, he chose his gray pinstripe suit and a flashy red tie. He had called down an hour earlier for a reservation.

"Reservation for one," Jack repeated quietly to himself, making sure he had his room key in his pocket as he opened the door to his suite. "Sounds pretty lonely, Jack. I guess I'll just have to invite Jack Daniels, Johnny Walker, and Jim Beam to join me." He closed the door to suite 3418, double checked it, and walked down the deeply rich carpeted corridor to the elevators. As the elevator doors opened, Jack smiled again as he thought of the kiss he had planted on Lisa's forehead at this same spot just four hours earlier.

"Maybe I should have kissed her on the lips," Jack mused as he rode down to the lobby, "But that would have really been asking for a major crap-storm."

The Madison Room was every bit as elaborate and ornate as Jack had imagined. Jack thought the food must be great as he noticed the dining room was very crowded at this late hour on a Thursday evening.

"Of course, this is New York," Jack thought, "The city that never sleeps and 9:00 p.m. is early for many of these people." Then, he had a second thought that sent a small shiver down his spine. "Maybe these people are all guests, and they're just eating here in the safety of the hotel for the same reason I am. We fear for our lives!"

After hearty portions of a delicious steak and lobster platter with all the trimmings, complemented by four scotch and waters, Jack declined on the cherry cheesecake.

"I'll have my dessert in a glass at the bar," Jack said to his waiter, nodding his head in the direction of Bannigan's. "Check, please."

Jack signed for the meal, left the tip in cash, and walked across the hotel lobby to Bannigan's. As soon as he entered, he spotted Avery Schneider sipping his usual brandy nightcap at the bar. Jack slipped onto an empty stool beside him. If Avery noticed Jack, he made no comment. His eyes were glued to the television again.

"It must be after 10:00," Jack said hoping to strike up a conversation with the elderly gentleman.

"Ten after ten," Avery replied, still not taking his eyes off the set.

"In for your nightcap, huh?" Jack asked, then ordered a scotch and water from the bartender.

"Same as always." Avery didn't appear to be very talkative tonight, and Jack was wondering if he should take it personally. "I've been thinking about your short fat guy in the brown suit," Avery finally said quietly, his eyes still focused on the TV screen above the bar.

"What about him? Was he a house detective?" Jack's curiosity was aroused.

"We don't have a house detective here. I think he was casing the place. There might be something about to go down. And I sure as hell would like to know what it is." Avery sipped his brandy.

Jack found himself staring at the screen, mentally repeating every word Avery had just said to him.

"You got any enemies, Mr. Kramp?" Avery's question caught Jack off guard.

"Huh, no. Not that I can think of." Jack's first thought was of Lisa. She was pretty upset with him. But that was after he saw the fat guy in the brown suit. Then Jack remembered Marsha's story about Buddy Shepard. He shuddered. He turned and faced Avery. "I'm just a first-time author for Brownstone Publishing," Jack said, fighting off slight attacks of panic and paranoia. "I can't imagine anyone wanting something from me. Or having a grudge against me. It's my first book. And I'm not rich."

"Steal some guy's woman, maybe?" Avery turned and gave Jack a sly smile.

"No way." Jack shook his head. "I haven't had a real date in the two years since my wife died."

Avery's smile disappeared. He took another sip of his brandy and turned his eyes back to the television. "Sorry to hear about your wife. She must have been pretty young." Avery's voice was gentle, but still matter of fact.

"She was forty. Died suddenly. Skiing accident."

"At least she didn't suffer for a long time. That's always a blessing."

Jack nodded. He felt a lump in his throat as he thought of Mary and that cold Sunday in late October. He stared at his drink, picked it up, and downed it. As soon as the empty glass hit the bar, Jack motioned to the bartender for another. He looked at his cell. It was 10:23. Jack turned his attention back to Avery, noticing that his brandy was almost gone.

"Are you sure I can't buy you another brandy, Avery?" Jack asked.

"No, sir. One a night is all I ever need. Besides, I've gotta be going pretty soon. Thank you, anyway."

"No problem," Jack replied, then thought of one more thing that was gnawing at him. "Does the name Buddy Shepard ring a bell with you?"

Avery quickly spun around on his bar stool and gave Jack a hard look, his eyebrows raised in suspicion. "Why? Did you know him?" Avery asked, the muscles in his cheeks tightening.

"No. I just heard about him this afternoon from an employee of Brownstone Publishing," Jack explained. "I understand he was killed a few years ago while working on a book here at the hotel."

Avery nodded slowly, stared down at his nearly empty glass, and began to speak as though he were reading a police report. "Bernard W. Shepard, age 59, Portsmouth, New Hampshire. Guest at West Park Plaza Hotel. Died sometime late Friday, April 7th, 2017 of multiple gunshot wounds to the back of the head. 38 caliber, possibly from an Astra A-60 handgun. Body found Monday, April 10th buried under debris in an alley near West 74th and Columbus, Upper West Side. Motive unknown. No weapon recovered or ballistics match up. Killer still at large. Case status; unsolved."

"Hot crap and coffee!" Jack exclaimed, sucking in his breath and feeling weak in the knees. "How do you remember all that?"

"I was working an extra shift here that weekend. Saturday morning, we got a report from one of your Brownstone editors that Mr. Shepard was MIA. And a good friend of mine from my old precinct was the lead detective on the case so we kinda worked together on it," Avery said quietly, then, and with a small smile, he added, "I might be staring at a 65th birthday soon, but I feel like I'm only fifty-five and still thinking like forty." He tapped his right temple with his finger, and his smile gave way to a soft laugh.

Jack studied Avery's face for a few seconds and finally asked, "What do YOU think happened to Buddy Shepard?"

Avery took a deep breath. "Well, robbery wasn't the motive. He still had his wallet with over a hundred and sixty bucks in it when they discovered the body." Avery scratched the back of his head and proceeded, "There's something else that's rather odd. His fingers on each hand were brutally smashed, either with a large hammer or a cinder block... or both. The coroner found tiny fragments of concrete embedded into the bones, tendons, and joints of his knuckles. The poor guy must have endured a great deal of pain. He was only about five-six and 138 pounds."

Jack winced and glanced at both of his own hands as they gripped the edge of the bar. "Tortured maybe?"

Avery nodded. "That's my thought. Somebody wanted something from him. Maybe some information they needed."

"Or maybe Shepard wrote something that someone else didn't particularly like," Jack said.

"Very astute, Mr. Kramp. But I still think there is more to it. Here it is, almost three years later and still no leads. Lots of dead ends, though."

"So what do we do about the fat guy in the brown suit?" Jack asked, clearing his throat and changing the subject.

"Not much we can do. But, he probably doesn't suspect there are two of us watching for him now." Avery shrugged his shoulders and chuckled as he added, "Heck, he might have just been up there trying to steal some hotel towels!"

Jack joined in Avery's laughter, hoping that might be the motive, but deep down, his sixth sense was still telling him that it was something more. Avery stood up and put his hand on Jacks right shoulder.

"Watch yourself, son. There are a lot of screwballs in this world, and New York has its fair share. We don't want you joining Buddy Shepard in that big library in the sky. Maybe I'll see you on Sunday?"

Jack remembered that Avery was off every Friday and Saturday. "Yeah, sure. Thanks, Avery, have a nice weekend.

Avery nodded, adjusted his hat, and walked briskly out of the bar. Jack caught his own reflection in the mirror behind the bar. He was mixed in between the house brands and the assortment of bar glasses.

"How befitting," he thought, "A family picture of an alcoholic." Jack lifted his scotch and water and toasted to himself. "Here's to you, Jack. Mary wants you to clean up your act and get on with your life." He spoke softly, yet four people around him turned their heads and heard every word. Jack downed the rest of his drink, threw a dollar tip on the bar, and headed back up to his suite. It had been a day from hell, and Jack knew there would be a few demons tormenting him tonight. Especially one; Buddy Shepard with his mangled, bloody fingers.

Chapter Eleven

Early Friday morning, rain and sleet were beating against the bedroom window of suite 3418. Somewhere on the street below, another siren was wailing toward its destination. Jack's eyes were wide open as he lay on his left side, watching the red numbers of the digital clock on the nightstand click off the minutes. The window drapes were open about six inches, allowing enough light from the skyline of Manhattan to enter, casting dim shadows around the room.

"My head feels unusually clear this morning," Jack thought, "especially after the half dozen scotches I had last night," noting that in two minutes Rita at the front desk would be calling with his 7:00 a.m. wake up call.

As Jack's thoughts turned to the various events that happened last night, he frowned and shut his eyes, trying to sort them out one at a time. He tried dealing with each situation separately, but yet, they were so entwined, he had difficulty focusing on any one individually. He was so deep in thought about Lisa, Tunnell, the book, the fat man in the brown suit, Marsha, Buddy Shepard, and Avery that when the hotel telephone rang just a foot away from him, Jack jumped, his heart pounding.

"Hello?"

"Good morning, Mr. Kramp, this is you wake up call. Have a wonderful day!"

"Thank you. You have a great day, too, Rita."

There was a giggle on the other end. Rita was enjoying her second morning of recognition from the handsome hotel guest.

"You're welcome, Mr. Kramp. I'll try." Then she added, "If you're planning to go out for breakfast this morning, may I suggest you take an umbrella and dress warm? There's a storm front moving through. Its forecasted to be like this most of the day."

"I appreciate the tip. Thank you, again!" Jack said good-bye to Rita and hung up. He slowly arose and went to the window, drawing the drapes wide open.

"You're right, Rita," Jack said aloud to the huge droplets of water and small coatings of slush already forming on the outside window ledge. "It's miserable out there today."

Jack shivered from the chill in the room as he stepped out into the main suite and turned the thermostat up. He went into the bathroom and turned on the shower.

"Another day in New York City, Jack," he said to himself through the steam starting to cloud the mirror. "Try to make the best of it, huh?"

It was 7:45 a.m. when Jack looked again at the nightstand clock. He was dressed in dark khaki slacks and a long-sleeved blue dress shirt. He didn't feel hungry enough to go out or even downstairs for breakfast. He turned on the radio and tuned in to a local news/talk station. Listening to country music had little appeal to him this morning.

Feeling restless, Jack wandered aimlessly around the big suite. He drew open the heavy drapes on the French doors, straightened up his desk, and filled the cassette tray in the printer with more paper. Finally, Jack gave in to a small whimper from his stomach and found the room service menu. He ordered up a large orange juice, a sweet roll, a fruit plate, and a copy of the New York Times.

As he waited for his breakfast to arrive, Jack picked up the box of proposed cover layouts and carried it down into the lower living room. He set the box on the floor and pulled six large sheets of paper out, spreading them face up on the coffee table. He let out a soft, approving whistle as he looked at the colorful graphic designs that Brownstone had created for the cover of his book. Each one was very dynamic and different from the others in color, style, typeface, and feel. Jack liked each one for many reasons and thought he would have a tough time selecting one if he had to choose immediately.

"It would have been a lot easier if you people would have just sent over two," Jack said aloud, standing over the coffee table and admiring the work of Brownstone's art department. He made a mental note to compliment Geri Parsons on the creative options if he had the opportunity.

"I'm definitely going to need help with this decision," Jack said. He decided to leave the six graphic renderings lay on the coffee table for Lisa. As he thought of Lisa, Jack looked at his watch. It was 8:06. He'd have enough time to eat, read a little of the newspaper, and start reviewing chapter fifteen.

"I should also use this time to figure out how to apologize to Lisa," Jack said, remembering the pain he had heard in her voice last night when he had mentioned Buddy Shepard. Suddenly, Jack snapped his fingers and headed to the telephone. He had an idea.

"Good morning, front desk, this is Rita."

"Rita!" Jack said enthusiastically. "This is Jack Kramp in 3418. I'm glad it's you. I need some more advice."

"Certainly," Rita responded eagerly.

"Where can I get fresh flowers at this hour of the morning?"

"Oh, goodness," Rita paused. "Our gift shop used to carry them, but I don't think they do so any longer. Oh! I know! Just over on Fifth Avenue and about 55th is a flower market that I'm sure opens early. Here, let me find the number for you."

Once Rita gave Jack the number, he thanked her and dialed it.

"Good morning, International Flower Markets, Sue speaking."

"Good morning, Sue, my name is Jack Kramp. I'm a guest at the West Park Plaza Hotel, and I need some flowers delivered here to my room before 9:00 this morning. Can you handle that?"

"Oh, I think so," Sue replied, hesitating. "It depends on what kind of flowers and how many."

"I need to say I'm sorry to a young lady. What do you suggest? Roses?"

"Are you romantically involved with her?"

"No, just a friend." Jack felt himself blush slightly. He felt like he was lying.

"Well, I have some fresh carnations, or... wait, some lovely orchids came in about an hour ago."

"Great!" Jack was excited. "Give me a large arrangement of orchids with all the greenery and ribbons and neat stuff that goes with them, OK?"

"Certainly," Sue said, smiling at the excitement in this early morning stranger. "That will be seventy-eight dollars, plus a fifteen dollar rush delivery charge. And I'll need advance payment with a major credit card."

"No problem," Jack said without hesitation. "It's suite 3418. And please hurry, I need them here before 9:00 a.m. Oh, and can you also include a blank note card with that?"

"Yes, sir. Can I get your name again?"

Jack repeated his name and suite number to Sue, gave her his American Express card number, and said a hasty good-bye. There was a knock on his door, and Jack knew it was room service with his breakfast. He looked at his cell. It was 8:20 a.m.

"This is going to be a close one," Jack said under his breath as he headed to the door to let in room service.

Jack scanned the New York Times as he munched on his fruit, a sweet roll, and sipped his orange juice. Every few minutes, he glanced at the time on his cell phone. Time seemed to be racing against him. There was a knock on the door at 8:41 a.m. He opened the door expecting to find a delivery person from the flower shop, but instead, it was a bellhop from the hotel. He was holding a large, green empty vase.

"Mr. Kramp?"

"Yes?" Jack said, looking from the young man's face to the empty vase and back, suspecting he knew what the vase was for, but wasn't quite sure how it came to be delivered to him ahead of the flowers.

"Rita at the front desk asked me to deliver this to you. She said you may be needing it."

"Oh, thank you. Thank you very much," Jack said as he fished a five dollar bill from his pocket and handed it to the bellhop.

"No problem, Mr. Kramp. My pleasure." The bellhop turned and left with a smile. Jack closed the door and carried the vase into the kitchenette where he placed it on the counter. He was about to return to his newspaper when there was another knock on the door. Once again, Jack looked at the time on his cell as he crossed over to the door, hoping it wasn't Lisa. Not yet, anyway. It was 8:46 a.m.

This time, it was the delivery person from International Flower Markets. The young lady looked cold and wet, but she smiled as Jack thanked her profusely for her speediness and gave her a five dollar tip.

Jack took the large white box and set it across the arms of Lisa's chair. Taking the blank note card and envelope out, he went over to his desk to find an ink pen. Jack sat down and stared at the empty card in front of him for a full minute, then finally began to write.

"Dear Lisa. Although you and I seem to mix about as well as oil and water, I want you to know that I could never have done all this without you. For that, I sincerely thank you. I suspect you have pain in your life. I should have never added to it. For that, I'm truly sorry. I also sense that, somehow, we will develop an unusual friendship that will go beyond these two weeks. And for that, I'm grateful."

Perplexed on how to sign it, Jack paused for a minute and watched the rain change over to snow, splattering on the terrace wall outside. It seemed almost natural to sign it "love," but consciously, Jack felt it was inappropriate. There was a knock on the door. Jack looked at the time. It was 9:00 a.m. sharp.

Jack looked back down at the note he had just written. He signed it, "Son of a Kramp, Jack," and hastily stuffed it into the envelope, scrawled "Lisa" on it and tucked it under the green ribbon on the white box. The knocking on the door became louder and more impatient. Jack raced across the room and flung it open.

"Hi," Jack said loudly as he looked at Lisa. She was wearing a large black raincoat with the hood up, covering most of her face. She was wearing gloves and held her briefcase in her left hand. Jack noticed dark circles under her eyes. Her hair hung loosely around her neck, the ends wet from the rain.

"Morning," Lisa mumbled as she walked past him to her desk. She set her briefcase down on the floor, took off her raincoat, and went to the hall closet. Jack closed the suite door and leaned against it, clasping his hands behind his back, watching her every move.

When Lisa returned to her desk, she noticed the large white box laying across the arms of her chair. She stared at the box, shot a quick glance at Jack, then reached for it and placed it on her desk. Jack remained at the door, unconsciously holding his breath.

Lisa's back was to him, but Jack knew she had opened the card and was reading it. She stood motionless for a very long time. It was an eternity to Jack. He watched her arms moving as she untied the ribbon and opened the box. She carefully removed the orchid arrangement and held them in her arms as though they were a newborn child. Lisa picked up the note from her desk and read it again. She turned completely around to face Jack.

"Thank you," Lisa murmured softly. Jack blinked and looked again, this time focusing on her face. Huge tears rolled down each cheek. Her fresh eye make-up had begun to run with them. "Excuse me," Lisa said as she gently placed the flowers back in the box, set the card on top of them, and headed to the bathroom.

"OK, Jack, what's the next move?" Jack mumbled to himself as he slowly walked toward the kitchenette to get the vase Rita had sent up. He filled the vase half full of warm tap water and brought it to Lisa's desk. He looked at the flowers in the box. They were beautiful. The colors were in direct contrast to the weather outside and the black turtleneck sweater and jeggings Lisa was wearing.

Jack sat down in his desk chair, kept his feet planted firmly on the floor, and folded his hands in front of him. He waited for Lisa to return from the bathroom. As Lisa entered the room again, she wore a weak smile. "She looks tired, but at least more relaxed than yesterday," Jack thought.

"That was really nice of you," Lisa said as she approached her desk, "But really, it wasn't necessary."

"You're welcome, and yes, it was. We sort of had a bad day yesterday, and last evening was even worse. Let's just work on our edits and try not to get in each other's way. We can maybe work on the friendship part later." Jack's speech was slow and deliberate. He had turned it over in his mind ever since she had come through the front door.

"OK," said Lisa, slowly nodding, not quite sure how she should react to Jack's last comments. "I'm sorry, too," she added softly.

"There's a vase for you to put the flowers in," Jack said, pointing to Lisa's desk.

"That was very thoughtful of you," Lisa said as she began to arrange the flowers in the green vase.

"Honestly, the vase was not my idea. I called Rita at the front desk this morning and asked her where I could order flowers this early. I guess she just assumed we would need it," Jack replied, making another mental note to thank Rita for her thoughtfulness.

Lisa nodded, but made no further comment. She was still recovering from the shock of Jack Kramp sending her flowers and writing an apology. Then, a slight sadness overtook her. "Damn him," she thought. "Can't he see that he's just making the situation worse?" Lisa turned her back on Kramp, sat down at her desk, and switched on the Mac. The orchid floral arrangement sat on the far edge of her desk, becoming the catalyst of an internal struggle for Lisa Lisignoli. Part of her wanted to scoop up the flowers and squeeze them tightly against her chest, letting the fragrance embrace her very being. The other part of her wanted to rip them apart and throw them over the outside terrace wall where they could fall thirty-four floors to the street below and be run over by a thousand cars. A few feet away, Jack Kramp worked on his edits for chapter fifteen, completely unaware of the possible fate that may await the orchids he had ordered just an hour earlier.

Chapter fifteen turned out to be the longest and most difficult part of the manuscript to edit. Jack and Lisa passed paragraph after paragraph back and forth between them. Each page was marked up in red ink, pencil, and yellow highlighter. They discussed the entire chapter, sentence by sentence, word by word. Occasionally, they would look back at a preceding chapter to review a scene so that it flowed smoothly into the current pages.

After laboriously tearing apart chapter fifteen and putting it back together, they were satisfied with the clean-up. When they finished with the final corrections of the last paragraph, it was already 12:45 p.m. Both Jack and Lisa were exhausted.

Jack stood, did his usual hands-above-the-head stretch, and walked over to look out the French doors. Lisa disappeared into the bathroom to freshen up. There was over an inch of snow on the floor of the terrace. Jack thought back to how warm it had been the day before.

"Guess I won't be eating out there today," Jack said as he shivered from the draft seeping in between the two doors.

"What?" Lisa had returned and was standing behind him, just in front of her desk.

"Just talking to myself," Jack said, flashing a small embarrassed smile at Lisa. "I said I won't be eating lunch out on the terrace today like I did yesterday."

"Not unless you're channeling an Eskimo and order up a couple pounds of whale blubber," Lisa said returning a tired smile. Jack noticed much of her make up was now gone.

"She has a great deal of natural beauty," Jack thought as he studied her face. "Want some lunch?" Jack asked.

"Yes," Lisa said as she sat down to find chapters sixteen and seventeen. "I think I'd prefer a salad. Shall we order up room service and work through lunch?"

"Fine with me," Jack shrugged his shoulders and walked over to the counter where he had left the room service menu.

"What kind of salad?" Jack asked.

"Um... spinach would be nice if they have it. If not, just a garden salad. With oil and vinegar, please."

Jack nodded at her and dialed room service. He ordered Lisa's spinach salad with the appropriate dressing and a ham and cheese sandwich for himself. He also requested a six pack of diet Pepsi to be sent along with their meals.

Lisa found a duplicate of chapter sixteen, handed it to Jack, and went down into the living area where she eased herself into the deep love seat. She tucked her feet under her, pulled out her red pen, and started to read. Jack followed, surprised that Lisa hadn't mentioned the cover designs strewn across the coffee table in front of her. He sat down on the sofa to her right and looked at her, his pencil behind his ear and a yellow highlighter in his right hand. Lisa felt Jack watching her. She looked up at him and returned his gaze. She thought his eyes looked even more blue today.

"What?" she finally asked, giving him a quizzical look.

"The covers," Jack said, nodding his head in the direction of the coffee table. Lisa looked at the six colorful graphic designs spread out on the coffee table and bolted upright.

"Oh, crap! I forgot about those yesterday!" she groaned nervously.

"Marsha called last night to ask about them," Jack explained. "She said she was going to leave you a message on your office voice mail."

"I haven't checked my messages yet this morning," Lisa said.

"Well, I think she and some woman named Geri Parsons wants us to make a selection or suggestions or something with these. I'm not quite sure."

Lisa nodded. "We should select one, write out any suggestions we might have, and send them back. I think they want them by Monday."

"So, pick one," Jack said as he made a sweeping motion with his hand over the layouts.

"It's not quite that simple. We need to spend some time and study each one individually, away from the others. Each cover needs to be judged on its own merit and how it reflects the storyline of the book. We need to identify if it has good shelf appeal. A bad cover can kill a great book almost as easily as a great cover can sell a mediocre book."

"Really?" Jack was genuinely interested in the process.

"Well, there is a little bit more to it than that, but when it comes to cover selection, it's not something we do in just a couple of minutes. Maybe later on this afternoon, once we get through chapter seventeen, we can spend some time to evaluate and at least narrow the field down a bit." Lisa stifled a yawn and settled back into the love seat with the manuscript.

"Are we still working tomorrow morning?" Jack inquired, turning his attention back to Lisa.

"I believe so," replied Lisa, not looking up from her pages. She paused, turned her eyes toward Jack, and added, "Is that a problem?"

"Nope," Jack answered. "Just making sure." He, too, settled back into his sofa and turned his attention to the pages in front of him. Jack read the first paragraph, paused, and looked over at Lisa again.

"What about tonight?" he asked.

"What about it?" Lisa asked, not taking her eyes off her page.

"The Brownstone party with Marsha tonight at Bradburry's."

"Yes. What about it?" she murmured again, still concentrating on her edits.

"Are you still going?" Jack asked, knowing deep down he would be disappointed if her answer came back as a negative.

Lisa sat up straight, took a deep breath, and stared into the unlit fireplace just ten feet in front of her. "Do you want me to go?" she asked quietly.

Jack was not prepared for this question. He hadn't anticipated that Lisa's decision would be in anyway based upon his preference. He looked at her. She continued to stare, focusing on something in the space ahead of her. Jack was sure she was holding her breath. Not a single cell moved in her body for several seconds. Jack searched for the words while the silence between them became more awkward.

"Yes," Jack finally said, "I want you to go." He paused again, and added softly, "I want you to go with me."

Lisa turned and looked into Jack's face. He thought he saw moisture in her eyes, but she blinked it away. Her shoulders sagged as she exhaled a deep breath.

"OK," she almost sounded relieved. "I probably didn't have much choice in the matter, anyway. But, I wanted to know how you felt about it. I'll be here to pick you up at 7:30. Sharp. The dinner party begins at 8:00. We'll limo over."

"Limo?" Jack repeated, with surprise in his voice.

"Sometimes Brownstone goes first class," Lisa said through a tired smile. "And tonight is one of those times."

As Jack thought of the limo, the formal dinner party, and his relief knowing that Lisa was going with him, there was a knock on the door. Room service had arrived with their food. But, a nervous knot started to tighten in his stomach.

They ate in silence, each reading sections of chapters sixteen and seventeen, making notes as they read. Lisa yawned loudly at one point and smiled at Jack as he looked over and raised his eyebrows at her.

"She's not exactly going to be the life of the party tonight," he thought. "She'll be sleeping by 9:00 p.m."

Lisa handed Jack eight pages; four to proof her edits and four to rewrite with her suggestions. She went back up the steps to begin inputting other corrections on the computer.

At 4:10 p.m., Jack finished up his section. He stood, flipped off the barely audible news/talk radio station, and walked up to turn his rewrite over to Lisa. He found her leaning on her right elbow, head on her hand, with her nose just inches from the screen. Her eyes were half closed. He gently nudged her left arm.

"Hey, sleeping beauty. I think this just about does it for seventeen."

"I wasn't sleeping," Lisa mumbled. "I was meditating."

"Yeah, just like I was Santa Claus over there at the fireplace just now, sticking my finger in my nose, and trying to go up the chimney," Jack replied, chuckling as he stepped back from her desk.

Lisa smiled at him and slowly sat upright in her chair. She pushed her hair back from her face and took a deep breath.

"I'll just enter these and then we'll review those cover designs," she said with little energy left in her voice.

"No you won't," Jack said, gently taking the pages he had just completed from her hand. "You're going to go home and get some sleep before the dinner party tonight. I'm going to enter these on the Mac. The layouts can wait until tomorrow morning when we are both fresh. Now go on, get out of here."

Lisa looked up at him in disbelief. She began to protest, but Jack gently took her by the right arm and escorted her to the closet to retrieve her coat.

"I do know how to run an Apple computer," Jack reassured Lisa. "All three of my kids are brilliant on a Mac. They taught me. I primarily learned from my daughter the hard way. She has little patience for imperfections, or my short memory."

Lisa smiled at Jack as he opened the door for her. "Sometimes I find it difficult to imagine you being a father," she said, "But I'll bet you're good at it."

"Sometimes my kids find it difficult to imagine me being a father, too, but I try," Jack said, laughing at his own comment. This was the first time Lisa had ever spoken of family. Especially his family. There was an unfamiliar feeling of comfort and hope deep inside Jack's heart. His sixth sense told him this was a good thing.

Lisa said good-bye and promised to be back at 7:30. She made Jack promise to be ready, thanked him again for the flowers, and left his suite. He closed the door, turned to look at the floral arrangement on Lisa's desk, and broke into a boyish grin. "I think you pulled it off, Jack," he said to himself as he crossed over to the computer. "I think you might be off her shit-list. For now, anyway," he added as he sat down and reached for the eight pages on the edge of the desk.

As Jack Kramp began to type the last corrections of the day, he started to hum quietly. A few minutes later, he was softly singing an old Beatles tune from 1964. "Yeah you, got that somethin', I think you'll understand..."

Chapter Twelve

Jack finished typing the corrections for chapter seventeen and added them to their *Loose Cannons* master jump drive. He printed the pages, proofed them, and stacked them neatly on the corner of Lisa's desk near the vase of orchids.

A rumble from his stomach caused Jack to look at the time. It was almost 5:00 p.m. He switched off the computer, took one last look at the floral arrangement, picked up the telephone, and dialed the front desk.

"Good afternoon, front desk, this is Lawrence, may I help you?"

"Is Rita there?" Jack inquired.

"I'm sorry, sir, she has left for the day. Oh! One moment, sir, she is passing right in front of me." Jack could hear Lawrence calling Rita's name in the background. In a few seconds, she was on the phone and slightly out of breath.

"This is Rita, may I help you?"

"Rita, Jack Kramp here, suite 3418. I want to thank you for having the forethought to send up that large vase this morning. We put it to good use."

"Well, you're quite welcome, Mr. Kramp. I'm so happy it worked out for you. We have dozens of vases stacked up in our storage room, so I always look for ways we can use them. How were the flowers?"

"They were awesome!" Jack said enthusiastically. "She loved them." Jack hoped Rita wouldn't ask him who "she" was.

"Oh, I'm so happy! Well, I'm terribly sorry, but I do have to catch a bus. I stayed on the desk an extra hour to help out. We had a large group of late check-ins due to the inclement weather."

"No problem. Thanks again, Rita!" Jack said good-bye and hung up. He crossed over to the French doors to stare at the lights across the Manhattan sky-line. He watched the traffic snarls on the city streets below and large snowflakes as they drifted through the air, floating down to become dirty slush.

"Somewhere out there is a very unusual woman," Jack whispered to himself as he looked back at the skyline filled with dots of lighted windows. "And I'm afraid I'm starting to care too much."

By 7:15, Jack Kramp was completely dressed and ready for dinner. He had called his children and told them he would be at a restaurant called Bradburry's and he'd have his cell phone with him as well. After being assured that every-thing was fine on the home front, Jack hung up and paced nervously around the suite. Twice, he reached for a beer but always quickly put it back. Jack had a very empty stomach, and he didn't want to be light-headed when he met the executives from Brownstone.

"I've already made a fool out of myself with Peter Tunnell by phone. I don't want to go two for two," Jack thought, trying to decide what he should do about his rumbling stomach.

Suddenly, he remembered the two yogurt bars he had stuffed in one of his pockets from Sunday's flight. He went into the bedroom and checked the pock-ets of his slacks. Nothing. After searching his suit cases and his dresser drawers, Jack finally found the missing yogurt bars in the left hand pocket of his trench coat. He scratched his head, trying to remember when and how they got there.

Jack chewed on the yogurt bars with all the apprehension of a lamb going to slaughter. He looked at the time and noticed it was almost 7:28 p.m. He made a mad dash to the bathroom to brush his teeth one final time.

"Why am I so damn nervous?" Jack asked himself in front of the bathroom mirror. He had selected his best suit; a solid black double breasted with a black and gold tie. Prior to going into the bathroom, Jack carefully laid the coat across the bed to avoid any water spots.

"Foaming at the mouth, Kramp?"

Jack flinched in surprise as the voice behind him broke into deep and hearty laughter. He quickly turned, his toothbrush still in his mouth, and toothpaste trickling down his lower lip. Lisa was standing in the doorway of the bathroom, smiling. She was also stunning. Jack returned her smile and swallowed, forgetting about his mouthful of toothpaste. It burned his throat going down, but he ignored it.

"You promised you'd be ready," Lisa said. She leaned on the door frame, the warm smile still on her face.

"I was. I mean, I am," Jack said as he turned back to the sink, spit, and wiped his face with a towel. "I was eating an airline snack. You look terrific!" Jack couldn't keep his eyes off of Lisa's reflection in the mirror as he washed his hands. She was wearing a long red dress with small straps. Her hair was pulled back and piled neatly up behind her head except for a few black curly strands hanging down near each ear. She wore long gold earrings along with a small diamond and gold necklace that sat perfectly above the plunging, yet tastefully revealing, neckline of the dress. A heavy red and black cape dangled in her right hand, almost touching the floor. She clutched a small black purse in her left hand. Her makeup was perfect. Turning to face her, Jack swore that this was not the same woman he had been working with for the past five days. He fought to regain his composure as Lisa spoke again.

"Thank you. It's amazing what a couple hours of sleep in the late afternoon can do for a person."

"Well, I don't know about that, lady," Jack said slowly as he leaned back on the bathroom counter and folded his arms in front of him, toothbrush still in his right hand. "You sure do look fine, but you'd better get out of here quickly," he continued, forcing a frown. "My editor is coming to pick me up at any minute to go to some fancy-schmancy dinner party downtown. I hate to say it, ma'am, but I think you've got the wrong room."

Lisa wrinkled up her nose at Jack, but continued to smile. He enjoyed taking in her entire beauty one more time, from head to toe.

"I must have looked terribly tired today," she said, "Thank you for making me go home early. I would have never made it through tonight had I stayed here and worked."

"No problem," Jack said. "You let yourself in?"

Lisa nodded. "I knocked about a half dozen times. I thought you were either in the shower yet or..." Her voice trailed off as she looked at Jack. She thought he looked handsome in his perfectly starched white tab-collared shirt and exquisite tie. She noticed his black dress pants and blushed slightly as she wondered what sort of long, muscular legs were underneath the fabric.

"Sleeping?" Jack said, finishing her sentence.

"What? Oh, yes," Lisa said, tearing her attention away from Jack's groin and back to his face. She forced a wider smile.

"I know I'm early. I ordered the limo to pick me up ahead of schedule because traffic is horrible with the snow. Fortunately, the driver made good time, so, here I am. I think our driver is from the NASCAR circuit."

Jack laughed and nodded. He hoped Lisa hadn't caught him staring at her cleavage. Jack thought maybe he should compliment Lisa on her necklace, just in case, but then changed his mind as she spoke.

"We had better get going, Jack, the limo is waiting," Lisa said as she turned to walk back through the bedroom. "Where is you dinner jacket?"

"On the bed," Jack called to her as he hurriedly sprayed on a little more Polo cologne. He stepped out of the bathroom and walked to the bed where Lisa was holding his suit coat for him. He slipped into it and turned to face the mirror above the dresser. Lisa stood between the mirror and Jack. Without saying a word, she reached up, straightened out his coat collar, and adjusted the knot on his tie. Her attention to perfecting his attire felt very natural to Jack, yet, her very closeness to him took his breath away. He looked into her green eyes. She returned his gaze for a few brief seconds, a small approving smile revealed her perfect white teeth. Jack clenched his hands into fists at his sides. He resisted the sudden urge to put his hands around her small waist and pull her close to him.

Lisa finished with his tie and paused. She felt the warmth of his blue eyes, and the thought of kissing his full lips unexpectedly flashed through her mind. She panicked, then quickly stepped back and away from him. She had been too close and they both sensed it.

"You might want to wear your trench coat," Lisa called over her shoulder to Jack as she walked out of the bedroom toward the front door. "It's quite cold outside."

Jack looked at his trench coat and decided against it. He caught up with her at the front door. Lisa gave him a questioning look and glanced over at his trench coat still hanging in the closet.

"I'm from Minnesota. I'm used to the cold," Jack explained through a chuckle. "Besides, we're just going from the hotel to the limo to the restaurant and back, right? How cold can that be?"

As Lisa waited in the hall, Jack stopped in the doorway, quickly turned, and walked back into the suite to grab his room key off the table. He grinned as he double checked to make sure his room was locked.

"What's so funny?" Lisa asked, looking up at him with a warm smile as they walked down the corridor toward the elevators. Jack told her how he had locked himself out of his room the night before as he had walked her down to the elevator during her safety sermon. He explained how he had to go down to the front desk and was almost forced to show his birth certificate to get an extra key.

"You got exactly what you deserved!" Lisa said. She laughed and jabbed Jack in the ribs with her elbow as they stepped inside the elevator.

As he told her the story, Jack thought about the little fat man in the brown suit and how he had two conversations with Avery Schneider about the incident. He decided not to tell Lisa any of it. He was content to walk with this beautiful woman through the crowded lobby and out to their waiting limo.

"This author shit ain't too bad," Jack said quietly to himself as the driver opened the back limo door and helped Lisa inside. "I could learn to like this."

Once inside the limo, Jack began to relax. There was a sense of comfort having Lisa sit next to him. He thought she looked like a princess with her thick, warm cape now wrapped around her body and pulled up around her neck. Her earrings sparkled in the soft interior lights of the limo.

"So do her eyes," Jack thought, adjusting his large frame in the seat, and turning slightly to his left, so he could look more directly at her.

"Would you like something to drink? I believe the bar in here is well stocked," Lisa said, nodding to a small cabinet with glass doors along the wall, just ahead to Jack's right.

"I think I'll pass," Jack said, noticing a hint of surprise on Lisa's face as she turned her head towards him. "I'm starving, and I think any kind of booze in me right now might make me do strange things at dinner."

"Oh, and you're thinking that would be a new experience for all of us, Jack?" Lisa teased with a small laugh. "You? Do something strange? We've read your book, remember? I think you may have invented strange!"

"Thanks a lot," Jack said, wearing a pretend look of pain. He leaned forward and opened one of the glass doors of the small refrigerated cabinet.

"Change your mind?" Lisa inquired.

"No, I was just looking for... ah, yes, here we go. Good non-alcoholic bottled water. Would you like something?"

"No, but thank you. You go ahead." Lisa leaned forward and handed him a glass off a small wooden rack to her left.

Jack sipped his spring water. He clutched the armrest on the door with his right hand as the limo suddenly swerved left. The unexpected turn caused Lisa to nearly fall into Jack's lap, spilling the glass of water onto their shoes. They both laughed as they righted themselves and inspected for any water spots on their clothing.

While they waited at a traffic light, Jack suddenly turned to Lisa and spoke. "You're Italian, right?"

"Half. Why?" Lisa gave him a questioning look.

"I was just wondering where you got your green eyes?"

"My mother was Irish," Lisa replied quietly.

"Was?" Jack repeated. "What is she now, Swedish?"

"She's dead," Lisa said flatly, turning her head away from him to gaze out the window on the opposite side of the limo.

There was a long period of silence as Jack mentally kicked himself for trying to be funny. He had ended up being insensitive and hurting someone, again. Lisa spoke first, her head still turned as she continued to stare out the limo window on her left.

"We lost her a year ago this past summer. Massive heart attack while jogging. She had just turned sixty."

"I'm really sorry to hear that, Lisa," Jack said softly, gently placing his right hand on her right forearm. "And I'm very sorry for joking about it before."

"A week before her death, she had a complete physical. The doctors told her she was in excellent health." Jack sensed she was controlling her tears. Lisa continued, speaking softly, "It all came as quite a shock to us."

"Who is us?" Jack asked, feeling like he should slowly change the subject.

"My father and I. We're all that's left."

Jack hesitated, waiting for her to continue. Lisa turned and looked at Jack. There was deep sorrow in her misty green eyes. Jack nodded, fighting the urge to ask her what she meant by "all that's left." He turned his head and looked out his window on the right side of the limo. Lisa sensed his question. She felt his right hand on her arm and placed her left hand on top of it.

"I had an older brother. He was a Navy pilot. He died during a training exercise in the Persian Gulf. We all took it pretty hard. Then, when mom died, my father just sort of... " her voice trailed off. Lisa squeezed Jack's arm and closed her eyes, leaving her sentence unfinished.

Jack felt her pain. He understood it. He knew what it was like to lose someone you love very much. You can make some of the pain and emptiness go away sometimes, but never completely. It's always there. And somehow, you learn to treasure it. It helps you remember and appreciate the one you loved, and lost, even more.

Jack watched Lisa' eyes close as her hand tightened on his. He slowly lifted his left arm up and curled it around her small shoulders, gently pulling her closer to him. She tilted her head to lightly rest on his shoulder. They rode in silence during the remainder of the limo ride to the restaurant while Jack thought of all the things she had just told him. He wondered about her father. Obviously, even though he was still alive, there was something painful for Lisa when it came to her relationship with him. Jack's keen sixth sense once again told him that he would eventually learn more. There was an unusual closeness rapidly developing between Lisa and him. He felt it. Plus, he saw something in her that he had never seen before; a gentler, softer side. And that surprised him.

Lisa relaxed in the warmth and comfort of Jack Kramp's large arms. She felt like she could curl up and go to sleep, but yet, she wanted to be consciously awake so she could enjoy these precious, rare moments of feeling secure and safe.

"He's actually like a big teddy bear," Lisa thought to herself as she felt his chest rise and fall as he breathed. "I think he's got a big heart." Suddenly, a small terror entered her thoughts. "And I'm not going to be the one to break it." A slow sadness replaced her feeling of safe comfort. She prayed, half-heartedly, for their quick arrival to the restaurant.

When they arrived at the restaurant, Lisa sat up and took a minute to look at her hair and makeup in a small lighted compact she had pulled from her clutch purse. Jack waited for the driver to open the door before stepping out. He extended his hand to assist Lisa. Once outside, Lisa turned to the limousine driver. "Plan for an 11:45 pickup," she instructed. "If there is a change in time, I'll call you."

Jack held his arm for her as she turned and they entered Bradburry's. He was thinking that it was going to be a later night than he had planned. His stomach gave a small growl.

"Hope we eat soon," Jack thought, noticing the time was 8:05 p.m. on a large grandfather clock in the massive lobby. The restaurant ahead of them had an aristocratic feeling of being tastefully expensive.

"I think you'll really like this," Lisa said as they were ushered down a long open corridor toward a small private room just off the main dining room. "It's one of the finest restaurants in New York."

"I'm sure glad I'm not picking up the tab for this shindig tonight," he said, grinning at Lisa.

"Oh, but you are, big guy!" she said, smiling back coyly. Jack stopped in his tracks to look her in the eyes. A small panic seized him as he wondered if they accepted Visa. "Indirectly, of course," she quickly added, appreciating the look of relief that spread across Jack's face. "Zing!" she said, laughing and jabbing her finger into his chest.

"Let's go, funny lady," Jack said, chuckling under his breath as he took Lisa by the arm and hurried to catch up with the maitre 'd.

As they walked, Jack noticed large, open arches lining the inner wall of the corridor. On the other side of the arches was a spacious, chandelier-adorned dining room, a massive dance floor, and a complete orchestra. There were at least a dozen couples dancing.

They suddenly turned right and entered a smaller, private dining room. There was a large, round white linen covered table in the center of the room with ten place settings. Eight people were already seated. Jack immediately recognized Marsha Morrow as one of them. All eyes turned toward Lisa and Jack as they entered. Then, almost as if they had rehearsed it, they all stood up simultaneously. Jack grinned broadly, suppressing a deep laugh at the majestic scene before him.

"I'm sorry we're late," Lisa said as she removed her cape. As Jack helped her out of it, he noticed a small coat rack in the far corner of the room and walked over to it. When he returned, Lisa extended her hand out to him and pulled him around the table, making introductions. Jack was introduced to Niki Jones, a young woman who looked barely thirty. She was Brownstone's Production Manager. He was introduced to Bob Malock, the Director of Marketing, and his wife, Barbara. When Lisa introduced him to Geri Parsons, the head of Layout and Design, Jack took the opportunity to compliment her.

"The cover designs you created are really great. I'm having a difficult time choosing one," Jack said sincerely, wearing a warm smile.

"Well, thank you, Jack," replied Geri. "I must confess, though, I had a lot of help. I'm sure we'll all be able to agree on the best one in a day or two."

Jack nodded and continued down Lisa's greeting line. Marsha Morrow was her friendly, beautiful self. Her husband, Geoffrey, was almost as tall as Jack, but about ten years older. His hair was gray and he looked rather distinguished. "Just like a reliable stockbroker should look," Jack thought.

Peter Tunnell didn't look anything like the man Jack had imagined from their one lengthy telephone conversation. He was short with a dark complexion. He looked as if he was close to sixty, but in very good physical condition. His long black shoulder-length hair was flecked with gray and in direct contrast to the baldness on top of his head. He wore thick wire rimmed glasses, and he had a wide smile that seemed to cause his entire face to wrinkle. Jack noticed his extraordinarily large hands. He was a powerful man. Jack instantly thought that maybe he had been a boxer in his younger years. Peter's wife, Cindy, was at least twenty-five years younger than her husband. She was a gorgeous blonde with a deep voice. Jack also learned that she was quite intelligent, too, contrary to his first stereo-type impression. Cindy was an English professor at NYU.

Once the Brownstone party of ten was seated again, two young men in tuxedos took their drink orders. Lisa ordered a glass of white wine. Jack ordered a plain coke, which caused Lisa to look at him with raised eyebrows, but she said nothing.

The dinner conversation centered around Jack's book, the storyline, and his subtle humor within the plot. There was a variety of dialogue surrounding production deadlines, edits, rewrites, other books by other authors coming up, and current best sellers. Jack found all of this to be very interesting.

As Jack thought about leaving New York in a week, he felt oddly sad. Lisa would be working on another rewrite with someone else. He would be back home in Minneapolis and life would go on. When he thought of Lisa in a hotel suite with the next writer, Jack became confused over what he was feeling. He recognized it, even though it was quite strange to him. It was a sense of jealousy.

The group around the table seemed genuinely interested in Jack's home state of Minnesota and proceeded to ask him questions about where and how he lived. They were also intrigued with the details of his radio career as a morning air personality. There was a great deal of discussion about the similarities between publishing and the broadcasting business. Jack was surprised to discover that Peter Tunnell and Bob Malock had been to northern Minnesota just last spring on a fishing trip in the Boundary Waters Canoe Area.

At one point over dinner, Marsha had the entire table laughing as she described the water fight scene in suite 3418 when she arrived to visit Lisa and Jack a few days earlier. Lisa and Jack exchanged embarrassing glances and grinned sheepishly at the other dinner guests.

They were eating an apple cobbler with a hot caramel sauce for dessert when Peter Tunnell stood up and gently tapped his fork against his water glass, gaining the attention of everyone at his table. He cleared his throat and slowly began to speak.

"As you all know, Brownstone Publishing has developed a reputation over the years for taking risks. A great percentage of these calculated risks have resulted in successes, some of them major. We evaluate each risk prior to taking it, to be sure, but sometimes, something, or someone..." Peter paused and looked directly at Jack who shifted uncomfortably in his chair. "...comes along with a piece of work that bears immediate attention. Immediate action. Now, I have conversed with every person who has read Jack's manuscript for *Loose Cannons*. Several of you are right here in this room. I must admit that I have only read, and, I might add, thoroughly enjoyed, the first twelve chapters fresh out of editing. Jack graciously filled me in on the rest of the book the other night. It has an unusual blend of action, romance, humor, and mystery set against the backdrop of the old west. It's a refreshingly rare piece of fiction that will have mass reader appeal. I truly believe we have the makings of a best seller here."

Peter paused again and carefully looked at each person around the table before he continued, "Therefore, I, we, have decided that we are going to take a gut-feel risk and take Jack Kramp's book, *Loose Cannons*, directly into hardcover and promote the friggin' hell out of it! Twenty-five thousand copies; first run!" Peter's voice rose in a crescendo as he ended his sentence.

There was a brief silence and no one at the table moved. Marsha Morrow was the first to let out a squeal of delight, jumping up and throwing her arms around Jack. Everyone seemed to be up and moving at once to congratulate him. He was numb from the sudden excitement and change of events. Jack looked at Lisa. She was smiling and nodding at him in approval. He suddenly became aware that her left hand was casually resting on his leg, close to his right knee.

Peter Tunnell came around the table and began pumping Jack's hand, expressing enthusiastic congratulations. He put his right hand on Jack's shoulder and waved the group to sit down with his left.

"Of course, Jack, there are a couple of strings attached to this deal," he said, grinning and turning to peer at Marsha over the top of his wire rims. "There always are, you know." He turned his attention back to Jack.

"We'll want you to sign an extended contract with Brownstone. You'll have to produce at least two more manuscripts within the next eighteen months. Deal?"

Jack looked up at Peter, around the table, and then finally to Lisa. Everyone's eyes were on him. "Well, that depends," he said slowly, searching for words.

"On what?" asked Marsha, leaning toward him.

"I'll only agree to the deal if I can be assured of having Lisa as my rewrite editor on each manuscript." Jack was sure he heard a couple of small surprising gasps of air from those around the table. He thought one of them may have even come from Lisa seated next to him.

"Lisa?" Peter had turned his gaze to her. She continued to smile. She put her head down momentarily and looked at her lap. When Lisa returned her gaze to Peter, her smile had broadened.

"Sure," Lisa said, "Why not? I'm becoming used to daily adventures with Jack." She looked around the table, a familiar confidence had returned to her voice. "You all know how I feel about paperbacks. But now, since Jack's book isn't a paperback any longer, I'll do it. But, he has to promise the next one will be good enough to go right to hardcover." Lisa laughed aloud, everyone at the table joined in with her, including Jack.

Two chilled bottles of champagne and ten fluted glasses arrived at the table. Several toasts were made to the pending success of *Loose Cannons*. At one point, when the attention had finally turned away from Jack, Lisa lifted her full glass of champagne and touched it against Jack's.

"Here's to your success, Jack. May it never go to your head."

"Our success," Jack corrected her. "And, I doubt that it will as long as you're around to keep my ego in check." They smiled warmly at each other and sipped their champagne.

"OK, everybody, let's go cut a rug!" Peter Tunnell announced loudly after draining yet a third bottle of champagne. He rounded up everyone and herded them out to the dance floor.

Geri Parsons and Niki Jones said their good-byes as couples paired up on the edge of the dance floor. The Morrows and the Malocks followed Peter and Cindy Tunnell out to the middle of the crowded floor, leaving Lisa and Jack standing in a cloud of uncertainty. It was an awkward moment as Jack looked from the crowded dance floor to Lisa and back to the floor. Lisa's gaze had followed her associates as they made room among the graceful, happy throng of moving couples.

"Shall we?" Jack finally said, offering Lisa his right arm, having found nerve from a final large swallow of champagne. She nodded without looking at him, set her glass down on a nearby ledge, and started walking out to the dance floor. Jack followed Lisa as they threaded their way into the center of the crowd in rhythmic motion. She slipped easily into Jack's arms as the orchestra played a slow, unfamiliar song. Jack soon found the right timing and gracefully moved Lisa around the floor in a leisurely waltz. He appreciated how well she glided with him, in spite of his large feet.

The band changed tempo to a rumba and without hesitation, Jack swung Lisa around and remembered the steps perfectly. He watched Lisa's smile widening as they whirled around the floor. Jack tried hard to remember the last time he had been dancing. "It must be years," he thought. He was wondering if he was smiling as much as Lisa. He was having fun and desperately hoped she was, too.

"What time is it?" Lisa asked Jack as they caught their breath during a slow tune from the forties.

"11:30," Jack said in surprise as he pulled his cell from inside the breast pocket of his dinner jacket. He had danced with Lisa the past eight dances, determined not to let her off the dance floor. He was enjoying himself and he sensed she was equally relishing the music and their compatible movements. Jack's intuitions were correct.

"The limo will be here in fifteen minutes. If you'd like to stay longer, I should call the driver," Lisa said softly as she looked up into Jack's blue eyes.

"It's up to you," he replied. "Do you want to stay?"

Lisa nodded her head slowly up and down, never taking her eyes away from Jack's. "I think they quit playing at 12:30. Peter will want to have a hot brandy nightcap with us. Shall I say 1:15 for the limo?"

"Sure," said Jack, chuckling. "I feel fine. I could dance all night."

Lisa flashed a grin at Jack and led him off the dance floor. Using Jack's cell, she called the limo company while Jack watched the upper crust of New York City dance, retrieve coats, and call for taxi cabs and limos.

As Lisa predicted, the orchestra stopped playing exactly at 12:30 a.m. The Brownstone party returned to their dining room. The group had dwindled down to just six of them; Peter and Cindy Tunnell, Marsha and Geoffrey Morrow, plus Lisa and Jack. The Malocks had left at midnight for home and their three visiting grandchildren.

"Let's go to the bar and have a nightcap," Peter said, putting his arms around the shoulders of Marsha and Jack. Lisa smiled and flashed a knowing look at Jack. He nodded and winked at her. Jack's cheeks hurt. He realized that he probably hadn't stopped smiling since he arrived at the restaurant.

Inside the dimly lit bar, the six of them found a small round table in an even darker corner. The brightest light emanated from a candle in the center of the table which cast soft, dark shadows over their faces.

"Hot brandies, all around," said Peter, making a large circular motion with his arm. Jack noted that Peter was a "take-charge" kind of guy. He had a great amount of respect for Peter. He had earned it.

"I ran into Frank at lunch today, Lisa," Peter said, turning his full attention to her. "He said to give you his love."

Lisa gave Peter a sobering look along with a nod that acknowledged his statement, but she said nothing. Jack eyed Lisa, but she gave him no indication that she was going to expand on Peter's message or tell Jack who Frank was. The conversation drifted to sports, and Jack smiled to himself when Peter told him that he had done some boxing in college.

"What about you, Jack?" Marsha Morrow asked. "Did you play any sports in college?"

"Just a little basketball. I played football, basketball, and baseball in high school, but I was a little awkward because of my geeky height and lanky stature," Jack replied. They all stared at him with small smiles, expecting him to explain. Jack cleared his throat and decided to go on.

"I hit six-three during the summer of my junior year in high school. I added one more inch the summer before college. I've been six-four ever since," he said, laughing to cover up his embarrassment.

At 1:15 a.m., the nightcap party in the bar broke up, and everyone headed for home. The white limo was waiting outside the restaurant for Lisa and Jack. They were surprised at how the outside temperature seemed to have risen during the time they had been inside. Most of the snow had already turned to slush.

"Chinook winds," Jack commented as they entered the limo.

"What?" Lisa inquired as she settled herself next to Jack in the back seat of the limo, sitting even closer to him now than she did during the ride down.

"Chinook winds," Jack repeated. "They're winds that warm everything up. The wind was from the northwest earlier tonight. Now they're circling and coming from the opposite direction. It might be a nice weekend after all."

"So, let's see, Mr. Kramp, you're not only an author, an on-air personality, and a basketball player, but you're also a meteorologist?" Lisa teased.

"Nope," Jack said as he grinned happily, pleased with himself that he was able to impress Lisa. "I had a smart grandmother."

Fifteen minutes into the ride home, Lisa pointed to a building just two blocks west off the street they were on. "That's my condo building. I'm on the 15th floor."

"Really?" Jack peered out the window and tried to gain his geographical bearings. "Wait a minute," he said, "How far are we from the hotel?"

"About ten, maybe twelve minutes, why?" replied Lisa.

"Well, if you live right over there, why aren't we just dropping you off? The driver can get me back to the hotel. It makes no sense to have you ride all the way up there and then back here again."

"Oh, it's no problem," Lisa said, but Jack could hear the hesitancy in her voice as she processed his logic.

"Look, you're tired," he reasoned, "In seven and a half hours we both have to be bright eyed and bushy tailed to edit and select a book cover. Come on, Lisa, let's drop you off now. It's on the way."

Lisa finally nodded in agreement, unable to argue with Jack's common sense. She was feeling very exhausted. It had been a long day and a most enjoyable night.

Jack picked up the intercom telephone and called up to the driver, giving him directions to turn left and head over to Lisa's condo.

When the limo pulled up in front of Lisa's building, Jack didn't wait for the driver to open their door. He opened the door immediately and helped Lisa exit. He walked her to just inside the front entry near her security door where they stood facing each other for an awkward moment, neither one speaking.

"I had a wonderful time tonight, Jack," Lisa finally said, looking up into his baby blues.

"So did I. You're one helluva dancer, Tiger-Lady!"

"You're pretty limber yourself, in spite of your... what did you call it in the bar tonight? Oh, yes, your 'geeky height!'" Lisa flashed a big smile at Jack. He stood watching her, not wanting the evening to end.

"Good night, Lisa," Jack said, knowing that she was tired and time was ticking away on the limo.

Lisa stood on her tiptoes, reached up, and put her right hand around Jack's neck. She pulled his head down toward her and gently kissed his left cheek. Jack just stood there in total surprise, his face frozen in a soft smile. There were several seconds of pure magic between them. Nothing moved in the world. Not one thing stirred except their distant hearts.

"Good night, Jack," Lisa said, then turned, found the lock pad with her electronic pass key, and walked into her building, never turning back to look at him. Jack's eyes followed her until she disappeared out of sight around a corner. Still smiling and feeling the warmth of her kiss on his cheek, Jack made a cherished memory of those few seconds that had just happened between them. He pulled the lapel of his coat toward his nose. The scent of her perfume lingered.

Feeling like a young school boy after his first date, Jack skipped down the steps two at a time and darted back into the waiting limo.

"Home, James," he said, knowing full well the driver's name wasn't James. Jack didn't care. Something was coming alive in him again. He had a wonderfully strange feeling of rebirth. For the first time in two years, Jack Kramp felt there was a possibility he could love again. He could love someone in the way he had loved Mary, only different; very different.

Chapter Thirteen

Jack's wake up call came at exactly 8:00 a.m. Saturday morning, precisely as Jack had requested just a few hours earlier. From a deep, contented sleep, Jack fought his way to semi-consciousness and finally answered on the third ring.

"Good morning, Mr. Kramp," a man's cheerful voice greeted him, "This is your wake up call. It's 8:00 a.m. Have a wonderful day!" Jack mumbled a thank you, hung up the telephone, and rolled over onto his back. As he became fully awake, he sensed the faint scent of Lisa's fragrance from the evening before. He wondered where it was coming from. Suddenly, Jack jerked and looked at the pillow next to him, leaning on his elbow.

"Whoa!" he said to himself. "I thought maybe I had way too much champagne and last night didn't end the way I had remembered. For a second, I thought that Lisa had come home with me! Now, don't I feel like a damn fool?"

Jack crawled out of the massive bed and stretched. He grinned as he thought of his sudden panic just a minute earlier to look for Lisa beside him.

"I actually wish she had been there," Jack said aloud as he walked toward the window and threw open the drapes. Bright sunshine lit up the room, and Jack noticed the snow had turned the streets below into small rivers of brown slush. There were already people walking leisurely in Central Park.

"Must be warming up," Jack thought as he headed for the bathroom to shower. "Maybe after lunch I'll get out and see more of this Big Apple."

Jack hastily showered and shaved. After a full minute of standing in front of the massive dresser, he finally selected a pair of blue jeans, a maroon sweatshirt, and dug out his only pair of sneakers. As Jack wandered out of the bedroom and into the living area, he thought about his children. Picking up his cell from the desk, Jack began to grin as he thought about sharing the good news of his book going to hardcover. The phone rang six times. Jack looked at the time; 7:25 in Minnesota. He wondered where all three kids were at this hour on a Saturday morning.

Feeling his stomach rumble again, Jack shrugged his shoulders and hung up the phone. He grabbed his room key, locked up, and headed for the elevators. "I'm afraid it'll be just orange juice and granola for you this morning, big fella," Jack said as he patted his stomach in the empty elevator. "You had a feast last night, and you're starting to look like a small, slightly pregnant elephant." As Jack thought about calories, he noted with a certain amount of pride that he had gone over twenty-four hours without a beer.

"Progress, Jack," he said as he exited the elevator and walked toward the Garden Cafe. "Progress, one day at a time."

By 8:50 a.m. Jack was on his way back up to his room with his stomach still crying for more. As he crossed the large lobby, he glanced toward the front entry. He stopped instantly, frozen in his tracks as he recognized a short little fat man talking hurriedly and making frantic gestures with his hands to a tall, thin man with long, black oily hair. Mr. Slick, as Jack quickly nicknamed him, was wearing a tailored gray suit. Jack thought he also noticed a thin mustache. Mr. Fat Face wasn't wearing his brown suit today, Jack noted. He was dressed in khaki slacks and a dark brown jacket. The pair went through the revolving door at the front entrance. Positive it was the same short fat man he had seen darting down the back hall on his floor just two mornings ago, Jack instinctively turned and headed toward the front entrance.

"Let's see where they're headed," Jack thought as he pushed his way through the revolving door. Once outside in the bright morning sun, Jack stood on the sidewalk, looking up and down the street in both directions. The hotel doorman walked over and asked if he could get a taxi for him. Declining, Jack walked fifty feet north up Central Park West, constantly turning his head, looking for the pair of suspicious characters. He glanced across the street at Central Park just in time to see the two men turn a corner behind some hedges. Jack's inclination was to follow them into the park, but he knew it was close to 9:00 a.m. and he had to meet Lisa. Jack softly cursed under his breath and headed back to the hotel. The thought of a dead Buddy Shepard flashed through his mind.

As he reached the hotel's front entrance, a cab pulled up and Lisa got out, paid the cab driver, and arrived at the front doors at the same time as Jack. Surprised at the unexpected encounter, they both looked at each other for a split second and burst into laughter.

"Out for a morning stroll?" Lisa asked.

"Just getting some fresh air after breakfast," Jack said, hoping his smile would cover up the fact that he had really been out chasing unusual suspects. As they rode up to the 34th floor in the elevator, Lisa and Jack talked about the party the night before.

"So how does it feel to have a potential best seller, Jack?" Lisa inquired with a broad grin.

"It feels great! I haven't had much time to think about it. It hasn't fully sunk in yet up here," he replied, tapping a finger to his head. Lisa rocked from side to side in front of Jack as though she were trying to see something around the back of him.

"Well, it still looks like the same size," she said.

"What does?" Jack asked, half turning around to see if there was something on the elevator wall behind him that he had missed earlier.

"Your head!" Lisa exclaimed. She broke into a deep laugh and elbowed Jack in the ribs as they got off the elevator and walked down to his suite. Once inside, Lisa walked directly to her desk and turned on the Mac. Jack opened the curtains over the French doors, started a pot of coffee, and switched on the radio. He changed the station from country music to a big band format. It reminded him of dancing with Lisa the night before. She had taken off her tan leather jacket and draped it over the love seat. Wearing blue jeans, white running shoes, and a gray sweatshirt with her sleeves pushed halfway up to her elbows, she looked ready to play a game of touch football.

"At last, we finally got our wardrobe in sync," Jack said as he came up from the living room and nodded in her direction. Lisa looked down at her attire and then at his.

"We almost match!" She grinned, turned, and opened her briefcase. Jack assumed his favorite position in his desk chair, feet up on the desk, legs crossed. Placing his hands behind his head, he watched Lisa shuffle the pages of his manuscript back and forth. She paused suddenly and pulled the vase of orchids toward her. Lifting them to her face, she took a deep breath, inhaling the fragrance of the flowers and greenery surrounding them. Still holding the vase of orchids in her hands, she turned to face Jack.

"They are quite beautiful. Thank you again, Jack. It's been a long, long time since anyone has given me flowers."

"Well, if they haven't, they've all been fools. You should have flowers every day," Jack said quietly, realizing that his voice engaged minutes ahead of his brain again.

Lisa flashed a quick smile at Jack, feeling a small blush rising in the dark complexion of her cheeks. She turned back to admire the flowers again and missed Jack's neck and face turn a tinge of red, too. Lisa set the orchids back on her desk, a little closer to her this time.

"They mean more to me today than yesterday for some reason," she thought. Remembering the dancing last night with the big handsome Minnesotan seated behind her, she murmured quietly to herself, "He's an unusual character, but one thing is for certain, he's a true gentleman."

They worked on chapter eighteen until 11:00 a.m. With six pages left, Lisa and Jack decided to take a break and narrow down their selections from the book cover proposals. While Jack collected two diet Pepsi's from the refrigerator, Lisa sat down on the love seat and leaned forward over the six layout designs. She looked up at the fireplace across from her.

"Jack, I think I have a couple of push pins in my briefcase, would you mind getting them?"

"No problem," Jack said, heading toward her desk. As he riffled through her briefcase, he noticed a small red book entitled "Brownstone Confidential Employee Directory." He picked it up, paused for a second, then placed it back where he had found it and grabbed four red push pins.

"We'll pin each design up separately on the rough wooden mantle above the fireplace," Lisa said. "We'll discuss the pros and cons of each element as they relate to the entire story line of the book. We'll give each layout a letter grade of A, B or C in each of five categories: color, eye appeal, typography, representative graphic, and over all style. That should help us narrow these first six down to two and then, finally, to one. OK?" Lisa spoke while pinning up the cover designs. She turned, looked at Jack, and waited for him to answer. He was grinning at her from his seat on one of the sofas.

"Sounds fine to me. You've done this a time or two before, huh?" Jack teased as Lisa stepped back and sat down on the love seat.

"A few," Lisa replied, concentrating on the cover layouts hanging in front of them.

After a great deal of discussion, Lisa and Jack narrowed their choices for the cover of *Loose Cannons* down to two. They hung them side by side on the mantle and decided to leave them there while they gave themselves a breather by finishing up the last six pages of chapter eighteen.

"Shall we order room service for lunch?" Lisa asked Jack as they each took three pages and assumed their usual positions at their desks.

"How about Louie's Pizza?" Jack suggested.

"OK," Lisa replied, nodding readily, "I haven't had pizza for a couple of weeks. Do you know the number?"

"Got it memorized," Jack said, tapping his temple again with his index finger. "What do you like? Veggie?"

"How did you know?" Lisa asked, her eyes wide in amazement.

"Lucky guess," he replied. Jack ordered a large veggie pizza. A voice with a heavy Italian accent on the other end said it would be about thirty minutes. Jack glanced at his cell. It was 12:30 p.m. "The day is going by fast," he thought. When Jack returned to his desk, Lisa turned toward him with a serious look on her face.

"I've been wanting to ask you something, Jack," she said somberly.

"Shoot," Jack replied, wondering from what field her question might come out of this time.

"How did you know about Buddy Shepard?"

Jack paused and gave her a hard look. He had to make a decision. Either dodge the bullet or tell her the truth and possibly have Lisa become angry at Marsha. Jack decided the truth was always best. He told her in detail about his phone conversation with Marsha the other night. He also relayed the conversation he'd had with Peter Tunnell that same evening. Lisa listened intently, nodding occasionally. She smiled openly at the way Jack could spin a tale. Although

Jack's thoughts turned to his serious conversation with Avery Schneider about Buddy's murder, he decided that it wasn't the time to go into that situation.

"I'm sorry I berated you so harshly the other night, Jack. It's just that Buddy used to wander around the streets alone at all hours of the day or night. I didn't want history repeating itself. I didn't want anything happening to..." she paused, swallowing hard, "...to you."

Jack nodded, thinking as long as this seemed to be the time for confessions, he might give it a try with a question of his own.

"Understandable. So who's Frank?"

Surprised by his question, Lisa raised her eyebrows for an instant. Jack thought he saw a hint of fire in her green eyes immediately followed by bits of moisture. She sucked in a deep breath and finally spoke softly, her eyes focusing on the tips of Jack's shoes.

"Frank Lisignoli. My father. We haven't spoken to each other for over a year. Shortly after my mother died, he went berserk. He became an alcoholic, although I've heard he's been in treatment now for a few months. He's also become even more of a workaholic, practically living at the office day and night. I hear through friends that the only time he ever leaves is to visit the grave sites of my mother and my brother, Brian."

Jack nodded, not moving a muscle as his heart felt her pain. His intuitions were correct; there was emotional pain in the life of Lisa Lisignoli.

"What does your father do for a career?" Jack asked, pushing the envelope a little further. Lisa tilted her head back and forced a smile, knowing that Jack Kramp might fall out of his chair when he heard her answer.

"Are you ready for this, Jack?" she asked, leaning toward him so as not to miss any part of his reaction. "He's the CEO of Tanner and Whitehall, one of the largest publishing companies in New York and a direct competitor of Brownstone's."

Jack's mouth gaped open at the news, his eyes wide from the shock of discovering yet another twist in the personal life of Lisa Lisignoli. "So that's how you... I mean, you're really good, and..." Lisa nodded as Jack continued to struggle with his words.

"I grew up in the business. I've wanted to be in publishing all my life. Being a senior editor in rewrite is as close as I've come. So far, anyway," Lisa said with a thin smile.

"You'll write a best seller someday," Jack told her confidently. "I know you will. You have plenty of time. Look at me, I'm forty-six, and I feel like I'm just beginning. Hell, I am just beginning!" Jack was on his feet pacing, his voice rising from all the recent excitement.

"Maybe someday," Lisa said, grinning as she watched Jack pacing the floor, throwing his hands in the air as he punctuated each sentence with a wild gesture.

There was a knock on the door. Jack glanced at the time on his cell phone and walked toward the door, calling over his shoulder to Lisa.

"It's the pizza. There's more Pepsi in the refrigerator. Or if you'd like a beer..." Jack let his voice trail off as he opened the door and took the pizza. He paid cash, closed the door, locked it, and returned to his desk with the pizza in hand.

Lisa was waiting for him, having cleared off the top of his desk to make room for the pizza and placed napkins on each corner. Jack put the pizza down in the center of the desk and stepped back, surprised to see Lisa holding out a can of beer for him in her right hand.

Jack stared at the beer and hesitated, not saying a word.

"You can have one," Lisa said, a soft smile on her lips. "But only because I'm joining you. If you try to drink two, I'll have to break your arm. Seriously, I will."

Jack looked over at the other can of beer already opened in Lisa's left hand. He took the beer from her, popped it open, and sat down at his desk. He lifted his beer to her in a toast, and Lisa touched her can to his.

"To surprises," Jack said quietly, tilting the can to his lips.

"May they always be pleasant ones," Lisa added, winking at Jack and taking her first swallow.

It was a little after 2:00 p.m. by the time Lisa and Jack finished their pizza and the last six pages of chapter eighteen. Lisa entered the corrections on the computer and backed them up on the jump drive while Jack finished up the final proofing of the pages they had corrected earlier that morning.

"There," Lisa said with satisfaction as she ejected the master jump from the Mac. "Eighteen down, only a few more to go." She stood, switched off the Mac and the printer, then turned to look at Jack who was already seated on the love seat in the living room area. He had his feet resting on the coffee table, reclining with both hands behind his head, and fingers locked. He stared at the final two options of the cover designs still hanging from the fireplace mantle.

"So, which one?" Lisa asked, coming to a halt behind Jack and the love seat.

"I don't know. How long do we have?" Jack continued to study the two designs.

"Monday. Noon, at the latest," she replied. "The sooner we inform Geri of our selection, the better."

Jack sighed as he stood up, shaking his head. He walked around the love seat to Lisa, gave her a tired smile, and walked up to the French doors. He opened them wide and stepped out onto the terrace. The bright sun filled a cloudless sky. The air felt crisp, but Jack thought it was still well over forty degrees, maybe even fifty. He stood near the outside terrace wall. Taking a deep breath, he looked down at Central Park sprawling out below him.

"It's really warmed up since last night." Jack heard Lisa's voice behind him. He turned to find her standing in the doorway. He nodded in agreement and turned his gaze back to the park below.

"What are you so deep in thought about?" Lisa asked as she moved next to him, looking up at his face with wide, questioning eyes. He gazed southeast over the East River toward Brooklyn and Queens. As he watched aircrafts adjust their flight patterns as they prepared to land at JFK International to the southeast, Jack thought about going home. In less than a week, he'd be on one of those winged specs that were climbing up and banking over the Atlantic and heading west. A sudden, unexplainable sadness spread over Jack. A cold loneliness began creeping back into his heart. He shrugged his shoulders and turned his attention back to Central Park.

"Let's go for a ride," he said unexpectedly.

"What?" Lisa responded, looking confused as she looked deeply into his blue eyes.

"Down there," Jack said, pointing over the ledge toward the park. "Let's grab one of those carriages and let 'em take us through the park, or wherever it is they go."

Lisa looked from Jack down to the park and back again. Jack could feel the hesitancy in her as he noticed her body stiffen ever so slightly.

"Now?" she asked.

"Why not? We aren't going to start chapter nineteen until Monday morning, right?"

"No..." Lisa said slowly. "It's just that I..."

"I'm sorry," Jack interrupted, "You probably have other plans this afternoon, I just thought that since..." His voice faded.

"No, no that's fine. I really didn't have any other plans. Okay. Sure. Let's go," Lisa said, recovering from the initial shock of Jack's startling invitation.

"Okay, then," Jack said, smiling as he turned and gently cupped his right hand on her left elbow and walked her back into the suite. He closed the French doors and helped Lisa with her leather jacket. He walked briskly over to the small closet and grabbed his trench coat. Lisa smiled at him, looking at the black trench coat with Jack's sweatshirt and blue jean ensemble.

"Sorry," Jack apologized. "It's all I have. I didn't think I'd have much time for recreation or sightseeing, so I didn't bring a casual jacket."

"You're fine," Lisa said through a warm chuckle. "As long as you have money, they really don't care how you're dressed in Central Park."

The conversation was light as they rode the elevator downstairs to the lobby and made their way across Central Park West to the carriage station. The one hour ride was one hundred fifty-five dollars. Lisa offered to pay for it, but Jack wouldn't allow it. She wanted to repay Jack for her half, but he remained steadfast.

"My treat," he said as they climbed into the open carriage. "You can be my tour guide, though."

Lisa nodded and grinned as she settled herself in the large leather seat of the black coach. Once Jack adjusted his large frame next to Lisa, she spread a thick plaid blanket over their legs and lap. Jack enjoyed rediscovering the forgotten aroma of a horse and leather. Mingled with the soft scent of Lisa's perfume along with the fresh, late autumn air and the warm sunshine, Jack Kramp was feeling as though he was experiencing a new life, or at the very least, a small rebirth of an emotion he had buried two years ago.

"So this is Central Park," Jack said as the horse-drawn coach began to meander through the paved trail inside the park. "Right in the middle of one of the biggest cities in the world. It looks huge! Hard to imagine."

"It's eight hundred and forty acres of grass, trees, shrubs, flowers, and rolling hills. Plus, depending on the time of day, a few muggers, drug pushers, murderers, and other people of ill-repute," Lisa said, smiling as she watched Jack stretch his neck around in all directions, trying to see everything at once.

"Fifth Avenue runs just on the other side. Park Avenue is a block over from that," Lisa continued. "Avenues run North and South. Streets run East and West."

"Where's Broadway?" Jack asked.

"Just behind us, to the south. Actually, Broadway is the longest and best known street in New York City. It starts south, down in the Financial District and runs north and northwest all the way through Manhattan. The Empire State Building is at the corner of Broadway and Avenue of the America's, about fifteen blocks that way," Lisa said, pointing south over her shoulder.

"And you live south, right?" Jack asked, looking back over his shoulder and trying to remember where the limo had dropped her off last night on their way home. Lisa nodded, smiling as she watched Jack thoroughly enjoying the sights.

"I live over near 9th and West 52nd," she replied.

"Did you grow up there?"

"No," Lisa said, slowly shaking her head, "My parents had an older home on the Upper East Side, right over there about six to eight blocks," she said, pointing. "It's not far from the river. It had belonged to my grandparents on my father's side. He sold it last year and moved to a penthouse in the garment district, not far from Madison Square Gardens."

Lisa chatted openly about Manhattan. Jack listened with a great deal of interest, looking out and around between quick glances at Lisa. "There are over one-point-six million people here in Manhattan, all living in an area that's just thirteen and a half miles long and a little over two miles wide."

Lisa pointed out several areas of interest around Central Park: the Zoo, the statue of Hans Christian Andersen, Cleopatra's Needle, and several colleges that bordered near the east side. On the way back to their starting point, Lisa pointed in the direction of St. Patrick's Cathedral at Jack's request.

"It's really only about a dozen blocks away, fourteen max. It's on the corner of Fifth Avenue and 50th, across from the Rockefeller Center. "Why the interest in St. Patrick's, Jack? Are you into Neo-Gothic architecture or are you planning on seeing the Archbishop while you're here?" Lisa asked teasingly.

"Nope," Jack said simply. "I just needed to know where to attend Mass on Sunday."

"So, you're Catholic," Lisa said slowly, nodding as though she should have known, but yet somewhat surprised at this latest revelation.

"You're not?" Jack asked in surprise, feeling he might have assumed incorrectly.

"A huge percentage of the population here is Italian, Jack, and nearly everyone of them is Roman Catholic. Of course I'm Catholic. I just haven't gone to Mass for awhile."

"How long?" Jack asked impulsively, then instantly regretting the question.

"Two years," Lisa said, flatly. "Except for the funerals."

"Have you ever attended Mass at St. Patrick's Cathedral?" Jack asked, thinking he was changing the subject.

"I was married in St. Patrick's," Lisa said, looking away from Jack.

"No shit?" Jack exclaimed in utter surprise.

"Well," Lisa responded slowly while turning back to grin at Jack's abrupt, yet naturally sincere profanity. "No, I didn't see any 'shit,' but there were a couple of assholes there. I think they were friends of the best man."

Jack threw his head back and roared with laughter. His outburst spooked the horse which suddenly jumped, lifting his front legs off the ground. The driver quickly pulled on the reins from his carriage perch. He yelled something harshly at the horse, turned to give Jack a nasty look, and proceeded with the final one hundred feet to the carriage station.

Descending from the carriage first, Jack turned to hold out his hand for Lisa. As she started to climb out, her feet became entangled in the plaid blanket. Jack reached up with both hands and caught her as she fell forward into his arms. Lisa felt very small in Jack's brief embrace as he gently set her on the ground in front of him.

They both laughed as they crossed the street toward the entrance of the hotel. Jack glanced at the time on his cell as they walked through the revolving doors.

"What time is it?" Lisa inquired as they headed toward the elevators.

"3:55 p.m."

Lisa silently nodded. A serious expression came over her as they rode the elevator up to the 34th floor. Jack noticed her quietness, but said nothing.

Once back in the suite, Lisa cleaned up her desk, picked up the pages of chapter eighteen from the printer tray, and stuffed them into her briefcase. Jack watched her closely. He had a question he really wanted to ask her, but he just stood near the front door of the suite waiting. His trench coat was hanging open and his hands were jammed into the front pockets of his blue jeans.

After waiting for her to turn around from her now tidy desk and look at him, Jack began to speak slowly, "Lisa, I was wondering if we could maybe have dinner tonight somewhere. I really enjoyed the ride with you in Central Park this afternoon, and I thought maybe we could go back downtown, you know, to try a famous Chinese or Italian restaurant, your choice," his voice trailed off. Jack's hopes diminished when he saw the sober look on her face. He already knew Lisa's answer as she pursed her lips together and cocked her head to one side.

"Oh, I'm terribly sorry, Jack. I do have other plans. I am meeting someone at 6:00 p.m. Perhaps another time?" Lisa turned her back and quickly picked up her purse. Slinging it over her shoulder, she walked toward him and the door.

"I'm leaving my briefcase here. I won't need it this weekend," Lisa said as she reached for the door handle and opened it. She forced a smile and added, "And I really enjoyed the ride in the park this afternoon, too, Jack. Thank you very much."

Jack nodded, forcing a weak smile to cover up his disappointment. "I should have never asked her to dinner on such short notice," he thought. "Maybe she was right, maybe I am just a country bumpkin."

"See you bright and early Monday morning, Jack."

"9:00 a.m., right?"

"Like always," Lisa said, flashing a quick smile and stepping out into the hall. "Bye."

"Take care, Lisa," Jack said as he leaned on the door frame. He watched her walk down to the bank of elevators. Lisa stood near the elevators for several seconds. She smiled and looked back at Jack. When the elevator arrived, she waved at him and disappeared. Jack closed the door and leaned on it. He noticed the room had become darker in just the past few minutes. The sun was setting. Or maybe it was because Lisa had left. Jack ambled over to Lisa's desk and sat down. He looked at the vase of orchids still sitting on the far corner.

"It was fun while it lasted, Jack," he said aloud to the French doors. "I'm going to quit thinking about her while I'm ahead."

As Lisa crossed the main lobby of the hotel, she found herself pausing and turning to look back at the elevator that had just brought her down 34 floors. She fought the impulse to retrace her steps, even though there was a small, inner voice calling her back. She put her hand to her throat as she suddenly realized that the small, quiet voice summoning her back to suite 3418 was coming from somewhere within the depths of her own heart. She shook her head vigorously in an attempt to stifle the soft, uncontrollable sobs that seemed to be growing louder. Then, the strong-willed, always-tough Lisa Lisignoli clenched her teeth, turned, and walked quickly out of the revolving hotel doors. She hailed a cab and forced herself not to look back.

Chapter Fourteen

Jack reclined at Lisa's desk for the next half hour, his feet up on the corner, watching millions of lights come on across the east side of the Manhattan skyline through the windows of the large French doors. Lost in thought, Jack was unaware of the darkness that had slowly enclosed the room.

A siren wailing on the street below suddenly brought Jack Kramp back to full consciousness. Surprised at the now darkened room, he bolted upright in his chair. Collecting his thoughts, Jack slowly stood and carefully crossed over to the kitchenette to find a light switch. In the semi-darkness, he noted a small flashing red light coming from the telephone on the counter. Jack flipped the light switch and called down to the hotel operator for his message. His children had called him at 3:00 p.m. Guilt spread over Jack as he recalled that he had been enjoying a carriage ride with Lisa at that time.

"I should have been here," Jack said aloud as he dialed home with his cell. "What if something happened and they needed me?" He looked at the time. It was 4:20 p.m. in Minnesota.

"Hello? Dad?" Tammy answered the telephone brightly.

"Tammy!" Jack blurted out, fighting a small panic in his voice. "Is everything alright?"

"Hi!" Tammy exclaimed. "Yeah, everything is fine. Why?"

"You guys called a few hours ago, and I was out. I just saw the message light, and I was worried."

"Oh, no. We're fine, Dad. Really. We didn't get home until almost 2:00.

"I called you guys early this morning. There was no answer. Where were all of you?"

"Jim had Michael and me up by 6:00 this morning. We all went to the supermarket before it got crowded. It cost us over a hundred and sixty dollars. It took us forever to unload all the food and unpack. I think we had sixteen bags."

"Growing teenagers have to eat," Jack chuckled. "How is the money holding out?"

"I think we are down to about fifty dollars. Jim says he'll probably have to go to the bank with your cash card on Monday."

"That's fine. How's Michael doing with basketball?"

"Real good. I think he's going to be a starter in his first game a week from Tuesday night. You'll be home for that, won't you Dad?"

Tammy's last comment almost sounded like a plea. A wave of loneliness rolled over Jack as he listened to his daughter. He wanted to go home and be with his kids. He wanted to leave now.

"Yeah, of course," Jack said. "Tell Michael I won't miss it."

They talked about several other things. Jack felt like he was talking to Mary again as he listened to Tammy. Her voice was soft, caring, and wonderful, just like Mary's. And she also knew how to take tough, maternal responsibility for the family the way Mary always did.

Tammy explained that Michael was down the block at a friend's house, and Jim was due home from the library any minute. Jack promised he would call tomorrow morning so he could talk to all of them. He was about to say good-bye when he remembered one of the reasons he had called earlier. He told Tammy about the dinner party last night at Bradburry's Restaurant and Peter Tunnell's announcement that Brownstone was going to publish his book in hardcover. Tammy squealed with delight at her father's good news. She asked how soon it would be out, and Jack told her of the tentative plans to do a preliminary debut and book signing during a weekend in December at the Mall of America. Tammy congratulated her father several times. Together, they shared the joy of his possible success. After a half hour, they finally said good-bye.

Jack stood in silence for several minutes after hanging up. He counted the days until he would see his children again. He thought of how much he missed them and how many times in the past two years he had abandoned them to wallow in his own self-pity. The overwhelming guilt caused Jack to reach into the refrigerator and pull out a beer. Without hesitating, he punched the tab and took a long swallow.

Jack carried his beer into the bedroom and placed it on the nightstand, noticing that it was already 5:35 p.m. He took off his sweatshirt and stuffed it into an already full laundry bag. His jeans followed.

"I better call the hotel's laundry service," Jack said as he kicked off his sneakers and jammed his white sweat socks into the bulging bag. He wrinkled his nose and dialed the telephone for guest services. They promised to send someone up immediately to pick up his laundry. A woman assured Jack it would be returned, fresh and clean, by tomorrow at noon. Jack thanked her, carried the bag out of the bedroom, set it down just inside the front door, and returned to take a shower.

As the hot water splashed his body, Jack thought about what he was going to do with the rest of his evening. He finally resigned himself to the fact that he would just grab a hamburger downstairs in the Garden Cafe, have a couple of drinks in the bar, and come back up to watch a Saturday night movie on television.

Jack finished his beer and slowly selected his wardrobe: a pair of navy dress slacks and a blue and white crew neck sweater. He switched on the television in the bedroom and half-listened to CNN as he was getting dressed. Suddenly, a black and white photo on the screen caught his attention. He turned up the volume on the TV to hear the announcer saying that the man pictured had escaped from a Georgia prison two months ago and was still evading capture. He'd been serving time for armed robbery, assault, and extortion. They believe he may be in the area of Atlantic City and possibly headed to his former home in the New York area.

Jack studied the photograph intently. There was a vague familiarity to the man in the photo. He knew he had recently seen someone who resembled him, only without the full beard. Jack's eyes widened and a knot developed in his stomach as he slowly recognized the man on the TV screen as being Mr. Slick, the man he had seen earlier that morning talking to Fat Face down in the hotel lobby.

"It's gotta be him. I never forget faces or voices," Jack said to himself as he switched off the television. He thought about calling the police, but he wondered if they would believe him. He thought of Avery Schneider, but remembered he wouldn't be working again until tomorrow afternoon. And, there's always the possibility he could be wrong. It was doubtful, but he could be totally mistaken.

Jack chewed his lower lip nervously as he turned off the bedroom lamp and walked into the other room. He took his room key off the table in the kitchenette and slipped it into his pocket. Checking the time on his cell, he noted that it was only 6:30 p.m. Jack slowly walked over and stood in front of the French doors. Pausing to look over the city one final time, he reached up and closed the heavy drapes. Seeing Central Park below reminded him of the carriage ride he had taken with Lisa that afternoon. Once again, an emptiness engulfed him as he turned and headed toward the front door of suite 3418.

As Jack neared the door, there was a gentle rapping. He opened it to find a young, attractive Asian woman in a crisp hotel uniform. She informed him she was there to collect his laundry. Jack plucked the bag off the floor and handed it to her. She smiled, said good night, and disappeared down the short hall just outside of Jack's suite.

As Jack prepared to leave, the room telephone rang. He turned and looked at it, wondering who might be calling him on a Saturday night in New York City.

"Hello?" Jack said cheerfully.

"Jack?" He instantly recognized Lisa's soft voice on the other end.

"Lisa!" His heart began to pound a little harder and faster.

"Yes, it's me," she said slowly.

"What's up?" Jack inquired, trying to disguise the hope in his voice.

"Well, I was just wondering if you've already made plans for this evening?"

"Plans?" Jack's mind was racing. "Oh, heck no. I was just going downstairs to the Garden Cafe to have a burger or something. Why?"

"Well, I was hoping your dinner invitation was still open. I... I've changed my mind." Lisa was struggling to find the words. To Jack, she sounded like she was almost regretting the call.

"Dinner would be awesome! Where are you? I thought you had to meet someone at 6:00?"

"I'm just a few minutes away. I did. It didn't work out," Lisa said reflectively, then added with a soft, forced chuckle, "Well, maybe it did."

"Do you want me to meet you somewhere?" Jack asked.

"No. Just stay there, Jack. I'll be over in less than ten minutes, if I can get a cab. Stay in your suite. I'll come up."

"What shall I wear?" Jack asked, becoming embarrassed by his own question.

"We'll dress you accordingly once we decide where we're going," Lisa replied with warm laughter in her voice. "Just please, stay there. OK?"

"OK, I'll stay right here," Jack said.

Lisa said a hurried good-bye, and Jack was left alone once again, still holding the receiver, relishing in his sudden good fortune. For the next fifteen minutes, Jack Kramp paced nervously around his suite.

"Why?" he kept asking himself. "Why did she abruptly change her mind? And who'd she meet at 6:00? And what did or didn't work out?"

There was a knock on his door and Jack rushed to open it. He found Lisa standing there wearing a long, black coat. Her black hair hung around her shoulders in large waves. He caught a glimpse of gold chain earrings dangling from her ears.

"She looks as lovely as she did last night at the Brownstone dinner," Jack thought. The sight of her took his breath away. He flashed her a big grin and invited her in. Once inside, Lisa turned to Jack and smiled. She looked up at him with her bright green eyes, her voice soft and rich.

"I'm truly sorry for all the confusion tonight, Jack," Lisa said. "I really did want to have dinner with you, but I had this previous..." she paused as her voice trailed off. Jack returned her steady gaze and waited. "...engagement. It was a mistake. A big mistake. Thank you for letting me join you at the last minute." She looked down at the floor briefly, then back up at Jack. "Thank you," she said again in a near whisper.

Once again, Jack felt the urge to throw his arms around Lisa and pull her close to him. Instead, he slowly nodded his head and smiled at this incredibly beautiful and unbelievably talented woman. In a very short time, she was making quite an impression on him, one that he suspected would last him a lifetime. He knew Lisa was hurting, and he was somehow destined to help her in some way. Lisa Lisignoli came into his life from a different world with a distant heart.

"So what do you feel like eating, Jack?" Lisa asked as she took off her coat and tossed it in her favorite spot, the back of the love seat.

"In case you haven't noticed by now, I eat almost anything," Jack replied, patting his stomach. He took a deep breath as he gave her another appreciating look. She was wearing a black ruffled blouse complimented by a gold neck chain. A short, tight black skirt with a wide black and gold belt and cross-strapped heels completed her attire; a sexy ensemble set off her curvaceous figure and sent a new kind of fiery hunger through Jack's flesh.

"There is a great little place down in Chinatown," Lisa said, thoughtfully. "Or, I know of a couple wonderful restaurants in Little Italy. What do you crave? This is New York, Jack. We have almost anything you can imagine."

"Chinese sounds super. Or some good Italian would be great, too," Jack replied. "You pick the place. I am but a stranger here."

"OK, Jack, Chinese it is," Lisa said, pulling her cell phone from her coat pocket to search for the number. "I'll see how soon we can get a reservation."

"Uh, just one thing. I don't especially care for raw fish," Jack said reluctantly as she began to dial. Lisa looked up at him and smiled.

"I believe you're thinking of sushi. That's Japanese," she replied, her smile becoming larger, showing her perfectly white pearly teeth. After a brief conversation with the restaurant, Lisa hung up and flashed another grin at Jack.

"We have reservations for 8:00. We better go down and grab a cab. It's going to take us a good thirty to forty minutes to get down there." Lisa reached for her coat, and Jack helped her into it.

"Wait. Am I dressed appropriately for dining in Chinatown?" Jack asked.

"You're fine, Jack. Like I said, if you have money, almost anything goes in New York. Strict dress codes are nonexistent in most places, except in the more upscale restaurants."

The speedy cab ride to Sammie Wang's in Chinatown was filled with quick starts, sudden stops, and plenty of weaving in and out of heavy traffic. At one point, Jack feared for his life as their driver squeezed the cab between two large trucks. Lisa seemed unconcerned as she pointed out famous buildings and landmarks along the way.

Once inside the restaurant, they were immediately seated at a four-top table near a back window. The small, ornate dining room was very crowded. Jack noted there were nearly as many food servers scurrying about as there were patrons dining.

"Wow. The service should certainly be good here," Jack said as he glanced around the room. The aroma of freshly brewed teas filled his nostrils. Steam rose up from delicious platters of seafood, pork, beef, noodles, and fresh vegetables from the tables around them.

"And the food is exquisite!" Lisa exclaimed. She was beaming. Once again, she enjoyed finding a way to impress this tall stranger from the Midwest.

Just as their dinners were served, a man and a woman were seated at the table directly across from them. Jack caught a quick glance at the woman and thought he had seen her somewhere before.

As Jack started to run the woman's image through his memory bank, he caught his breath as he watched the man about sit down. He was a tall African-American with an athletic build. As he pulled his chair back to sit, the bottom of his gray sport coat caught on the back of the chair long enough to reveal a shoulder holster and a handgun. The man nonchalantly covered it up, adjusted his large frame in his chair, and began talking to the woman across from him.

Frowning, Jack stared at his generous portions of Kung Pao shrimp and fried rice in front of him. He was thinking about the woman and the man with the gun when his thoughts were interrupted by Lisa.

"What's the matter, Jack? You don't like your dinner?"

"No. I mean, yes, it's great," replied Jack. He looked at Lisa, then leaned forward and whispered to her. "Do a lot of people in New York carry handguns?" he asked.

Lisa stared back at him wide-eyed, pausing with her chopsticks full of food halfway to her mouth. She grinned at Jack, leaned forward, and whispered back. "Why?"

"Well, don't look now, but that guy in the gray sport coat across from you has a holstered handgun under his coat, left arm."

Lisa sat back and placed her chopsticks down on her plate. She gave Jack a long, hard look, trying to determine if he was serious or if this was another one of his little jokes.

"Are you certain?" she asked quietly, her eyebrows raised.

"Positive," Jack nodded, "And I think I've seen the woman with him someplace before, too. But I can't get a real good look at her. Maybe her hair is styled differently. Something..."

"Well, don't stare, Jack," Lisa said quietly as she casually glanced over at the couple just a few feet away. "The gentleman is most likely a police officer or something of that nature."

"Or with the mob," Jack said seriously.

"Don't let your imagination run away with you, Jack," Lisa said, forcing a light-hearted laugh. "Just because you're a writer doesn't mean there's danger and intrigue at every turn."

"Okay," Jack said, joining in Lisa's laughter. "You're probably right. Let's eat. It's freakin' delicious."

"Well, good evening, Mr. Kramp!" A woman's voice interrupted Jack's concentration on Lisa and his dinner. Upon hearing her voice, Jack instantly knew who she was. He turned and looked directly at the woman seated to his left.

"Well, hello Rita!" Jack exclaimed, a small sigh of relief released with his breath.

"I thought perhaps it was you when we first came in, but I wasn't positive," Rita said, flashing a smile at Lisa and Jack.

Lisa looked back and forth from Jack to the couple. She slowly recognized Rita as one of the employees she often saw behind the front desk at the West Park Plaza Hotel.

"Rita, this is Lisa Lisignoli, senior editor with Brownstone Publishing," Jack said, offering an introduction.

"I thought I recognized you, too," Rita said, smiling at Lisa. "I've seen you in the hotel often. It's very nice to meet you personally. I'm Rita Burgess."

"It's a pleasure to meet you as well," Lisa said, smiling genuinely back at Rita.

"This is my husband, Corey," Rita said as she motioned her hand toward the man seated across from her.

Jack leaned across the aisle and stretched out his hand, pumping the strong hand of Corey Burgess. Again, he noticed the gun under Corey's left arm as the large, muscular man leaned forward and to his left to accept Jack's hand with his right. Corey's eyes followed Jack's gaze to his gun.

"I'm an officer, NYPD," Corey said to Jack, offering a simple explanation for his concealed weapon.

"Corey is a lieutenant," Rita said with pride in her voice. "He's been with the force for over twenty years."

Jack and Lisa nodded. Corey Burgess smiled and looked down at his menu again, slightly embarrassed by his wife's openness.

The two couples conversed over their dinners from across the aisle. Jack and Lisa found Lt. Burgess to be a warm and friendly human being. He was rather quiet, but very intelligent and took his job on the police force very seriously. Rita was a delightful bubble of energy. Her smile seemed to never leave her face, and she always found something good in everything and everybody. At one point, the conversation turned toward keeping the streets of New York safe. Jack commented that he had met one of the hotel's security guards, Avery Schneider, one night in the bar earlier this week.

"Avery is quite a gentleman," Corey said quietly.

"So you know him, huh?" Jack inquired.

"I served under Captain Schneider for fifteen years. He was sort of forced into retirement. But now I think he's much happier working security at the West Park Plaza."

Surprised that Avery had been a police captain, Jack inquired more about the elderly gentleman. They learned that Avery was a graduate of West Point, and he'd been wounded three times in action while on the police force. He has a large family, and he is completely devoted to his wife, who was recently diagnosed with early stages of multiple sclerosis.

When it came time for dessert, Lisa and Jack invited Rita and Corey to join them. Jack insisted that all four desserts be added to his bill.

It was a little after 10:00 p.m. when Lisa and Jack said good-bye to Rita and Corey Burgess outside Sammie Wong's restaurant. Lisa and Jack hailed a cab and headed back up toward midtown.

"The night is young, Jack. What would you like to do now?" Lisa asked as she moved closer to him in the back seat of the cold cab.

"Let's go dancing," Jack replied, grinning at her. He noticed Lisa was shivering from the cold so he put his big left arm around her and pulled her closer to him. She said nothing, and Jack was hoping Lisa didn't resist. He wanted her to be close to him out of her desire, and not because she was simply cold.

"The Blue Diamond on West 57th," Lisa called to the cab driver.

"What's that?" Jack asked.

"Trust me," she said, flashing a smile up at him, then gently letting her head rest on his shoulder.

The Blue Diamond turned out to be yet another pleasant surprise for Jack. It was a dance club that catered to the baby-boomer generation, playing rock and roll from the fifties, sixties, and up through the mid seventies. For the next two and a half hours, Jack and Lisa danced to music from the Beatles, the Rolling Stones, the Bee Gees, The Doors, The Who, Mamas and Papas, and even a few tunes by Bob Dylan and Elvis.

"Damn, this is fun!" Jack said as he dragged Lisa over to the edge of the dance floor to catch his breath. "It's been a long time since I've heard many of these songs."

"Well, it ain't country, honey, but it's the best I could do on short notice," Lisa said through a mimicked sultry, southern drawl.

"What time is it?" Jack asked as he started to reach in his pocket for his cell phone. Lisa grabbed his wrist with her right hand and stopped him.

"The night is young, Jack, and so are we. Let's dance!" Lisa pulled him back out onto the crowded dance floor and slipped into his arms, softly singing along with Bobby Vinton's "Blue on Blue."

Jack closed his eyes, held Lisa tight, and guided her around the floor. They threaded their way through hundreds of other couples who were reliving fond memories of younger years, better times, and happier lives. But Jack Kramp wasn't recalling an old memory, he was making a new one.

"Another late night," Jack said as the cab finally pulled up in front of the West Park Plaza.

"Actually, it's early morning, Jack. Or are you still in your Minnesota time zone?" Lisa teased, still slouched in the back seat next to him.

"My stomach feels like it's in the hunger zone," Jack said as he reached for the door handle. "I worked up an appetite from all that dancing. Want to come up and see if we can get some snacks?"

Lisa looked up at him, her green eyes wide, searching his face for any sign of an ulterior motive. Finding none, she nodded her head in the affirmative.

"Sure, for some reason, I'm wide awake," Lisa said, attempting to sit up straighter in the cab. Jack stepped out and fished in his pocket for cab fare. "And I'm hungry, too," she added.

Back up in suite 3418, Lisa headed into the bathroom to freshen up. Jack called down to the front desk to find out where he might get some food at such a late hour. To his surprise, he learned that the hotel's room service was on duty twenty-four hours a day.

"Only in New York," Jack said as Lisa came back into the kitchenette and leaned against the counter, just a few feet from him.

"What's only in New York?" she inquired.

"Only in New York can you get room service any time of the day," Jack said, shaking his head in disbelief. "Good grief, it's 2:00 a.m. Doesn't anyone ever sleep?"

"Oh, it's not just room service. We can get pizza, Italian pasta, Chinese, Indian, deli sandwiches, almost anything you want. And no, sleep is a luxury. Why do you think they call it the city that never sleeps?"

"I think I know why no one ever sleeps in New York," Jack said, "They're too afraid they'll miss something! This country boy wants to eat. What do you suggest?" Jack asked, rubbing his empty stomach.

"Do you like reuben sandwiches?" Lisa asked Jack as she walked to the love seat and dug her cell out of her coat pocket.

"You mean with sauerkraut, mustard, and all that good stuff?"

"Yes, on fresh pumpernickel bread."

"Sounds great," Jack said as he headed down into the lower living room. "But where the heck do you get those at this hour?"

"I think I know of an all night deli not far from here that delivers. I'll give them a call. But just one thing, Jack," Lisa paused.

"What's that?"

"It's on me. I'm buying. You paid for everything this evening."

"Last night," Jack corrected her.

"Last night, plus the carriage ride yesterday afternoon. This one is on me, Okay?"

"Okay," Jack said reluctantly. He turned his back to her while she dialed the phone. In a moment, he had a warm fire dancing in the fireplace and soft music on the stereo system. He ambled up the three steps and pulled open the heavy drapes on the French doors. Jack was surprised at how many lights were still on in buildings all over the city.

"We're all set. Two reubens and an order of waffle fries will be here in less than twenty-five minutes. I ordered Cokes for us," Lisa said as she walked down into the lower area and sat on the love seat facing the French doors.

"Good," Jack said. He joined her on the love seat. They sat in silence, each lost in their own thoughts as they looked out over the city. Finally, Lisa spoke.

"Jack?"

"Yeah?"

"Would you mind turning off the lamp? It's much easier to see the lights of the skyline."

Jack reached up and turned the knob on the floor lamp next to the sofa. The room became buried in semi-darkness except for the small fluorescent bulb above the sink in the kitchenette. For the first time, Jack noticed all the other lights in the suite were off.

"Lisa must have turned them off," Jack thought to himself as he turned to look at her. She was staring out the windows of the French doors, the pupils of her green eyes were larger than ever with the soft lights of the skyline reflecting on them. Jack watched her. Once again, he felt his breath being taken away by her fine facial features and natural beauty.

"I've lived here all my life, Jack," Lisa said. "And so often, I've taken the beauty of this city for granted. Then, once in awhile, I see it through someone else's eyes, and I appreciate it all over again."

Jack stared at Lisa as she spoke, but he remained silent. She turned and looked at him.

"Thank you for letting me see the beauty again, Jack. You've been a real eye opener for me this past week, in more ways than you can ever imagine." Lisa's voice was silky. She found his hand with hers and slowly locked her fingers in his.

"You've been a real source of inspiration for me, too, Lisa," Jack said. "I've really enjoyed the last couple of days. You are a very unusual woman." Lisa continued locking eyes with Jack. "And a very beautiful woman," he added, "Inside and out."

"Thank you," Lisa murmured, giving Jack's hand a small squeeze.

Their sandwiches arrived and they ate in the velvety darkness of the room. Lisa and Jack talked of past dreams, bitter disappointments, and heart breaks. They shared secret hopes of future fantasies and fearful nightmares. Jack told Lisa the story of his twenty-three year marriage to Mary, concluding with her sudden, accidental death. She asked him about his three children, so Jack spent a great deal of time telling her about them and their achievements.

"You must be so very proud of them," Lisa said.

Jack nodded and then asked her about children.

"I've occasionally thought about having a child. When my husband and I were first married, we discussed it a few times, but both of us were active in our careers and it never seemed to be the right time. Then the divorce happened. Now, my biological clock is ticking. Actually, it's banging as loud as Big Ben! I'm thirty-eight, and the prospect of having a child doesn't look very promising. When I was growing up, I used to dream of having four kids in a big old house and doing the mommy-thing along with a writing career. It's funny, even sad, how our dreams slowly vanish with time, isn't it?"

"They can be shattered in an instant, too," Jack added remorsefully. Lisa nodded, knowing Jack was referring to Mary's unforeseen death.

There was a comfortable silence between them. Jack kicked off his shoes and propped his feet up on the coffee table. When he sat back, Lisa nestled herself next to him. He put his right arm around her, his hand resting on her forearm. He became aware of her hand on his knee. With her head resting on his right shoulder, Jack was enjoying the tropical fragrance of her hair.

"Lisa?" Jack asked softly.

"Yes, Jack?" she responded, tilting her head up slightly.

"I'm curious. What happened to your 6:00 p.m. engagement last night?"

There was a lengthy pause as Lisa collected her thoughts. She was determined to give Jack the absolute truth.

"A long time ago, I met a man by the name of Delano Morrison. He's a journalist and a foreign correspondent with The New York Times. I lived with him for about six months. It was about a year after my divorce. He moved to Berlin on assignment last December. He also moved in with a young French woman who is a photographer of some sort." Jack detected a faint bitterness in Lisa's voice. "He was back in New York this week. That's who I've been meeting for lunch. I wanted to see him tonight one last time, just to make sure."

"Just to make sure?" Jack questioned, sounding a little confused.

"Just to make sure he was completely out of my system. And I realized that he was when I hugged him good-bye last night. Right after I broke off the date before it even began. There is nothing left between us. We both know it, and I couldn't be happier about it because I now have closure and I can finally move on. He's one of the reasons I swore off men as my New Year's resolution."

Jack said nothing. He pulled Lisa closer and held her a little tighter in his arms. Several minutes passed with neither of them speaking.

"I feel safe with you, Jack," she said suddenly, not moving any part of her body. "It's hard to explain. I haven't felt like this in a long, long time. Maybe never."

"That's good," Jack replied softly. "I'm not too sure I can tell you exactly how or what I'm feeling right now, but I can tell you that whatever it is, it's very, very good."

"Good," Lisa whispered. Jack looked out at the million lights of Manhattan, Queens, and Brooklyn. He thought about the young woman sitting next to him. The woman he was holding. Her breathing had become slow and deliberate.

"Either she's deep in thought or she's fallen asleep," Jack thought. He carefully let his face fall down into her hair. "Yeah," Jack whispered aloud, "It's very, very good."

Chapter Fifteen

Sharp pains in Jack's right shoulder and spine made him jerk, causing his head to tilt backwards. He slowly became aware of the numbness spreading down his arm as he tried to flex his fingers. He opened his eyes to faint rays of pink shadows filtering in through the windows of the French doors. Lisa was still next to him, her head on his chest as he lay slouched down on the sofa in almost a total prone position, his feet still draped on the coffee table in front of them. Jack gently took a deep breath and wondered if he would disturb Lisa's sleep if he lifted his right arm and rotated it in an attempt to get some feeling back into his muscles and joints. He was still clearing the cobwebs out of his brain when Lisa stretched out her legs that had been curled up beside her.

"Jack?"

"Yeah?"

"Are you awake?" she asked sleepily.

"Yeah, I just woke up."

"Me too."

Jack returned his gaze to the French doors. He squinted, closed his eyes, and squinted again. "Hey, what's that funny light outside?" Jack asked curiously.

"Well, I don't know what you call it in Minnesota," Lisa said chuckling, "But it happens here in New York every twenty-four hours. We call it dawn!"

"Oh God!" Jack exclaimed as he rotated his right arm in mid-air to get the circulation going again. "We must have fallen asleep!"

"No kidding, Jack!" Lisa said, sitting up and brushing her hair away from her face. "It's almost 7:30."

"Don and Phil," Jack said, slowly pushing himself up on the sofa and rubbing his eyes.

"Who?" Lisa asked, looking at Jack. She was always amazed at how Jack's brain could take sudden, unexpected turns toward a completely new subject.

"The Everly Brothers, Don & Phil. They had a song out in the fifties that applies to our situation here."

"Huh, 'Bye Bye Love?'" Lisa guessed, smiling at Jack with one eye closed.

"Nope. 'Wake Up Little Suzy!'" Jack replied, laughing as he checked Lisa's cell on the sofa arm to verify the time. "And aren't you a little too young to know those songs?"

"My mother had stacks of old forty-five records. She'd often play them for my brother and me when we were very young," Lisa said as she stood and excused herself to the bathroom.

Jack finally found the energy to stand, stretch, and shuffle stiffly to get his blood flowing to all the parts of his body that were still in a light coma. He flipped off the switch to the stereo and hit the cancel button on the remote for the fireplace. As the flames slowly flickered away, Jack looked around the room. The loneliness was there again, an emptiness that Jack could not describe to himself on that bright, early Sunday morning as he stood barefoot in suite 3418. He shook his head and walked up the steps to the kitchenette to make a pot of coffee, pausing briefly as he passed by the French doors. Miles away, the tip of the sun was peeking over the Atlantic.

The freshly brewed coffee spread it's aroma throughout the suite. Jack Kramp stood in front of the French doors, watching the sun bursting behind the eastern skyline. His hands were thrust into their familiar security pouches; the front pockets of his slacks. His sweater was rumpled and his hair disheveled. Jack was totally unaware of Lisa standing in the doorway between the bathroom and the kitchenette, watching him. Crossing her arms in front of her, and remembering how smoothly the large man danced, she recalled how wonderful he smelled and how he had gently held her. Lisa stood motionless, watching the sun's infant rays spread across Jack's solemn face, highlighting the wrinkled lines of wisdom on his forehead and glinting off the few silver strands of hair along his temples.

"There stands a man who is trying to learn how to love again," Lisa thought as she continued to watch him. She took a deep breath. "And, so am I."

"It's beautiful, isn't it?" Lisa said as she quietly joined Jack at the double doors.

"Stunning," Jack said, not tearing his eyes away from the changing sunrise before him. He casually circled his arm around Lisa's waist and placed his palm flat against her stomach.

"I made coffee for you," Jack said, smiling down at Lisa.

"Thank you. It smells delicious."

"Pour yourself a cup. I'm gonna hit the head," Jack said and ambled toward the bathroom door.

"Hit the head," Lisa repeated quietly, laughing to herself as she watched the big man disappear into the bathroom. "He's so... so..." Lisa searched for the words, knowing that she was talking aloud. "Natural!" She nodded confidently to herself as she reached for a cup and poured herself a steaming cup of coffee.

Jack returned to the kitchenette to find Lisa sitting in her desk chair, her feet propped up on the corner of her desk, her legs crossed. She was sipping her coffee and watching the rising sun. Flashing a grin at her, Jack tweaked her toes as he walked by, causing her to jump.

"No wonder you sit like this all the time, Jack. It's really quite comfortable. I'll bet it would be even better if I wasn't wearing a skirt!"

Jack nodded, noticing her shoes still laying near the coffee table. He chuckled as he thought how the two of them had fallen asleep sometime after 3:30 that morning. He stepped back and looked at Lisa again. Clasping his hands behind the back of his head, Jack began to stretch, raising himself up on his toes.

"So, Tiger-Lady, will you get into any code of conduct trouble with Brownstone?" Jack asked with a mischievous grin.

"For what?" Lisa looked at him in surprise, her green eyes wide.

"For sleeping with one of their writers," Jack said, snorting as he laughed at his own joke after placing emphasis on the word sleeping.

Lisa smiled at him. She looked down into her coffee for a moment, then back up at Jack with a serious expression.

"I want you to know something, Jack. I have never dated any of our writers. What happened here last night between us was an accident. Nothing inappropriate. We simply fell asleep. I've never done that before, so please don't tease me about it. You're beginning to make me feel..."

Jack frowned at her. He started to offer an apology, but Lisa continued.

"...cheap."

Jack stopped stretching. He leaned against the wall next to the French doors and gave her a long, hard look. Lisa returned his stare, refusing to blink. Jack began to speak slowly, his husky morning voice seemed to warm up the room, as though it was fueled by the rising sun behind him.

"Lisa, I've met a lot of women in my life. All kinds. And I can think of several hundred words that I would use to describe you. But I'll tell you here and now, cheap isn't one of them. You are, without a doubt, one of the classiest people I know. I want to be able to call you a friend for a long time. A good friend. If I've offended you in any way, I'm sorry. I guess when you've been in the broadcasting business for as long as I have, you become a bit calloused. When things start to hurt too bad or become complex, I tend to make a joke out of them. It's a defense mechanism. It's how I'm wired." Jack watched her as he finished his last sentence. Lisa never took her eyes off him. Jack could feel himself breathing heavier.

"This week started out very confusing for me," he continued. "It took me three days just to get over being afraid of you. I was angry. I became confused. Then, I got drunk. And you threw me another curve, and now..." Jack turned his head and gazed out the window, hoping to find the strength to say how he felt by staring at the top of a distant skyscraper. "And now, I feel like I'm about to make a damn fool out of myself because every time you walk out of a room, I miss you." Jack turned to look back at Lisa. She slowly lowered her head and stared into her half empty coffee cup.

"I know, Jack," she said in a half-whisper. "It's been hard for me, too. I was angry with you because you're too nice and because I'm afraid that I'm starting to care for you. I really like you and, quite frankly, it's scaring the hell out of me. I've been terribly hurt twice before. I'm not emotionally strong enough to go three for three."

Jack walked over and eased himself down on the corner of Lisa's desk next to her feet. He found her green eyes with his. Reaching out his left hand, he found hers and gently pulled it away from her coffee cup. With their fingers entwined,

Jack spoke again. "I'd never hurt you, Lisa. You've apparently had more than your share of pain in life, and so have I. We come from very different worlds. If we go down any road together, let's go slowly. I'm just as scared as you are."

Lisa nodded in agreement. Jack watched her blink back tears. This was not an easy moment for either of them.

"I think I better go home. We both need to get some sleep," Lisa finally said as she stood. "Some real, restful sleep," she added as she grinned and winked at Jack. He nodded and slowly ambled down to the lower living area to retrieve Lisa's shoes and coat.

"Thank you," Lisa whispered as she slid into her shoes and glided into her coat simultaneously.

"So, Jack Kramp, what are your plans today?" Lisa asked, tucking her purse under her arm and placing her hand on the door knob. Standing just a few feet behind her, Jack threw his hands up in the air and shook his head.

"I'm not sure. I thought I'd walk over to noon Mass at St. Patrick's Cathedral. After that, maybe I will grab some lunch and do some sight-seeing. I've only seen downtown at night so far, you know," Jack replied. "I'd like to see more of New York during the day. Maybe, if the weather is decent, I'll go out to Ellis Island and see Miss Liberty."

Lisa nodded and stepped closer to Jack. She smiled as she looked up at him. Reaching up with her right arm, Lisa pulled Jack's face down to hers. She softly brushed his lips with hers. Jack wrapped his arms around her small waist. Their eyes locked for a few tender moments, then Lisa slowly pulled away.

"Be careful, Jack," Lisa said as she turned and slowly backed toward the door. "I'll see you tomorrow morning, OK?"

Jack was still reeling from the warmth of Lisa's body next to him and feeling lightheaded from her short but very sweet and unexpected kiss. In that instant, Jack knew from the pounding of his heart that everything he thought he might have felt for Lisa was absolutely true. Jack was falling in love with her, and he consciously searched his soul for any warning lights. He could not find a single one.

"Jack?" Lisa was still standing near the open door, preparing to leave.

"Sorry," Jack apologized, "I was just thinking. Yeah, tomorrow. 9:00 a.m." He winked and pointed his index finger at her. "Sharp!"

Lisa smiled one last time, winked back, and was gone. Jack stood looking at the door that had just closed. He felt a sudden coolness in the room, but there was a fire in his heart.

Jack shuffled into the bedroom and threw off his sweater, casually tossing it on top of the dresser. He flopped down on the king-size bed, noticing that it was almost 8:00 a.m. Reaching over to the night stand, he dialed down to the front desk and requested a wake up call for 10:30.

"Two and a half hours should help. Then, it's a shower, call the kids, grab some food, attend Mass, and try to find a reason to see Lisa again today," Jack mumbled to himself. As he began to drift into a land of needed slumber, his final conscious thoughts were of Lisa's pleasant kiss.

At exactly 10:30 a.m., Jack's telephone rang. He caught it on the third ring, mumbled a thank you for the wake-up, and rolled over onto his back. He slowly swung his legs over the edge of the bed and brought himself into an upright position. Jack scratched his head as he sorted through the mesh of memories that were clogging his brain. He slowly stood and stumbled to the bathroom where he splashed cold water on his face.

"There," he said to his slightly rumpled mirror image, "I think I'm awake." Jack walked back into the bedroom and resumed his position on the edge of the bed. He picked up his cell phone and dialed his home number. Jim answered.

For the next fifteen minutes, Jack enjoyed conversations with his three children. He realized how much he missed them. He loved his children dearly, and he made a solemn vow that he would make up for all the time he had missed with them over the past two years. And he'd start the minute he returned home. But for now, delightful conversations by telephone was as close as he could come.

It was 10:50 by the time Jack ended the phone conversation and found his way to the shower. He dressed in a dark navy suit complimented by a flashy red tie. He also noted that he was down to his last clean white shirt.

"Thank God my laundry will be coming back this morning," Jack grumbled as he hunted for a matching pair of socks amongst the chaos in the dresser drawer. A few minutes later, Jack grabbed his trench coat, double checked to make sure he had his room key, and headed down to the lobby. During the elevator ride down to the lobby, Jack closed his eyes in an attempt to remember exactly how to get to St. Patrick's Cathedral. Lisa had told him it was just ten to twelve blocks southeast, somewhere near Rockefeller Center. Jack's rumbling stomach reminded him that he'd forgotten to eat breakfast.

Outside in the warm sunshine, Jack headed south to West 57th. He fumbled in the pockets of his trench coat until he found his pair of sunglasses. He was pleased the bright sun had warmed the temperature. Jack also noticed the sidewalks were far less crowded with people than on a normal business day.

At the corner of West 57th, Jack headed east and walked briskly to Fifth Avenue where he turned and walked the seven blocks south to St. Patrick's Cathedral. As Jack climbed the steps to the church, he glanced at his watch. It was only 11:35 a.m. Jack was pleased that he would have a little bit of time to walk around the famous church and see the magnificent neo-Gothic structure up close.

Twenty blocks away on the fifteenth floor of the Arcadia apartments, Lisa finally gave up on the sleep that had eluded her since she came home. Even a long hot shower when she arrived home earlier hadn't helped her relax enough to drift off. She looked at the clock on her antique dresser for what seemed like the hundredth time. Once again, Lisa had a strange feeling that, with each passing minute, she was wasting precious time. She was missing out on something wonderful in her life. There were small pains of panic in her stomach. Her ears were ringing with the same inner voice she had struggled to ignore late yesterday afternoon in the lobby of the West Park Plaza Hotel, right after she had left Jack in suite 3418.

"I can't believe I'm doing this," Lisa murmured as she flung back the sheets and stood in front of her large oval mirror above her dressing table. She sat and began applying her makeup.

Twenty-five minutes later, Lisa was dressed and in a cab weaving her way north on Fifth Avenue. She was faintly aware of her heart beating faster than normal. For Lisa, doing the unexpected and unplanned was very unusual. But her entire world seemed to have become unusual since Jack Kramp wrote his way into her life.

The choir and congregation had started the second verse of "Gather Us In" when Jack briefly noticed the woman in a tasteful blue and white speckled hat and navy blue coat slip into the pew to his far right. The priests and processional were finding their places on the altar. Jack continued to sing quietly, but his thoughts were not on the words printed in the hymnal. His nose told him he knew the scent of the woman sitting a few feet away. He recognized that particular fragrance. Jack turned his head slightly to get a better look. The woman was holding her hymnal up in front of her face. He could only see the top of her sunglasses peeking out from under her broad rimmed blue hat. At least four feet separated them as they stood. Not wanting to stare, Jack turned his attention back to his hymn.

"Well, it's going to be difficult to concentrate," Jack thought. "Of all the women in New York, one wearing Lisa's distinct perfume has to sit near me."

The song ended and the priest made the Sign of the Cross in unison with the masses of people. He asked that everyone take a few minutes and greet the people around them. An old man on Jack's left shook his hand and simply nodded his head. Jack was seated about one-third of the way back on the right side, near the wall. The woman in blue remained standing to his right at the very end of the pew. Jack turned to the woman in blue and offered his right hand. He watched as a blue gloved hand accepted his. As he found her face, she smiled and spoke from behind the huge, dark round sunglasses.

"Good morning, Mr. Kramp," she greeted him with a soft voice.

"Lisa?" Jack said, in total surprise. She pulled her sunglasses down toward the tip of her nose. Her green eyes flashed a warm radiance at him as his gaping mouth slowly closed and spread into a large smile.

"What the. . .?" Jack asked, still trying to recover. Lisa moved closer to him in the pew. "How did you..." he stuttered.

"You're actually pretty easy to find," Lisa whispered as she leaned into him. "Someone as tall as you stands out in a crowd, Jack."

They sat down. The lector began the first reading, but Jack didn't hear a word. He just looked at Lisa. She was staring ahead, wearing a smug smile.

"Why'd you come?" Jack whispered out of the corner of his mouth.

"I thought you may need a tour guide this afternoon," Lisa responded softly, smiling but keeping her eyes on the altar. "Besides, I thought it might be a good time for me to start attending Mass again."

"I'd love it if you showed me around," Jack said, nodding with enthusiasm, then lowering his head quickly as an elderly woman in the pew ahead of them turned around and gave Jack a look that said, "Shut your mouth."

Lisa found Jack's right hand with her left. There was a kindhearted comfortableness that embodied them as they sat in that massive, holy structure. They didn't speak again during the Mass. There was no need for words. Lisa and Jack became acutely aware of the healing process that had begun through a silent, heart-to-heart feeling of compassion.

Lisa Lisignoli and Jack Kramp spent the rest of the sunny New York Sunday afternoon together. The temperature climbed to over fifty degrees, which was very unusual for early November. They walked, talked, and laughed often. They ate lunch at a small French bistro and visited historic Broadway. Jack was impressed with the old charm of the Empire State Building and Lisa giggled at his impression of King Kong. By 3:30, they were on their way to Ellis Island and the Statue of Liberty. After, they strolled the plazas near Wall Street and learned the history in and around the new One World Trade Center. Later in the evening, they buttoned up their coats and wandered along the docks of the Hudson River. Jack was thoroughly enjoying the sights, sounds, and smells of New York City. He appreciated it's charm and diversity. Lisa couldn't remember the last time she felt so valued; cherished for who she was and what she knew. Lisa treasured the special moments as she watched the world she had known for over thirty-eight years unfold anew through the eyes, mind, and mouth of Jack Kramp. It was a day of new beginnings and fresh memories in a fascinating, old city.

"Are you hungry?" Lisa asked as they caught a cab in front of the American Stock Exchange.

"Starving," Jack replied, peeking at his cell. "No wonder, it's dark already. It's almost seven. I can't believe where the time went."

Lisa nodded. She felt exhausted, but extremely happy. She turned and looked up at Jack's face in the dim light of the cab.

"How about Italian?" she asked. "I know this great place in Little Italy where you can get delicious, authentic Italian and the wines are superb."

"You haven't steered me wrong yet, Lisa, lead on!" Jack said as he made a sweeping motion with his hand in front of him. Lisa gave the driver the address of the Italian restaurant. They arrived in less than ten minutes and were seated immediately.

Lisa was sipping her second glass of wine when she cocked her head and gave Jack a long, hard look through squinted eyes.

"How do you do it, Jack?" she asked quietly.

"Do what?" Jack responded, stuffing another large, savory meatball in his mouth.

"How do you take everything in stride? Nothing really seems to rattle you. When a surprise does come along, you recover very quickly. You adjust to changing situations quite easily and meet any challenge head-on. And I'm wondering, how you do it?" Lisa spoke very slowly, never taking her green eyes away from Jack's blue dancing pools. Jack returned her gaze, took a sip of his wine, then folded his hands under his chin with both elbows on the edge of the table before he began to speak.

"I'm not sure I have a real clear-cut answer for you, Lisa," he began. "I guess I just believe that the ultimate tragedy in any life here on earth is death. Anything beyond that, any adversity, the unexpected, any problem preceding death, is merely an inconvenience." Jack amazed himself at the off-the-cuff forthrightness of his answer. He had never verbalized these particular thoughts before, but now he suspected they were always deep within, waiting for the right time.

"An inconvenience," Lisa repeated, slowly nodding, yet grasping for a deeper understanding. Jack barely heard her, but he nodded.

"What's the worst that can happen?" Jack asked. "Somebody dies." Answering his own question, he proceeded, "If you back up from that point, everything else that's bad or unforeseen is just an inconvenience, a stumbling block that teaches you to fully appreciate everything and everyone around you on your way toward death."

Lisa gave Jack a warm smile. She continued to be shocked at the emotional depth of this new big stranger in her life. "I think someone once said that we shouldn't fear death as much as living an unfulfilled life," Lisa said, wishing to continue this interesting topic with Jack. "Do you think most people are afraid of death, Jack?"

"Yeah," Jack said, picking up his wine glass again. "I'm sure there are millions out there who are afraid of dying. And maybe just as many who wish they were dead because they haven't figured out how to live a productive and fulfilling life. I agree with Woody Allen. "It's not that I'm afraid to die, it's just that I don't want to be there when it happens." Jack chuckled loudly and sipped his wine.

"You're wise beyond your years, Jack Kramp," Lisa said, still smiling approvingly at his answers.

"Hardly," Jack said with a short laugh. Then his face turned serious again. "To me, wisdom is an entirely separate trait. After all those years of college, research papers, visits to dozens of libraries, reading hundreds of books, browsing internet websites, and decades of my own ups and downs, I've come up with a philosophy of my own: acquired information does not necessarily translate into knowledge, nor does the accumulation of vast knowledge guarantee wisdom. Wisdom is only measured by your own yardstick of right and wrong, good and evil, from birth to death. What happens to you is far less important than what happens within you."

"Wow!" Lisa exclaimed. "Where did you come up with all of that?"

"Listening to idiots with Ph.D.'s!" Jack chuckled. "Let's change the subject. All this philosophical talk of death and wisdom, or lack thereof, is ruining my appetite!"

"Well, I happen to think you're an intellectual philosopher," replied Lisa. "And humble, too!"

"Humility is the only virtue a person can never be proud of," Jack said with a loud laugh.

Lisa joined in on his hearty laughter, but she continued to be mystified and intrigued by the wonderful way his mind worked.

"He's truly going to be a great writer someday," Lisa thought to herself. "But in order for him to realize his own vast, hidden talents, I'll have to try guiding him in a direction other than the western genre."

"So, what's the storyline of your next book?" Lisa asked, changing the subject at Jack's request.

The time flew quickly for Jack and Lisa as their conversations drifted from one topic to another. They both declined on dessert and noticed the restaurant was nearly empty. Lisa insisted on picking up the check for dinner while Jack stepped outside to hail a cab. It was after 8:35 p.m. when Jack said good-bye to Lisa on the front steps of her apartment. They had decided to call it a night since both of them were extremely tired from Saturday's carriage ride, the long night of dinner, dancing and discussions afterward and today's lengthy tour of New York City.

Lisa and Jack clung tightly together in each other's arms for a full minute before whispering good-bye. It was a kind, wonderful minute. Both Lisa and Jack knew the other was feeling something special as a result of them being there, together, at that precise moment. Jack bent down and gently kissed Lisa's full lips, holding his big hands on her small back. Her knees went weak, her heart did wild backflips, and her breathing became non-existent. Jack could feel his own breathing becoming irregular. Lisa turned and felt herself float through the door of her building. She paused to look back one last time. Smiling, she blew Jack a kiss with her right hand. He watched as she turned the corner and headed for the elevator.

Jack's racing pulse finally returned to a normal rhythm during the cab ride back to his hotel. It was a cab ride he would never remember because only a small part of him was consciously there. For the most part, Jack Kramp was already living years away, lost in a fantasy fog of beautiful dark-haired children with bright green, loving eyes.

Chapter Sixteen

Bannigan's was extremely crowded for 9:45 p.m. on a Sunday evening. Jack suspected most of the patrons had checked in that afternoon. They all looked the part of traveling business people; professionals who wanted a good drink and friendly conversation prior to going up to a strange room to sleep before tomorrow's boardroom battles and face-to-face sales calls.

With every bar stool occupied, Jack finally found an empty high-backed booth near the rear of the bar. It was one booth away from the entrance to the storage room. He ordered his usual scotch and water and slipped out of his trench coat. The bar crowd seemed to be louder than normal. The boisterous din was in direct contrast to his quiet day with Lisa.

Jack suddenly focused his attention on the conversation he overheard coming from the booth directly behind him.

"Listen, her old man is gonna pay. She's his only daughter," mouthed a nasal voice with a Brooklyn accent.

"Yeah, but from what I hear, if assholes could fly, he'd be a jet." The second voice was raspy, almost a hoarse whisper. Jack thought he detected a slight southern accent.

Becoming more intrigued with the conversation of the two men, Jack heard a third voice in the same booth. A deep, rich booming voice as large as the Grand Canyon.

"OK, so how we gonna do this?" the deep voice asked. Jack sat straight up, his back pressed firmly against the inside of the booth next to the wall. He was straining to hear the conversation over the rise and fall of the other loud conversations around him.

"We got it all figured out," replied the Brooklyn nasal cavity. "This woman has very definite routines. She comes here every morning at exactly 9:00 AM and goes to the 34th floor. She did it every day last week."

Upon hearing this, Jack froze, his hand gripping the low-ball glass in front of him. "Is this a coincidence? Were they talking about Lisa? Couldn't be!" Jack's mind became sharper as he thought about the three strangers in the next booth.

"See, she's working with some writer in suite 3418. The room is on the top floor at the end of the hall. I saw the guy once. Tall fella, but nothin' to worry about. He won't even know what happened," Brooklyn said confidently.

Jack's heart began to pound loudly. They were definitely talking about Lisa. And him!

"When she shows up at 9:00, POW! We'll be waiting for her. You guys nab her before she gets to the door of the suite. I'll give you a plastic bag with cotton balls soaked in chloroform. She'll go out like a light and down like a sack of potatoes. You'll be dressed in a maintenance man's uniform. You'll be in a laundry guy's uniform. Just dump her into the big, dirty laundry cart that I'll have waiting in the little hallway. I'll make sure you have a few old sheets to cover her with just in case anyone gets curious. Wheel her around the corner and through the double doors. Take the freight elevator to the first floor delivery entrance. I'll be waiting in a white delivery van. It'll have a sign on it that reads 'Mabel's Dry Cleaning.' You'll have three to four minutes, max."

Jack sat motionless in the tall booth, feeling ill. His sixth sense went into overdrive. He desperately wanted to get a good look at these men, although he already suspected the identity of two of them; Mr. Fat Face, the guy in the brown suit, and Mr. Slick, his partner whom Jack had seen in the lobby yesterday morning. Turning in the booth slightly, Jack realized he could see the reflection of the three men behind him. By watching the side mirror on the end of the back wall of the bar directly across from him, he had a pretty good view. His suspicions were confirmed. Mr. Fat Face, the apparent ringleader, sat on one side of the booth by himself. Fat Face had the nasal voice with the thick Brooklyn accent and was giving the orders.

Jack held his left hand cupped up to his forehead and studied the men via the mirror. Fat Face had about three sets of double chins that hung over an equally thick neck. A large, unlit cigar hung limply out of the corner of his mouth, bobbing up and down whenever he spoke. Slick was well dressed in a three piece gray suit with a black tie. Sporting a thin mustache, he had long, dark side burns and wore lots of gold. When he spoke, it was a raspy whisper with a slight southern drawl. Jack was almost certain this was the same man he had seen on CNN last night, the one who escaped from a Georgia prison a couple of months ago.

The third man was a total stranger to Jack. He was extraordinarily large and was sitting on the inside of the booth next to Slick. His huge frame took up so much space that Slick had to sprawl his feet out into the aisle. Brute, as Jack nicknamed him, had all the makings of a bodybuilder or perhaps a professional wrestler. He wore a green sleeveless vest over a black turtleneck, his wrists and hands were covered with tattoos. There was a large scar across his forehead and he had thinning blonde hair. Jack continued to squint cautiously in the mirror, cursing himself for not getting the recommended prescription eyeglasses last summer. The conversation in the booth progressed.

"How do we know the hallway is going to be empty?" Brute asked. "And what do we do if other people are around?"

"It's not very likely. Housekeeping doesn't start making their rounds until 9:30 or so. Like I said, the suite she goes to is at the far end of the hall. You'll both be in uniforms. If anyone gets nosey, just tell them she fainted and you're going to take her down stairs to an ambulance the fastest way. The freight elevator!" Fat Face was obviously pleased with himself. "Nobody will suspect a thing!"

"Where are we taking her?" Slick asked quietly. Jack pressed his ear against the wooden back corner of the booth, straining to hear.

"An old warehouse over in Jersey. We give the old fart three days to come up with the ten mill, if he doesn't, they find her body floatin' down the Hudson." Fat Face said with an evil laugh.

"And you're sure he's gonna pay?" Slick drawled again with a note of uncertainty.

"He'll pay," replied the confident Fat Face. "I spent nine years working for that son-of-bitch at T and W, and he's gonna pay."

"What day is this goin' down?" Brute boomed loudly.

"Lower your damn voice!" Fat Face screeched softly through his nose. "You want the whole frickin' place to hear?" Fat Face leaned over the table, looking back and forth between Brute and Slick. "Tuesday," he said in a nasal whisper. "Tuesday morning. I've got some details to take care of yet tomorrow. We'll meet in the parking garage downstairs, level three, at 8:15 sharp, Tuesday morning. I'll have an empty tool box for you to carry." Jack watched Fat Face point at Slick. "I'll have your uniforms, too. You can change in the back of the van before going up."

"What about a piece?" Slick asked slowly, but deliberately.

"Yeah, you'll each need one, just in case. I'll have a couple of guns for you in the van with the uniforms. And if something goes wrong, just remember, kill the broad. No matter what happens, she dies. Immediately. Understand?" Fat Face was grinning, turning his head back and forth as he studied the other two men's faces.

"What about the ransom note?" Slick asked.

"Me and DM got it handled. Just call me tomorrow around 4:00 at Cal's. I'll let you know then if everything is set for Tuesday morning. Anymore questions?"

"When do we split the ten million, Tork?" Brute asked, trying to keep his voice low, lest he be reprimanded again by Fat Face.

"As soon as her rich daddy pays. Just as soon as he makes the drop, we make the split. And then we all get out of town as fast as we can." Fat Face grinned again. "I can't wait 'till Franky sees the damn note. He's gonna shit little green textbooks."

Jack suddenly became aware that he was sweating profusely. He picked up his scotch and took a long swallow. Setting his drink down, Jack slumped in the booth, his right ear pressed hard against the back of the booth near the wall. With his left hand cupped over his forehead, he became aware of his heart pounding rapidly in his chest.

"And you two better not screw this up like you did a few years ago with that little Shepard prick," Fat Face said with a sneer.

"Buddy Shepard? Hey, me and Jag thought he'd taken the bait and the money. How the hell were we supposed to know he'd turn out to be a chicken at the last minute and write it all out for the cops?" replied Brute.

"Well it's a damn good thing you got to him first or we'd all be doin' hard time," said Fat Face, then added, "By the way, what'd you ever do with the gun?"

"Still in the trunk of my old Buick," answered Mr. Slick. "Hasn't run for years. It's parked and covered in my Aunt Rosie's barn up near Lake Pleasant. Don't worry, nobody will ever find it."

Fat Face stared at both of them intently and finally said, "You better hope not. Or I'll take the both of you out myself."

"What does this broad look like again?" Brute asked with a devilish grin, wanting to change the subject. Jack shuddered as he watched the big man rub his hands together.

"Oh, she's extremely beautiful!" replied Fat Face. "She's about five-five, five-six, slender, good body, long dark hair. You'll know her when you see her. Why? You planning something special for her?"

"Never know, Tork," Brute said, his grin widening even more. "Three days in a big empty warehouse can get pretty damn lonely."

Fat Face raised both his hands in the air and exhaled deeply in exasperation. He wore a crooked grin, showing his dirty yellow teeth between the layers of fat around his cheeks.

"You make sure you get her to the damn warehouse. After that, just keep her alive 'till we get the cash. Then, you do whatever you want with her," Fat Face chuckled. "In the meantime, DM is going to watch her. If she does anything out of the ordinary, we might have to put it off until another time."

"What about the writer-guy in suite 3418?" Slick drawled thoughtfully. "Won't he get suspicious when she doesn't show up?"

"We have that figured out, too," Fat Face replied, starting to wheeze. "I've got Shirley calling him about ten to nine. She's going to pretend she's a secretary with Brownstone and calling to tell him his editor is running late and won't be there until noon. That'll give us plenty of time to disappear."

"Timing is everything in something like this, Tork," Slick persisted in his slow southern accent. "What if that big guy from the suite shows up or is in the hall at the same time as the broad. What do you want us to do with him?"

"If he gets in the way, take him out or take him with you, whatever you think you gotta do," sneered Fat Face. "I really don't give a shit about him, just as long as you get Franky's kid."

Jack stiffened, his heart was thumping rapidly in his chest. He leaned forward with his elbows on the table, head in his hands.

"This is real," Jack thought. "This is really happening. It's not my imagination. It's not the booze. These are real guys with real plans to kidnap Lisa, hold her for ransom, and probably kill her. And if I get in the way, I'll be dead, too."

Jack's mind raced. He needed to tell someone about this. He had to get to the authorities immediately. He thought of Avery Schneider and Lt. Corey Burgess. Somehow, he had to find them, and quickly.

"I gotta go," Brute said. "I gotta get back to the gym."

"Yeah, I better get movin', too," said Slick. "I'll call you tomorrow at four."

The three men emerged from the booth slowly. Brute and Fat Face were struggling to stand. Slick stepped a few feet back from the booth, rubbed his thin mustache with his thumb and forefinger and glanced in Jack's direction. Sensing the three men were going to pass by him, Jack lay his head down on his arm and closed his eyes. He wanted the appearance of being totally drunk and passed out to avoid any suspicion that he had been listening to their conversation.

Once the three men left the bar, Jack sat up straight. His heart was still pounding, although there was a slow calm spreading over him as he collected his thoughts and started to develop a plan.

Connie, his server, stopped to ask him if he'd like another scotch and water. Jack immediately declined. Instead, he found a pen in the pocket of his trench coat, opened a cocktail napkin, and started feverishly making notes. He wanted to recap every point of the conversation. Closing his eyes, he let his mind replay the meeting between the three men in the booth behind him, attempting to remember it word for word.

Jack looked at the time on his cell and noticed it was already 10:15 p.m. He stood, left a tip on the table, threw his trench coat over his arm, and walked out of the bar. Jack crossed the lobby and to the front desk.

"Good evening." A young blonde woman behind the desk greeted Jack with a big smile as he approached. "Can I help you?"

"Yes, you can," Jack said, with a faint return smile. "I need to see Avery Schneider, your security guard."

The blonde's smile faded and was replaced by a frown that brought her thin eyebrows together. "I think he went up to the fifth floor a few minutes ago. Is there a problem?" she asked as she pulled a red cell phone from under the counter.

"I think there may be one," Jack said grimly.

"I'll call him," she said without hesitation. "Are you a guest with us?"

"Yeah, tell him I'm Jack Kramp from suite 3418. I need to talk with him right away."

"Hello, Avery?" the blonde said, turning to look at Jack. "This is Marti at the front desk. I have a Mr. Jack Kramp down here. He's a guest in 3418 and he'd like to see you right away." There was a pause as Marti listened to Avery on the other end. "OK, I'll tell him." Marti set the cell down and looked at Jack. "Avery's on his way down. He said he'll meet you in the lobby in two minutes."

Jack thanked her and walked quickly toward the massive lobby where he spotted Avery getting off the elevator, heading toward him. As soon as Avery saw Jack looking at him, he jerked his head and nodded to his right. Jack followed him through a door across from the elevators marked 'Employees Only' and down a short, brightly lit fluorescent hall. At the end, Avery walked through another door labeled 'Hotel Manager.' Jack was just a few steps behind him. They stepped inside a small, plush waiting area. A large glass office immediately ahead of them was dark and the door was closed. An empty receptionist desk was on their left. To the right, Jack noticed a small, frosted glass-walled conference room with a round table and five chairs. Avery flipped on the light and motioned Jack inside. Avery shut the door and sat down, Jack followed.

"I take it you saw the short fat man tonight," Avery began, surprising Jack. It was the first time he had spoken.

"Yeah, and two of his friends," Jack nodded.

"Me, too," Avery said, leaning back in the chair and crossing his legs. "I saw the three of them going into the bar about an hour ago as I was waiting for an elevator. I have a strong feeling there's something going down."

"There is," Jack said flatly, his throat suddenly feeling dry.

"Tell me what you know," Avery stated as he pulled a small notebook and an ink pen from his shirt pocket.

Taking a deep breath, Jack pulled the folded cocktail napkin out of the pocket of his trench coat and placed it on the table in front of him. He relayed the entire story from beginning to end. He told Avery all about the conversation he'd just overheard between the three men in the booth behind him in Bannigan's, including their brief discussion concerning Buddy Shepard and the location of the gun used to kill him.

"And you're sure this guy, Slick, as you call him, is the same man you saw on CNN last night?" Avery asked, raising his eyebrows.

"Almost positive," Jack replied.

"And the fat guy said he worked nine years for..." Avery scanned his notes, "... T and W?"

"It's got to be Tanner and Whitehall, a local New York publishing company. Lisa's father, Frank Lisignoli, is the CEO. Remember, Fat Face kept referring to a 'Franky.' It's gotta be the same guy, Lisa's dad. It all fits. That's why Fat Face was up on the 34th floor near my suite the other morning. He was casing the place."

Avery nodded in agreement. He stuck the pen behind his ear and rubbed his jaw with this right hand. He was deep in thought. Jack watched him intently, trying to think of any detail he might have missed. Avery flipped through his notebook again.

"Tuesday morning," he said slowly. "Tork, Jag, Cal's, Shirley, Frank Lisignoli, somebody named DM, ten million, fake uniforms, Mabel's Dry Cleaning van, a warehouse in Jersey plus armed and dangerous. Not much to go on, but certainly enough puzzle pieces to get started. And maybe a break through in the Buddy Shepard case, too. A Buick in a barn at Aunt Rosie's near Lake Pleasant. Wow."

Avery stood and returned the notebook to his pocket. He studied Jack's face for a moment.

"Wait here. I'll be right back," he finally said.

"What do we do now?" Jack asked, hearing the fear and panic building in his own voice.

"I'm working on it. Just sit tight. I'm going to call a friend from my old precinct. He's a detective with the NYPD."

"Lt. Corey Burgess?" Jack automatically asked the question without thinking.

Avery stopped in mid-stride at the doorway and spun around to face Jack with his eyebrows raised, eyes wide in surprise.

"How did you know?" he asked stiffly.

"Lisa and I met him and his wife, Rita, last night down in Chinatown. We happened to be having dinner in the same restaurant."

Avery relaxed his shoulders, nodded, and gave Jack a small smile.

"Sit tight," he said again before disappearing into the next room. Through the small crack in the open door, Jack could see him leaning on the edge of the reception desk while talking on the phone. Jack folded his hands in his lap and shut his eyes.

"Things aren't looking good here, Jack," he muttered to himself. "We have got to warn Lisa."

Fifteen minutes later, Avery returned. He sat down across from Jack and casually put his hands on the edge of the table.

"Here's what we are going to do for now. They're putting two undercover officers on duty to watch Lisa Lisignoli. Burgess is getting an emergency court order to place phone taps on her phone and her father's phones at his home, cell, and office. Also one for your hotel suite. It's a little after 10:00, Jack. Burgess is coming over here to talk with us. It'll be at least an hour or so before he can get here. I suggest you go back up to your room and wait. I have to call my wife and tell her that I'm going to be late. I'll give you a ring when he gets here. Maybe we'll just come up and meet with you in your suite, if that's OK?"

"That's fine," Jack replied quietly. He started to feel better now that there was some immediate reaction to his story. He stood and followed Avery out of the office, down the hall, and back out into the lobby. Jack crossed over to the elevators and pressed the UP button.

"Life was so simple this afternoon," Jack thought as he waited. His next thought sent a river of fear rushing through his veins. "What if I would have just gone up to bed and not stopped in for a drink? I would have never known."

The time passed at a glacial speed for Jack as he paced the floor in suite 3418 during the late Sunday evening hours. At 11:50 the telephone rang. Jack ran across the suite to get it, expecting it to be Avery. It wasn't.

"Hi!" Lisa's warm voice greeted him. "Are you in bed already?"

"Nope," Jack said, surprised at how calm he sounded.

"Where have you been?" Lisa inquired. "I tried calling earlier but you weren't in your suite."

"Oh," Jack forced a laughed, "I stopped into Bannigan's downstairs for a nightcap. I ran into Avery Schneider. We got to talking and I lost track of time. Sorry."

"No problem, Jack. I just became a little concerned. I wanted to call and thank you for a very wonderful afternoon. I really enjoy being with you."

"I had fun, too, Lisa." Jack nervously looked at the time on his cell. "How did you like the Mass at St. Patrick's?" There was a long pause. He could hear Lisa slowly take a deep breath.

"It was nice, Jack. I think I'll go again sometime soon."

"Good." Jack didn't want to seem rude in anyway, but he was afraid that Lt. Burgess and Avery would be calling or knocking on his door at any minute, and he wondered how he would explain the late night intrusion to Lisa.

"Well," Lisa yawned, "I'm in bed and feeling very sleepy. I think I'll say good night."

"Yeah, I'm pretty exhausted, too. I'm heading for bed soon as well," Jack said, somewhat relieved that the conversation was coming to an end.

"Good night, Jack. See you tomorrow morning at 9:00 AM."

Jack winced. He thought of the plot to kidnap Lisa. And she was making it easy for them because she was always so damn punctual.

"Good night, Lisa," Jack said softly. "Thanks for calling. Sleep well. I'll see you tomorrow."

Jack hung up the telephone. He ambled down into the living area and eased himself into the love seat. His cell told him it was 12:05 a.m. He reached over and picked up the fireplace remote from the coffee table. He soon became engrossed in deep thought about Fat Face, Slick, Brute and all those other names he had overheard during their conversation. He also felt confident that Avery and Lt. Burgess would figure out a way to keep everyone safe. He sensed help was on the way.

The silence in suite 3418 was broken by the ringing of the room telephone. Jack jumped to get it. Once again, he glanced at his cell phone. It was 12:18 a.m.

"Jack, it's Avery. We're on our way up, if it's not too late for you."

"Not at all, come on up," Jack replied, rubbing his eyes. He couldn't remember if he had fallen asleep or had just been in such deep thought that he wasn't totally conscious.

Moments later, Jack opened the door. Avery, Lt. Burgess, and another gentleman walked in. Jack shook hands with Corey Burgess and turned his attention to the stranger. Corey made the introductions.

"This is my partner, officer McKay. Bill, meet Jack Kramp." Jack shook the powerful hand of Bill McKay. He was a short, stocky man with closely cropped red hair and green eyes. There was little doubt in Jack's mind that he was one hundred percent Irish. Jack closed the door and invited the three of them to sit down in the lower living room.

"I can order up some soft drinks from room service or make some coffee if you'd like," Jack offered as they each took a seat. They declined.

"OK, Jack," Avery said, "I want you to tell Lt. Burgess and officer McKay everything you told me downstairs a little while ago."

Jack nodded and began to repeat the entire conversation. He occasionally referred to his notes on the cocktail napkin. Burgess and McKay scratched hastily on their notepads while Jack spoke. Suddenly, Avery's cell phone rang. Everyone turned and listened as Avery responded to the call.

"Yes, 3418. Come on up. You need to hear this." Avery hung up and turned to look at Burgess. "I think we need to have Terry Cole in on this, too. He's on duty tonight." Burgess nodded in agreement but said nothing. Avery turned and looked at Jack.

"Terry Cole is another security guard here at the hotel. He has the shift right after mine tonight, but he normally works days. There are seven of us from Midwest working here. We'll be cooperating with the NYPD on this case."

Jack nodded his understanding and continued his story. At one point, Corey Burgess went into the kitchenette and began talking on his cell to someone in his precinct.

"Get me everything you can on someone named Tork who used to work at Tanner and Whitehall. It's a book publishing firm. Books. It could be a nickname or a shortened version for a first or last name. He apparently worked there for approximately nine years, but we don't know how long ago. Also, do a run on any place, bar, tavern, restaurant, barbershop, or whatever, called Cal's. Oh, and see what you can get on a DM. That's right. D as in dog. M as in Mary. It could be someone's initials. And have dispatch pull a current bulletin on Jagger Tormain. Yeah, the guy who escaped from that Georgia prison a few months ago. We believe he's in the vicinity. I'll need everything you've got first thing tomorrow morning. I'm writing my initial report tonight. Yeah, possible kidnapping and extortion plot. Not yet. We just learned of the planned attempt. What about the taps? Good. Thanks, Mulvaney. I'll talk to you tomorrow morning if not yet tonight."

Burgess returned to his place on the sofa. Jack finished repeating the rest of the conversation, especially concerning the details he'd heard about the Buddy Shepard murder.

"Do you know Frank Lisignoli?" Bill McKay asked Jack.

"Never met him. I didn't even know who he was until yesterday when Lisa mentioned him," Jack replied.

Terry Cole joined them as they discussed how they might proceed. At one point, Corey Burgess turned to Jack with a very serious look and spoke softly.

"I have to warn you, Jack, all of this better be on the up and up. You may have to take a polygraph."

"You think I'm lying about all this shit?" Jack asked incredulously.

"No, I don't. Not in the least," Burgess replied firmly. "But if the things you've told us don't start checking out, you could be in serious trouble."

"And when you find out that all of it's true?" Jack queried.

"Then you and Lisa are in serious danger." Jack nodded, understanding exactly what Lt. Corey Burgess was telling him.

They all stood. Burgess looked at the group. He pulled back his sport coat and placed his hands on his hips.

"I'm going to brief Captain Marinaro on this situation first thing tomorrow morning. I think we'll have a better chance of putting these gentlemen away if we can apprehend them in the act. We'll probably use an undercover policewoman for a Lisa look-a-like on Tuesday morning. As far as the other details, we'll have to work them out tomorrow. Our officers will keep Lisa under tight surveillance tonight and they'll be around here tomorrow, just in case this Tork fellow and his boys have a sudden change in plans and move the abduction up a day." Burgess turned and addressed Jack. "We'll want to meet with you tomorrow night. I'm going to pay a visit to Frank Lisignoli tomorrow morning and apprise him of the situation."

"What about Lisa? Shouldn't she know?" Jack asked.

"For now, we won't tell her," replied Burgess. "No need to panic her until we have a plan in place. I think we may need your help, though, Jack. Avery will let you know where and when we'll meet tomorrow night. Do NOT tip off Lisa. For the next day or so, she needs to continue her normal routine. If she doesn't, she may tip off Tork that something is up. We want to nail these guys, OK?"

"OK," Jack said, his stomach suddenly doing flips again.

The four men said their good-byes and left the suite. Jack flipped off the fireplace, turned out the lights, and walked into the bedroom. He immediately noticed his clean laundry had been delivered. His socks and underwear were neatly folded, wrapped in plastic, and stacked on top of the dresser. His starched and pressed shirts hung in the closet in plastic bags. The clock on the nightstand read 1:15 AM. Jack removed his suit, tossed his shirt, socks, and underwear in a new laundry bag, and headed for the shower. Even though he was exhausted, Jack's mind was still wide awake. Jack was going over the events of the evening for the fifteenth time in his head. A plan was forming. Although Jack knew the responsibility of this case was now in the hands of the New York Police Department, he had an idea of how to spoil the kidnapping plot and still catch Fat Face, Slick, Brute, and the rest of them. He just had to convince Lt. Burgess and the rest of the officers to listen to his plan. Jack crawled into bed and stared at the ceiling. He continued to turn his plan over in his head, trying to think of every small detail. It had to work and it had to work perfectly or people could die.

Chapter Seventeen

Jack was up early, showered, and dressed by 6:30 on Monday morning. He tried to ignore the butterflies in his stomach as he rode the elevator downstairs for breakfast in the Garden Cafe. The small restaurant was crowded at that early hour and Jack ended up waiting for a table. Finally seated in a small booth near the kitchen, Jack ordered waffles, sausage links, and a large orange juice. While he waited for his food, he glanced at the faces seated at the tables around him. There were tired faces with red eyes, but they were all total strangers. Not one of them looked familiar to Jack. He was almost relieved. He ate hurriedly and returned to his suite. He tried concentrating on the news in USA TODAY, but his mind kept drifting back to the kidnapping plot.

Anita knocked on his door earlier than usual and came in to clean his room. She was her usual cheerful self. Jack walked around her large supply cart, carefully looking it over.

"You need something extra from in there, Mr. Jack?" Anita asked as she restocked the kitchenette.

"Nope," Jack replied. "I was just looking. What's under here?" he asked, lifting a heavy brown drape on the one side of the cart.

"Oh, there is just the linens we put in the rooms. Sheets, pillowcases, towels, you know, yes?" Anita replied. Jack knelt down and stuck his head under the cloth. He noticed there were four shelves and they were adjustable.

"That also means they're removable," Jack mumbled to himself as he stood up. He estimated the space under the cart to be about two and a half feet wide, four feet high, and five feet long. The side opposite the drape was made of a light stainless steel panel.

Jack watched Anita disappear into the master bedroom with her arms full of fresh linens. He lifted the drape on her supply cart again for a final peek. Satisfied, Jack made a mental note and crossed over to the French doors. He opened the large heavy drapes and noticed it was mostly cloudy.

"Typical Monday," Jack muttered as he unlocked one of the doors and stepped onto the terrace. An icy chill from an eastern wind drove him back inside instantly. After closing the door and locking it, he walked down into the living area, flipped on the radio and found his favorite country station just in time to hear the morning air personality tell everyone it was 8:15. Anita reappeared from the bedroom, flashed him a smile, and pulled her vacuum cleaner off the end of her cart. She dragged it after her, heading back into the bedroom. The room phone rang and Jack bounded up the three steps to answer it.

"Hello?"

"Good morning, Jack! It's Marsha!"

"Well, good morning," Jack replied, grateful to hear a friendly voice. "What's up?"

"Oh, I was just calling to remind you and Lisa that we really need those cover designs back today. And be sure to send your suggested improvements along with your top pick."

"We have them narrowed down to two," Jack said, happy to be thinking about something else other than Fat Face. "Lisa said we'll finish up the selection process this morning."

"Good. When you're finished, have Lisa call us. Jo or someone will come over to pick them up. Or perhaps you and Lisa want to deliver them? You've never visited our offices, have you, Jack?"

"No, I haven't. But I'd sure like to stop in sometime before I leave."

"We'll have to arrange it. We aren't far from the hotel. Our offices are just down on Avenue of the Americas, near 34th street, only a block from the Empire State Building."

"Oh, yeah," Jack said. "Lisa pointed out your office building to me yesterday."

"Yesterday?" Marsha asked, sounding a little confused.

"Yeah, she, uh... she sort of gave me a tour of Manhattan yesterday afternoon. We went to the observation deck of the Empire State Building."

"You did?" Jack could tell that Marsha was wearing a big, knowing smile on the other end of the phone. She suspected there was more going on in suite 3418 than just rewrites and edits.

"By the way, Marsha," Jack cut in, wanting to change the subject. "I want to sincerely thank you for the dinner party the other night. I really enjoyed myself."

"Oh, wasn't it marvelous!" she exclaimed. "We think it's so exciting to have your very first book come out in hardcover. Peter thinks a lot of you, Jack. This morning he told me he thought you were... let me see, how did he say that? Oh, yes. He said you were a 'rare commodity.'"

"Great," Jack said solemnly, "I'm right up there with corn, pork bellies, and soybeans."

"Oh, Jack," Marsha giggled, "You know what he meant. He's counting on you to turn out a number of best sellers for Brownstone over the next few years. You may even have to quit your day job!"

"Well, let's just see how we do with this one first," Jack replied with a nervous laugh.

"It'll be sensational," Marsha said confidently, "I have a very good feeling about *Loose Cannons*. It's a winner!"

"I hope so," Jack said. Suddenly, he thought of something. "Listen, Marsha, does the name Tork or the initials DM mean anything to you?"

There was a long pause on the other end of the line as Marsha turned the names over in her mind.

"No, I'm sorry Jack, I don't believe I've ever heard either of them. Why?"

"No reason. I just heard a story about them last night in Bannigan's here at the hotel. I thought they might have been some colorful local characters or something."

"Sorry, Jack, I'm drawing a blank."

"No problem," Jack replied. "Listen, as soon as Lisa arrives, we'll get right on those covers and have them over to you before noon, OK?"

"Sounds wonderful, Jack! Take care and we'll see you soon! Good-bye!" Jack said good-bye and hung up the telephone. He was always amazed at Marsha's high level of energy and enthusiasm. He could tell she was not only very dedicated to her job, but she also thoroughly enjoyed it.

Jack crossed over to his desk and flipped open his briefcase. He looked for the next chapter in preparation for today's edits. Anita emerged from the bedroom, returned her vacuum cleaner to her cart, said a friendly good-bye to Jack, and left his suite. The telephone rang again. Jack jumped to get it.

"Hello?"

"Jack Kramp?"

"Speaking."

"Good morning, Burgess here. Is Lisa there yet?"

"No. Not yet. She always shows up at exactly 9:00."

"Good. Then I have a few minutes to bring you up to date. Do you have time?"

"Shoot," Jack said, cringing at his careless comeback.

"Never say shoot to a law enforcement officer," Corey chuckled, "Some of us get trigger happy."

"Sorry," Jack mumbled. "What'd you find out?"

"OK, here it is," Corey said, taking a deep breath. "We believe Tork is Mick Thorkmon. He worked for Tanner and Whitehall for a little over nine years in their accounting department. He fits your physical description of him. He was terminated about four years ago. Frank Lisignoli caught him with his fingers in the cash drawer."

"Embezzlement?"

"You got it. He was charged, but skipped bail before the trial. We've been looking for him for the past three and a half years."

"What about Tormain?"

"Jagger Tormain. The one you call Slick. We're betting it's him. Our street sources tell us he's been seen in New York City as late as last Friday. We still don't have anything on the big guy with the scar on his forehead. The one you call Brute. We have four officers checking all the local gyms, and our computer files are running at full speed looking for a profile match."

"Anything on DM?"

"Nothing. But we've got a list of places called Cal's. One of them is a sleazy bar on the lower East side near the docks. We're checking it out."

"When are you seeing Frank Lisignoli?"

"I just got off the phone with him. I called him at home. I'm meeting him at 9:30 in his office. I briefed him, but he wants all the details. He said he also wants to meet you."

Jack gulped. A lump had suddenly formed in his throat, and the butterflies in his stomach were no longer flying in a tight formation.

"Jack?"

"Yeah?"

"The wire taps will all be in place by 10:00 this morning. If you get any strange calls, keep them on the line for as long as you possibly can so we can run a successful trace."

"OK. Anything else?"

Corey Burgess paused and took another deep breath and a sip of hot black coffee. "Well, there is one more thing. I spoke with a few people this morning who knew Mick Thorkmon. They don't think he's intelligent enough to plan an operation like this by himself. We think there's someone else who is the true brains behind this group."

"DM?"

"Maybe. Did you happen to think of anything else overnight that you might have forgotten to tell us?"

"No. I'm sure I covered everything. Why?"

"Just looking for more clues about DM. If we are going to nail the little buzzards, I want to make sure we get the big vulture, too!" Corey chuckled at his own analogy. "Oh, and you should also know we've sent out an alert and copies of our reports to the FBI."

"Whew! What time and where are we meeting tonight?" Jack asked, shifting uncomfortably as he leaned on the counter in the kitchenette.

"Not sure yet. Avery comes on duty at 2:00 p.m. I'll try to get to him shortly thereafter. He'll let you know somehow."

"Tell him to be careful contacting me so as not to tip off Lisa," Jack said.

"Will you two be working late on your book tonight?" Corey asked.

"I don't think so. If she suggests it, I'll figure some way out of it."

"OK. We'll keep you posted. Oh, and Jack?"

"What?"

"I apologize if you felt I was inferring that we didn't believe you last night. This city is full of crackpots. We just needed to make certain you weren't one of them."

"Well, you can go ahead and check me out. They know me in Minneapolis."

"We already have," Corey laughed aloud. "They love you in Minneapolis. And so does Peter Tunnell over at Brownstone. You're squeaky clean, Jack, not even a traffic ticket! A reputation for a warped sense of humor maybe, but there are no outstanding warrants for you anywhere!"

Jack took a deep breath. The New York Police Department had investigated him while he slept. Somehow, it was a comforting thought for him. At least they were thorough. He and Corey Burgess exchanged good-byes. Jack had thought about mentioning his plan to Corey, but decided against it. He still had a few details to work out. He wanted to make sure he had all the bases covered before he outlined it for them during their meeting later that night. There was a knock on the door. Without looking at the time, Jack knew it was 9:00 a.m. and Lisa had arrived. He recognized the rhythm of her knock. A small panic seized him as he reached for the doorknob.

"What if I heard wrong and Fat Face and his goons were coming on Monday?" Jack thought. "What if they changed their mind?" He quickly flung the door wide open, causing Lisa to jump with fright in the process. He grabbed her by the arm and pulled her firmly inside the suite.

"Jack!" she protested as he kicked the door shut behind him and locked it with his free hand. "What the hell is wrong with you?" Jack forced a smile and relaxed his grip on her arm.

"I just couldn't wait to see you!" he said.

Lisa frowned at him, a confused look in her eyes. She stepped back and removed her coat. "It's cold out there this morning," she said as she draped it over Jack's waiting hand. Jack nodded and slowly ambled over to hang her coat in the closet. Lisa watched him, sensing there was something different about him this morning, but she couldn't put her finger on it.

"Marsha called earlier," Jack said. He turned and leaned on the frame of the closet door, his thumbs hooked in the pockets of his pants. "She was wondering how we were doing on the cover selection. I told her we had it down to two. She'd like them back by noon with our final selection and any recommended changes. You're supposed to call Jo for a pick up when we have 'em ready."

"OK," Lisa replied, nodding and glancing at the two finalists still hanging from the fireplace mantle. "Well, let's do it now."

Jack walked stiffly across the room and followed her down the three steps into the lower living area. Lisa sat on the love seat, directly facing the fireplace and the two cover selections. Jack took his favorite position on the sofa to her right.

"What do you think this morning?" she asked him, never taking her eyes off the graphic cover composites.

"The one on the right," Jack replied firmly. He surprised himself with his own decisiveness. Lisa turned her head and studied Jack's face. Her eyes slowly narrowed. There was something in his voice. A nervous tightness, and she sensed it even more strongly now than before.

"Why?" Lisa asked slowly. "Both of them tied in our scoring within the five categories. Why that one?"

Jack turned his attention back to the cover on the right. He closed his left eye, opened it, then repeated the process with his right. Taking a deep breath, Jack began to speak, never looking at Lisa sitting to his left.

"I like the orange and golden yellow background at the top. The man dressed in the black western-cut suit, white shirt, and string bowtie is pretty classy. I like the way he is leaning on the edge of a fence rail with his left elbow supporting him and his right arm hanging down at his side. Notice how his arm pushes his coat open enough to reveal the pearl handled revolver in the black holster strapped on his hip? I think the top one third of the partially exposed book in his right coat pocket is very subtle. You can almost read the words, How to shoot. The expression on his face shows a lot of things: sadness, toughness, intelligence. Yet, when you look at his eyes, there is understanding, warmth, and laughter. And his lips have just an inkling of a smile. It's just the right touch of whimsical intrigue I'm looking for. Plus, seeing only the shadow of a woman in a dress behind him is pretty cool. You see it subliminally. It doesn't detract by sticking out like a sore thumb. I like the overall positioning of the graphic and the title. The man is positioned on the right side of the cover and the bold, black title pops against the bright reddish orange background on the left. It sort of gives one a representation of Hell. That's why it's got my vote."

Lisa let out a soft gasp of surprise. She had been looking back and forth between Jack and the cover as she listened to him explain why he had chosen the one on the right.

"You never cease to astonish me, Kramp!" Lisa exclaimed. Jack winced and looked at her. He was wondering what happened to her informality of calling him Jack. Suddenly, she was back to calling him Kramp again. "I really have to agree with everything you said," Lisa continued. "Actually, you pointed out a couple of things that I'd missed. So is that it? Is that our recommendation?"

Jack shrugged his shoulders. "Unless you like the other one better," he replied, his voice flat and matter of fact. The cover for Jack's book really didn't seem to be a priority to him at this moment. Keeping the woman seated next to him alive was foremost in his mind.

"No," Lisa said, searching Jack's eyes for tell-tale signs of what was really going on in his head. "The other one is just a shade too ominous. It has too much black in it. It doesn't give us the undertones of humor that you've carefully woven into the storyline. Let's go with your choice."

"Our choice," Jack corrected her. Lisa stood, walked over to the mantle, and removed the two cover comps. Holding them in front of her, she studied their choice as she walked back up to her desk.

"I'm going to make a few notes on this. Then I'll call Jo to come over and pick them all up for Marsha. Could you please get started on the first few pages of nineteen?"

"Sure," replied Jack as he stood and drifted to his desk. He fumbled through his briefcase until he came up with chapter nineteen. He glanced at Lisa. She gave him a quizzical look, but decided not to say anything. Jack sat down, assumed his usual feet-up-on-the-corner position, and attempted to read the words in front of him. However, the words made little sense, they were being crowded out by his plan.

"There," Lisa said suddenly, satisfied that her notes were clear to the graphic arts department. Jack looked up momentarily and then returned to his papers. Lisa stood, found her cell phone in her coat to call Brownstone and left an order to page Jo for a pickup. After hanging up, she leaned on the frame of the closet door. With her hands on her hips, she stared at Jack. She bit her lower lip and crossed directly to him. Jack looked up at her, startled by her sudden appearance.

"What's wrong, Jack?" she asked softly. Jack detected a certain firmness in her question.

"Nothing," he responded. "Why?"

"Because you've been a little off this morning. You're distant. You're body is here, but your mind is miles away. Yet, you said you missed me when I first came in. You're acting strange, Jack." Lisa caught herself giving him a quick smile. "Well, stranger than usual."

Jack let the pages on his lap fall to the floor. He slowly stood and took one step toward Lisa. He reached out his arms and gently pulled her close to him. She allowed herself to be buried into his massive arms, nestling her cheek against his warm chest.

"I did miss you," Jack whispered. "You're right. I'm just a little off this morning."

"What did you do last night?" Lisa asked, closing her eyes and enjoying the safety and security of Jack's tender strength. "You look really tired. You're eyes are red and there are bags under them. You didn't go to bed, did you?"

"Yeah," Jack whispered, fighting the fear that he may choke up. "I went to bed. But I couldn't sleep. I was thinking about you. And about us."

"I know, Jack. I woke up around 4:00 a.m. and I was thinking about you, too. I don't know where this is going between us. Half the time I'm afraid I won't ever see you again, the other half, I'm worried that I will. I don't know what to do."

"Then we'll do nothing," Jack said quietly. "We'll make no future plans. If we can't have anything beyond now, at least we've had these days." Lisa slowly eased herself back from Jack and stared into his blue eyes. She nodded slowly, understanding exactly what he had said.

"Well, I guess if we want to see each other again soon, you better get your butt back to Minnesota and write another bestseller," Lisa said with a weak smile, blinking back her tears. Jack laughed, draped his right arm around her shoulders, and slowly ushered her back to her desk.

"There won't be another book if we don't get this one finished and to the proof-readers," he said. "Remember, they want it to be on the presses within two weeks."

Lisa nodded and sat down. She flipped on the computer and began searching the files for her copy of chapter nineteen. She knew Jack was telling her the truth. But she still had a small doubt, surmising he wasn't telling her everything. There was still something else rumbling around in Jack's head. And the thunder was getting louder.

"Well, he'll tell me when he's ready," Lisa sighed to herself quietly as she started the reread. "I hope."

Jo arrived at 10:45 to pick up the box of artwork for the cover. She was in and out in minutes, barely speaking to either Jack or Lisa.

While Jack was working on the first nine pages, Lisa started her portion of edits in the middle of the chapter. She was unaware that Jack was doing two things simultaneously. He had a second sheet of paper under his pages with several notes on it. As Jack read and corrected the chapter, he would pause occasionally and carefully make an unrelated note on a piece of paper under his edits. It was his anti-kidnapping plan. He had to have it refined by the time he met with Lt. Burgess, Avery, and officer McKay later that evening.

Lisa and Jack worked in silence. The sky outside the French doors became even more cloudy and gray. A northeast wind rattled the doors often enough until Jack rose and closed the heavy drapes, drowning out the noise and stopping the draft. As Jack returned to his desk chair, he passed behind Lisa. He let the palm of his hand gently brush her left arm and shoulder while his fingers grazed her long black hair that rolled in soft waves down to the middle of her back, like silk in a graceful breeze. She reached up with her right hand and caught his. She held it briefly, gave it a tender squeeze, then returned to the keyboard in front of her. She never looked at him. She didn't have to see his face to feel the tenderness pouring from his heart.

It was 12:15 when Jack stood, rubbed his stomach, and stretched his large frame over his desk. "I'm hungry. Want some lunch?" he asked. Lisa finished typing another sentence before answering.

"Yes," she replied, leaning over to turn on the printer.

"Shall we order something up from room service?" Jack asked, heading for the menu on the counter.

"Well. . ." Lisa slowly turned in her chair to face Jack in the kitchenette.

"What?" Jack asked, his arms stretched out waist high in front of him, palms up. Lisa wrinkled her nose and threw him a smile.

"Let's go out and grab something," she said. "I need some fresh air and exercise. How about lunch at The Basket?" A small panic gripped Jack. He thought about Tork and his goons. One of them was probably out there right now, watching their every move.They may be hoping for a chance to grab her at any moment instead of waiting for tomorrow morning.

"The Basket?" Jack repeated. "That's kind of far. And it sounds pretty cold out there." He nodded in the direction of the French doors.

"Don't be silly, Jack," Lisa laughed as she headed for her coat. It's just around the corner on 59th, near Columbus Avenue. Come on, the fresh air will do you some good. Besides, I thought you were such a hearty Minnesotan and used to the cold!"

Jack forced his feet to move in Lisa's direction toward the closet. She pulled his trench coat off the hanger and held it for him. Jack reluctantly slipped into it and took his room key off the table. Lisa watched him, again sensing a renewed apprehension.

"What's the matter," she asked, reaching for the door handle, "I thought you liked to explore New York."

"Yeah," replied Jack dryly, "I just love being trampled to death on my way to lunch."

"Oh, come on now, it's not that bad," Lisa laughed. "I'll walk in front of you!"

"You'd be better off walking close behind me," Jack muttered under his breath as he followed her out the door and into the corridor, his thoughts turning once again to Tork and the boys. He nervously glanced up and down the empty hall.

"What?" Lisa asked, leaning toward him as they walked briskly down to the elevator.

"Nothing," Jack mumbled. "I said I'd better close the door behind me."

As they waited for the elevator to arrive, Lisa studied Jack's face again, looking for any clues as to what he was really thinking and refusing to tell her. She was oblivious to the fact that a door opened down the hall, just twenty-five feet from Jack's suite, but across the corridor. A man in a white shirt and dark tie stuck his head out, looked down the hall, and saw Jack and Lisa waiting at the elevator. He quickly ducked back into his room. Lisa, intently focusing on Jack Kramp, missed it. But Jack noticed, and his heart and brain began to pound in unison as questions sprang up and whirled around in his head.

"More of Tork's guys? DM? One of Burgess's men from the police force? Or just a hotel guest who's a little nosey?" Jack turned these questions over in his mind, looking for answers. He had none.

"Jack?"

"Huh?" Lisa's voice brought Jack back from his deep, fearful thoughts as he stood motionless just outside the elevator.

"Are you coming?" She was already inside the elevator, holding the door, and waiting for him. Jack quickly stepped into the elevator. They rode down in silence, lost in their own private thoughts. Lisa and Jack were both concerned for the other, but for very different reasons.

Over lunch, Lisa tried a new approach in another attempt to get Jack's mind back on track. She knew he was preoccupied with something else. She thought that perhaps discussing possible storylines for his next book might help him relax.

"Have you given any thought to your next manuscript?"

"Nope," Jack replied, chewing on his hamburger.

"Are you going to try another western? Maybe a series with the characters you've already established in *Loose Cannons*?"

"Maybe. I don't know. I haven't thought that far ahead."

"How about a romance? A modern romance spiced with a lot of comedy?"

"Yeah, maybe." Jack glanced nervously around the crowded restaurant for the tenth time.

"Or maybe you should try your hand at a murder mystery. You know how to develop a good plot. Maybe introduce a funny character who solves a murder unconventionally. You could keep your unique writing style and center it around a bunch of characters in an extortion ring!"

Jack began to choke on one of his French fries. He grabbed his water glass, his face turning bright red as he gulped for air and poured water down his throat. Jack blinked back the tears of panic and pain that filled his eyes during the sudden episode. He became aware of several people seated at tables around him pausing to stare. Jack coughed, raised his right arm, and managed a weak smile. He waved at the people around him to indicate he was fine. Once again, Jack surveyed the crowded restaurant with apprehension.

"Are you expecting someone?" Lisa asked suspiciously. She leaned back in her chair and clutched her napkin with both hands in exasperation.

"Nope," Jack replied. "I'm just embarrassed about choking in front of all these people. I noticed nobody rushed to my rescue."

"Don't worry. A few more seconds, Jack, and I would have performed the Heimlich maneuver on you. But if you don't start paying attention to me, I'll choke you myself!"

Jack's gaze finally returned to Lisa's face, his eyes meeting hers. She had a smile on her lips, but he could tell she was serious about the attention part. Jack wanted to take Lisa's hands and tell her everything he knew about Tork and the conversation he had overheard last night in the bar. He wanted her to know about Corey Burgess and the investigation, but Jack promised the NYPD to keep his mouth closed, especially to Lisa. He smiled at her and winked.

"Sorry, I guess I'm just not as comfortable in New York City as I thought I was. You're right, it's not Minneapolis or St. Paul. It's a lot more frightening" Jack replied, going for a cover up.

"Bull!" Lisa said tersely, but continued to return his smile. "There's something going on up there and I know it." She pointed to the middle of Jack's forehead.

"I've just got a little personal problem," Jack said with a heavy sigh. "I'm in the process of working it out." It was the truth. Once again, Jack had told her the truth and Lisa knew it. She decided to give it one more try.

"Do you need money? If you do, I'm sure I can get you a second advance on your book. You'll get another check in three weeks or so, once they start shipping, but I know I can get you something now if it will help."

Jack laughed and waved her off. "No, it's not money problems. I'm fine. It's just a good friend of mine. They've got a little unexpected problem, and I'm sort of involved." Jack bit his lip, afraid he may have said too much.

"OK, just let me know if I can help in any way," Lisa said softly, still looking at Jack with a great deal of concern.

"I will. Let's get out of here."

Jack walked Lisa briskly back to the hotel. He kept his eye on the door of suite 3417 as they passed by, but he neither heard nor saw anyone. Once inside his suite, Lisa and Jack immediately went to work and finished off chapter nineteen. By 3:00 p.m. Lisa was entering their final changes into the computer. Jack had begun to peruse chapter twenty when the room telephone rang. He jumped out of his chair and raced to answer it.

"Hello?"

"Jack, Avery here."

"Yeah, what's up?"

"Lisa with you?"

"Yeah."

"8:00 tonight. Your suite, okay?"

"Sounds fine. I'll look forward to it."

"See you then. Bye"

"Bye." Jack hung up the telephone, flashed a grin at Lisa, and returned to his desk.

"Who was that?" Lisa finally asked.

"Uh, that was Avery. We're going to catch the last part of the Knicks game on TV tonight when he gets off duty." Jack knew it was a small lie.

"Why don't you just tell me the truth, Jack?" Lisa demanded, her green eyes flashing anger at him as she spoke. Jack froze. The hair on the back of his neck stood straight out.

"How did she know? I must have tipped her off somehow, " he thought to himself. "What?" he finally asked out loud, stalling for time to think.

"You're going down to Bannigan's to meet Avery for drinks, aren't you?" Lisa asked. Relief spread over Jack as he understood her question.

"Yeah," he laughed. "Well, that too."

Lisa nodded and gave Jack a quick all-knowing smile. She had caught Jack red-handed and was proud of herself. She gave Jack ten pages of chapter twenty and told him to get to work.

Jack grinned to himself. He had dodged a bullet. Now Jack only hoped he could save Lisa from a real one.

Chapter Eighteen

It was nearly 6:00 p.m. by the time Lisa received Jack's final corrections on chapter twenty. She placed them next to the computer keyboard and turned in her chair to face him.

"I'll input these tomorrow morning," Lisa said, looking at Jack's tired expression. "I'm going home to catch up on all the things that I didn't do this past weekend. And Jack, you better get some sleep tonight. You're starting to look like hell," she added with a grin.

"Okay," Jack said as he uncrossed his legs, stood, and followed Lisa to the closet to help her with her coat. "I'll escort you downstairs," Jack said. He draped his right arm around her shoulders as they headed toward the door.

"No, you don't have to do that," Lisa protested, giving him another quizzical look.

"I have to go down anyway," Jack said, checking to make sure his room key was still in his pocket. "I need some gum." He winked and gave her a warm smile and a quick hug with his right arm.

"Gum?" Lisa repeated, raising her eyebrows with a dubious look.

"Yeah, it beats the heck out of chewing tobacco. It's healthier, and you don't have to spit!" Jack laughed heartily. Lisa set her jaw and gently clenched her teeth. She slowly shook her head at Jack but said nothing. She knew there were many things he would have to explain to her sometime and this was just one more oddity to add to her list.

As Jack opened the door to his suite, he casually looked out into the corridor. There was no one in sight. Behind him, Lisa paused to look back toward her desk.

"I'll leave my briefcase here," Lisa said. "I won't have an opportunity to work tonight anyway." She turned and walked out ahead of Jack. He was thankful she hadn't noticed his quick inspection of the hall. They rode the elevator down to the lobby in silence. Jack walked Lisa through the large vestibule and waited with her while the doorman procured a taxi. It was already dark, but the wind had subsided since the afternoon. When the cab arrived, Jack turned and faced Lisa. He gave her a quick hug.

"I'll call you later," Lisa said, smiling while ducking into her cab. Jack returned her grin and nodded. The driver closed the door, jumped behind the wheel, and they were gone.

"Great," Jack muttered as he walked back through the revolving door and into the lobby. "She's going to call me later. With my luck, it'll be right about the time Burgess, Avery, and the other officers are there."

Jack found a quiet table in one of the corners of the Garden Cafe and ordered the evening special. His thoughts returned to formulating his plan, turning the details over in his mind while he picked at his food. Satisfied his plan was finally organized, Jack signed for his dinner and strode down the hall to Bannigan's Bar. Selecting an empty bar stool far away from the other people in the bar, he ordered a beer and studied his cell. It was 6:50. Jack sipped his beer slowly, considering the options and alternatives of his plan while he carefully scrutinized the people coming in and leaving Bannigan's by using the large mirror behind the bar.

Suddenly, with his beer glass tilted to his lips, Jack paused. A familiar figure across the hall from the bar caught his attention. Through the large doorway of Bannigan's, Jack could see Tork talking on one of the hotel house phones just outside the restrooms. Jack squinted, trying to focus on the short fat man. Tork turned his back slightly to Jack, but he continued to make wild gestures with his left hand as an unlit cigar in the corner of his mouth bobbed up and down as he spoke. Jack set his beer back down and folded his arms in front of him, never taking his eyes off Tork.

As Jack continued his surveillance, another familiar figure appeared. Avery Schneider walked casually by the entrance to Bannigan's. Jack's first instinct was to get his attention, but he noticed Avery had already turned his head and was looking directly at Tork. Avery slowly ambled by him and disappeared from view down the hall.

After Tork hung up, Jack noticed him grinning to himself, pausing for a moment to readjust his cigar, then casually stroll toward the elevators. Jack turned in his bar stool as Tork disappeared out of sight. Avery was about ten steps behind Tork, walking as though he was just strolling the massive lobby.

Jack stood, gulped down the rest of his beer, tossed a tip on the bar, and headed toward the door. He paused just inside the bar, looked out toward the lobby and spotted Avery standing in front of the elevators. Tork was nowhere in sight. Jack walked swiftly to the elevators and Avery, glancing around the nearly empty lobby one last time.

"Did you see him?" Jack asked quietly out of the corner of his mouth while looking straight ahead at the elevator doors.

"Yup," Avery replied. "He went up."

"Up?" Jack repeated.

"Yup. My guess is we'll find him on the 34th floor."

Jack nodded in agreement. The elevator arrived and Jack and Avery got on with five other guests. Neither spoke as they rode to the 34th floor. Once off the elevator, they looked up and down the empty corridor. As they walked toward Jack's suite, Avery leaned toward Jack and whispered, "Wait in your room."

Jack nodded slightly. When they arrived at Jack's suite, he quickly unlocked the door and slipped inside. Avery continued down the corridor toward the small hall leading off to the right to the stairwell, the laundry room, and the freight elevator. Jack leaned against the inside of his door, straining to listen over his own heavy breathing.

Several minutes passed. Jack thought he could hear a faint knocking down the hall. He bent his head and peered through the small peep hole in his door. He could barely see Avery standing outside the door of suite 3417. The door opened and Avery stepped inside. Jack waited, leaning his back against the door. He jumped abruptly when there was a knock on his door behind him. He checked the peep hole again. It was Avery. Jack threw the door open and Avery stepped quickly inside, shutting the door hastily behind him.

"Did you see him?" Jack asked in a near whisper.

"No," Avery replied. "But I'm sure he was up here. The freight elevator was going down to the basement and parking garages when I got back there. There was also cigar smoke in the short hall, so he must have lit up. I called down to the kitchen. One of the night cooks coming on duty saw him get into a white van parked in a handicap space. He remembered him because he noticed the lit cigar, and this entire hotel is a non smoking property."

"Did it say 'Mable's Dry Cleaning' on it?" Jack asked.

"Don't know. He didn't say. I'm going to talk with him in a few minutes. He might have gotten a license number or something, but I doubt it. He wouldn't have had any idea that he should be watching for someone suspicious. He just remembered the fat guy with a cigar getting off the freight elevator and into a white van."

"Think he was up here scouting the layout again?"

"I suspect he was," nodded Avery. "I noticed one of those big yellow laundry carts sitting outside the supply room. Normally they're locked up. Either it was left out by accident or Tork placed it there for his boys tomorrow morning. I'm going to check with the head of housekeeping when I go back downstairs."

Jack wanted to ask Avery about his visit to room 3417, but decided he'd wait and see if the security officer brought it up first. Avery checked his watch and turned back toward the door.

"It's 7:20," he said. "I'm going to try and get a few more answers before our 8:00 p.m. meeting up here. I checked with Lt. Burgess' men. They're holed up in 3417, just down and across the hall. Been there all day, I guess. They haven't seen anyone yet." Avery's eyes twinkled at Jack a bit. "Although, one of them says he's pretty sure you saw him earlier today. He was checking out the hall this afternoon when you were at the elevators with the Lisignoli woman."

"Yeah, I saw him," Jack grinned slightly. "At first, I thought he might be with Tork. I was hoping he was one of us." Avery nodded and smiled back at Jack. He mumbled a good-bye and left. Jack locked the door behind Avery and immediately walked over to his desk where he pulled out his plan. He sat down and began to make additional notes. Suddenly, Jack stood and crossed over to Lisa's desk. He paused and looked at her briefcase on the floor. Picking it up, he placed it on her desk and opened it.

"I might as well try to find her home and cell numbers now instead of asking for them later when she calls," Jack said aloud to the empty room. "She might get suspicious."

Jack quickly found what he was looking for. It was the small, red Brownstone Confidential Employee Directory he had seen on Saturday morning when he was looking for the push pins. He flipped it open, found her name alphabetically, and jotted her telephone numbers down on his planning sheet. As he replaced the directory, his eye caught sight of a larger black book. It was Lisa's appointment book. He held it in his hands for several seconds, debating whether or not he should open it. Curiosity finally won out, and he flipped it open to the previous week. He wanted to know what kind of notes she might have made about him. Once spread open, her calendar showed all seven days of the week on it, one week at a time. Last Monday had a line clear through it, from nine to five, with his name written on it. The same notation was used for the rest of the week. There was another note for Friday night's dinner party. Jack flipped to the current week and found the same schedule for Monday. He flipped back to the previous week and was about to close the appointment book when he saw smaller printing within a circle around 12:30 on Monday. It said, "Lunch - DM." Jack almost choked. He turned on Lisa's desk lamp and placed the pages under it to study them more carefully, his hands beginning to tremble.

"Damn!" Jack cursed softly. "She knows DM! She was having lunch with the same person who is plotting to kidnap and probably kill her!" Panic seized him. Jack carefully searched each day and found the initials DM again. This time, they were penciled in next to a circled 6:00 p.m. Saturday evening. Feeling weak, Jack slumped into Lisa's desk chair, holding her black appointment book half open on his lap.

"Delano Morrison," Jack said quietly to himself in disbelief. "Her ex-lover is out to get her. He's involved somehow. Maybe he decided if he can't have her, he'll get revenge and get some of her daddy's money."

He picked up his pen and wrote "Delano Morrison" behind the initials DM on his note sheet. He paused for a moment to search his memory, then added a question mark and "foreign correspondent/The Times." Slowly rising from Lisa's desk, Jack switched off her lamp and folded his notes. He tucked them in his top shirt pocket and glanced at his cell phone. It was 7:35. He walked over to the hotel phone and dialed room service.

"Good evening, this is Jack Kramp in suite 3418. I'd like to order up a dozen cans of soda. Make it four regular and four diet Cokes, a couple of Seven-Ups, and a couple of root beers. And, do you have a large bag of pretzels? Good. That's fine, send those up, too."

Jack thanked the friendly voice on the other end and said a quick good-bye. He walked down into the living area and sat on the love seat. He picked up the remote for the fireplace off the coffee table and started the gas log to take the chill out of the room. Taking his folded notes out of his pocket, Jack began to review them one last time before the arrival of Lt. Burgess, Avery, and the rest of the officers.

At 8:05 p.m. Jack greeted four men and one woman at the door of his suite; Lt. Corey Burgess, Avery Schneider, Officer McKay, Detective Sheldon, the plain clothes officer from suite 3417, and an attractive, slender, dark haired officer named Linda Stinson. Each took a seat on the furniture surrounding the coffee table as Jack offered the soft drinks from the tub of ice on the service cart. Only Avery declined, but he helped himself to pretzels from a large glass bowl in the center of the coffee table.

"We all know why we're here," Burgess began. "We are going to make a serious attempt to prevent the kidnapping of Lisa Lisignoli, thwart the extortion plot of Mick Thorkmon and his accomplices, and make several arrests. Here is what we have so far."

Burgess gave the background and updates on both Tork and Jagger Tormain. He outlined the events of the past several hours, including the phone taps that were now in place. Avery filled them in with the recent sighting of Tork by he and Jack earlier that evening.

"The night cook didn't get a license number off the white van," Avery said. "And the laundry cart sitting out in the hall was a mystery to the housekeeping staff. The police still haven't been able to get a lead on Brute, but the FBI is scouting out barns near Lake Pleasant for a '93 Buick registered to Tormain. They're looking for an Aunt Rosie and are determined to find enough evidence to charge both Jagger Tormain and Brute for the murder of Buddy Shepard."

"We have a couple of officers watching a tavern on the lower east side called Cal's," said Burgess. "We flashed photos around of Thorkmon and Tormain, but nobody's talking."

"Anything on Shirley or Mabel's Cleaners?" asked Detective Sheldon.

"We have nothing on Shirley. She might be Thorkman's girlfriend. There are six dry cleaning establishments in the greater New York area listed as Mabel's Dry Cleaning. We are checking each of them. So far none have reported a white van being stolen."

"What about DM?" inquired Avery.

"Zippo," Burgess said, shaking his head. Jack, who had remained silent, shifted his position on the corner of the love seat. He cleared his throat and the men looked at him.

"I think I might have something on DM," he said quietly. Everyone focused their attention on him with a bit of surprise in their eyes. Jack told them how he had looked in Lisa's briefcase for her telephone numbers and then snooped through her appointment book. Jack walked over to Lisa's desk, picked up her appointment book, and handed it to Burgess. He also relayed everything he knew about Delano Morrison from what Lisa had told him. Corey Burgess, with appointment book in hand, stood and walked up to call his office in the kitchenette.

"Mulvaney? Burgess here. I'd like you to get me everything you can, as fast as you can, on a Delano Morrison. He's an overseas correspondent with The New York Times. Yes, I'm here at the West Park Plaza, suite 3418. Call my cell as soon as you have something." Corey hung up and rejoined the group of men.

"Are you still planning to use one of your officers in place of Lisa Lisignoli?" Jack asked.

"Yes, that's me," Officer Stinson spoke for the first time. "I'm going to be Lisa tomorrow morning," she said. Jack nodded, he had suspected that. Officer Stinson was approximately the same height and almost had the same hair color and figure as Lisa.

"Good," Jack replied. "That'll work perfectly in my plan." Once again, all eyes turned to Jack in surprise. He walked over and stood in front of the fireplace.

"Do you have a specific plan on how to get these guys tomorrow morning?" Jack asked Burgess.

"A basic outline. That's why we're all meeting here now, to work out the details. Do you have a suggestion or a plan?" Corey asked with a bit of skepticism.

"I think so," Jack replied. "It's just an idea I'd like to share with all of you, if you don't mind."

"Okay. Let's hear it," Burgess said, settling back into his seat and crossing his legs as he, Avery, and McKay took out their ink pens and notebooks.

"Okay," Jack said, taking a deep breath, "Here it goes. We know that Delano Morrison, or someone with him, is probably watching Lisa. If Lisa does anything out of the ordinary, it may tip them off. That means Officer Stinson will have to leave Lisa's apartment dressed like her and cab it over here, arriving precisely at 9:00 AM. It also means we can't have the real Lisa leaving at the same time as Stinson. I think I can get Lisa over here earlier, maybe by 7:30 or so. Since they lived together for six months, Delano Morrison knows she is not a morning person, and he most likely will not be watching too intently for her to leave at that hour."

The five officers nodded in agreement. Jack pulled his notes out of his shirt pocket and glanced at them briefly.

"Okay, I thought maybe we could put an officer in here with Lisa and me. We'll fill Lisa in on everything that is happening when she gets here early tomorrow morning. I know officers are already set up just down the hall in suite 3417, but maybe two more officers can be hiding on the second landing going up to the roof in the stairwell exit just down the hall. I also think we need somebody closer to Stinson as she gets close to the door of my suite. I took a look at one of the housekeeping supply carts this morning. One side is open and just covered by a curtain. We can easily remove the inside shelves and place another officer inside."

Avery and Corey both frowned at Jack, trying to determine how the supply cart worked into the plan. Jack continued, "We can put the supply cart just outside my door. That way, Stinson is covered by somebody other than Sheldon and company who are a good twenty-five feet away down the corridor in 3417. That gives us at least seven against two, which is pretty good odds."

"When Slick, excuse me, Jagger Tormain and Brute make contact with Stinson, thinking she's Lisa, Sheldon and his partner will have to run like hell to help her. If needed, the officer under the supply cart will be able to assist Stinson sooner. When Sheldon sees Brute and Tormain coming near my door, they'll either have to send some sort of signal to the officers waiting in the stairwell or have those guys come out promptly at 9:00. I also suggest that we have a wide angle peephole installed in the door of suite 3417 so Officer Sheldon has a better view of the main corridor and my suite. I suspect they'll be coming up the freight elevator. Remember, they'll both be armed and won't hesitate to shoot any of us."

Jack turned and looked directly at Burgess. "I'm sure you've already thought of this, but you'll need a couple of undercover vehicles downstairs in the parking garage to get Thorkman. If Brute and Tormain don't show up within a short period of time, he's going to bolt. The only thing I haven't figured out yet is how or where we can get to Delano Morrison."

When Jack finished outlining his plan, he was feeling weak and out of breath. He nervously stuffed his hands in his pants pockets and leaned up against the fireplace mantle. There was a dead silence in the room as the five seated officers looked at each other. Finally, Corey Burgess spoke. "That's quite a plan, Mr. Kramp. It looks like you've pretty much thought of everything."

Jack grinned and looked at the floor. "I've had about twenty-four hours to think of nothing but a plan," he replied.

"Well, I think it's a great plan," Bill McKay said, looking around at his fellow officers. They all nodded, still in shock over Jack's thorough outline.

"Are you sure you never did any police work?" Avery Schneider asked, a slow grin spreading over his face. Jack shook his head. Burgess's cell phone rang, and he went into the kitchenette to converse with Mulvaney from the precinct. After a few minutes of jotting down notes, Corey rejoined the men in the lower level.

"DM?" Officer McKay inquired.

"Yes," replied Corey Burgess, looking over his notes. "He is a very interesting gentleman. Delano has won several awards for his journalism and is held in high regard at The Times. He also owns property in New Jersey," Corey paused before delivering the rest of his news. "An old warehouse that he inherited from his father."

Bill McKay let out a slow, soft whistle. Avery, Sheldon, and Stinson leaned forward.

"There's more," Corey said with a grim look on his face. "Delano has an older sister."

"Shirley," Jack said instinctively. Corey nodded.

"Shirley Morrison Thorkmon."

"Mick Thorkman's wife." Bill McKay said with a note of confidence.

"Ex-wife. She filed for divorce shortly after he was arrested for embezzling over three hundred grand from Tanner and Whitehall. But, word on the street is that they've been seen together as recently as last Saturday afternoon."

"Where does she live?" Stinson asked.

"Her last address was on the Lower East Side. She lived in a small apartment over Cal's Tavern and Pool Hall. She hasn't been seen around there for several weeks, though."

"Aren't we going to pick up Delano Morrison for questioning?" inquired Sheldon.

"Can't," Burgess replied. "Not yet anyway. That could easily tip off Thorkman. We'll have to wait until their little operation gets underway here. I'll have him placed under constant surveillance. We'll pick him up tomorrow morning. By the way, he's booked on a noon flight back to Paris."

"How convenient," Jack mumbled. Avery and McKay nodded in agreement.

"I'll take care of the peep hole expansion in room 3417," Avery said as he stood. "And I'd also like to be here in the room tomorrow morning with Jack and Lisa."

"I'll be here, too," Bill McKay chipped in.

"Okay," Corey said as he rose and placed his hands on his hips. "I agree with Jack. Avery and McKay are in here. Sheldon and Donner will be in suite 3417. We'll put Johnson and Duncan in the stairwell. I'll have three units lined up downstairs to get Thorkmon."

"Who's under the supply cart?" McKay asked.

"I'm going under the cart in the hall," Burgess replied matter of factly.

Jack raised his eyebrows in Corey's direction. He looked at the tall African-American from head to toe. Corey caught Jack's review of his stature.

"Something wrong, Jack?" he asked, a half-smile on his face. He knew what Jack was thinking.

"It's going to be a damn tight squeeze for you to get under that supply cart," Jack said, returning Corey's grin. "It's about four feet high and five feet long, but it's only two and a half feet wide. By the time you manage to squeeze your way out of there to help, it'll probably be all over."

"He's right, Corey," Avery said, "I know the kind of cart Jack's talking about, and you're just too damn big. You'll look like an elephant climbing out of a Volkswagen."

"Let me go under the cart, Lieutenant," Bill McKay begged. Lt. Corey Burgess paused for a minute. He turned his back on everyone in the living area and slowly walked up the steps. He turned and looked at them all again, his chin resting in his right hand.

"Okay," Burgess said reluctantly, "Bill, you're under the cart. I'll be in here with Avery. Sheldon, we'll put Donner with you in room 3417." Corey gave Jack a long look. He turned his head toward the bedroom for a moment, then back to Jack.

"You've got a very good plan here, Jack, but from here on in, it's entirely a police operation. So I'm asking you to stay out of sight and out of the way. Okay?"

"Fine with me. I'm allergic to bullets anyway," Jack said with a weak laugh. Everyone else chuckled as well.

"I thought perhaps we should have Lisa secured and protected by U.S. Marshals downstairs somewhere, but if anyone sees her moving around, it could blow the whole set up," Burgess said quietly. Then looking directly at Jack again, he added, "I want you and Lisa to stay in the bedroom and stay low until it's all over, understand?" Jack nodded.

"Avery," Jack said, turning his attention to the security officer, "Anita, from housekeeping, usually shows up early to clean my room. Will you please make sure she stays out of sight? I don't want her mixed up in this or hurt in anyway."

"Yup. I'll be here by 6:00 tomorrow morning. We will make sure the head of housekeeping keeps Anita out of the way and that there's an extra supply cart available with the shelves removed."

"Let's all be careful how much we tell and who we tell about this operation," Burgess cautioned everyone in the room. "We don't know who Thorkman may have contact with here at the hotel." They each gave him an understanding nod.

By 9:45, everyone had left suite 3418, leaving Jack feeling alone and exhausted. He shut down the gas log in the fireplace, picked up the empty soda cans, and brought the pretzels up to the kitchenette counter. The phone rang.

"Lisa," he said to himself as he reached over to answer it.

"Hi Jack, it's Lisa." The warmth of her voice relaxed Jack.

"Well, hello!" Jack said, adding energy to his forced enthusiasm. "I thought you'd be sleeping by now."

"I'm just now getting ready for bed," Lisa giggled. "I had to be a domestic engineer tonight. It's not one of my favorite duties. Are you going down to meet

Avery soon for a drink?"

Jack remembered he had told Lisa he was going to watch the Knicks game with Avery to cover up the phone call Avery had made to his suite earlier that afternoon.

"Yeah, pretty soon. I'm just going to have one beer and call it a night. I'm really tired, and I need to get to bed at a reasonable hour."

"You're right, Jack, you better get rested. We have to wrap up everything by Wednesday. Thursday and Friday will probably be filled with last minute meetings with various people at Brownstone. I spoke with Marsha tonight. She wants to meet with you to go over the contracts for possible film rights and your extended publishing contract on Thursday."

"Good," Jack said. He eased himself up on the kitchenette countertop and sat with his legs dangling in front of him.

"You're quiet again tonight, Jack. What's wrong? Is it your friend?"

"Yeah, well sort of. We think we have the problem worked out. I'll know tomorrow." Jack swallowed hard as he thought about the danger that awaited all of them the following morning. He decided to change the subject, but only slightly.

"Have you heard from Delano Morrison lately?" he asked, closing his eyes and biting his lower lip, wondering if he should have even mentioned his name.

"Why, no," replied Lisa, a note of surprise in her voice, "Why do you ask?"

"I was just curious," Jack chuckled nervously, searching for a logical and believable excuse. "Actually, I was feeling a little jealous."

"Jealous?" Lisa laughed, even more surprised at his personal candor. "There really isn't any reason to be. He is out of my life."

"Are you sure?" Jack asked, persistent in fishing for any more clues from her regarding Delano Morrison.

"Positive. He's changed. He's different, now," Lisa said slowly, looking for a new description of him.

"What do you mean?"

"His entire personality is colder. Even though he tried to cover it up with flowers, hugs, and smiles, I could see through him. He's not the same man I lived with a year ago. He kept asking me a lot of strange questions about my relationship with my father. He was never interested before. I found that odd, too." A confidence returned to Lisa's voice. She had finally voiced her feelings aloud to someone else. She knew she was right about the change in Delano, and it felt wonderful for her to share these thoughts and feelings with Jack.

"Maybe the rich French food doesn't agree with him!" Jack wanted to turn the conversation to something lighter.

"Maybe," Lisa chuckled on the other end. "How about you? Where did you eat tonight?"

"I had lasagna downstairs in the Garden Cafe." Jack felt the conversation starting to lag. He wanted to say other, important things to the woman on the other end, but he sensed the timing wasn't right. The thoughts he wanted to so desperately share with her would have to wait for another time. "If there is another time," Jack thought to himself.

"Well, I better let you get ready to leave. Doesn't Avery get off at 10:00?"

"Yeah. He's off at 10:00. Listen, thank you for calling. I'll see you tomorrow morning, okay?" Suddenly, Jack was in a hurry to get off the phone. He wanted to review his plan again. Fear drove him to think that maybe he had overlooked something.

"Okay, Jack. Sweet dreams. I'll see you at 9:00. Goodnight."

"Goodnight, Lisa. Until 9:00 tomorrow," he whispered. He hung up the telephone. "Or earlier," he added, mumbling quietly to himself. Jack slid off the counter and flipped the lights off in the suite. He walked into the bedroom, turned on the nightstand lamp, and noticed it was 10:05. Jack sat on the edge of the bed and dialed home. A heaviness burdened him as he thought how this might be his last conversation with his children.

"It could very well be my last if something goes wrong and my plan doesn't work perfectly tomorrow," Jack said aloud as he heard the phone ringing at the large, white two story in south Minneapolis.

Chapter Nineteen

With his head propped in his hands, Jack was sitting on the edge of the bed in only his boxers when his 5:00 a.m. wake-up call came from the front desk. He picked it up on the first ring, murmured a soft thank-you to the man on the other end, and slowly placed it back in its cradle. Staring at the telephone as though it were an instrument of death, Jack was trying to determine when to call Lisa. He had to give her enough time to arrive at the hotel by 7:30. And he knew she was not an early riser.

"6:10," Jack finally mumbled to himself. "That should give her enough time to get ready, grab a cab, and be over here by 7:30."

Jack headed to the bathroom to shower and shave. As the hot water hit him, he kept hoping that he would wake up to find the past thirty hours were just a bad dream; no Tork, no Jagger Tormain, no Brute, no plot. He hoped it was nothing more than a vivid imagination of a slightly drunken writer who is often visited by nightmarish monsters in his sleep. However, as he stepped out of the shower, he knew that it was all too real and too frightening. Jack resigned himself to the fact that whatever happened at 9:00 a.m. this morning outside his suite, it would once again change his life forever. He remembered the cautionary words of Corey Burgess.

"You got it, Lt. Burgess," Jack said aloud as he hunted for a pair of socks. "Lisa and I will stay in the bedroom until it's over. Hiding."

Jack wrinkled his eyebrows into a hard frown as he thought about the plan he had shared last night with Corey, Avery, and the other officers. "I wonder what they would have come up with?" he asked himself. "I should have listened to them first. They're the professionals." Jack was suddenly regretting becoming so involved. Then he thought of Lisa.

"Caught between a damn rock and a hard place," Jack muttered as he slipped into a pair of blue jeans. He pulled on a gray sweatshirt, laced up his tennis shoes, and walked to the edge of the bed.

Jack watched the clock slowly tick toward 6:10 a.m. He glanced at his scribbled out plan on the tattered and folded paper laying on the nightstand. He picked up the telephone and dialed Lisa's number. She finally answered on the fourth ring.

"Hello?" Her voice was groggy and horse. Jack had obviously awakened her.

"Lisa, this Jack," he said, trying to sound angry and demanding.

"Jack?"

"Yes," he snapped. "Jack Kramp." He hated having to use such a harsh tone of voice with her, but he knew it was necessary.

"Oh. What time is it? What's wrong?" She struggled to come out of her deep sleep and clear her head.

"It's ten after six and there is plenty wrong."

"What do you mean?" Lisa struggled to a sitting position. She opened her eyes and brushed her long hair back with her left hand.

"The book. Me. You. All of it. I'm calling the whole damn thing off. I'm going home. Brownstone can take the damn manuscript and stuff it!"

There was a long pause. Lisa shook her head to clear it, trying to understand what Jack had just said. "What?" She was wide awake now.

"You heard me. I've changed my mind. I want out!" Jack raised his voice intentionally.

"What the hell is wrong with you, Kramp? Are you drunk?" Lisa was becoming angry.

"I'm as sober as the hair on my ass," he bellowed back. "And I want you to get over here right away and help me figure a way out of all this. I've booked a flight for 11:00 a.m. back to Minnesota."

"Jack," Lisa said, speaking calmly, thinking she might be able to reason with him to find out what was really going on. "What happened? Did something scare you? Why are you acting like this?"

"I don't want to get into it over the telephone. We've got some talking to do. Just get your butt over here now!"

"Now?" Lisa echoed. "Wait, how about if I call Marsha and have her meet us there at 9:00, we could..."

"Leave Marsha out of this," Jack interrupted. "This is between me and you. If you're not here in an hour, I'm leaving!"

"Okay, okay, Jack. Calm down," Lisa said, confused, yet pacifying him. "I'll be there as quick as I can. I don't know WHAT is going on with you, but you had better have some damn good reasons for your behavior."

"Just get over here as soon as you can," Jack pleaded.

"I'll be there in forty-five minutes. Just stay there," she said hurriedly. "Please, just stay there."

"Forty-five minutes," Jack repeated. "Hurry."

"I will," assured Lisa. She hung up the phone and sat for a few seconds, collecting her thoughts. Suddenly, she bolted out of bed and raced for her bathroom.

"He's crazy! A nut job!" Lisa kept muttering under breath while she showered. "He's flipping out. Something's been upsetting him since Monday morning. No, wait. He even sounded strange and apprehensive Sunday night on the phone." In her mind, she tried to organize Jack's unusual behavior during the past two days. Lisa ran a brush through her hair and clipped it back, threw on jeans, a sweater plus her leather jacket, and was on her way down to hail a cab by 6:43 a.m.

Jack called Corey Burgess at his precinct within five minutes after he hung up from talking to Lisa.

"Jack! What's up?"

"I just spoke with Lisa. She should be over here in less than forty-five minutes."

"Good. I'll alert our men outside her apartment to watch for her. They'll make sure she arrives at your hotel safe. She takes a cab, right?"

"Yeah, I think so."

"Okay. They'll follow her. How did you get her to come over two hours early?"

"I threw a writer's tantrum," Jack said with a nervous chuckle. "I told her I was quitting and going home to Minnesota this morning."

"I'll bet that got her attention," Corey laughed quietly. "By the way, I just got off the phone with Avery. He is all set with the cart. Anita will be going through an employee review downstairs with her supervisor, so she won't be in any danger."

"Good. When are you guys coming over?"

"I'm on my way. The rest of the officers should already be there. They're meeting with Avery in suite 3417. I'll see you in your room a little after 7:00. We'll brief Lisa together."

"Okay, but just so you know, she'll probably be pissed as hell at me for jerking her around this morning. Be prepared for her hot temper."

"I can handle it," Corey said grimly. "I'll see you shortly."

They exchanged good-byes, and Jack walked out into the main area of the suite to open the heavy drapes on the French doors. Sunlight streamed in and brightened the room. As the time ticked by, Jack began to feel more confident about his plan. His worries seemed to dissipate with the warmth of the sun. He turned to the kitchen counter and called down to room service, ordering pastries and fruit. A few minutes later, he watched the coffee pot beginning to perk. He glanced nervously at the time on his cell. It was 7:00 a.m. sharp, and he hoped Corey would arrive before Lisa.

"In two hours, it'll all be over with," Jack sighed quietly as he picked up a half dozen cups out of the kitchen cabinet and placed them next to the coffee pot. There was a knock on the door, and Jack crossed over to peer through the peephole. It was Avery Schneider. Jack quickly opened the door and Avery stepped inside. As Jack closed the door, he glanced out into the corridor and noticed Corey Burgess getting off the elevator, so he waited for him. Corey spotted Jack in his doorway as well.

"Hi, I'll be right in," Corey called softly. "I need to have a few words with Sheldon and Donner first. Is Avery in there yet?"

Jack nodded.

"Lisa?"

Jack shook his head. "Any minute, I suspect."

"Okay. I'll be with you shortly." Corey turned and walked a few feet back down the corridor to the door of suite 3417. It opened for him before he had a chance to knock. Jack closed his door and turned his attention to Avery.

"Coffee?" Jack offered.

"Yup. Just black."

"I've got some pastries and fruit on the way up."

"I've had breakfast," Avery said as Jack handed him a cup of hot coffee. "Is Lisa on the way?"

Jack nodded as they heard another knock on the door. Jack checked the peep hole again and opened it for room service. He quickly took the tray, signed for it, and closed the door again.

"Burgess should be here soon," Avery said. He was standing in front of the French doors, looking out over Central Park and sipping his coffee.

"Yeah," Jack replied. "He's already up here. He just stopped to talk with the officers in room 3417."

"I just came from there myself," Avery said quietly. Jack sensed Avery was a little apprehensive this morning by his lack of conversation. Corey Burgess gently rapped on the door and Jack let him in. Corey glanced around the room, greeted Avery, and helped himself to coffee and a donut.

"Lisa's not here yet?" he asked.

"Not yet," Jack replied. He glanced at his cell again. It was 7:10. "Think there's trouble?"

Corey pulled his two-way radio from his belt to call the officers in the car following Lisa's cab.

"They just pulled up in front of the hotel," Corey said, relaying the information to Jack and Avery. "One of the officers is going to follow her in. He'll be carrying a briefcase and will ride the elevator up with her. Once off the elevator, he'll proceed down the corridor in the opposite direction from this suite and wait in the far stairwell, just in case one of 'em tries to go down that way."

As Jack checked the time again, Lisa arrived at the door. She pounded loudly, her anger fueled by her thoughts of how ridiculous this entire ordeal was during the cab ride over to the hotel. Corey Burgess, being the closest to the door, opened it and ushered her in. Lisa stared at him in complete surprise as he greeted her. She shot Jack a hard look as he leaned against the kitchen counter. Noticing Avery near the French doors, her eyes widened further. A look of confusion came over Lisa's face as she quickly looked from Jack to Corey to

Avery and back to Jack.

"Exactly what's going on here?" she demanded, her green eyes narrowing, her jaw firmly set.

"I think we should sit down," Corey replied softly, gesturing toward the lower living room. "I'm afraid we have some news that may upset you."

"What sort of news?" Lisa glanced at Jack nervously, looking for a clue. He smiled weakly at her.

"It'll be okay, Lisa," Jack reassured her. "Lt. Burgess will give you the whole story. Want some coffee?"

"Yes, thank you," she said, hesitating for a moment, then following Corey and Avery down into the living area. Jack poured up a fresh cup of coffee for her, slowly walked down, and perched on the arm of the love seat. Lisa sat in the center of the love seat, Corey on one sofa and Avery on the other.

"We have very good reasons to believe that your life is in danger," Corey began, "But, I also believe we have the situation under control."

In great detail, he slowly explained Thorkmon's plot to kidnap her. Lisa listened intently, glancing often at Jack as Corey told her how Jack had come to overhear the kidnapping and extortion plan. Her eyes widened in disbelief and her olive skin turned pale as she slumped back in the love seat. When Corey informed her that Delano Morrison was suspected as the mastermind behind the entire plot, her hands covered her mouth in shock.

"So that's why you've been acting so strangely," Lisa said slowly as she looked at Jack. He nodded, but waited for Corey to continue.

"We had to get you over here early. Jack came up with a brilliant plan last night," Corey said. "In just over an hour, an undercover policewoman impersonating you will be leaving your apartment building and arrive at this hotel. It has to appear like nothing is out of the ordinary. She most likely will be followed."

"So, your frantic call to me this morning was just a way to get me over here early?" Lisa asked incredulously, looking directly at Jack.

"I'm sorry," replied Jack, nodding. "It was the only way I could think of to get you over here immediately. Forgive me?" Lisa nodded slowly. Corey told her about the rest of the plan and reassured her of her safety.

"We have twenty-four officers working on this case. Twenty-five if you count Murdock who is with your father in his office."

"My father?" Lisa asked in surprise.

"I want an officer with your father for protection in the event someone tries to get to him directly. There may be more people involved in this thing than we know." Corey spoke frankly, sensing Lisa was a strong woman who could take the truth across the board.

"I find it extremely difficult to believe that Delano is behind this," Lisa said sadly, shaking her head. "Have you questioned him yet?"

"Not yet," Corey replied, "But we're keeping a close eye on him. He's booked on a noon flight to Paris."

"You know," Lisa spoke thoughtfully, looking back and forth from each man. "Delano is, or was when I knew him, quite a gambler. He was always betting on sporting events. He made very good money at The New York Times, but yet, he was often broke. More than once I loaned him money. As a matter of fact, I think he still owes me about nine hundred dollars."

"Maybe he is deep into somebody's pockets either here or over in France," Avery said, rubbing his chin. "Gambling addiction and overwhelming, unpaid debts can make a person do some pretty awful things."

"Well, we expect to apprehend them all this morning without incident," Corey Burgess said confidently, "Starting with Thorkmon, Tormain, and the Brute, as Jack calls him. The action starts right outside in about an hour from now." He studied his watch. "Thank God we moved all the guests off this floor."

"You did?" Jack asked with surprise. He suddenly felt guilty for not having thought of the safety of other guests.

"We told them we were doing some renovating up here," Avery said.

"We didn't expect you to think of everything," Corey said. He smiled at Jack, suspecting that he might be mentally kicking himself.

By 8:00 a.m. Lt. Corey Burgess had all his men in position around the hotel. At 8:45, Bill McKay went under the housekeeping supply cart, now positioned just across the corridor from the door of suite 3418. At the same time, officer Stinson, posing as Lisa Lisignoli, was hailing a cab in front of the Arcadia apartments. Two hundred feet away, a tall, well dressed man in a dark green Jaguar watched Lisa enter a Yellow Cab and head for the West Park Plaza Hotel. He pulled in behind the cab and followed, unaware that a blue four door sedan with two New York City detectives were traveling a safe distance behind him.

At exactly 8:50 a.m. the telephone rang in suite 3418. At the door, Corey Burgess motioned for Jack to let it ring three times before picking it up. Lisa was already tucked away safely in the bedroom. She sat on the edge of the unmade bed, her hands clasped in her lap, her head down. Avery Schneider was at his post, just outside the bedroom door. He was waiting for Jack to complete the phone conversation so he could close the door with Jack and Lisa securely on the other side. His job was to protect them at all costs. At the start of the fourth ring, Jack Kramp picked up the telephone. "Hello, this is Jack."

"Good morning, sir, this is Janice over at Brownstone Publishing. I'm calling on behalf of Lisa Lisignoli."

"Yes, Janice," Jack said very slowly, stalling for time so the call could be traced. "Didn't I meet you the other day when I was in the office?"

"Uh, no, I'm sorry, I don't think so..." said Janice, unprepared for Jack's response.

"Oh, sorry," Jack interrupted, "I get all those people around your office mixed up. Uh, wait a minute, can you hold on? I've got a pot of coffee boiling over here, just a minute."

The woman on the other end started to protest, but to no avail. Jack held the telephone receiver in the air and banged the coffee pot around on the counter for a few seconds. Across the room, Corey grinned at Jack and gave him a double thumbs up.

"Sorry about that," Jack babbled on. "I'm not used to this new fangled automatic coffee pot. This is the second time this week that I've boiled it over. I must add too much water or something."

"Sir? Sir?" Sir!" On the other end, Janice was nearly shouting, trying to cut into Jack's continuous chatter.

"Oh, yeah, you must have called me for one reason or another. That's right, you said you were calling on behalf of Lisa Lisignoli. What's up?"

Jack looked at Corey, his eyebrows raised. Corey made circular motions with his hands in front of him, indicating he should keep the conversation going.

"Ms. Lisignoli isn't feeling well this morning and will not be able to meet you at nine. She asked me to call you. She said she'd try to make it over to see you later this afternoon."

"Oh my goodness!" Jack exclaimed. He grinned at his own enhanced performance. "Is she all right? What's wrong? She seemed fine last night. I hope she's not too bad. We've got a lot of work to do today. But if she is too bad, tell her not to come over at all, I sure as heck don't want to get sick. Can I have her number? I'd like to call her, just to see how she is so..."

"Sir. Sir!" Janice finally cut in again, "I'm sorry. I was just asked to give you her message. That's all I know."

"What about her home telephone number?" Jack persisted.

"I, uh, we are not allowed to give out that information," she said nervously. "Good-bye, sir." Shirley Morrison Thorkmon, pretending to be Janice, quickly hung up. A sick feeling of fear spread through her. She felt as though she should run, but it was too late. The phone call was already traced and two uniformed patrolmen were racing toward a small apartment in Queens to arrest her.

Corey's radio beeped. He waved Jack into the bedroom with Lisa, and Avery immediately closed the door. On the other side, with his right ear pressed against the door, Jack heard Corey whisper to Avery that Tormain, wearing a maintenance uniform, had just appeared on the floor with a tool box. He was kneeling down on the hall floor, just six feet outside the door to suite 3418 under the pretense of repairing an electrical wall socket. Avery entered the bedroom with Lisa and Jack and locked the door behind him.

Seconds later, Brute came around the corner from the small hall pushing a large yellow cart used to collect dirty laundry. There were two sheets and a blanket in the bottom. He left the cart just to the right of the door of suite 3418, directly across from the supply cart housing officer Bill McKay. Brute casually strolled over toward Tormain and engaged in light conversation. At exactly 8:59 a.m. Officer Stinson, looking like a twin sister to Lisa Lisignoli, stepped off the elevator and walked toward suite 3418. She paid zero attention to the maintenance man or the large man in the Mabel's Dry Cleaning uniform. Neither of the men looked at her, until she stopped outside the door to Jack's suite.

Brute quickly pulled a hand towel soaked in chloroform from a small plastic pouch inside the front of his coverall. He swiftly moved in on Stinson from behind, throwing his left arm around her neck in a choke hold while at the same time covering her face with the towel in his right hand. Tormain was directly behind him, looking up and down the hall, preparing to help Brute lift her limp body into the yellow laundry cart and cover her up.

Instinctively, Stinson elbowed Brute in the ribs and placed her right leg between his legs. Pushing herself back into him, she threw him off balance by bracing her left foot against the door of 3418 and simultaneously butting him in his chin with the back of her head. It worked, slightly. A surprised Brute dropped the towel off her face. Stinson took a deep breath and nailed him in the crotch by swinging her right fist downward and back. She heard him groan under the shout of Officer Bill McKay who suddenly emerged from under the nearby supply cart.

"Police! Freeze!" McKay shouted. Tormain wheeled around, a forty-four caliber pistol in his right hand. He fired, hitting Bill McKay in the left shoulder. McKay fired back twice, catching him in the right hip and thigh as Tormain turned to see Donner and Sheldon running down the hall toward him. Tormain fired two more shots, Donner went down against the wall with a heavy thud, the bullet entering his left shoulder just above his heart. Sheldon fired, hitting Tormain in the neck. Tormain jerked his gun around and clubbed McKay in the head, knocking him out before his fourth bullet grazed Sheldon's temple and ripped off the top of his left ear. Officer Woo emerged from the nearby stairwell firing his pistol at Tormain. The first bullet struck the base of his skull, and Jagger Tormain died before his body hit the floor.

Hearing the gunshots from inside suite 3418, Lt. Corey Burgess flung the door open and crouched down in time to see Brute clubbing Stinson in the face with his handgun, his back to the door of the suite. Blackburn, the second officer from the stairwell, attempted to grab Brute's left arm, but Brute landed a powerful blow to the officer's head, rendering him unconscious. Stinson jammed her right knee into Brute's crotch and slammed the palm of her right hand forcefully into his nose. Reeling, he fell backward into Burgess, sprawling them both on the floor just inside the suite. Stinson fell forward into the laundry cart. Corey's gun flew out of his hand from the unexpected impact of the two hundred and eighty pound man and landed on the second step leading down to the living area. Burgess was quickly on his hands and knees, attempting to get up. From his position, flat on his back, Brute kicked the door shut, rolled quickly to his left and caught Corey under his chin with the barrel of his gun. Still kneeling, Corey went over backwards again and slumped headfirst down the steps into the living area. Blood spurted from a deep gash under his chin.

From his post inside the bedroom, Avery Schneider opened the door and was already moving to aid Burgess, his gun drawn. Jack shoved Lisa down between the bed and the wall and told her to stay there as he ran toward the open bedroom door.

"Freeze!" Avery barked at Brute as Corey's limp body lay motionless on the floor in the lower level. Brute turned and fired three shots. His first bullet shattered the light above the fireplace, the second one caught Avery in his left forearm, and the third buried itself in the doorframe of the bedroom. Avery fired at close range, putting a bullet in the left shoulder of Brute who lunged forward and tackled the security officer by the legs, pulling him down.

In a split second, he was on top of Avery. Brute raised up on his knees and slammed the gun barrel down toward Avery's skull. Avery saw it coming and twisted away just as the gun caught the carpet near his left ear. Brute grunted, placed his left knee in the middle of the old man's chest, and raised the gun to strike again.

Jack Kramp watched in horror as Brute swung his gun at Avery's head and missed. He saw him raise his arm for the second attempt. Before he fully realized what he was doing, Jack raced the eight feet toward Brute. Because Brute was focused on the targeted head of Avery, he never saw Jack coming at him. Nor did he see the toes of Jack's right foot as they buried themselves deep into his throat. Brute's eyes bulged as he searched blindly for the source of the sudden and severe pain in his adams apple. Jack quickly regained his balance, turned, made a fist with his right hand and hammered it into Brute's right temple. Brute rolled off Avery to his right and fired twice at Jack, both bullets lodging in the door of the entry closet. As blood poured from Brute's mouth and he gasped for air while on one knee, he pointed the gun at Jack's chest and repeatedly pulled the trigger. Hearing nothing but empty clicks from Brute's weapon, Jack turned again, suddenly aware of the shouts of the other officers in the hall who were now pounding on the door of the suite. He leaned over, pulled down on the handle, and jerked it open. Brute, gurgling and coughing, eyed Corey Burgess's gun still laying on the second step of the living room. Avery scrambled to his knees, found his gun, and poked it into the back of Brute's head.

"Go ahead, you bastard," Avery whispered hoarsely, "Just give me any excuse to pull the trigger."

The next hour and a half were a blur of confusion. A dozen officers filled the room, along with five paramedics, and a general practitioner from the hotel. Tormain's body was taken to the precinct's morgue for identity verification. McKay, Donner, Stinson, Sheldon, Woo, Blackburn, and Avery were taken to a nearby emergency room for treatment of their injuries. In addition to the bullet wound in his left arm, Avery also had two broken ribs and a cracked sternum. Brute, having been read his Miranda Rights, was also taken to the hospital, handcuffed and under heavy guard. His larynx was crushed, he had difficulty breathing and kept losing consciousness. Corey Burgess was given twelve stitches on-site by an EMT. Although his chin and jaw were severely swollen, the police lieutenant insisted on staying on the scene to gather details for his report. Corey's wife, Rita, left her position at the front desk as soon as she heard her husband had been injured. She sat next to him on the sofa, her hand on his knee.

One of the paramedics packed Jack's right hand in ice. He severely sprained three fingers and his right wrist when he punched Brute's head. Four out of five toes on his right foot were bruised and swollen from the impact of connecting with Brute's esophagus with his Nike.

Lisa sat on the love seat in emotional shock. Tears slowly streamed down her face as she struggled to regain her composure from the violent ordeal. Jack sat on the sofa opposite Corey, relating the events to him after the lieutenant had taken the blow from the barrel of Brute's gun. Occasionally, Jack would lean over and touch Lisa's right arm with his left hand. She would give him a slight nod and a weak smile. She felt an unexplainable new union with this big, gentleman who had just saved her life.

They received word that Mick Thorkmon had been arrested in the parking garage. He had offered little resistance. For her part, Thorkmon's ex-wife, Shirley, was already booked and waiting downtown for further questioning. Delano Morrison was arrested as he was leaving his hotel with his luggage. He gave a full and complete confession to the arresting officers during a mental breakdown as they brought him into police headquarters.

The Wrap: Weeks later, after undergoing psychiatric evaluations, Delano Morrison was found mentally incompetent and unable to stand trial for his part in orchestrating the attempted abduction of Lisa Lisignoli. Five months after the highly publicized trial of the Thorkmons' and Clipper "Brute" Sullivan, who were each sentenced to lengthy prison terms, Morrison's body was found in the garden of a minimum security sanitarium in upstate New York where he was a patient. He had been brutally executed. Members of organized crime were suspected, but his killers were never found. Evidence of his gambling habits suggested that he owed a great deal of money to one of the syndicates. Clipper "Brute" Sullivan never regained the use of his voice box and could only speak in whispers for the rest of his life.

The FBI located the 1993 Buick owned by Jagger Tormain in an old barn near Lake Pleasant. An unregistered handgun was found under the spare tire in the trunk, and ballistics matched it to the slugs taken three years earlier from Buddy Shepard's skull. The only fingerprints on it belonged to Clipper Sullivan, leading authorities to believe that even though Jagger Tormain may have been directly involved with the murder of Buddy Shepard, Tormain was apparently clever enough to frame Sullivan alone for the actual killing. While in prison, Sullivan was also charged with first degree murder and is awaiting trial.

The West Park Plaza Hotel, and especially suite 3418, was besieged by reporters, hotel staff, and management. The hotel's maintenance staff assisted the police in removing the slugs in suite 3418 and repairing the damages. Professional carpet cleaners were standing by and waiting for the NYPD's crime unit to finish their investigation before they came up to shampoo the bloodstains out of the carpet in the corridor and the suite. Police Captain Anthony Marinaro arrived from the local precinct and took a position on the arm of the sofa next to Lt. Burgess. He asked a few questions, but allowed Corey to follow through with a complete verbal report.

At 11:20 a.m., in the midst of the havoc, a large bearded man with a dark complexion and wearing an expensive, tailored suit quietly entered 3418 unnoticed. He stood in the far corner of the kitchenette, hands clasped behind his back, patiently waiting for the crowd to thin before he would make his move.

Chapter Twenty

It was just prior to noon before the assortment of people left suite 3418. Only Lisa, Jack, and three members of the hotel cleaning staff remained. As Jack closed the door behind Corey and Rita Burgess, he suddenly noticed the tall bearded man standing in the kitchenette and immediately went on a defensive edge. Jack glanced nervously at Lisa on the love seat. Her back was to them. The large, well-dressed stranger smiled at Jack. He crossed over to him, his right hand extended.

"Mr. Kramp? I'm Frank Lisignoli." His deep voice echoed around the suite, causing Lisa to swiftly twist and look up, surprised at the unanticipated appearance of her father.

"Nice to meet you," Jack said. With his right hand still wrapped in an ice pack, Jack gripped the soft hand of the large man with his left hand. Jack was apprehensive about the sudden presence of Lisa's father and the added stress for her. "I've heard a lot about you," Jack added, with a nervous smile.

"I'm sure you have. And if it was from my daughter, I'm afraid all of it's true," Frank replied softly. "I've been hearing some very nice things about you, though, Mr. Kramp."

"It's Jack," Jack corrected him.

"Okay, Jack. Lieutenant Burgess holds you in very high regard. Both Lisa and I are deeply indebted to you for uncovering this… " Frank paused. He looked over at Lisa with soft, kind eyes. "This unbelievable and most unfortunate kidnapping and extortion plot."

"It was accidental. Coincidental, actually. If I hadn't stopped into Bannigan's for a nightcap on Sunday evening, I'm afraid we'd be having a very different conversation right now. Would you like to sit down?" Jack gestured toward the living area. The large man hesitated, glancing once again at Lisa who hadn't uttered a word since he had announced his presence.

"I was deeply concerned for my daughter's safety and came over to personally thank you," Frank sighed. "I've been extremely distressed about this entire situation since I first learned of it yesterday morning from Lieutenant Burgess. I even hired private bodyguards to keep an eye on her. Of course, not knowing of your plans, I became somewhat fearful when they told me she left her apartment at 6:50 this morning." He paused and gave Lisa a warm smile, then added, "You see, my daughter is not known to be an early riser and for her to be up and moving at that hour of the morning was quite unusual."

Jack nodded. He looked at Lisa and raised his eyebrows. Feeling helpless, he thought the next move should be hers. She glanced from Jack to her father and back to Jack before finally speaking.

"Why don't you have a seat, Dad?" she asked quietly, nodding her head in the direction of the sofa on her right.

"Are you sure?" Frank asked, searching her green eyes for further encouragement.

"Please," she replied coolly.

Jack, hobbling from the pain in his right toes, followed the large frame of Frank Lisignoli down to the lower living area. Jack sat on the sofa to the left of Lisa, opposite her father.

"I've heard the basic story," Frank Lisignoli began slowly, leaning forward, his hands folded in front of him. "If the two of you are up to it, I'd like to hear it all."

Jack and Lisa exchanged looks, then nodded in unison. Before either had a chance to speak, one of the cleaning crew announced it was going to get very noisy in the suite while they worked to remove the stains from the carpet. The hotel management had offered to move Jack and Lisa to another suite, but they declined. They felt a certain nostalgia in suite 3418. It was where they had begun their rewrite and editing work and it was where they were determined to finish it, on time. Upon hearing of the pending racket from the carpet cleaning machines and the workmen who had suddenly appeared to replace the shattered light fixture above the fireplace, Frank suggested they go to lunch.

"And I insist on both of you being my guests," Frank said as Lisa slowly rose. She still had on her leather coat. Jack limped over and retrieved his trench coat from the closet.

"How is your hand, Jack?" Frank inquired as they made their way slowly to the elevators.

"I'm not sure yet. My fingers are throbbing a little," Jack grinned.

"How did you injure your foot?" Frank asked, punching the elevator button.

"My toes are bruised," Jack said, his grin widening even more. "I tried to drop-kick a pair of two hundred and eighty pound tonsils across the room this morning."

"Same guy who ran into your right fist?" Frank chuckled.

"Same guy," Jack replied grimly. "Biggest, rock-hard S.O.B. I've ever seen."

Lisa spoke for the first time since they had left the suite.

"He would have killed all of us if Jack hadn't been there." She turned and faced Jack as the elevator arrived. "By the way, I really haven't said thank you for everything you've done."

Jack hung his head modestly and shrugged his shoulders. The trio rode the elevator down to the main lobby in silence.

"Shall we get you a wheelchair?" Frank volunteered as he watched Jack limp along toward the front entrance of the hotel.

"Oh, no thank you. I'm not incapacitated, just inconvenienced."

"Jack has an interesting philosophy, Dad," Lisa said, looking up at her father as they waited for the doorman to call them a cab. "He believes the ultimate tragedy in life is death. Everything preceding that is merely an inconvenience." She looked over at Jack. "Did I get it right?"

"Even better than the first time I said it," Jack grinned. Frank gave Jack an understanding smile. The two men were beginning to develop a certain amount of respect for each other as they climbed into their cab. Lisa, seated between her father and Jack, felt very small. She also felt very safe.

"Where to?" asked the young cab driver.

"Roberto's on 34th and Broadway," replied Frank. He reached inside the breast pocket of his wool suit for his phone. "I'll call ahead and get us a table."

Lunch at Roberto's was superb. Jack was surprised he had his appetite back. Lisa and Frank teased him about his generous consumption of garlic bread while they waited for their entrees to arrive.

Although Jack did most of the talking, Lisa interjected comments of her own as they relayed the entire chain of events. They started with Jack's visit to Bannigan's on Saturday night and lead up to the violence, trauma, injuries, and death in the corridor and inside suite 3418 shortly after 9:00 this morning.

Frank Lisignoli took in every word. He asked a question or two, but was mainly silent as the tale of the plot unfolded. He was horrified at the thought that, not only had a former employee stolen money from him, but they would also collaborate with a former significant other of Lisa's to take his only daughter, extort even more money from him, and most likely kill her in the process.

"We're all very fortunate," he finally said, after the server had removed their empty plates. Jack and Lisa nodded in agreement, lost in their own thoughts of what could have happened. Frank leaned over and placed his large hands over his daughter's who was seated across from him, her own hands curled around a cloth napkin on the table in front of her.

"How have you been, Lisa?" he asked softly. "I've missed you."

Lisa looked at her father, tears welling up in her beautiful green eyes. The lack of sleep, along with the exhausting events of the morning and the hurtful pain of the past, finally surfaced. She choked back a reply and put her head down, unable to say anything. She slowly pulled her right hand out from under her father's and placed it on top of his. Jack, sensing this should be a private moment between father and daughter, excused himself.

"I'm going to the bar for a bit. You two need time to talk, and I need a drink to kill the pain," Jack said, grinning as he held up his bandaged fingers and the ice pack which had melted into cold water. He stood and limped away.

Jack had ordered his second double scotch and water when Lisa tapped him on the shoulder. He glanced at his cell, startled to see that it was already 2:15 p.m.

"Let's go. My father is waiting in the lobby to say good-bye. He's going to walk a couple of blocks to an appointment."

Jack nodded, took a large gulp of his drink, threw a five dollar tip on the bar, and slid off his stool. He took Lisa by the hand as he hobbled toward the front entrance.

"How did things go in there for you?" he asked, nodding toward the dining room as they passed by.

"Quite well, actually. We are having dinner tonight. We're attempting to heal things between us."

"That's really great, Lisa," Jack said warmly, giving her hand a comforting squeeze. "I'm happy for you."

In the lobby, Frank Lisignoli shook Jack's left hand with his own while putting his right hand on Jack's shoulder and looking him in the eye.

"We owe you, Jack. I really don't know how to thank you enough," Frank said softly, his eyes were damp. "If there is anything I can do, name it."

"You've already thanked me, sir," Jack said. "Just having Lisa safe is good enough for me. I'm happy Burgess, Avery, and all those officers were there to help. They're the real heroes. Although, I feel terrible that a few of them were injured. I understand some of them were hurt pretty badly."

"It could have been much worse," Lisa said. "Now that I've had time to think about it, we're all very lucky to be alive." She turned to Jack. "I, too, am sad about the injuries sustained by Avery, Corey, and the other police officers. Remind me to send them all flowers. I think I heard that Avery, McKay, Sheldon, and Donner are all in the same ward at St. Francis Hospital."

"What about officer Stinson?" Jack asked, vaguely remembering her face after the attack. "Brute had beaten it pretty badly."

"I heard she had twenty-some stitches. I think they treated her in the emergency room and sent her home," Lisa said, frowning, trying to sort out the various news that had filtered her way after the morning's commotion. "I also heard she gave Brute a pair of matching bruised testicles from her repeated blows with her knees!" she added, grinning broadly.

Frank Lisignoli said a final good-bye to Jack. He leaned over and gave his daughter a quick hug, brushing his cheek against hers. Lisa smiled at her father and said she was looking forward to dinner. He waved one last time and walked briskly up the street.

"Nice guy," Jack commented as he hailed a cab from the curb in front of Roberto's.

Lisa nodded. "He's more like he was prior to my mother passing away. There's still a sadness there, but his apathy and self-centeredness is gone." She bit her lip, then added, "I think."

As Jack and Lisa entered the cab, Jack had an idea. He turned to Lisa, his eyes wide, his voice excited, and said, "Hey! We only have a few chapters left to edit, correct?"

"Six, I think, why?"

"Well, if we work hard on them this afternoon… " Jack paused, forming his thoughts into words. "What time is dinner with your father?"

"8:00," Lisa answered.

"Okay, so, if we work hard this afternoon and tomorrow, we should be able to finish, right?"

"I would hope so. We have to turn in our final edits by Thursday morning. Peter has proofreaders standing by to work through the weekend if necessary. I could come back to the hotel and we could work tonight, after dinner with my father."

Jack waved her off. "No, no, it will get too late. I don't want you rushing through dinner. It's important that you and Frank take your time and mend your fences."

"Mend your fences," Lisa repeated, smiling and looking out her window of the cab. "So what's your point?" she asked, returning her attention to Jack.

"I'd like to stop by St. Francis and see Avery, McKay, Sheldon, and Donner. It'll only take a few minutes. Maybe we can buy them chocolate or flowers downstairs in the gift shop before we go up. Besides, I think I need to get some stronger aspirin or some sort of painkillers for my hand. It's starting to really throb."

"Okay, Let's do that, Jack," Lisa said, smiling softly. Her color had started to return to her face which had been pale since she walked into suite 3418 this morning and found Jack, Avery, and Corey. Lisa leaned over the seat and gave the driver instructions to take them to St. Francis Hospital.

Lisa had heard correctly. Avery Schneider, Bill McKay, Mike Sheldon, and Joe Donner were in the same four bed ward on the seventh floor of St. Francis. They were quite surprised to see Lisa and Jack enter with four large green plants, one for each of the officers.

"How is everyone?" Jack asked with sincere concern.

"We've enjoyed better days," Avery replied with a grin. "But at least we're still on the green side of the grass!" He noticed Jack's limp and rested his eyes on Jack's bandaged right hand.

"That big ass had a real hard head, didn't he?" Avery said through a crooked smile. Jack nodded. "At least you shut him up for awhile," Avery continued. "We heard he might never talk again, thanks to your huge friggin' foot!" Avery broke into a grim laugh. "Guess he lost a lot of blood on the way to the hospital, too. He's still in intensive care."

"Yeah, I hear you kicked the shit out of his larynx," Bill McKay said. "Good for you. I hope he never does talk again. His partner drilled me in the shoulder. Pretty clean, though. I'll be able to go home in a day or two."

"When will you three be released?" Lisa inquired, looking back and forth from Avery to Sheldon to Donner.

"Doc says he'll probably let me get out of here tomorrow," Avery replied. "They want to keep me here overnight for observation. I got lucky. The slug went clean through my arm." Avery lifted his left arm and indicated the point of entry just above the top of his wrist. He then turned his arm to show where the bullet exited on the back side, just below the elbow. "My ribs and cracked sternum will have to heal on their own at home."

"Donner wasn't as lucky," Bill McKay said in a near whisper, nodding to the man in the bed across from him.

"I took one in my left shoulder," Donner said hoarsely. "Shattered a bone. They're going to have to put a pin in it once the swelling goes down. I'll be here close to a week."

"What about you, officer Sheldon?" asked Jack to the man in the bed next to Donner, his head wrapped in a white gauze bandage.

"Hoping to get out of here tomorrow," he replied quietly. "The bullet just grazed my temple. Another half inch and we wouldn't be having this conversation. Doctors are worried about infection. And my ear is missing a piece but at least I can still hear."

"I'm sorry," Jack said, surveying the room of four brave men who had sworn to serve. "Thank you for all your help. We really appreciate it."

"Occupational hazard," Joe Donner said with a shrug of his right shoulder, a small grin appearing on his face. "I've been on the force for seven years. It had to happen sometime. My number just came up this morning. And none of us suspected Tormain and Sullivan would be that nuts to try and take on all of us at once."

Jack nodded and turned to look at Lisa as she spoke with Avery. Jack wondered about the kind of men who are attracted to the service of law and order. They had to accept more harsh realities than ordinary people. Police officers take huge risks for granted everyday. Some, like Donner, recognizing the fact that one day, their number will be up.

It was 3:40 when Jack and Lisa said good-bye to the four police officers and caught a cab back to the West Park Plaza Hotel. After stopping in the gift shop of the hotel to buy ibuprofen for Jack, they rode the elevator to the 34th floor. They found the suite spotless. It had been thoroughly cleaned, repaired, and painted. The smell of industrial cleanser and fresh paint hung heavily in the air. Jack opened the French doors to allow fresh air inside.

"I'll finish inputting chapter twenty. It'll take me less than an hour," Lisa said as she settled down at her desk. She turned on the Mac and flipped on the printer. "Maybe you can start on twenty-one?"

Jack took the first seven pages of chapter twenty-one off her desk and found his own chair. With highlighter and pencil in hand, he leaned back, propped his feet up on his desk, and began to read.

Lisa turned slightly at her desk and studied Jack for a long time. In just eight days, this man from Minnesota had made a significant impact in her life. He saved her life just hours ago. And now, he sat there, acting as if nothing traumatic had ever happened today. He was already working toward tomorrow. Both of them knew that tomorrow was filled with uncertainty. But Lisa Lisignoli, senior editor for Brownstone Publishing of New York, was certain of one thing, she had fallen deeply in love with Jack Kramp.

"Loving together and living together are two separate issues," Lisa mumbled to herself as she studied the computer screen in front of her. "He's right. We're from two different worlds. I don't know how it could ever work between us."

A few feet away, Jack Kramp's mind concentrated on the printed words before him, but his heart was trying to read the feelings he had for Lisa. He knew his feelings were becoming stronger and more clear as each hour passed that he was with her.

"How in the hell could I ever get her to live in Minneapolis?" Jack mused as he glanced at Lisa. He grinned. "Maybe she'll like Minnesota if I can get her to visit." There was a forced glimmer of hope glistening deep in his heart.

"What does this say?" Lisa asked Jack, holding a page of the manuscript in front of him. "I can't read it."

Jack squinted at his scribbling in the margins. He looked up at Lisa and smiled, somewhat embarrassed.

"I can't remember," he said slowly.

"What do you mean?" Lisa persisted. "You wrote it."

"Yeah, but with my left hand." Jack held up his bandaged right hand and pointed to it with his left finger.

"Oh, I'm sorry, Jack. I forgot," Lisa said apologetically. "How is the pain?"

"I think I froze my fingers," Jack replied. "I'm going to take some more ibuprofen. I forgot to ask for something stronger when I was at the hospital this afternoon." He stood and walked toward the closet and his trench coat, hoping he had left the small bottle in one of his pockets.

"It's 6:45," Lisa called after him. "I'm going to have to leave in a few minutes. I'm going home to change before meeting my father."

Jack turned and leaned against the door frame of the entry closet. He thrust his hands in his pants pockets and grinned at her.

"What is that look for?" Lisa inquired from her desk chair.

"I was just thinking. I'm happy for you. I hope you two work everything out tonight."

"So do I, Jack. I want my father back, the one I knew when I was growing up."

"You'll have him back, I'm sure. I can tell he loves you very much."

Lisa nodded. She gave Jack a small smile and returned her attention to the computer screen. Jack began going through his coat pockets in search of the painkillers.

Lisa finished her inputs on chapter twenty-one. She stood, switched off the computer, leaned over, and flipped off the printer. Jack limped toward the kitchenette. Grinning at Lisa, he held the palm of his left hand open to reveal four tablets.

"These should help," Jack said as he stopped at the sink and filled a cup of water. Lisa nodded, walking over to him.

"Let's take a look at your hand," Lisa said as she gently took his right wrist and slowly unwrapped the bandage. Jack stared deeply into her large green eyes. They looked like matching pools of perfect emeralds. "Can you flex your fingers?" Jack was suddenly conscious of Lisa asking him a question.

"Huh?" Jack said, knowing he hadn't heard her. Jack had become lost in Lisa's eyes and his own dreams.

"Your fingers. Can you move them?" she repeated. Jack looked down at the fingers on his right hand. Only his pinkie looked semi-normal. The other three fingers were swollen to twice their size. They were turning black and blue with shades of green and purple around the edges. He slowly started to move them. They felt clumsy, stiff, and bulky. It was painful, but Jack was pleased with the dexterity with which he was able to at least wiggle them.

"They aren't real pretty, but at least they're not broken," he chuckled. "I think they're a little smaller than this afternoon when I changed the ice packs."

Lisa slowly lifted Jack's hand with the swollen fingers toward her face. She bent her head and softly kissed his knuckles. Jack placed his left hand on the nape of her neck. She looked up at him, her eyes wide, her full lips slightly parted. He lowered his head and kissed her, slowly and tenderly. She responded by melting into his arms, her left hand still holding his injured fingers. Lisa reached up and circled Jack's neck with her right arm, and they both felt the passion exploded between them as their bodies became molded together. Their passion was forged by the emotions they had been denying for days.

Lisa's breath became rapid and hot against Jack's neck. He wasn't conscious of his breathing, but he was keenly aware of the warmth of Lisa's body next to his, the taste of her lips, and the scent of her hair. They pulled apart for a split second to find each other's eyes, then their lips met again, exploring the rampant fire of their inner desire. Lisa buried her face into Jack's massive chest. Wells of tears flowed from her closed eyes and immediately soaked the front of his sweatshirt. Ignoring the pain in his right hand, Jack encircled her small back with his large arms. He held Lisa and let her softly cry, feeling the stress and tension of the day drain away from her. With his head bent, Jack ensconced his face in Lisa's beautiful long black hair.

"I'm sorry, Jack," Lisa sobbed. "I just don't know... today was... and my father... and now, there's you and..."

"I know," Jack said softly. "I know."

Their timeless moments of tenderness and understanding were suddenly interrupted by the ringing of Jack's cellphone on his desk. Jack groaned. Lisa stepped back, tearing herself away from his embrace. She turned and rushed into the bathroom. Jack grabbed the telephone on the third ring, already knowing who was on the other end.

"Hello?"

"Daddy?" An excited, familiar voice filled his ears.

"Hey! Tammy! How is everything?" Jack asked enthusiastically, staring at the bathroom door. He was torn between his children and the woman on the other side of the white door.

"We're fine, Dad. How are you?" Tammy replied, sensing a distraction in her father's voice.

"Uh... fine, Tammy. You're sure there is nothing wrong?"

"No. Did we catch you at a bad time?"

"Well, sort of, Tammy. Listen, would it be okay if I called you back in just a few minutes? I'm just finishing up here," Jack said. "I have so much to tell you."

"Okay, Dad. We'll be here. Take your time," said Tammy, understandingly.

"Give me ten minutes or less," Jack said apologetically. "I'll call you right back, I promise."

They said good-bye and Jack hung up. Striding stiffly toward the bathroom, he knocked on the door just as Lisa opened it. She managed a petite smile.

"Are you okay?" Jack asked softly, his palms on her shoulders as they stood facing each other in the doorway. He searched her eyes.

"I'll be fine," Lisa said. She stood on her tiptoes and gave Jack a hug, whispering in his ear, "I've got to go."

Although Jack didn't want to let Lisa go, he gradually released his left arm from around her waist. He draped his right arm around her and walked her toward her coat, flexing his right fingers as he limped along. In front of the small closet, their eyes locked again, a comfortable warmth engulfing them.

"I'll walk you down to the lobby," Jack said as he helped Lisa with her leather jacket.

"No, you won't," Lisa said firmly. "You are going to get off that foot." Jack nodded, knowing she was right.

"By the way, not that it's any of my business, but who was on the phone?" she asked.

"My daughter, Tammy. I'm going to call my kids back in a few minutes."

"Good," Lisa said as she placed her fingers on the handle of the door. "Just do it sitting down with your foot up and," she paused and glanced at his hand, "Your right hand up, too!"

Jack chuckled as Lisa opened the door. They stood facing each other for a brief second. Once again, the warmth between them began to burn and the unexpected sexual tension became uncomfortable.

"Well, take care of yourself tonight," advised Jack.

"I will," Lisa responded softly. "Good-bye." Lisa put her index finger to her lips and then placed it on Jack's.

"Bye," Jack said. He felt his heart begging her not to leave.

Jack stood in the doorway of suite 3418 and watched Lisa walk down the corridor to the elevators. She waved and smiled at him one last time before stepping into the waiting elevator. Jack remained in the doorway for a few more minutes. He studied the floor, thinking about all the events that had ensued just ten hours earlier. To Jack, it felt as though it was a lifetime ago. He thought about Jagger Tormain, dying just a few feet from where he stood. He remembered Brute and all the faces of the officers who had assisted in the violent arrest. Jack slowly shook his head and closed the door.

"Only the bad guy died," Jack said to himself as he hobbled toward the bedroom. "For the rest of us, it's just an inconvenience."

Smiling thoughtfully as he remembered Lisa's orders, Jack switched on the bedroom lamp and lay down on his bed. He noticed it was already 7:10. Jack dug his cell phone from his pocket and auto-dialed his home number. Holding his right hand toward the light of the lamp, he looked at his distended and contused fingers.

"Just an inconvenience," Jack repeated as he heard the first ring on the other end.

Chapter Twenty-One

Throbbing pain in Jack's right hand brought him out of a deep, troubling sleep. With his heart pounding, he opened his eyes and tried to remember where he was. Jack's mind was racing. Panic made his entire body tense as he shook the cobwebs from his foggy brain and began collecting his thoughts.

Flexing his right hand slowly, the increased pain sharpened his memory and he began to relive the events of the day. The lamp on the nightstand was still on. The digital clock read 9:42 p.m. Groaning, Jack struggled to a sitting position on the edge of the bed, rubbing his eyes and running his fingers through his hair with his left hand. As his feet hit the floor, he became conscious of a rhythmic pain emitting from his right toes. He was aware his shoes were off, but he couldn't remember removing them. Still fully clothed in his sweatshirt, jeans, and white socks, he sat on the bed pondering his next physical move.

"You're in bad shape, Jack," he grunted to himself as he looked back at the clock. Noticing his cell on the nightstand, he tried remembering how long he had talked with his children earlier that evening. Jack couldn't recall what time it had been when he had hung up after telling them the entire story of the plot to kidnap Lisa and extort ransom money from her father. He grinned to himself as he imagined Jim and Tammy's wide eyes as he told them about the capture of Brute and the death of Jagger Tormain. Toward the end of their conversation, Jack recalled that Tammy made him swear he wasn't just telling them a tall tale.

"It does sound pretty friggin' far fetched," Jack muttered as he struggled to a standing position. He stretched as best he could and shuffled slowly into the bathroom to take more ibuprofen. Jack cursed softly under his breath as he attempted to open the bottle with his one good hand. He washed two tablets down with a full cup of water and stumbled toward the toilet.

"This is worse than a hangover," Jack said as he painfully removed his clothes and turned on the shower. He looked at his face in the mirror. He saw dark circles under his eyes and a thick, black stubble on his face.

"You look like hell, Jack," he said as he turned and stepped gingerly into the shower. As the hot water, shampoo, and soap covered his aching body, Jack began to feel better. He suddenly became aware of his hunger. He thought of the Garden Cafe downstairs and winced as he remembered his sore toes. He resolved to stay in his suite and order a pizza from Louie's.

By 10:30 p.m. Jack was seated on a sofa in the lower living area, his right foot propped up on the coffee table. He watched CNN on the television as blue and yellow flames danced around the gas log in the fireplace. Munching slowly on his pizza and sipping a beer, Jack was finally relaxing. Wide awake and fully conscious, his thoughts drifted from Lisa to Mary to his children at home in Minneapolis. He thought of Avery in the hospital, Corey Burgess, and the lifeless body of Jagger Tormain. And Jack pondered on the massive, unexpected warmth of Lisa's estranged father, Frank Lisignol. One by one, the details of the day went through his mind, each being filed away in his memory bank; like little notes you'd stuff in the slots and drawers of an old pigeon hole desk.

Jack finished his pizza and sat watching the news from around the world on television. He flipped through several local channels, hoping to catch the story of the attempted kidnapping of Lisa. He found none. Midway through his third beer, Jack began to feel restless. He stood and hobbled up the steps to the French doors. He slowly drew open the heavy drapes and looked out over the lights of the city. Taking a big swallow of his beer, Jack felt tears welling up in his eyes, a large knot constricted his throat. Surprised, Jack caught his reflection in the glass of the small square windows before him. He lifted his can of beer in a toast toward the windows of the French doors.

"Okay, Mary, you're right as always. It's time I move on with my life," he said quietly. "You've been after me for years to get my priorities straight. I will start now."

Holding the can of beer between his right forearm and the right side of his chest, Jack bent the small aluminum pull-tab back and forth with his left hand until it finally broke off. He slipped it into the front pocket of his dress slacks, took the can in his left hand and walked toward the kitchen. Standing over the sink, Jack poured the remainder of the beer down the drain. He tossed the empty can into the recycling bin next to the waste basket.

"Endings and beginnings," Jack whispered as he limped back down toward the sofa. He picked up his pizza box along with the two other empty beer cans and carried them up to the kitchenette.

A sudden heaviness came over him as he realized that he would be leaving New York in three days. He slowly lumbered back down to the living area and turned off the TV. He watched the fire flicker around the gas log for a few more minutes, then picked up the remote and switched off the flames. Jack painfully climbed the three stairs, closed the heavy drapes over the double doors, flipped off the lights, and limped into the bedroom. He carefully removed his bathrobe and hung it up, wincing now and then from the pain radiating from his right hand. Jack took two more ibuprofen and crawled into the massive bed. Glancing at the clock, he noted that it was 11:48 p.m.

Reaching to turn off the lamp, Jack hesitated. He picked up his cell phone, closed his eyes, and dialed the number by memory with his left hand while propping himself up in bed with two large pillows. As it rang, Jack's heart began to sink and he thought about hanging up. After the fourth ring, a voice answered.

"Hello?" Lisa answered hurriedly.

"Lisa," Jack said softly. "Did I wake you?"

"Jack?" Her voice filled with surprise.

"Yeah, it's me."

"Sorry, it didn't sound like you. No, I wasn't even in bed. I just arrived home a few minutes ago."

"So," Jack spoke slowly, searching for a conversation starter. "How did things go tonight between you and your father?"

"Things went very well, Jack," Lisa said confidently. "He's making every effort to get his life in order. He's been in treatment for several months."

"That's good," Jack replied, thinking about the beer he poured down the sink thirty minutes ago and his silent vow.

"He seems tired, though," Lisa said thoughtfully.

"It could be just the strain of the past few days," Jack said.

"I hope so. By the way, my father wants us to join him for dinner tomorrow night. Can you make it?"

"Sure, I'd like that," Jack replied, a hint of excitement creeping into his voice.

"My father is quite impressed with you, Jack. And, I can tell you from experience, it takes a great deal to impress him. He has very high standards."

Jack felt himself flush from the compliment, yet his chest swelled with pride. He was equally impressed and intrigued with Lisa's father.

"I think he's a great guy, too," Jack said.

"He is. I'm seeing him in a different light now," Lisa said quietly. "More as a person rather than my father. It's quite an emotional adjustment for me."

"Sometimes we become so caught up in our own sorrow, we tend to forget what other people are going through," Jack said kindly. "You lost a mother and a brother, but your father also lost a wife and a son, and through your own individual suffering and pain, you somehow lost each other."

"You're right, Jack. I was selfishly looking to him for comfort and understanding when he needed me for strength and support."

"Well, it sounds like things are headed in the right direction for the two of you," Jack replied, not wanting to get into another long conversation about death and dying. "When life showers us with adversity, I guess we just need to dance in the rain," he added thoughtfully.

"You're so much deeper than I had ever imagined, Jack. It's a gift to the point of being unnerving at times, but still, it's quite impressive. I'll remember that one, too," Lisa replied quietly.

"Sometimes thoughts just spew out of my mouth without me thinking about them first," Jack chuckled. "And once in a great while, they even make sense!"

"There are two more things, Jack," Lisa said slowly.

"What are they?" he asked, sensing her nervousness.

"Well, I received a letter from a publisher today. They've accepted my manuscript. I had submitted it in July under the pseudonym of Carolyn Conners."

"Hey! That's awesome!" Jack exclaimed as he sat upright in bed. "What's the title?"

"*A Good Time to Cry*," Lisa replied softly.

"So, what's the problem?" Jack asked, sensing Lisa's distress on the other end.

"The publisher." Jack barely heard her over the lump bulging in her throat.

"Who is it?" he asked.

"Tanner and Whitehall," she replied. "I guess at the time I was angry with my father, and I sent it to them because I felt I had something to prove."

Jack let out a soft whistle. "Balls on a goose! What'd your father say?"

"I didn't tell him," Lisa said. She paused, then added, "Yet."

"Wait. He doesn't have a clue his publishing company is going to produce his own daughter's book?" Jack asked in surprise. "Are those the two things?"

"No," she replied. "That's only the first."

"What's the other?"

"My father wants me to come and work with him at Tanner and Whitehall."

"Wow! In what capacity?" Jack asked curiously, taking a deep breath.

"He's asked me to become the managing editor for one of their new imprint divisions."

Jack whistled again. "What are you going to do?"

"I don't know, Jack," she whimpered. "I just don't know."

"What do you think Brownstone will say?"

"I'm sure Peter Tunnell wouldn't be real happy. But, I think deep down, perhaps he's always known there was a possibility of me joining my father."

"Is there a rule that your current employer, being a publishing company, can't produce a book by one of their own editors?"

"Not necessarily a rule, Jack," replied Lisa. "It's more a question of ethics. Unless the book was about rewriting, editing, or publishing, maybe. I just don't know. I guess I'll have to sit down with Peter in a few days and discuss it all with him. And I'd also have to look into my contractual obligations as well as my non-compete agreement."

"What about your father?" Jack asked.

"Well, I suppose I'll have to have a few lengthy conversations with him, too. What would you suggest?"

There was a long pause as Jack thought about the new situation. He grinned suddenly, thinking how strange it was that Lisa was asking him for advice.

"I guess if it were me," Jack replied slowly, "I'd make up my own mind first about what I really wanted to do with the rest of my life. What would make

ME happy and be the most rewarding for ME. And, since blood is thicker than water, I'd probably discuss it with my father first. I think he'd be hurt if you discussed your options with Peter Tunnell before you ran everything by him."

"You're right," Lisa said, taking a deep breath and relaxing a little. "I need to make up my mind and determine what I really want to do."

"After all, you do have three choices," Jack said matter of factly.

"Three?" echoed a slightly confused Lisa.

"Yeah," replied Jack. "One, you stay employed at Brownstone and continue to write. Two, you go to work for your father and try to find the time to write, or three, you retire from the publisher's rat race and do nothing but write."

There was dead silence on the other end as Lisa pondered the three obvious choices Jack had just presented. Choice number three had not entered her mind as an option. A small spark ignited deep within her soul as she quietly considered this as a real possibility. A picture suddenly flashed through her mind. She was seated at a computer in a small study while lazy snowflakes drifted outside her window. In the distance, she could see the silhouette of the Minneapolis skyline.

"Lisa?"

The sound of Jack's voice brought her back to the present. She smiled at her sudden thoughts of an unintended future. She couldn't tell Jack. She wouldn't tell Jack.

"I'm here," Lisa said. "I was just thinking."

"Well, you certainly have a lot to think about," Jack declared, "But you also have to get some sleep. We have one day, tomorrow, to finish the last five chapters. I need you well rested so we can crank them out."

"I know, Jack," Lisa replied with a tired giggle. "Let's get an earlier start tomorrow. Say, 8:00 in the morning?"

"8:00 instead of 9:00?" Jack asked in surprise. "Isn't that a little too early for you, Lisa?"

"Don't worry about me. I can rise earlier when I have to. I'll see you at 8:00. Why don't you order some breakfast up for us."

"Sounds great. What would you like?"

"Pancakes!" Lisa said with a spirited, husky voice. "I've been craving pancakes and strawberries for days!"

"You got it!" Jack laughed. "Pancakes it is for tomorrow morning."

"And plenty of hot tea," Lisa added.

"Hotcakes and tea," Jack repeated with an exaggerated British accent. "Oh how royal of us!"

"Say good-night, Jack," Lisa interjected, laughing at his impromptu dialect.

"Good-night, Jack," he replied, still using his English voice.

"8:00 a.m. sharp," she repeated more seriously, but still wearing a warm smile.

"8:00 a.m. sharp. Hot cakes and tea with Miss Carolyn Conners. I shall certainly make arrangements for it, post haste." Jack couldn't let go of his newly acquired British accent.

"Good-night, Jack," Lisa said with a soft whisper. "I... I really... appreciate you."

There was a slight pause on Jack's end. He sucked in his breath.

"Good-night, Lisa," he whispered. He heard the click on the other end. Jack reached over, hung up the phone, and turned off the lamp.

"I love you," he whispered quietly in the darkened room. Jack Kramp burrowed down under the covers and tried to forget about his aching hand and sore toes. His thoughts were only of Lisa. He imagined her typing at her computer in a small study while lazy snowflakes drifted outside her window. In the distance, she could see the silhouette of the Minneapolis skyline.

Breakfast arrived promptly at 8:00 a.m. the next morning. Jack arose an hour earlier and waited. He felt ready for the new day, having dressed in a yellow sweater and navy slacks. Jack thoughtfully transferred the pull-tab from his last can of beer from the pocket of his gray slacks he had worn the previous night and tucked it into the right front pocket of his navy pants. Jack paced nervously, continually glancing at the time. He changed the water in the vase that still held the colorful orchids he had given Lisa a few days ago. The open drapes allowed the morning sun to enter through the windows on the French doors, brightening the room. At 8:05, Jack recognized Lisa's knock on the door of his suite. He quickly hobbled across the room and opened the door wide.

"Sorry I'm late," Lisa said breathlessly as she hurried inside. "I had trouble getting a cab." She clutched a file folder in one hand and carried a large, paisley colored garment bag slung over her other shoulder.

"Breakfast is served," Jack grinned as he helped her out of her black trench coat and hung it in the entry closet along with her garment bag. He watched Lisa walk over to the small table where Jack had placed the tray of stainless covered plates. Noticing her trim figure in bright blue slacks and a matching blue sweater, Jack forgot all about asking her the reason for the garment bag.

"It smells delicious!" Lisa said, turning to look at Jack. She flashed him a wide, beautiful smile. Lisa had taken extra time with her make-up and hair that morning, she wanted to look perfect for this man who had suddenly become a very important part of her life. Her efforts did not go unnoticed by Jack. Without saying a word, he crossed over to where she was standing and gently took her in his arms. Offering no resistance, Lisa looked up at him knowingly. He bent down and kissed her. She returned his embrace and tender kiss, holding him tightly.

"Good morning," he whispered softly, planting yet another kiss below her ear on the side of her neck.

"It certainly is," Lisa said, pulling back and winking at him.

Jack released his left arm that had encircled Lisa's small waist. "We better eat before our food gets cold," he said. Lisa nodded and began to uncover the plates of pancakes and strawberries.

Lisa and Jack began reviewing chapter twenty-two over breakfast, each taking eleven pages and only making small talk between edits. Taking the last sip of his tea, Jack stood and crossed over to his desk, limping only slightly.

"How are your toes?" Lisa asked as she followed him toward her desk.

"These little piggies went to market and had the hell beat out of 'em by the butcher," Jack replied, laughing as he sat down in his chair and lifted his right foot in her direction. Lisa laughed aloud, a pleasant twinkle in her eyes. "Actually, they feel much better this morning," he added.

"What about the hand?" Lisa inquired as she crossed over to him and held out her right hand, insisting Jack place his bruised fingers in her palm.

"Stiff," he responded, flexing them slightly as he gently lay them in her small hand.

"Can I get you some pain meds before we continue?"

"Nope, I just had some about an hour ago. Let's get these chapters done. What time are we having dinner with your father tonight?"

"8:00 p.m. unless he hears from us. I told him we'd probably have a long day. That's why I have the garment bag. I'd like to change clothes and freshen up here, if you don't mind."

Jack nodded, turning slightly in his chair and looking over his right shoulder toward the closet where he had hung the forgotten bag. He wondered what sort of exquisite dress it held. He turned his attention back to Lisa.

"Where are we planning on having dinner?" Jack asked.

"My father is meeting us here in your suite at ten to eight. I think he's planning on the three of us dining down in the Madison Room. It's very good." Lisa paused, glancing solemnly out the windows of the French doors. She took a deep breath, turned to Jack with a weak smile, and asked, "Have you eaten there yet?"

"Just once, I think it was last Thursday evening. It was very good. I think."

"What do you mean, 'you think?'" Lisa frowned at him.

"That was the night of disasters. I ended up talking to Marsha, you, and Peter Tunnell in successive phone conversations. Afterwards, I went down and ate in the Madison Room. Immediately after that, I went into Bannigan's Bar for about a half dozen more drinks. But I think I remember the food being excellent. How about you? Do you eat in the Madison Room often?"

"I used to," Lisa said quietly. "I haven't been there since..." she hesitated, searching for the words and strength to continue. Jack waited patiently. "Since the night Buddy Shepard was murdered," Lisa said with a distinct sadness in her voice, "He, Roy Kinter, one of the other editors from Brownstone, and I had dinner together. That was the last time."

Jack nodded, understanding Lisa's reluctance to face a past still filled with unpleasantness. "We can easily go somewhere else," he offered.

"No," Lisa shook her head firmly. "I want to eat there again. It's a wonderful restaurant. I have to stop hiding from ghosts."

"Okay, then," Jack smiled warmly at her. "We'll go down and face the memory of Buddy Shepard together."

"Thank you," Lisa whispered, nodding her head. She looked at her computer screen and sighed deeply. "We better get to work."

"I'm on it," Jack grinned, holding a freshly sharpened pencil up with his left hand.

For the next four hours Lisa and Jack worked feverishly on the edits and rewrite for chapters twenty-two and twenty-three. Working against a tight deadline, they took their individual responsibilities seriously. Their only communication was concerning the business at hand, and it was rapid and to the point.

They were interrupted around 9:30 by a light knock on the door. Jack stood and headed toward the door when Anita slowly opened it. She smiled shyly at Lisa and Jack as she dragged her supply cart behind her into the room.

"Do you mind if I clean now, Mr. Jack?" she asked.

"Come in, come in!" Jack said, waving his beckoning hand at her.

"You hadda little excitement here yesterday, no?" Anita asked as she stacked fresh towels from her cart into her arms.

"Lots of action," Jack said, smiling at Anita as he settled back into his desk chair and propped up his sore foot. Anita nodded, smiled, and hurried about her work. She was finished and gone in less than fifteen minutes. By 12:30, Lisa was ready to add their corrections to the jump drive. Jack stood and slowly crossed over to the counter in the kitchenette where he picked up the room service menu.

"Shall we order up and keep going?" he asked.

"I don't think we have much choice," Lisa replied, without looking up from her screen. "We have only a few hours to complete the last two chapters."

"And the epilogue," reminded Jack.

"And the epilogue," repeated Lisa. "How many pages?" she asked as she flipped open her briefcase and began searching.

"Five or six, I think. What would you like to eat?"

"Just a salad and a couple of breadsticks for me," Lisa replied. Jack nodded. He dialed room service and ordered Lisa's salad, oil and vinegar dressing, plus breadsticks. For himself, he ordered a steak sandwich and a glass of tomato juice.

Jack had just returned to his desk chair and put his feet back up on the corner of his desk when the room telephone rang again. Lisa glanced at Jack and motioned for him to stay seated.

"I'll get it," she said rising and walking toward the phone. "You keep that foot up. Hello?"

"Lisa?"

"Speaking," Lisa replied in her business tone.

"Good afternoon, Lisa, it's Marsha."

"Hello, Marsha!" Lisa winked at Jack.

"I was just heading out for lunch but I wanted to call and see how things were going. I understand you had just a terrible fright yesterday."

"It was pretty awful..." Lisa's voice trailed off.

"Oh, honey, I'm so sorry. Is there anything I can do?"

"No, I'm fine, really. Jack sprained three fingers and some toes during the fight."

"Oh, yes! I hear he was quite the hero! We are so proud of him. And we're so very grateful you're safe."

"How did you know about it?"

"Peter Tunnell called me into his office this morning. He had just finished a phone conversation with your father. Apparently, Peter knew something was going on. The police told him a little about it on Monday. We're all dying to hear the entire story. I understand your father was rather vague with Peter on details."

"Well, maybe we'll have a chance to do that sometime," Lisa replied, wishing to change the subject. Marsha took her cue.

"The other reason for my call is that I'm wondering how your edits are going. I'm sure the terrible trauma of yesterday has put you two behind schedule."

"Not really," Lisa said, shooting a quick look at Jack. "We're just starting the last two chapters and plan to have them and the epilogue completed by this afternoon or early evening. We'll deliver the jump drive and printed copies tomorrow morning."

"Excellent!" exclaimed Marsha. "Shall we set it for 10:00 a.m.?"

"That will be fine," replied Lisa, "We'll be there."

"Wonderful! We'll look forward to it. We'll give Jack the grand tour, and maybe we can go over the contracts with him at lunch. Please give him my regards, won't you?"

"I will. And, I'm sure lunch will be fine." Lisa hung up the phone and grinning at Jack, she walked back to her desk while filling him in on the details of the conversation he missed.

"Tomorrow is going to be a whirlwind for us around Brownstone, Jack," said Lisa. "We have to deliver the final corrections and jump drive to Marsha by 10:00 a.m.. There will be a tour, a luncheon to discuss your future book contracts, and a meeting with production. You should wear a suit. They may want to do a few publicity shots. Then on Friday, you better plan to be in our offices again for a PR meeting. We'll need to go over printing schedules and plans for a debut at the Mall of America in Minneapolis just prior to the Christmas holidays."

"Will you be there?" Jack asked suddenly.

"I can try to be with you in most of the meetings."

"No, not tomorrow. I meant during the launch of my book in Minneapolis?" Jack persisted.

Lisa took a deep breath and exhaled slowly as she looked deep into his blue eyes. "I don't know, Jack. That's Marsha's job. I'm sure she'll be there. It's really not my department."

"I'm not asking you to come in a professional capacity. I'm asking if you will be there... for me. With me." Jack restated his question slowly, quietly. There was a long pause as they once again locked eyes. "I'd like you to be there," Jack finally added.

"I don't know, Jack. I just don't know. I'll have to see what my schedule is like during that time." Lisa turned and stared out the window. Jack waited, disliking the odd silence between them and her blunt uncertainty.

The stillness of the suite was broken by the arrival of room service with their food. Lisa and Jack brought their meals to their desks. Jack began working on trouble spots within chapter twenty-three as Lisa finished the input of twenty-two on the Mac. By 2:45 p.m., she was starting the final edits on the second half of chapter twenty-three. They settled into the familiar routine that they had come to know over the past several days. Jack made no further mention of Lisa coming to Minneapolis. He resigned himself to just be happy for the moments he was able to spend with her in the present.

At one point, Lisa casually opened her appointment book, careful not to let Jack see she was looking ahead to her schedule for mid-December. It looked fairly open. At 3:40, Jack hobbled over to the hotel phone and ordered a six pack of diet Pepsi from room service.

"I need some caffeine to stay awake," Jack muttered as he hung up the phone and glanced over at Lisa. She nodded as he disappeared into the bathroom, dug two more ibuprofen out of the bottle, and shuffled back to his desk.

"Pain level high?" Lisa inquired, turning to look at him.

"These should take care of it," Jack said stoically, placing the tablets on his desk, waiting to wash them down with the soon-to-arrive Pepsi.

"Are you certain you feel up to going tonight?" she asked, suddenly feeling that Jack had become indifferent toward her.

"I'll be fine, really. I'm looking forward to dinner with you and your father," Jack said, forcing a small grin.

"He feels greatly indebted toward you. I know he's looking forward to dinner this evening as well."

Jack nodded, wanting to say something more. He wanted to be taken out for dinner because of who he was as a person and not because someone felt they owed him something, so he silently clenched his teeth and held his tongue.

Lisa rose and answered the knock of room service at the door. She took the six pack of Pepsi, handed Jack one, set one on her desk, and placed the other four in the small refrigerator. She noticed the remaining beers, but said nothing as she returned to her desk. Jack was deep into his rewrite, looking a bit clumsy as he made corrections with his left hand cocked at a right angle over the manuscript pages. Lisa sat down at her desk, turning her attention back to her section of chapter twenty-four.

"I can't let this happen," Lisa thought as she tried to focus on the pages in front of her. "I can't let this man into my life any further than he already is. It just will not work. I have enough decisions to make between my father, my job, and my career. I don't want to have to make a choice with Jack." She turned and looked at Jack out of the corner of her eye, her heart pounding a little harder, a little faster.

"And yet," Lisa mumbled to herself, "Maybe I no longer have a conscious choice as far as Jack is concerned. It might be too late. My heart may have already made the choice for me."

Chapter Twenty-Two

How much time do we have?" Lisa asked Jack as she came out of the bathroom. Jack was standing with his back to her, staring out the windows of the French doors at the lights below, lost in deep thought. While Lisa finished inputting the changes of chapter twenty-five and the epilogue, Jack had showered and changed for dinner. He was dressed in his black double breasted suit with the bright red tie.

"Jack?" Lisa called to him a second time as she hunted in her garment bag for a pair of shoes. "The time?"

"Huh?" Jack turned suddenly and started to reach into the breast pocket of his jacket for his cell. His eyes fell upon Lisa across the room. He stopped, arm in midair, and let out a soft whistle as he abruptly exhaled. She was standing in front of the entry closet, a pair of shoes dangling from her right hand.

"You look incredibly beautiful," Jack said in a near whisper as he gazed at her. She was wearing a dark green strapless dress that showed off her bare shoulders, the neckline plunging just far enough to reveal the delicate crease between her shapely breasts. The dress was short, accentuating her perfect legs. Lisa's hair was brushed impeccably smooth, flowing behind her neck and down her back. It was pulled together on top and held in place by a gold clip. She wore a small emerald pendant surrounded by a gold setting and a pair of matching emerald earrings.

"Thank you," Lisa replied with an appreciative smile, "But please stop drooling long enough to give me the time. I can't find my watch or my cell phone."

"It's 7:40," Jack said as he tore his eyes away from her long enough to glance at the time on his cell.

"My father will be here in ten minutes or less," Lisa said as she scurried toward the bathroom again. "I have to finish my make up. Then, I'll be ready." She paused in the doorway and gave Jack a serious look. "Are you okay?" she asked.

"Yeah," Jack replied pensively. "I was just thinking. It feels odd to be done with the book."

Lisa nodded. "It often feels like that, especially for first time authors. You may experience a wide range of emotions, from joy and elation to sadness and melancholy. You'll likely go through a few mood swings for a day or two. I've seen it hundreds of times."

"Great," replied Jack dryly. "I write a book and then I'm forced to go through male menopause." Lisa wrinkled her nose at him, gave a quick smile, and disappeared back into the bathroom.

Jack returned to watching the lights of Manhattan, Queens, and the Bronx. He winced slightly as he tried to wiggle his sore right toes that were crammed into his snug black winged-tipped shoes. A knock on the door caused Jack to flinch. He limped quickly across the room and peered through the peephole at the large frame of Frank Lisignoli. Without hesitation, Jack opened the door.

"Good evening, Jack," Frank greeted him warmly, remembering to shake with his left hand as Jack stepped back and invited him in.

"Nice to see you again," Jack replied.

"Is Lisa ready?" Frank asked as he looked at his watch. "We have reservations downstairs for 8:00."

"She'll be ready on time," Jack chuckled as the two men walked down into the lower living area and sat down.

"I'm sure she will. My daughter has developed a wonderful habit of being extremely punctual, almost to the point of being obsessive-compulsive," Lisa's father replied with a large grin.

"So I've noticed," Jack said.

"I suspect you have. The only time her punctuality fails slightly is in the morning," Frank continued. "The earlier it is, the later she becomes."

"That's not true any longer, Dad." Lisa's voice behind them caused Jack and her father to quickly turn their heads to look at her.

"You look very lovely this evening, my dear," Frank said, smiling and nodding his head as he rose. Jack remembered his manners and stood as well.

"You're pretty dashing yourself, Father," Lisa replied, returning his smile. "I like the black bowtie. Nice touch."

"Thank you," he said, "But I can't compete with Jack here. He looks exceptionally dignified, especially with that bright red tie."

"Sometimes I clean up pretty good," Jack said, slightly embarrassed. "The bright tie keeps me from falling asleep."

"He's certainly not expecting any exciting topics during our dinner conversation tonight, is he?" Lisa teased, winking at her father. The three of them laughed aloud.

"Shall we?" Frank asked as he walked up the three steps and held his arm out for his daughter.

"Where is your coat, Dad?" Lisa inquired as she hooked her arm through his elbow.

"I've already checked it downstairs at the restaurant when I confirmed our reservations." He turned and looked at Jack several steps behind them. "Coming Jack?"

"Yes, sir," Jack said, "I just have to grab my room key." He stepped gingerly over to the small table and tucked the key into his inside suit coat pocket. He followed Lisa and her father out of the door and closed it tightly behind him, making sure it was locked.

"How are your foot and hand doing, Jack?" Frank asked as they walked slowly toward the elevators.

"Improving gradually," Jack replied smiling at the two of them.

"We finished the edits and rewrite of Jack's book about an hour ago," Lisa said to her father. "And, thank God Jack didn't injure his hand last week. His penmanship with his left hand is, shall we say, quite unique?"

"Quite awful," Jack corrected her. He flexed his right hand and noticed he had more mobility in his fingers. He reached up and gently brushed the pocket of his white shirt, making certain that he had remembered to tuck in four ibuprofen before leaving the bathroom.

As they entered the elevator, Frank turned and looked at Jack.

"So, if your manuscript is finished, how soon will you be heading home to Minnesota?"

Jack glanced at Lisa, a knot forming in his stomach as he thought about leaving. She caught his eyes, then quickly looked away, watching the floor numbers click off on the overhead panel in the elevator. Frank pretended not to notice the exchange of looks between them, but it peaked his curiosity.

"Well," Jack said slowly, taking a deep breath. "I understand we'll be in meetings over at Brownstone for the next two days. I think my flight is around 10:00 Saturday morning."

"There's a lot more to publishing a book than just writing it," Frank nodded. "I'm looking forward to reading yours, Jack. Peter Tunnell told me this morning he believes it's a potential best-seller." Frank chuckled and gave his daughter a squeeze with his large arm around her shoulders. "Your boss likes to rub my nose in your successes from time to time."

The threesome were seated in the center of the elaborately decorated dining area of the Madison Room. Jack observed at least three servers waiting on them at all times. He tried to recall if he had that kind of attention the other evening when he dined alone.

"Maybe they know Frank Lisignoli," Jack thought to himself. "The maitre'd certainly gave us first class attention."

"May I bring you cocktails?" a young, well-dressed waiter asked them as soon as they were seated and their water glasses were filled.

"I'll have a small carafe of white wine," Lisa said, "A chardonnay, please." Jack motioned for Frank Lisignoli to order next.

"Ginger ale for me, please," Frank said confidently.

"I'll have the same," Jack added quickly, rubbing the small aluminum pull-tab in his pants pocket between his left index finger and thumb. Lisa shot an odd, questioning look at him. Her father had picked up a large menu and was carefully inspecting each selection, suddenly appearing oblivious to his daughter and Jack's brief eye contact. Jack pulled the small aluminum tab out of his pocket and casually placed it on the table in front of Lisa.

"What's that?" Lisa whispered quietly as she leaned toward him.

"The pull tab off my beer last night. My last beer. My last alcoholic drink," Jack whispered back. "I'm keeping it as a constant reminder that I've quit."

"Good for you!" Lisa whispered excitedly as she sat back in her chair, flashing him a broad smile.

Frank Lisignoli peered over his open menu at them. A large, white smile appeared through his heavy black beard. He'd become keenly aware something was going on between his daughter and Jack Kramp, but he made no inquiry. He sensed there was more to their relationship than their joint professional endeavors of editing Jack's manuscript. True, Jack was scheduled to leave New York City on Saturday morning, but Frank Lisignoli had a strong feeling he hadn't seen the last of Mr. Jack Kramp. There was a new softness in his daughter's eyes whenever she looked at this big stranger from Minnesota. A silky glow he had never witnessed before. And he suspected it was going to be something truly wonderful for her. Finally.

Their dinner conversation ran the gamut of topics. Frank was deeply interested in Jack's background and growing up in Minnesota. Jack was intrigued by Frank's diverse career experiences.. He learned Frank graduated from Yale and became an overseas correspondent with CBS during the Vietnam Conflict. After the war, Frank did a stint as a writer with the New Yorker, then as a rewrite editor for a small publishing company in New Jersey. He joined Tanner and Whitehall in 1988 as an editor in one of their imprint divisions. Rising quickly through the ranks, Frank Lisignoli was promoted to Publisher and CEO seven years ago by the retiring Walter Whitehall.

Frank went on to share stories of his youth, growing up across the East River in Brooklyn. With a great deal of pride, he also spoke of the childhoods of his two children, Lisa and Brian. Occasionally, Lisa would chime in with a related story. With deep sorrow, Frank told of Brian's sudden death during the Persian Gulf War and of his wife's unexpected heart attack just a few months later.

Jack's interest spiked as he closely followed Frank's account of becoming an alcoholic and the painful steps to recovery during the past several months of rehabilitation.

The more Jack learned about Lisa's background from Frank, the more comfortable he felt about being with her. Lisa had graduated in the top twenty of her class from Yale and spent most of her career working in three other publishing companies prior to arriving at Brownstone.

"For years I've begged Lisa to come work with me at Tanner and Whitehall," Frank said, "But she is extremely stubborn. She has always insisted on making it on her own."

"It's better that I don't work for you, Dad," Lisa interjected. "This way, I'm not subjected to the other employees resenting me because I'm favored as Daddy's little golden girl." Jack looked from Lisa to Frank and back. He sensed she was trying to tell her father something about the decision she was wrestling with, but he wasn't certain.

"Well, maybe someday, Lisa," her father grinned at her, refusing to give up on his persuasive dream of her joining him at Tanner and Whitehall.

"Let's have some espresso, shall we?" Lisa replied, deliberately changing the subject.

By 11:25, Jack and Lisa were saying good-bye to her father outside the coat check room. Frank excused himself, explaining he had a board meeting and breakfast at 7:00 a.m. the next morning, and it was now long past his bedtime. He gave Lisa a long, warm, smothering bear-hug, shook Jack's left hand firmly, then proceeded to smile and wave one final time as he headed through the lobby to catch a cab.

"Your coat is up in the suite," Jack said turning toward Lisa as they slowly walked to the elevators. She nodded.

"My father had a wonderful time tonight," Lisa said thoughtfully as they stepped into the elevator.

"So did I," Jack said. "He is really a down-to-earth, intelligent human being."

"I could tell there was a high-level, testosterone-rich, male-bonding event going on between the two of you," she said, grinning broadly at him.

"What about you?" Jack inquired, gently taking her right hand in his left.

"Oh, my father and I have been bonding off and on for years!" Lisa joked through a deep chuckle.

"You know what I meant," Jack said, grinning at her evasiveness. "Did you have a wonderful time?"

"Yes, I did," she said softly, looking into his blue eyes. "You know I did."

The elevator slowly came to a halt on the 34th floor. Jack and Lisa stepped out and walked arm in arm down the corridor to suite 3418. Jack awkwardly fished the room key out of his coat pocket with his left hand and opened the door. Upon entering, Lisa kicked off her shoes and headed down to the lower living area. Uncertain about what to do next, Jack tossed the key on the small table, removed his jacket, and took off his tie. Lisa stood facing Jack, leaning against the back of the love seat. She searched his face, looking for clues as to what he was thinking.

"Are you tired, Jack?" she asked.

"Not at all. I'm actually wide awake, thanks to that cup of high octane espresso. How about you?"

"I'm not sleepy either," Lisa replied. She rubbed her arms with her hands. "I am a little chilly, though. Can we have a fire?"

"Certainly," Jack said as he quickly shuffled down to the lower living area and found the remote to the gas log in the fireplace. In seconds, colorful flames were dancing around the ceramic log. The fans kicked in and they could feel warm air flowing from the vents just under the mantel. Seated on the love seat, Lisa curled her shapely legs up next to her body and stared at the flickering fire in front of her. Jack found a soft classical radio station and limped back up the steps to the refrigerator. Without glancing at the remaining beers, Jack pulled out a can of diet Pepsi and popped the top.

"Would you like a Pepsi?" he called to Lisa.

"No, thank you," she said. "I'm fine."

"I need to take a couple more pain meds," Jack said, lifting the Pepsi can in her direction. The two ibuprofen he'd taken earlier during dinner had long since worn off. He removed the two remaining tablets from his shirt pocket, popped them in his mouth, and washed them down with a large swallow of soda.

Jack hobbled back down to the living area, slipped off his shoes, and sat down on the love seat next to Lisa. He propped his feet up on the coffee table in front of them.

"You couldn't tell him, could you?" Jack asked softly.

"Tell who what?" Lisa replied, attempting to avoid the direction she knew Jack was planning to take the conversation.

"You couldn't tell your father about your book," Jack stated. He grinned at her. "Frank has absolutely no idea that his publishing company has just accepted the printing rights to his daughter's manuscript. I think that's pretty incredible."

"Incredible? Or terrible?" Lisa asked, turning to look into Jack's eyes.

"I said incredible. Not terrible," Jack said gently.

"What should I do, Jack?" pleaded Lisa.

"Talk to him. Tell him everything."

"When?" she asked nervously, biting her lower lip.

"Soon. Tomorrow. The sooner, the better."

"Are you sure, Jack?"

"I'm sure," Jack said firmly.

Lisa leaned over and placed her head on Jack's left shoulder. He slipped his left hand into her right and they clasped fingers.

"I don't know if I can do that," she whispered.

"Sure you can," Jack said confidently. "Do you want me to go with you when you tell him?" Jack waited during Lisa's long, thoughtful pause.

"No," she finally said softly. "I have to do it alone."

"You'll do just fine." Jack gave her hand a reassuring squeeze.

"I'm so afraid of hurting him, especially if I decide not to work with him at Tanner and Whitehall."

"He'll understand, Lisa. I know he will. And you know he'll understand, too. He'll want whatever you want as long as you're happy. And deep down, you already know what you want."

Lisa instantly sat erect, pushing herself away from Jack. There was a hint of anger in her green eyes as she pulled her hand from his. She stared into his blue eyes and pursed her lips together.

"And what do I want?" she quietly demanded. "How do you know what I want, Jack Kramp?"

Surprised by Lisa's reaction, Jack stared at her, his eyes wide. He wasn't certain what he had just said that caused her unexpected fiery outburst. He looked at the fireplace a minute before answering her. Jack sensed the truth. He had realized it for several hours now, but it became very clear to him just in the past few minutes. Jack looked directly back into Lisa's deep green eyes.

"You want to write, Lisa," he replied slowly. "You want to do alone what you've been helping everyone else do for years. You want to author a collection of your very own best sellers. You have words, stories, ideas, thoughts, and an abundance of emotional, literary music within you that needs to come out. If it doesn't, you'll eventually burst. And you'll spend the rest of your creative life feeling empty and unfulfilled."

Lisa sank back into the love seat, closing her eyes. She let out a deep sigh. Lisa's body was close to Jack's, but she was not touching him. They both remained silent for a full minute, waiting for the other to speak.

"And how do you know this?" Lisa finally asked, her eyes still closed.

"I just know. Intuition," Jack said assuredly, shrugging his shoulders, unable to explain his sixth sense. "You're an awesome writer. You're doing a grave injustice to yourself by sharing your expertise with other people to make them look good. You should be writing by yourself, for yourself, and you know it."

For more than five minutes, an awkward silence echoed between them. Jack studied the flames flickering around the gas log, causing large shadows to twist and flutter around the semi-darkened room. With her eyes still tightly closed and her breathing shallow, Lisa remained passive. She finally spoke, slipping her right hand once again into Jack's left. "You're right," she whispered. "You are absolutely correct. I want to write more than anything. But..." she paused.

"But? But what?" Jack softly repeated, pulling his hand from hers and slowly putting his left arm around her bare shoulders.

"But I'm so damn afraid," Lisa choked.

"Afraid of what? You've already had a manuscript accepted. That must tell you something!" Jack was confused.

"I'm afraid of not being good enough to do it all the time. Can I support myself by just writing? What happens if I wake up some day and I don't have any more ideas left? What if my creative well runs dry or I get writer's block? What if I fail?"

Jack pulled Lisa closer to him. He thought about her questions. Without consciously thinking about his answers, he let his inner voice take over.

"First of all, creative people have an endless reservoir of ideas. It's like breathing. It becomes second nature to them. They only run into trouble when they start thinking too hard about it. Like when one starts thinking about their own breathing, they start to hyperventilate. As long as your right brain and your left brain function in unison, and as long as there is a small electrode igniting each creative thought, you will have an idea that will explode into a terrific manuscript. You'll have hundreds of ideas. Some will be better than others, but you will never be at a loss for them."

Jack looked down to find Lisa watching him, hanging on every word. He took a deep breath and went on. "And as far as failure goes, so what? Do you think everything you write is going to be on the New York Times Best Seller list? Success only comes through failure. Sometimes we get lucky. I was lucky.

Real lucky. But I'm not on the Best Seller list, and I may never be. I may not be so lucky the next time. My next book might suck sheep shit. But if you don't try, you don't have the chance to fail. But you also won't have the chance to succeed either. Look at Mark Twain, Agatha Christie, John Grisham, Louis L'Amour, Stephen King, Danielle Steel, Walt Whitman, James Joyce, Edgar Allan Poe, and hundreds of others. Do you think any of them were ever afraid of not having another good idea? Do you think any of them were ever afraid of failing? At first, many of them did, but they kept trying until they succeeded. And thank God they did, or our literary world would have been robbed of their entertainment and classics.

The Japanese have an old proverb that says; 'Fall down seven times, stand up eight. So don't use the worry of running out of creative ideas or failing now and then as an excuse with me, Lisa, it won't work. You're better than that. You're a writer and you know it. And a damn good one," Jack paused, looked into the fireplace once more, then slowly added, "End of sermon."

Once again, Lisa was silent. She snuggled closer to Jack, her head on his chest. Jack let his cheek brush against her soft hair. He enjoyed her fragrance and the tenderness of her small body next to his.

"Thank you," she whispered. "I needed that. I need you."

At 1:15 a.m., Lisa stirred. She had fallen asleep with her head in Jack's lap. Jack was lost in his own thoughts while watching her sleep. The fire in front of him and the soft music of Brahms made him dream beautiful dreams of sharing a life with Lisa. He felt they had already shared so much, and he also sensed that it was only the beginning.

"What time is it?" Lisa murmured, slowly opening her eyes and focusing on Jack's strong jaw.

"A quarter past one," Jack said, grinning at her.

"Oh," Lisa groaned as she struggled to a sitting position, "I have to go."

"Do you?" Jack asked softly.

"I should. Tomorrow is going to be a long day for us." Lisa slowly rose off the love seat and stretched, adjusting her green dress down around her thighs. She ambled sleepily up the steps and stood, looking down at her shoes. Jack joined her. He circled his arms around her waist and pulled her to him. She promptly placed her arms around his neck and stretched on her tiptoes to reach his face.

Their soft kisses quickly turned into unleashed passion. Their soft kisses turned into a passionate embrace while their tongues explored each other's mouths. Lisa and Jack's breathing became rapid and heavy.

"I really should be going," Lisa's hot breath whispered in Jack's ear.

"Do you have to?" Jack whispered back, his hands covering her bare back, his fingers becoming entwined in her long black hair.

"No," Lisa said, her breath becoming shorter as the fire within her raged out of control. Her body melted into his, their wanton desires no longer hidden from each other.

"Do you want to go?" Jack asked again, wanting to be certain he was reading her body language correctly.

"No," Lisa whispered, slipping her right hand down to Jack's hip, gently hooking her fingers into his belt and sliding them toward his buckle. She kissed him harder, her lips passionately begging him to delve into her secret passages of love. Jack found the zipper hidden in the seam on the back of Lisa's dress. He slowly and easily unzipped it. Lisa gasped from the sudden, unbridled freedom of her trembling body and let her tongue trace the lines of his ear, her breath hotter and more irregular.

In one swift, fluid motion, Jack reached down, scooped her into his arms, and carried her effortlessly into the bedroom. In the darkness, Lisa moaned in soft rapture and whispered his name. Jack heard his own rapid breath crashing against the silence of the pillows like waves on a deserted beach. Together, they moved deliberately toward an ecstasy neither had ever suspected would be there just days ago.

Chapter Twenty-Three

Early morning surprised the naked bodies of Lisa and Jack. Their interwoven limbs were molded together as they quietly slept under the warm covers of the massive king-size bed. Jack's eyes fluttered open to the rising sun casting a soft light through the window, making the bedroom float in shades of story-land pink. He felt Lisa's satiny hair brushing against his cheek, laying across his chest, and neck. Her delicate frame was half-draped over his while her perfume, mixed with the scent of their lovemaking, filled the room. Jack was afraid to move. Enjoying this unforgettable moment in time for as long as he could, Jack took a shallow breath as a smile slowly spreading over his face. Lisa turned her head slightly and gently kissed his chest, her right hand resting on his inner thigh.

"I love you," she whispered.

"I love you, too," Jack replied softly, his mouth dry.

"Please tell me we have time to lie here for awhile. I don't want to get up," Lisa said.

"We have time," Jack replied, glancing at the clock, noting that it was 7:22 a.m. He moved his right arm to fully enclose her bare shoulder, draping his bruised fingers on her right arm.

"I really don't want to know," Lisa said, "But is it 8:00 yet?"

"No, not yet," Jack answered, his voice husky.

"Good," Lisa said. "Let me know when it's almost 8:00. I need to go home, freshen up, and change clothes. We have to meet Marsha with the final chapters and the jump drive at 10:00."

"We have time," Jack said again, bending his head down and kissing Lisa lightly on her temple.

"Any regrets?" she whispered, lightly tracing the hair on his chest down to just below his navel with her finger tip.

"None," Jack replied with a firm conviction. "You?"

"No," Lisa replied. "Although, I must confess, I've secretly wondered what it would be like to make love to you since we had our carriage ride through Central Park last Saturday."

"Really?" Jack looked at Lisa and grinned as she tilted her head up to find his eyes.

"When did it all start happening for you, Jack?" she asked innocently.

"You mean, when did I first become aware it might be possible for me to fall in love with you?" Jack inquired, teasingly looking for a clarification from her.

"Yes," Lisa said.

"A week ago, Monday morning. The first time I ever laid eyes on you. I sensed it then, but I kept telling myself for days that it was absolutely crazy. I kept dismissing it in my rational mind as insanity, but my determined heart wouldn't listen."

"I know!" Lisa exclaimed, propping herself up on her left elbow and facing Jack, her right hand resting on the center of his chest. "I kept trying to erase you from my thoughts, but you were always there. And with every passing day I spent with you, it became harder to let you go."

"You're a wonderful person, Lisa," Jack told her as he placed his left palm on her cheek.

"Thank you," she replied softly, her eyes fixed on his, "So are you. You make love like you write!"

"What the hell does that mean?" Jack asked, surprised. "Full of mistakes? Now you want to edit our love making?"

"No," Lisa laughed, kissing him briefly on the lips, "You make love with a peppered passion, mixed with a little humor now and then. I love it." A sobering look came over Lisa's face. "I love you," she added softly as she let her head slowly drop back onto Jack's chest.

"Peppered passion," Jack repeated, chuckling as he held her tightly in his arms again. "I love you, too. Now I have another reason to call you a Tiger-Lady!" he added. Lisa let out a deep sigh, snuggled closer into Jack, and hugged him with a greater intensity.

"What do we do now?" whispered Jack. "Where do we go from here?" There was a long, pensive silence while Lisa seemed to almost stop breathing. She finally answered. "I don't know, Jack. All of this happened so suddenly. I don't want to think about it right now. There are too many other things. We'll need to take our time."

"We have the time," Jack said quietly. "It's the distance that could be our problem." Lisa nodded.

"What time is it?" she asked, hoping to change the subject.

"Ten minutes to eight," Jack said with disappointment in his voice.

"I have to go," Lisa said sadly.

"Do you?" he asked softly, holding her tighter.

"I better."

"Do you want to?" Jack persisted with a crooked grin.

"No," Lisa said with a giggle, "But it seems to me this is how we started last night. If I don't go now, I never will." They laughed aloud, their happiness matching the brightness of the sunlit room. Lisa slipped out of Jack's arms and bounced out of bed. Jack watched her perfect body disappear into the bathroom. He lay back, his hands behind his head, staring at the ceiling.

"Now what, Jack?" he asked himself in the sudden stillness of the empty room. "Now what?"

Lisa dressed and left within ten minutes. Jack, dressed in only his boxers, kissed her good-bye at the door as she hurried to catch the elevator and a cab home, her briefcase and purse in one hand, her garment bag in the other. Jack turned off the gas log in the fireplace and the radio. He walked back to the bedroom, noticing his toes were much better this morning. He flexed three fingers on his right hand, extending them out for inspection. They moved much easier, but their colors of blue, black, and yellow were a bit disgusting.

"Sex therapy for dexterity," Jack mumbled aloud as he stepped into the shower, wiggling his toes and fingers under the stream of hot water. He turned the water temperature hotter, watching the steam engulf him. With his head clear and feeling good, Jack was ready for a busy day at Brownstone. And for the first morning in two years, Jack Kramp was completely sober, truly himself, and in love again.

By 8:45 a.m., Jack had called home and spoke with his kids before they headed off to school. He dressed in his dark gray pinstripe suit and headed down to have breakfast in the Garden Cafe on the main level. His sizable appetite encouraged him to order a large breakfast special. Jack devoured his two eggs, sausage, toast, pancakes, and his large orange juice while scanning the headlines in The New York Times. Suddenly, in the upper corner of page twelve, he saw photos of Jagger Tormain, Mick Thorkmon, and Clipper Sullivan. Jack carefully read the detailed story of the arrest, injuries, and deaths of everyone involved with the kidnapping and extortion plot. Jack's name was mentioned twice, along with Lisa's, Frank Lisignoli, Avery Schneider, Lt. Corey Burgess, and all of his fellow officers. Funeral services for Jagger Tormain were scheduled for Monday in his home state of Georgia. Clipper Sullivan was charged and still under heavy guard while recuperating in the hospital's intensive care unit. Jack grimly tore out the newspaper article, folded it, and tucked it inside the breast pocket of his coat.

"Now there's something special for my scrapbook at home," Jack said quietly as he rose and picked up his check. Jack signed for his breakfast, left a tip, and crossed over to the elevators.

When he returned to his suite, Jack found Anita once again faithfully cleaning and straightening up. Embarrassed, he wondered if Anita noticed any telltale signs Lisa had spent the night with him. Anita gave no indication she suspected anything. Instead, she chatted on about the unusually warm weather for early November. She asked Jack if he would still be staying with them next week.

"No," Jack said reluctantly. "I'm leaving on Saturday morning."

"Oh, I'm sorry to hear that, Mr. Jack," Anita replied, smiling at him. "You are one of my most favorite guests!"

"Well, thank you, Anita," Jack said crossing over toward her and her supply cart as she prepared to drag it out into the hall. "I appreciate everything you've done for me. I may not see you again. I have meetings over at my publisher's tomorrow morning so, here, I want you to have this." Jack pulled two crisp twenty dollar bills out of his pocket and handed it to Anita."

"Oh, Mr. Jack, thank you!" she said excitedly, "But this is not necessary!" She tried handing the bills back to him.

"Yes it is," Jack insisted, folding his hand around hers and pushing it back toward her. "You take it and buy something nice for yourself!"

Anita carefully folded the cash and placed it inside the pocket of her uniform. She flashed a huge grin at Jack, repeated a half dozen more "thank yous," and disappeared into the corridor, gently closing the door behind her. Jack never saw her again.

Jack noted it was 9:20 on his cell phone. He went into the bathroom, brushed his teeth, and sprayed one more shot of cologne. He walked out into the main suite area and crossed over to his desk. Packing his briefcase, he carefully scanned both desks, sorting out the trash from the items he thought should be saved. It saddened Jack. He suddenly realized that he would never again see Lisa sit in front of her computer at that desk. Never again would he recline in his chair or prop his feet up on the corner of this small metal desk and watch Lisa work her magic on his manuscript. Another chapter in his life was closing, and for Jack Kramp, it felt as if it was the end of a book. He knew another book would open for him soon. He felt it, but he hadn't the faintest idea of the title. The uncertainty left him feeling very lonely.

Jack picked up his briefcase and walked to the small entry closet. He slipped into his trench coat and paused, looking around the empty, quiet, and solitary room. A room full of memories. A room full of awakenings.

"Life is fluid. Nothing ever stays the same," Jack said quietly in the stillness, hearing his voice echo through the vacant, lifeless space. He opened the door and stepped into the corridor. Closing the door firmly, Jack walked quickly down the hall toward the elevators, now hurrying to catch a cab to Brownstone Publishing. He was hustling to a series of meetings that would greatly change his future. Jack was rushing to meet Lisa Lisignoli, without whom, he suddenly felt there would be no future.

It was 9:55 when Jack finally arrived at Brownstone. Lisa was waiting for Jack in the lobby on the fourth floor. She greeted him warmly, but with a reserved professionalism in her manner. Lisa escorted Jack through a series of double glass doors to Marsha Morrow's office. Peter Tunnell was waiting for them along with Marsha and three other people. For the next several hours they went from floor to floor, stopping to introduce Jack to many of Brownstone's people who were already working behind the scenes to proof, print, distribute, and promote Jack's book. Through it all, Jack's head swam in a dozen uncharted rivers of decisions, information, and changing situations, often making him feel lost and confused amongst the flurry of activity.

Marsha, Jack, Lisa, and Peter were shown the final color proof for the jacket cover. Jack noticed the art department had made a few subtle alterations to the original mock-up, and he told them he thought they were great improvements.

They ate lunch across the street from Brownstone at a spacious restaurant named Gallo's. Peter and Marsha explained the terms of the contracts and copyrights with Jack. They wanted two more manuscripts from Jack over the next eighteen months, with each one between eighty thousand and one hundred-fifty thousand words. They encouraged him to take the contracts home with him and have them reviewed by his lawyer. Peter asked Jack for a third time why he didn't have a literary agent. Jack continued to tell him that he felt more comfortable handling his own affairs.

Another contract for the change from paperback to hardcover was also handed to Jack. He had to sign it before he left so they could continue with the production. Brownstone scheduled four proofreaders to perform a final review of his entire manuscript by 9:00 p.m. that evening. "We'll be on the presses by a week from Monday," Peter announced loudly, slapping Jack on the back as they left the restaurant and headed back over to their offices.

Throughout the day, Lisa would duck in and out of meetings, sometimes disappearing for nearly an hour at a time. Whenever she was with Jack, there was never any public display of affection, although twice, Jack caught her eyes and noticed there was still a warmth in them. Once, during lunch, she winked at him when she was certain no one else would notice. Most of the time, Lisa remained friendly yet completely professional. Jack tried to understand, but it bothered him a little. He felt she might be slowly withdrawing from him and their relationship.

At 5:15 p.m., Jo escorted Jack up to the 12th floor to Lisa's office, two doors down from Petter Tunnell's spacious corner office. Lisa was on the telephone, but she waved Jack in and motioned for him to have a seat.

While Lisa gave someone on the other end instructions about changing a deadline, Jack let his gaze travel around her office. It was approximately twenty feet by fifteen feet, slightly larger than most of the other offices Jack had seen today, but not as large as Marsha's or Peter's. Her enormous white desk faced the door. She was seated in a blue cloth high-backed chair, a large computer screen sat to her right on a matching white credenza. The large window behind Lisa provided a view of The Avenue of the Americas and the skyscrapers of Wall Street in the distance. There was another long, matching white bookcase under the window, lined with books. A wall of glass and a glass door gave Lisa a view of the busy corridors of Brownstone Publishing's 12th floor. Jack sat in one of the three matching blue arm chairs in front of her. The entire wall to Jack's right was lined with shelves, from floor to ceiling. Each shelf was bulging with books, reference materials, and manuscripts. Lisa's entire office was organized and purely professional, except for a small family photo on top of the bookcase behind her. Jack squinted at the picture. He could see Lisa, her father, a very attractive woman with light, golden brown hair, and a handsome young man in a Naval uniform, his hair the same color as his mother's.

Jack looked down at the plush deep blue carpet with the small flecks of gold woven into it. A sadness came over him again. This was her world, and he suddenly felt as though he were an intruder. Jack looked at the volumes of books overflowing on Lisa's bookcase. He wondered if he was just another writer to her. Someday, his book would sit next to the rest of them and Jack wondered if he and his book, like many of those now slightly dusty, would be half-forgotten by this beautiful editor.

"Neatly filed away in the library of her heart," Jack mumbled under his breath as he surveyed the office again.

"Thank you for waiting," Lisa said, smiling at him as she hung up. Jack felt his heart thumping loudly in his chest.

"Alone at last," Jack said, returning her smile and spreading his hands out wide in front of him.

"It's been quite a day for you," Lisa said, reclining back in her desk chair, slowly twirling a thin gold ink pen in her right hand. Her smile faded slightly. Jack mentally noted she did not respond to his comment about the two of them being alone.

"Yeah," Jack answered, "And it sounds like tomorrow morning isn't going to be any picnic here either."

Lisa sat up and pulled a sheet of paper closer to her. "You're scheduled for publicity shots at 10:30 on the sixth floor. Wear your black double breasted suit, but also bring along a couple of sweaters, dress slacks, oh, and maybe a pair of jeans as well."

"Are you going to be there?" Jack asked, holding his breath.

"I'll stop in for a few minutes. We have an editorial meeting at 9:00, and I have to meet with the manuscript review committee at 11:00." There was a professional hardness in her voice. It was the same hardness he'd heard the first time they met. Jack felt a small spear of ice pierce his heart.

"How about dinner tonight?" he asked. Pausing briefly, Lisa took a deep breath and quickly swiveled in her desk chair. Picking up a four-inch thick stack of bound papers from her credenza, she quietly said, "I don't think I can, Jack," Lisa said quietly. I have to read this manuscript. They want my opinion on it by tomorrow morning's meeting. I'm sorry."

Jack nodded. He suddenly felt himself standing up, trying to decide if he was feeling embarrassed, hurt, angry, or all three. The only thing Jack knew for sure was that he wanted to leave now.

Sensing his frustration, Lisa rose and walked around the desk, stopping just a foot in front of him. She looked up at him. Moisture was clouding her bright green eyes.

"Please understand, Jack, other than your rewrite and edits, I haven't had time to do any of my other work around here since the middle of last week. I normally come in on Sunday to catch up, but Sunday I was with you and..."

"I understand. But I didn't ask you to do that," Jack interrupted, feeling his jaw clench slightly. "You showed up in church, remember?"

"Jack..." Lisa said, her eyes and voice pleading. She was interrupted by a voice coming from her intercom.

"Ms. Lisignoli, Bruce Hannigan is on line three, he says it is very urgent."

"Take it," Jack said softly, nodding toward her telephone. "It's okay. Maybe we can talk later by phone."

"Okay, I'll take it," Lisa replied into the intercom after a slight hesitation. She turned, walked around her desk, and picked up the phone. She looked at Jack one last time with pleading eyes, then turned her back to dig through a lower drawer in the cabinet behind her in search for another schedule. When she turned around again, Jack Kramp was gone.

With his briefcase in his left hand and his trench coat draped over his right arm, Jack stepped off the curb in front of Brownstone's office building and jumped into a cab. He instructed the driver to take him to The Basket, the restaurant near his hotel.

"Might as well eat," Jack said as the cab pulled away from the curb in the semi-darkness. "Nothing better to do." He was sulking like a little boy who didn't get his way, and he knew it.

The half pound hamburger, French fries, iced tea, and apple pie ala mode helped fill the emptiness in Jack's stomach. But, the big knot was still there. He understood Lisa's workload and how she could easily be falling behind in her other deadlines because she had spent additional time with him. But he could not understand the sense of feeling forgotten, the warmth he'd felt from her earlier that morning now seemed absent.

"Maybe I'm yesterday's news," Jack mumbled to himself as he left the restaurant and joined the crowded sidewalks filled with late commuters heading home. As he walked slowly back to his hotel, he glanced at the large time and temp clock on the bank across the street. It read 38 degrees, and the time was 6:19. Jack winced, realizing the toes on his right foot were beginning to throb again. He had been on his feet quite awhile during the day, and his stiff dress shoes hadn't helped.

Jack entered the lobby of his hotel carrying his briefcase, his trench coat hanging off his shoulders. He headed for the gift shop and purchased another bottle of ibuprofen. Leaving the gift shop, Jack limped toward the elevators where he punched the "UP" button. He glanced down the marble corridor and heard music coming from Bannigan's. Abruptly, he turned and headed toward the music. Once inside the bar, Jack found a secluded booth away from the early evening crowd. He shed his coat, opened his briefcase, and took out a yellow legal pad. A young woman came over to take his order.

"I'll have a ginger ale in a tall glass, lots of ice," Jack said, giving her a smile. He dug into his left front pants pocket and retrieved the pull tab from his last beer. Placing it on the table directly in front of him, he began to write.

Absorbed in his fervent writing, Jack lost all track of time. He was into his third glass of ginger ale and had just flipped the tenth page of his yellow pad when he tapped his cell for the time. It was 9:15 p.m., and Jack slowly sat back and took a deep breath. He was suddenly aware that the bar was full of people with every available booth and bar stool taken. The noise level was a shock to his ears, and he wondered why he hadn't noticed the loud din of mixed voices and the tinkling of glasses earlier. He bent over his yellow pad once more, feverishly pushing all thoughts of Lisa out of his mind once again.

By 11:07 p.m., Jack's bladder felt like it was about to burst from the five tall ginger ales he had consumed. He quickly paid his tab and tucked the legal pad full of scribbles back into his briefcase. Picking up his trench coat, he stuffed the aluminum tab back into his pants pocket and rushed upstairs to his suite and a welcoming toilet.

Exiting his bathroom, Jack noticed the room telephone's red message light blinking on the nightstand next to his bed. He dialed the hotel operator. There were two messages from Lisa Lisignoli. One at 6:45 p.m., the other at 9:30 p.m. Jack slowly removed his suit and hung it up in the closet. He sat on the edge of the bed, staring at the phone. He finally sighed, picked it up, and called Lisa's work number. He got her voice mail. He dialed her home. After the fourth ring, Lisa's answering machine kicked in. Jack left a brief message. A small panic seized him as he wondered where she could be at this hour.

Jack took off his socks. Dressed in just his underwear and t-shirt, he headed toward the bathroom. As Jack reached for the shower knob, he thought he heard a faint knocking. He opened the bathroom door leading into the main suite to listen more closely. Someone was definitely knocking at his door at 11:35 p.m.. Jack hobbled swiftly to the door in the semi-darkness of the outer room, finding his way by the light emitting from the open bathroom door. He looked through the peephole. He unlocked the door quickly and flung it open.

"Where the hell have you been?" Lisa demanded, striding past him. Jack closed the door and found the light switch. He turned to face her. She stood in the center of the room, dressed in blue jeans, a sweater, and her leather jacket. Both of Lisa's hands were resting on her small hips. Fire was shooting from her eyes. Jack stared at her expressionless, saying nothing.

"Well?" Lisa challenged him again.

"I guess I should ask you that," Jack said calmly, folding his arms in front of him. "I returned your calls."

"When?" she raised her voice sharply. "I was home until twenty-five minutes ago when I left to come looking for you."

"I just got back to my room about five minutes ago," Jack explained slowly. "I heard your messages, and I returned your calls. My message is on your home answering machine."

"So where have you been for the past six hours?" Lisa repeated.

"Downstairs," Jack said reluctantly. He walked towards the desk where he had dropped off his briefcase during his rush to the bathroom. Jack wanted to arm himself for the impending Italian crap-storm.

"Bannigan's?" Lisa snapped, turning to watch him as he shuffled past her. "I thought you quit drinking!"

"I have," replied Jack, keeping his back to her. "I've had about 80 ounces of ginger ale." Jack flipped open his briefcase on top of the small metal desk.

"You just sat and drank ginger ale alone for six hours?" Lisa asked, finally bringing her voice down an octave.

"Yeah, right after I ate dinner alone at The Basket. But, I did something else to pass the time while I tried to keep from thinking about you," Jack said, slowly turning to face her, his yellow pad in hand.

"What?" Lisa asked, her voice softer and more curious.

"Here," Jack responded as he thrust the legal pad toward her, over a dozen pages filled with his handwriting. "It's an outline and notes for my next manuscript."

Lisa took the pad from Jack. She scanned the front page, then flipped to the second. She slowly walked down the three steps and sat down on the edge of the love seat, continuing to read the entire way.

"I can read this," she said, suddenly looking up at him.

"Yeah, why not?" Jack said, not understanding the question.

"I mean, you wrote all of this with your swollen right hand. It's not scribbled with your left," Lisa said slowly, her gaze falling to his hand hanging limply at his right side.

"Had to," Jack shrugged, "I tried left-handed, but it was just too damn difficult. So I popped about four ibuprofen and kept going with my right."

Lisa nodded and turned her attention back to the scrawling penmanship on her lap. She read swiftly, turning page after page. Jack slowly walked down and sat on the sofa to her left. He was aware he was still in his underwear and t-shirt, but after their previous night of intimacy, he felt it no longer mattered.

"This is very good, Jack," Lisa said quietly, keeping her eyes focused on the pages. She read for the next fifteen minutes, pausing once to look at Jack, but she made no comment. When Lisa finished, she slumped back into the love seat, clutching the yellow pad in both hands and holding it against her chest. Lisa closed her eyes momentarily. Jack quietly placed his bare feet up on the coffee table in front of him, leaned back with his hands clasped behind his head, and waited. He could tell she was both pleased and a little troubled.

"Do you have a working title for it yet?" Lisa asked softly, finally turning and looking directly at him.

Jack nodded, "I was thinking of calling it something along the lines of *The Left Side of Sanity*. Or maybe *The Shepard Files*." Lisa nodded her approval. She then frowned and flipped back to page six of Jack's notes on the legal pad.

"I don't understand this line." Lisa said. "You wrote 'Buddy Shepard was in deep. Way over his head with these guys. Until his conscience came alive and eventually caused his death.' What is that all about?"

Jack cleared his suddenly dry throat and folded his hands as he looked her in the eyes. "Burgess didn't want to tell you everything Tuesday morning because you had enough shock and stress to deal with that day. You see, Thorkman, Tormain, and Sullivan had planned to kidnap you three years ago, and they coerced Buddy Shepard to help them by offering him a cut of the ransom money."

Lisa gasped and put her hand to her mouth as the color left her face. "Buddy?" she asked in a hoarse whisper.

"Apparently Buddy changed his mind at the last minute and wrote a synopsis of the entire plot with the intention to turn it over to the N.Y.P.D." Jack went on, "The bastards somehow got wind of it before he could get it to the police. That's why they killed him."

"But why? Why didn't they go forward with their plans even after they murdered Buddy?" she asked weakly.

"Well, from what I understand, Tormain was picked up the next day by the Feds for an outstanding warrant in Georgia for armed robbery. Two days later, Sullivan was jailed for assault and battery at a bar in Soho. So the whole thing fell apart before they could get to you. But I guess the two of them hooked up again recently with Thorkman sometime in mid October."

"And you're absolutely sure Buddy Shepard was going to take the money?" Lisa asked, still in disbelief.

"The investigators are pretty positive he was involved," Jack replied. "See, Buddy and his wife were living an extravagant lifestyle. But they were struggling financially despite his wife's lucrative salary as a healthcare administrator along with Buddy's royalties from his books. I heard they even discovered evidence that Buddy made a deposit on a new sailboat just days prior to his murder, but his wife was completely unaware of it. So the pieces all fit."

A faint smile appeared on Lisa's face for the first time since she entered the suite. She shook her head, refusing to hear or even think about Buddy Shepard any longer. Lisa slowly stood and adjusted her jacket, the color returning to her face as she felt her years of guilt for Buddy's death finally disappear. Jack rose as well, and they faced each other.

"Well, I think you've got another winner here, Jack," Lisa said softly.

"Well, I never met a word I didn't like. And, we might have another winner," Jack corrected her. "And so much is based on true events. So, are you still upset with me?" he asked, raising his eyebrows.

"A little," Lisa said, a smile tugging at the corners of her lips. "But we'll talk about it tomorrow over lunch if I can steal you away from the Brownstone entourage. Shall we say 12:30?"

"Sure, why not?" Jack said, feeling her beginning to drift toward the door and out of his life again. Lisa handed the yellow pad back to Jack. When they reached the door, Jack put his arm around her, slowly bent over, and gently brushed her lips with his. Placing her hand on his left cheek, Lisa tenderly returned his kiss.

"Good-night," she whispered.

"Good-night, Tiger Lady," Jack said. He managed a small grin as Lisa opened the door and stepped into the corridor. He watched her head down the hall and returned her wave as she stepped into the elevator. He closed the door, locked it, and headed toward the shower. Under the spray of the shower head, Jack started singing Jimmy Buffet again, "If we couldn't laugh, we would all go insane."

Forty seconds later, Lisa Lisignoli stepped out of the elevator and walked through the lobby of the West Park Plaza Hotel. Just a few feet from the revolving door, she stopped abruptly. Cursing softly under her breath, Lisa wheeled around and walked briskly back to the elevator bank with spirited determination in each step.

With his eyes closed, Jack stood shampooing his hair in the shower. He didn't hear someone quietly enter his suite, remove their clothes, and toss them on his bed. He jumped in astonishment when the glass shower door suddenly slid open and Lisa stepped in. She pulled his head down to her's and embraced him as her lips found his. Over the steady sound of the running water, she whispered earnestly in his ear. "Damn you, Jack Kramp!"

Chapter Twenty-Four

Lisa awoke to the smell of freshly brewed coffee. She slowly opened her eyes and let them drift around the strange room. Alone in the large king bed, she recognized the scent of Jack's cologne still lingering on the pillows. Smiling, Lisa raised herself up on her elbows and noticed her clothes strewn across the floor near the bed, having been kicked off during their night of lovemaking.

"Coffee?" Jack asked cheerfully from the doorway, a steaming cup in his hand.

"That would be wonderful!" Lisa replied, sliding herself up and propping two pillows behind her back. She noticed Jack had already showered and dressed in a black pair of pants and a freshly starched white shirt. Lisa accepted the cup from him as he sat on the bed next to her. Jack grinned as he watched her take a sip of the hot coffee.

"It's almost 7:30," Jack said, "And you have a meeting at 9:00, right?"

Lisa glanced at the clock on the night stand. She looked back at Jack and nodded with a serious expression.

"I have to leave in a few minutes," she said sadly.

"Do you?" asked Jack, his grin widening.

"You know I do," Lisa replied with a smile. "Please, Jack! Let's not start that again."

"Why not?" Jack inquired softly, gently taking her coffee cup from her hand. He set it down on the nightstand and encircling Lisa with his arms, Jack leaned over and kissed her. Lisa returned his kiss, then slowly eased away.

"I'd love to stay, but I really need to go home. I have to shower, get dressed, review the rest of a manuscript, and be on time for the editorial meeting." Lisa drew her knees up to her chest and slowly swung her legs out of bed. Jack stood and stepped back toward his closet. He watched Lisa dress, appreciating her light olive complexion, long black hair, and her perfectly toned body. At the door of his suite, she gave him a hug and a quick kiss. She opened the door and headed down the corridor.

"I'll see you at 10:30 on the sixth floor for your publicity shots," Lisa called out to him over her shoulder. "Remember to bring a couple of wardrobe changes."

Jack gave her a thumbs-up signal with his left hand as he watched her enter the elevator. He closed the door and walked back to the bedroom to pack his wardrobe changes.

The Friday morning activities in the offices of Brownstone were even more intense than the previous day. Jack observed that every person moved around the offices at the same brisk pace. He arrived promptly at 10:30 to the publicity department on the sixth floor where he was immediately ushered into a small photo studio. A tall thin man named Marty with gray hair and a matching mustache began preparations for the photo session. Marty put Jack in several poses, adjusted the lighting, and clicked off shot after shot. Jack had just started posing in his third wardrobe change when he saw Lisa standing in the background. She waved at him and smiled. He returned her smile, held his position, and nodded his head.

Jack was finished by 10:50 a.m. and found Lisa waiting for him in the hall as he left the photo studio. Loaded down with his briefcase, a garment bag, and a small suitcase, Jack struggled through the doorway to meet her.

"That looked as though it went well," Lisa said as they walked toward the elevators.

"What's next?" Jack asked.

"Publicity. Just down the hall," replied Lisa. "They want you to review the press releases to make certain your personal information is accurate before sending them." She stopped just outside another set of offices. "Go through these doors and ask for Jennifer. I have to go to my 11:00 a.m. manuscript review meeting. Let's meet in my office at 12:20. We'll go to lunch. My office is on the 12th floor."

"I remember," Jack said. "12:20, your office. I'll be there."

"If you're not, I'll come looking for you," Lisa laughed softly as she turned and walked briskly toward the elevators, a stack of manuscripts tucked under her arm.

"I'll count on it!" Jack called loudly after her. Lisa turned, flashed him another smile, and then resumed her direction. Jack entered through the glass door and walked up to the front desk.

"Hi," he said to the young man seated behind the desk. "I'm Jack Kramp. I'm here to see Jennifer."

"Okay, Mr. Kramp, I'll tell her you're here," the young man replied. "Was she expecting you?"

"I believe so," Jack said patiently. "I was told I need to review some press releases before they go out." The young man nodded and called Jennifer's secretary. Within a few minutes, a young lady named Bonnie appeared and escorted Jack to a small conference room. Jack placed his garment bag over a chair, set his suitcase on the floor, and put his briefcase on the table.

Jennifer Tomkins, a tall blonde with bright blue eyes entered the room and introduced herself to Jack. She had a thick file with eight versions of advance releases that were scheduled to be sent out with the advance reading copies to all the major book reviewers within the next ten days.

"We just need to be certain everything we are saying about you is accurate," she informed him. "Please indicate any changes or corrections with this red pen. I'll come back and see how you're doing a little later." Jack nodded, took the folder from her, picked up the red pen, and started reading. He glanced up, suddenly aware that Jennifer hadn't yet left the room but was still standing in the doorway, staring at him.

"Something wrong?" Jack asked.

"Oh, no, I'm sorry," she blushed. "I was just thinking. I heard about you and Lisa Lisignoli this morning."

Jack felt his face and neck turn a deep red. "Does everyone know we've been sleeping together?" he immediately thought to himself. His pulse quickened as he grinned sheepishly at her.

"It must have been very frightening for both of you," Jennifer said, shaking her head. "I couldn't believe there was a plot to kidnap Lisa. And to think, you were lucky enough to be in the right place at the right time to overhear their plans. You are both very fortunate."

"Yeah, we are," agreed Jack. He sighed with relief as he realized that Jennifer was talking about the events of Tuesday morning and not his secret love affair with Lisa.

"It sounds like it would make a good book," Jennifer said, her smile appearing again.

"You never know," Jack replied. "Truth is stranger than fiction."

Jennifer nodded, promised to be back in less than an hour and left the conference room. Jack turned his attention back to the press releases, flexing his right hand occasionally to prevent it from becoming stiff. Overall, he found very little of the information in the press releases to be incorrect and was pleased with how they were written by Brownstone's publicity department.

By 12:15, Jack was on an elevator and riding swiftly to the 12th floor. He navigated his way to Lisa's office and found it empty. He dumped his bags and briefcase in one of her side chairs and went searching for a vending machine. He needed a cold soda to wash down a couple more ibuprofen. At the far end of a long corridor, Jack found a Coke machine and a much needed men's room. He walked slowly back to Lisa's office, nodding to the friendly Brownstone employees along the way. Once back in her office, Jack sipped his Coke and browsed the wall of books, searching for familiar titles.

"Your book will be in there within two to three weeks, Jack," a man's voice said from the doorway. Jack turned to find Peter Tunnell standing with his arms folded across his chest, his tie hanging loosely from his open shirt collar. Jack flashed Peter a big grin and sat on the front edge of Lisa's desk.

"Let's hope it's the first of many," Jack said.

"It will be, Jack, it will be," Peter nodded confidently. "Where is Lisa?" he asked, abruptly changing the subject.

"I think she is in a manuscript review meeting," Jack replied. "We are supposed to meet here in ten minutes. Shall I tell Lisa you were looking for her?"

"No, it's not important," Peter said with a wave. "I'll talk to her Monday. I'm leaving for the weekend."

Jack walked over and extended his left hand, holding the bruised fingers on his right hand up slightly as a reminder of his injury. "It was nice meeting you, Peter," Jack said.

"The pleasure's all mine, Jack!" Peter said, pumping Jack's hand enthusiastically. "I'm sure we'll see more of you in the coming months."

"I hope so," Jack said. "I've got to crank out two more manuscripts for you in less than two years."

"And that's just the beginning," Peter said, pointing his index finger at Jack. "I'm expecting more than that over the next several years. You take care of yourself, Jack." Peter turned to go, taking a step toward the door. Suddenly, he stopped and looked back at Jack. He had a soft smile on his face and a slight twinkle in his eye. "And take care of Lisa, too, will you?" Peter added.

"What do you mean?" Jack asked, stunned by Peter's request.

"She needs someone like you in her life, Jack," Peter said seriously. "I've known Lisa Lisignoli for a long time, and I can tell, there's something unique and magical between the two of you when you're together."

For the second time that day, Jack blushed. "Is it that noticeable?" he asked quietly.

"For me? Yes. To others? I seriously doubt it. Lisa wears a great poker face most of the time. It's often hard to determine exactly what she's thinking."

"Or feeling," Jack added.

"Or feeling," agreed Peter. "Just take good care of her."

"I'll try," Jack promised. Peter nodded, winked at Jack, then turned and disappeared down the hall.

Lisa arrived back in her office at 12:40 to find Jack scanning a handbook on grammatical revisions. Jack was unaware of her presence until he heard her speak.

"The butler did it," Lisa said, grinning as she crossed to her desk and dropped a stack of manuscripts on it. "But, he was from Minnesota and they found him not guilty!"

"Nice plot," Jack laughed as he tossed the book back on the shelf. "What's for lunch?"

"They say it's almost sixty degrees outside with abundant sunshine in a cloudless sky. How about a picnic?" Lisa asked as she removed her trench coat off the rack in the corner.

"Sounds great," Jack said. "Do I need to come back here after?"

"No, I understand they're finally finished with you," Lisa said, smiling as Jack helped her slip into her coat. "Until your next book."

"Okay," Jack replied. "Then I suggest we take a cab back over to the hotel and drop off my things. We can grab something from a deli and have a picnic as we take a carriage ride through Central Park." Lisa nodded in agreement and picked up Jack's briefcase. Together, they rushed to the elevators and downstairs to catch a cab.

The sunny afternoon picnic during their carriage ride through Central Park relaxed Lisa and Jack. They found comfort in each other's arms, laughter from each other's company, and an unspoken sadness as they realized this was their last day together. They enjoyed warm bagels with cream cheese and washed them down with hot coffee.

"I don't want this day to end," Lisa said quietly as she snuggled next to Jack near the end of their ride.

"It doesn't have to," Jack said. Lisa remained silent. She closed her eyes, and a soft smile caused a dainty dimple in her cheek. Jack looked over the sides of the carriage, enjoying the park around him, still beautiful even through the trees were bare, bracing themselves for the onslaught of winter. He looked down at the young woman next to him. "It doesn't have to end," he whispered again, mostly to himself.

"I'm afraid it does, Jack," murmured Lisa.

"Do you have any meetings this afternoon?" Jack asked as he looked at the time on his cell, noting it was already 2:05 p.m.

"No," Lisa replied slowly, already thinking ahead of Jack.

"Then, take the afternoon off. Spend it with me," Jack said with a note of confidence in his voice.

"Okay," Lisa said, flashing a warm smile at him. "As soon as we stop, I'll call my office."

"Calling in sick?" Jack grinned, raising his eyebrows.

"Calling in love," Lisa replied with a chuckle and jabbing him gently in his ribs with her elbow.

The rest of the afternoon and evening flew by quickly for Jack and Lisa. They found an arcade and played video games. Walking down Broadway, Lisa pointed out various shows and plays she had seen recently. They ate casually at a small Hungarian cafe across the street from the Metropolitan Opera House. By 8:00 p.m., they were slowly strolling arm in arm back to the hotel.

When they returned to suite 3418, Lisa and Jack immediately noticed the two desks, both chairs plus the computer and printer had been removed. The rest of the furniture in the living area had been rearranged.

"Well, it's official, Jack," Lisa said sadly, standing in the middle of the room. "Our work is complete."

Without saying a word, Jack crossed over to Lisa. He placed his arms around her and held her close, his face buried in her long hair. Lisa clung to Jack tightly as they both began sensing an unexplainable loss and a fear of an uncertain future.

"Will you come to Minneapolis?" Jack asked softly.

"I don't know, Jack," Lisa replied in a faint whisper.

"What are we going to do?" Jack sighed. "I wish New York wasn't so far from Minneapolis."

"Shhh," Lisa said, placing her finger gently on his lips. "Let's not talk about it. Let's not think about it. Let's just love for the moment right now."

"You mean live for the moment," Jack said faintly, then wishing he hadn't corrected her.

Lisa shook her head. "Love for the moment," she repeated, taking his hand in hers and leading him toward the bedroom.

It was 10:07 Saturday morning when Jack Kramp glanced at the lighted seatbelt sign as the Boeing 757 slowly climbed it's way out of Kennedy International. From his window seat, Jack watched Manhattan disappear behind him as the plane weaved around a large, dark cloud bank and began a gradual turn over the Atlantic to head west. Far below, a very lonely Lisa Lisignoli was standing at the curb waiting for a cab at the JFK terminal. It was a tearful good-bye for her and Jack, with many unasked questions and a few spoken answers. The only thing they were absolutely certain about was, against all odds, they had fallen deeply in love with each other.

Jack's head was filled with a mass of unrelated thoughts. He was riding an emotional roller coaster, his brain twisting up and down, deliberating over his children, Lisa, his book, his new outline, and every dramatic detail that had an affect on his life during the past fourteen days. His thoughts were interrupted by a flight attendant who asked for his drink order.

"I'll have a ginger ale," Jack said, knowing the pull tab was buried safely in the pocket of his dress slacks. He returned his gaze to outside the window, determined to pick up the memories where he had left them. A tightness settled in his chest. Taking a deep breath, he resigned himself to going back to his life prior to coming to New York. Before the rewrite and Lisa Lisignoli. Before nearly getting them all killed. Three things had changed for Jack in New York. He had fallen in love again, he had a renewed opportunity with his children, and he made a firm resolution to give up alcohol. As for a definitive future with Lisa, there were several obvious obstacles, but none of them impossible to overcome.

"Just an inconvenience," Jack said quietly to the clouds churning below him as he returned to his home in Minnesota.

Chapter Twenty-five

Eleven days later, Thanksgiving Day caught Jack Kramp by surprise. He quickly planned a family dinner at a local restaurant for his three children and himself. Jack had very little direct contact with Lisa since he returned home from New York. A dozen short texts and a few brief phone calls left Jack feeling lonely and perplexed about the future of their relationship. As Jack's family was leaving their home for the restaurant, the phone rang. Jack dashed back inside to answer it.

"Hello?" he said, slightly out of breath.

"Hello, Jack, it's me, Lisa." Jack quickly sucked in a deep breath. He had left her two messages on her cell within the past three days, and both had gone unanswered. "Jack," she said, "Are you there?".

"Yeah, I'm here," he replied dryly, stubbornness creeping into his voice.

"Are you in the middle of dinner? I get the distinct feeling you don't want to talk to me," Lisa said quietly.

"Gee, that's funny," Jack retorted. "I've gotten that same feeling from you since I left New York. What changed between us, Lisa?"

"Nothing. Look, I'm sorry, Jack. I've been very busy. It's our fiscal year-end and we are all under a lot of pressure here to wrap up loose ends financially," Lisa said. "Plus, I've had a great deal of personal decisions to make concerning my future as well." Jack continued to be silent. She decided to change the subject. "Did you receive your shipment of the advance copies of your book?"

"Yeah, I got 'em yesterday morning," Jack replied, attempting to keep his voice nonchalant.

"Well? Do you like them?" Her voice perked with hope and excitement.

"They're very nice. Thank you, I appreciate them."

"Jack, I also called to wish you good luck during the debut and signing of your book at the Mall of America. It's scheduled for a week from this Saturday, correct."

"Yeah. Thanks. Just what I like. Crowds," he said cynically.

"You'll do fine. Just be your charming self," Lisa said, attempting to lighten the mood. "I understand Marsha is flying to Minneapolis to assist you."

"I guess she is coming in late Friday night and going back to New York late Saturday afternoon."

"I wish I could have arranged my schedule to be there, Jack," she said softly. "I really do."

"Yeah. Just like I wish I would have kept drinking," Jack said sarcastically.

"How are you doing in that area, Jack?" Lisa asked, continuing to be as sweet as she could, knowing he was feeling quite neglected.

"Everyday, still sober as a doorknob," he said. "There've been a few nights when I wish I wasn't."

"I'm truly sorry Jack, but I'm going through a real difficult period in my life right now," Lisa said sadly.

"Aren't we all," Jack responded dejectedly.

"Someday, I hope I can make you understand, I..."

"Save it, Lisa," Jack interrupted. "Let's face it. We thought we wanted the same things, but it seems we can't have them. We're over a thousand miles apart, and I'm not just talking geographically. You were right at the start. It was just a damn western manuscript, and I'm from Minnesota. You have your life in New York. I have mine here in Minneapolis. We had a few laughs and shared a little love. We can let it go at that, okay? You can get on with your life with a clear conscience. You'll have no problems with me." There was a long pause of dead silence on the other end of the telephone.

Jack couldn't hear Lisa choking back her tears. "Is that how you really feel, Jack?" she asked quietly, trying to swallow the lump that had formed in her throat.

"What do you think?" Jack replied. He hesitated and took a deep breath. "Look, my kids are waiting for me in the car. Have a nice holiday season. Thank you for calling. Maybe we can have lunch the next time I'm in Manhattan. Good-bye." Jack placed the phone back in it's cradle, wiped a small droplet of water from his right eye, forced a smile, and headed outside to his family.

The launch of *Loose Cannons* was very successful on that second Saturday in December. During the busy pre-Christmas shopping day, Jack met hundreds of people and autographed dozens of his books for over seven hours, often feeling as though his hand was going to fall off. Marsha Morrow was a great help and delighted the waiting crowds with her outgoing personality. All the local newspapers ran news releases about their new native author and his book. One of them gave Jack a raving review in their new book section. A local television station covered a portion of the signing event, although Jack missed watching his forty-five seconds of fame that evening because he went to bed early, totally exhausted.

With Lisa seemingly absent from his life now, Jack threw himself into gathering research for his second manuscript. Having decided to use the title, *The Left Side of Sanity*, he diligently prepared a detailed outline to follow as he wrote. Using all the facts he could dig up concerning Buddy Shepard's murder, Jack spent hours on the web and interviewing people on the phone such as Avery Schneider, Corey Burgess, and several other NYPD officers involved in the case. He developed an interesting relationship with Joe Mackey, a police reporter with the New York Post. Joe had covered the Shepard case from day one and knew a great deal about the events and characters surrounding it. Jack was determined to tell the provocative story of Buddy Shepard's curious life and tragic death as accurately as possible and only fill in the blank areas with his own suppositions where necessary.

One day in mid December, Jack stayed home from work with a bad cold. A little after 5:00 p.m., Tammy's new cell phone on the hall table rang five times, and Jack struggled to get up off the sofa to answer it. Tammy ran by him quickly and grabbed it.

"I got it!" Tammy yelled as she looked at the number carefully and raced upstairs to her bedroom. Jack raised his eyebrows and gave a questioning look to Michael who was sitting in the recliner doing his homework.

"That happens a lot lately, Dad," Michael said. "I think she's got a boyfriend. She gets a call at least once a day. And sometimes, I think she even sneaks down to the kitchen later at night to talk on her phone."

Jack nodded and grinned to himself as he flopped back down on the sofa. His little girl was growing up. He reached for a tissue to wipe his nose and a couple of tears. But, he made a mental note to have a discussion with her about boys, etiquette, dating, and raging teenage hormones. It was a topic he felt ill-equipped to handle as a father, and he silently wished Mary or Lisa were here to discuss it with Tammy instead of him.

On December 18th, Frank Lisignoli called Jack's cell phone at 3:00 p.m., shortly after Jack returned home from the radio station. Shocked by his unexpected call, Jack was totally unprepared for any conversation with Lisa's father.

"Hello, Jack, Frank Lisignoli here. How are you? I hope I'm not disturbing you," Frank bellowed from his office in Manhattan.

"No, I'm fine, Frank, how are you? What's up?"

"Lisa. I just wanted you to know a thing or two," Frank's voice was kind, but Jack could tell he was serious about his news.

Jack swallowed hard. "Is she okay?" he asked quickly.

"She's okay, Jack. You know, of course, that we're publishing her book, *A Good Time to Cry*. We expect a release date within two months."

"Oh, that's good. Is she going to leave Brownstone and come to work with you?"

"I don't think she has any solid interest in working with me, Jack. I am quite certain she's leaving Brownstone, though."

"Is she going on her own to write full-time?"

Frank cleared his throat and paused for a few seconds to collect his thoughts. "I do believe that's the direction in which she's headed, but I'm not absolutely certain, so don't quote me on that one."

"What else?" Jack asked, feeling his pulse begin to race as his sixth sense told him Frank Lisignoli had more he wanted off his chest.

"My daughter is miserable, Jack. In case you don't know it or perhaps you are unsure, she's in love with you. For the first time in Lisa's life, she is deeply head-over-heels in love. It's not my place to meddle, but both of you are so damn obstinate, you're making each other miserable. And you're making me miserable right along with the both of you! Neither of you are communicating clearly with the other.

"Wait. How did you know I'm miserable without her?" Jack asked cautiously, his sixth sense now kicking into overdrive.

Frank paused again. "Well, you're sort of putting me on the spot here, Jack, but I guess you might as well know. I was over at Lisa's apartment for dinner last night. While there, I needed to make a private business call. As I was on the phone, I noticed a stack of invoices on her desk. Her telephone bill was on top. I couldn't help but see several calls to Minneapolis. I immediately assumed she had been talking to you. I asked her how things were with you two, but Lisa said she hadn't spoken to you since Thanksgiving Day."

"Well, that's true. I haven't heard from her in almost three weeks. Who the heck is she talking to here in Minneapolis?" Jack asked, his curiosity aroused.

"Well, let me first tell you that all the calls were made to a cell number. At least once, sometimes twice per day."

"But who? I didn't think she knew anyone here other than me," Jack said, totally surprised and bewildered.

"Well, I asked Lisa about that. I was very direct with her because I wanted some answers. Apparently, my daughter has developed a very pleasant relationship with your daughter, Tammy. She has even spoken with your oldest son, Jim? Yes, Jim, a time or two."

"But I..." Jack stammered, feeling completely mystified.

"Did you tell your children about Lisa?" Frank asked.

"A little," admitted Jack. "I told them how wonderful I think she is, but I never..."

"Perhaps you've spoken of her more than you know. Children can be quite perceptive. At any rate, Lisa has been able to keep up with what's going on in your world through Tammy. She has become very fond of your children, Jack, and she really hopes to meet them sometime soon. She told me so. Lisa feels you're shutting her out for reasons she doesn't understand. Perhaps you're still working through remorse from the loss of your late wife? And Lisa has placed herself under a great deal of pressure with her own life-altering decisions as well."

"I don't believe it," Jack said, finding a chair and sitting down before his weak and wobbling knees gave out from under him.

"Believe it, Jack. Without a doubt, my daughter is very much in love with you, but she's afraid to tell you. She is trying to figure out a way to make it work for all of you, apparently with a little help from your daughter. Lisa is terrified of making the wrong move and losing you. She told me that straight out. But let me ask you two questions, Jack, and I would appreciate candid answers."

"Go ahead, ask." replied Jack, a bit on edge.

"One, are you truly in love with my daughter? And two, can you envision a way to make this relationship work geographically?"

Jack was silent for about five seconds as he pondered Frank's two questions and formulated his answers. Taking a deep breath, he said, "Yes. And Yes. To both. I am in love with Lisa, and I do believe we can make it work. Somehow."

"I thought so, Jack," Frank responded. "I'm seldom wrong in my character judgements, and I knew I was right when it came to you."

Jack swallowed hard and said, "Thank you, Frank. That means a great deal to me. And just so you know, the feeling is mutual."

Jack and Frank conversed about the weather for another minute, then said good-bye. After hanging up, Jack sat there for a long time, staring at the kitchen floor, holding his head in his hands.

"You've been a fool, Jack," he said to himself as he picked up his cell phone and began typing a text message with his large fingers. It read: "I miss you. Congratulations on the release date of your first book. EVERYTHING is still just an inconvenience. Let's talk soon. Loving you from Minnesota. Jack"

After pushing SEND, Jack found the number and dialed Sue at the International Flower Market in Manhattan and ordered a large arrangement of orchids to be delivered to Lisa's office as soon as possible. He instructed Sue to simply write on the card: "Lisa, It's time. Love, Jack."

Jack waited patiently for several days and was disappointed when he heard nothing from Lisa. No phone call. No text. Nothing. Six days later, during the early morning of Christmas Eve Day, Jack was in his bathrobe and sitting in the kitchen drinking hot tea and reading the morning newspaper. Over 8,000 copies of *Loose Cannons* had been sold nationally during its initial two weeks on the shelves, and Jack was looking for a second review in the Arts & Entertainment section. It was a little after 7:00 a.m. and he was enjoying the peacefulness of the big house. His three children were still sleeping, and Jack was fighting an enormous emptiness that had engulfed him for days. Through it all, he had managed to avoid all forms of alcohol.

"Maybe my melancholy mood is because it's now our third Christmas without Mary," Jack mumbled to his mug half-full of tepid tea. "Or maybe it's because I got dumped by Lisa..."

Jack's thoughts were interrupted by the doorbell. He quickly rose and headed down the hall toward the front door, hoping to get it before it woke the children. As he passed by the stairway, he was completely unaware of his three children crouched near the top steps in their bathrobes, each wearing a wide smile. The doorbell rang for the second time as Jack reached the handle and flung it open. He found himself staring into the beautiful green eyes of Lisa Lisignoli. His mouth fell open, his mind went blank, and his legs became numb and refused to move. Jack became slightly aware of a taxi cab slowly backing down the driveway in front of his home. There was a stack of luggage on the steps next to Lisa. Jack's gaze caught a glimpse of a new pair of black and silver cowboy boots sticking out from under her black slacks. She was wearing a long, white coat. Her long black hair hung freely, a sharp contrast against the stark white background of the high coat collar. Lisa looked at Jack, a broad smile spreading across her face, exposing her perfectly white teeth.

"You're right, Jack. It's time," Lisa said softly.

From the stairs behind him, Jack faintly heard his three children say, "Merry Christmas, Dad," in unison. They were enjoying being a part of their father's special moments of surprise.

Jack's mouth started to move as he attempted to speak, but no words came out. He held out his hand and backed away from the door. Lisa stepped into the foyer and placed a finger on his lips to silence him. She reached her arms up and wrapped them around his neck, pulling herself up on her tiptoes until her lips found his ear. Lisa whispered softly, but to Jack, her voice rang through his head like a thousand beautiful silver bells.

"I am going to love you forever, Jack Kramp. You can ask me to marry you later, but for now, just hold me, Jack. I took the red eye last night to get here. I'm tired and extremely nervous so please, just hold me."

"Okay," Jack whispered back through a voice filled with choking emotion as he held her tightly. "Anything you want, Tiger-lady."

Jack's three children bounded down the staircase and stood next to their father. He introduced his children to Lisa and then pulled all five of them together into a group hug.

"Okay, guys," Jack said, trying to sound authoritarian but unable to hide his enormous joy. "Will one of you please explain to me how all of this came about?" as he gestured toward Lisa.

"Dad, we all could tell you were really unhappy. You talked about Lisa all the time, and we knew you really loved her and missed her. So the Friday after Thanksgiving, I found the number for Brownstone on the internet, then I called Lisa and left her a message."

"I called Tammy back in less than an hour, and we spoke for over two hours," Lisa said. "Your daughter is an absolute delight, Jack. And very convincing, I might add," she said smiling.

Jack turned to Jim and asked, "And were you involved with this set-up, too?"

"Well, Dad, that depends," Jim replied slowly, a crooked little grin forming at the corners of his mouth. "If you aren't upset with us meddling in your life, then yeah, I helped. If you're mad about it, then it was all Tammy's idea and I had nothing to do with it!" Everyone broke into uproarious laughter. Lisa noted that Jim had many of the same mannerisms as his father, right down to the mischievous smile.

Jack briefly glanced down at Michael who immediately threw up his hands and shouted, "Hey, don't look at me, I'm clueless!"

The five of them once again laughed as they stood in the foyer, each knowing in their own hearts they were becoming a family. A warm thought flashed through Jack's mind. "It had been a very long time since there was so much happiness in this house. Too long."

Three hours after the chaos of Lisa's surprise arrival at the Kramp home, things began to settle down for the five of them. Tammy and Jim were preparing to make pancakes and sausage in the kitchen while Jack helped Lisa with her luggage. He gave her a tour of their home, Michael tagging along with them, smiling and watching Lisa but saying nothing.

"It was built in 1957," Jack explained. "It's been remodeled and updated three times. The house has five bedrooms, four and a half baths, four fireplaces, and two offices. I've always thought four fireplaces were a bit over the top. Anyway, the house is just over forty-five hundred square feet, and you can't beat the location. It is close to the lakes and parks, downtown, and all sorts of restaurants and shopping."

"Are you trying to sell me your house, Jack?" Lisa teased, "You're sounding like a realtor and I'm not sure if I'm supposed to live here alone and you're planning to move or what!"

Jack exploded with laughter, encircled his arms around her and said, "No, honey, this is your home and I expect, no, I WANT, you to be here with us forever, so get used to it."

Later that afternoon, Lisa and Jack went out for a few hours to do some final Christmas shopping. They both wanted that night, Christmas Eve, and the next day to be the best Christmas in years for Jack's three children. As they were wrapping gifts behind closed doors in Jack's study, he slowly eased into a serious conversation with Lisa about his finances.

"Look, Lisa, I know this might take some getting used to for you. This isn't New York. It's not the pace you're used to in Manhattan. It'll be a slightly different lifestyle. Although I make a decent salary with my radio job, I can't see myself there forever. Getting up at 4:00 a.m. five days a week and getting to the studio by 5:30 is starting to drain me. And until my royalties start coming in and I get another couple of books published, I might not be able to provide all the things you've become accustomed to having or doing like you did in New York."

"We'll be fine, Jack, really," interrupted Lisa. "I don't make sudden or rash decisions. It took me over a month to process all my feelings and then make a solid plan for my professional life. This is what I want. YOU are what I want." She looked at Jack, giggled, and added, "I'm just not sure how I'm going to explain you to my friends back in New York!"

Jack furrowed his eyebrows in mock pain and laughed. "So exactly what IS your plan for your professional life, Lisa?" he asked quietly.

"I'm going to write. You were correct all along, Jack. Writing my own novels has always been my dream, not editing someone else's. I met with my father and Peter Tunnell. We worked out a nice contractual arrangement for my future manuscripts. Each publisher has the right of first refusal on my alternating submissions. It's fair for everyone. So, yes, I AM going to write. It just took your strength, encouragement, and wisdom to make me understand that. Thank you for bringing that to my realization." Lisa bit her lower lip and added, "And thank you for overlooking my short-comings and still falling in love with me."

"The pleasure is all mine," replied Jack. "And as far as your writing, I'll bet you already have at least a dozen future storylines tucked away in that pretty little Italian head of yours, if not already outlined on some laptop computer somewhere!" Lisa nodded and smiled. She was amazed at how well Jack really knew her in spite of only knowing each other for less than two months.

"So, until both of us start receiving royalties on a semi-regular basis," Jack started again, trying to bring the conversation back to his original finance subject, "Our bank accounts may not have the large balances in them as you are used to. I'm sure you made big bucks at Brownstone."

"I did alright," Lisa said, smiling smugly. "But, Jack, you really need to stop worrying about money. We will be just fine."

"I suppose so. I paid off the mortgage on this house with Mary's life insurance money. I've got close to forty thousand in the bank, and every month I make deposits into the kids' college funds, but still..."

"Okay, Jack, enough!" Lisa stopped him again by placing her right hand on his cheek. "We. Will. Be. Fine!" she said, slowly and deliberately. "And here is why. You know my father is pretty wealthy, right?"

"Yeah, I suspected he made good bank, but listen, I'll be damned if I'd ever ask your father for... "

"Geez, Jack! Let me say this as nicely as possible to you. Please shut up and listen! Yes, my father has money, but remember me telling you my mother was Irish? Well, she was the only child of Irish immigrants. My grandfather, Patrick Callaghan, came to America at age seventeen and eventually started a factory in Massachusetts. He made copper wire for electric motors, generators, and that type of thing. He also made a small fortune. Both my brother, Brian, and I were given trust funds from my maternal grandparents when we were twenty-one. When Brian died, his trust automatically transferred to me. When my mother passed, I inherited a good portion of her estate as well. Are you with me, Jack?" Lisa paused to give Jack ample time to process this new, personal information.

"Yeah," Jack replied slowly, his eyes wide and mouth open.

"Well, my uncle Tony, my father's only brother, is an attorney and financial planner. He is very intelligent and wise, and he's monitored my trust and invested it on my behalf for over fifteen years. Oh, and the wire factory is still operating and doing well. It's now owned and managed by my grandfather's youngest brother and still in the Callaghan family. I think they've expanded into making components for alternative energy systems like wind generators and solar panels, too. Anyway, I still receive a lovely dividend check each year from them."

Jack let out a long slow whistle and continued to stare at Lisa in disbelief. For the second time that day, he was unable to speak. Seated on a small love seat next to Jack, Lisa patted his knee and said, "You're speechless, Jack. That's a totally new experience for me! Aren't you going to ask?"

"Ask what?" Jack said weakly.

"How much money I have in my trust?"

"No." Jack replied, shaking his head slowly.

"Well, since you promised me this morning we are going to be together forever, I want you to know."

"You can tell me if you feel it's that important to you, but I will not ask," Jack said soberly. "And sure as hell don't tell the kids or they'll be making out new Christmas Wish lists!" he added with a nervous laugh.

"It's sizable, Jack. I haven't checked the numbers in over three months, but my best guess is the fund currently holds somewhere in the neighborhood of twelve to fifteen."

"Thousand?" Jack asked, knowing he was probably off by several digits.

Lisa laughed and elbowed him in the ribs. "No. Million." she said, her bright green eyes twinkling with delight at Jack's reaction. "Now, will you PLEASE stop worrying about our financial future?"

Jack slumped down in the love seat and closed his eyes. "I had no idea," he said.

"You look like your trying to decide whether to wet your pants or charge your cell phone!" Lisa said, watching Jack's facial expressions.

"Truth be told, I wouldn't mind if I happened to be wearing an adult diaper right now," replied Jack while struggling to sit up on the love seat. "Twelve to fifteen million? Snot on a camel's nose, that's huge!"

"Would it have made a difference if you had known? Would you not have fallen in love with me?" Lisa questioned, cocking her head to one side.

Jack sat straighter, his chin resting in the palms of both hands and elbows on his knees. "Give me a few seconds to think about that," he said, closing his eyes and becoming silent for several seconds. "Okay, here it is," he said, looking directly into Lisa's eyes.

"I'm sure I would have still fallen in love with you. That was probably inevitable. Involuntary. But I suspect, if I had known you were a miniature Chase Manhattan Bank, I would have never let you know how I felt about you. Good grief, I was already intimidated by you as *you*. I already felt you were way out of my league, and it was a long shot with you at best. So my answer is yes, it would have made a difference. And we most likely wouldn't be sitting here today if you had disclosed your wealth during those two weeks we were together in New York."

"But it's too late, Jack. We're here. And we're together now. I love you for who you are, and I know you love me," Lisa replied thoughtfully. "Because I have a few more bucks invested than you anticipated shouldn't change anything between us. The wonderful thing for me is that I completely trust you. That's why I wanted you to know."

"Maybe you shouldn't," Jack responded with his cute crooked grin Lisa had seen hundreds of times before. "But thank you for your honesty and trust. I will never let you down," he added seriously.

Lisa smiled, leaned over, took Jack's hand in hers, and planted a warm kiss on his cheek. They sat together in an understanding silence for nearly a half hour, their bodies, minds, and souls connecting once again, but this time, on an even higher level.

Jack finally stood up, kissed Lisa lightly on the lips, and excused himself to his upstairs bathroom. Lisa began to wander around his study and gathered more insight into this new man who had fallen unexpectedly into her dreams. Lisa smiled as she looked at the collection of memories from recent days and years gone by: softball trophies, autographed baseballs, family vacation photos, community recognition awards, Broadcast Excellence plaques, a dozen comedy books for his on-air shifts, and stacks of assorted magazines, especially GQ and National Geographic. Lisa giggled quietly as she thought about the dichotomy of the two publications and Jack's diverse interests.

Lisa sat down in Jack's black leather chair behind his desk and spun around to face the large window behind her. The sight of heavy snow hanging on the branches of the tall pines outside gave her a comforting feeling of serenity. As she stood and rounded Jack's desk, heading toward the kitchen to help Tammy, her eye caught sight of a white sheet of paper laying on top of the printer. She studied it, rereading it three times before it made sense to her and softly let out a gasp of astonishment.

Typed neatly at the top of the page, Jack had written, "Manuscript #3 Draft. Title: *PAGES, Distant Hearts. Different Worlds.*" Just under the title, it read "By Lisa Lisignoli & Jack Kramp." Six spaces down, he had begun the first paragraph.

"The fasten seatbelt sign lit up the overhead panel, and the pilot began announcing the conclusion of Delta flight 1705 from Minneapolis to New York. The sudden change in pitch of the jet engines and the soft chime of the seatbelt warning light brought Jack Kramp back from distant thoughts to instant reality. He fumbled with his seatbelt, knowing he hadn't taken it off since the Boeing 757 had jetted down the runway at Minneapolis-St. Paul International."

Jack stood in the doorway of his study, watching. Lisa, completely unaware of his sudden presence, remained frozen, her eyes refocusing on the sheet of paper in her hand again and again. She quickly realized their love story was about to come to life, not just for them, but for the literary world, too.

"Well?" Jack asked as he slowly crossed over to Lisa and took her in his arms. "I see you found number three."

Lisa looked up into Jack's blue eyes, wrapped her arms around his neck, the first page of number three still clutched in her right hand. She gently pulled his head down to meet hers and whispered, "Let our adventures begin!"

The End